THE LAKE HOUSE CHILDREN

GREGG DUNNETT

Ebook ISBN: 978-1-80508-552-2
Paperback ISBN: 978-1-80508-554-6

Cover design: Henry Steadman
Cover images: Shutterstock

Published by Storm Publishing.
For further information, visit:
www.stormpublishing.co

ALSO BY GREGG DUNNETT

Erica Sands Series

The Cove

The Trap

Standalone thrillers

Little Ghosts

The Wave at Hanging Rock

The Glass Tower

The Girl on the Burning Boat

The Desert Run

The Rockpools Series

1. *The Things You Find in Rockpools*

2. *The Lornea Island Detective Agency*

3. *The Appearance of Mystery*

4. *The Island of Dragons*

To the children with memories, the scientists with theories, and my brother, who thinks this is all a bit much.

ONE

It didn't always happen, but there were times when Jim McGee had an unusually acute sense of smell. He paused outside the interview room, already getting it—something burnt, flesh, perhaps hair? It smelt like the office did after one of his partner's famous barbecues, inviting half the station and then paying too much attention to refilling their drinks so that he turned the steaks black. But there had been no barbecue, and McGee knew the smell came from her, the woman who had passed through the doorway moments earlier. It wasn't a lack of hygiene. In the days immediately prior, while they had waited for her to recover sufficiently from the shock and the grief to hold this interview, he had caught the sharper smell of hospital soap. But somehow that burnt smell, carrying its notes of tragedy and death; it *lingered*. It cut through.

He hesitated still, his hand touching the door handle but not yet pressing it down. Something else about the case troubled him—but he couldn't quite grasp what it was.

gun a week before, the type of call you just prayed turn out to be an accident. Where the suffering of olved was so great, it would seem cruel if his role was to extract more misery from those who had made it out alive. But it had soon become clear that the blaze had been no accident. It had been deliberately set and timed so that the occupants of the building had no chance of escaping. There was no question this was a murder enquiry. But was the woman waiting behind this door the killer?

And yet, there was something else about this case that made it very different. After all, McGee had interviewed hundreds of suspects, spending thousands of hours listening to their stories, unpicking their lies. So what was it about this woman that perturbed him? What was it about this case? Could it be the scale of the thing? Four people, burnt to death? It seemed unlikely. McGee had worked on plenty of multiple murders over the years. Was it the unusually callous nature of the crime? Most murders happen in the heat of the moment, when the killer's actions can at least be partly blamed on the irrationality of anger; whereas whoever set this fire waited until their victims were asleep before striking. But this too wasn't that uncommon. Perhaps then it was the timing in terms of his own retirement? He had hoped, tentatively, that he might see out his service without another major case. But as he paused, hand still on the door handle, he knew it was none of the above. What unsettled him was simply the mystery that rested at the heart of the case. The things this woman—and the people around her—were saying simply *could not be true.* Yet she insisted they were. Why? And if so, how? Maybe today's interview would tell him. Or maybe it wouldn't.

"You alright?" Billy Robbins looked concerned. He of the barbecues, Robbins had been McGee's partner for over seven years now, which seemed hard to believe. McGee still thought of him as young and inexperienced, but the truth was that when McGee stepped down, Robbins would become the senior investigator with whomever he was paired up with next.

"You thought of something?" Robbins went on. Now he

looked hopeful. The last few days had thrown up many more questions than answers.

"Not exactly."

Robbins made a face. "Shame," he said. "Because I gotta bad feeling I'm about to get told the biggest pile of bullshit I ever heard."

McGee didn't answer. The smell was stronger now, and he realized it was on his partner too. Himself as well, probably. The fire department had finally declared the site safe yesterday, after the fire had smoldered for several days. He and Robbins had visited, picking their way carefully through the part-burnt beams and charred remains of furniture, of people's lives. He let his mind roam through it again now, as if he were back there.

"You sure you're OK for this?" Robbins asked again, looking closely at McGee. "I can take the lead if you want?"

But McGee wasn't ready to be put out to seed just yet. And Robbins wasn't yet ready to lead.

"I'm fine," the older man said.

McGee pressed down the handle at last, and stepped inside.

TWO

The woman was sitting at the table, waiting to begin. She was dressed in what McGee guessed were borrowed clothes from the hospital: a loose beige shirt and shapeless pants, chocolate-brown. He got the smell again, stronger now—burnt wood, plastic. With a fire that big, maybe you just couldn't quite get it out, no matter how hard you scrubbed.

Kate Marshall—married, but hadn't taken her husband's surname—was an attractive woman in her mid-to-late thirties, with dark hair and a slim, athletic figure. McGee had noted how she'd turned heads in the police station where he'd first seen her, even with her face a mask of grief. But it wasn't the woman's looks that now stood out, it was how defeated she appeared. She slumped in her chair, shoulders rounded. Strands of hair that had escaped from her ponytail hung still and listless. The only movement, McGee noticed, was her eyes darting left and right around the desktop, like a cat chasing a laser beam. Then she closed them, as if seeking relief.

McGee pulled out a chair opposite and sat down. He continued to watch her, thinking. And then she slowly drew her head up and looked right at him, holding McGee's gaze in a way he didn't expect. He looked back, trying to see behind her eyes, still tasting those burnt notes on his tongue. She stared back, threads of green running through the brown of her irises. From somewhere he felt a pang of sympathy for the woman, then took a breath to push it away.

Robbins sat down next to him, depositing his thick file of paperwork on the table with a loud *thwack* which caused Kate to glance towards him; McGee noticed this irked him for some reason, just a tiny amount. But then Robbins' lack of subtlety sometimes had that effect. McGee looked around the room. A video camera stood on a tripod in one corner, already recording. On another table, pushed against the wall, was a tray with a pump-action flask of coffee. He reached across, turned over a cup and filled it. He offered it to her, but she shook her head. He lifted one eyebrow at this but followed it with a slight shrug. He took a sip himself. It was bitter and too hot.

"How are you, Kate?" he asked, putting the cup down carefully so that the handle pointed at right angles to the table edge. He made his voice soft, sympathetic. Whether or not the woman had done anything criminal, she'd clearly been through a lot. "You get much sleep?"

For a moment Kate just sat there, head held loose, shoulders still stooped forward. Then she raised her head and turned those green-brown eyes on him once again.

"A little."

"That's good. They got you in that hotel across from the gas station?" They'd discussed holding her in the cells, but decided she was no flight risk. Not without her son.

She nodded.

"How is it? The room I mean. Not too bad, I hope?"

"It's OK."

Suddenly she attempted a smile. It was just a flicker, but McGee read from it what he could. She was either sending a signal—consciously or unconsciously—that she wanted to help them make sense of this madness, that she was cooperating. Or perhaps it was the mask of a cold, manipulative psychopath, who was simply feeding him what he expected to see. He'd seen plenty of both over the years. He let the matching curve on his own lips fade away.

"You sure about the coffee? We could be here a while."

She didn't answer. He watched her, before going on.

"You do understand why we're here? What we need from you?"

At this she nodded. "I need to tell you everything."

"That's right. From the beginning." He took another sip from his coffee, feeling the hit of the caffeine.

"I guess I could have a water then."

He nodded, and reached over again to the other table where a few plastic bottles of mineral water stood next to the coffee flask. McGee picked one up, twisted off the top and handed it to her. He saw that half-smile again as she took it from him. The politeness you'd expect from a nice lady who didn't deserve the horrific twist of fate which had befallen her. Or the calculating killer who'd engineered the situation and was now trying to worm her way out of it? It was his job to decide which.

He watched as she took a small sip. Then she placed the bottle down on the table and twisted it around on its base so that the label pointed directly back at her. McGee noted the action, matched to his own, and filed it away. He let his eyes rest on her face, waiting until she finally met his gaze.

"I'm ready," she said.

THREE

"Katherine Marshall,"—Robbins formally began the interview by reading her her rights—"you're not under arrest at this point. You're not under oath, but you should be aware that providing false statements to a federal agent is a federal offense, including in this interview. According to Title 18, United States Code, Section 1001, it is illegal to knowingly and willfully make any materially false, fictitious or fraudulent statement. Violation of this law could result in fines and/or imprisonment. Do you understand that?"

It took Kate a few moments to respond, but then she nodded. "I do."

Robbins stayed quiet, continuing to stare at her. McGee took over.

"You sure about that? What that means is that if you lie to us—even if we don't charge you with what happened the other night—you're gonna go to prison." He waited. "Are you sure you understand that?"

Kate held his gaze. "I'm not lying."

McGee matched her look, studying her eyes.

"Good," he said. He took another sip of coffee, content for a while to keep gazing at her, wondering if she would eventually look away. As if reading his mind, she suddenly did so.

"Where do you want me to begin?" Kate asked, now studying the water bottle in front of her.

He pretended to think about this, but then settled back in his chair. Sometimes you could read a suspect right from the beginning. Other times you couldn't. On this occasion they were here for the long haul.

"The lake house. Let's start with that. It came into your ownership recently; how exactly did that happen?"

He watched her again. Thoughts, emotions flickering across her face like a candle in a breeze.

"It wasn't just my ownership," she replied.

He held up a hand, acknowledging this point. "Tell us about it all the same."

"That was about three years ago," she said.

"OK then. Let's start there."

There was a long silence during which Kate hung her head. Then suddenly she looked up and began speaking. "Two years ago, we went to the lake house to visit Dad. I say 'visit,' the truth is he kind of summoned us."

"Who's 'we'?" Robbins interrupted, his pen hovering over an open notebook. "I need you to be clear on who you're talking about in each—"

"Neil and I," Kate cut him off. She nodded at McGee as if she understood how this had to work. "My husband, Neil, and our son Jack; he was just over two at the time." She fell quiet, as if picturing him at that age.

"It wasn't just us," she continued. 'My two sisters were there as well. Amber—she's the oldest of us. She came with her husband, Brock, and their twins, Aaron and Eva. They would have been..." She paused suddenly, seeing that Robbins was falling behind.

"Sorry," she said. "I'll slow down."

"Don't worry about me," Robbins told her.

Kate resumed, speaking a little more slowly this time.

"The twins would have been about eighteen then. Aaron and Eva," she repeated. "And then Bea—she's the middle sister, she's two years younger than Amber, but six years older than me. Bea was flying in because she doesn't own a car, and it's a long way from where she lives now."

She paused again. Robbins looked up from under his dark brows, as if unsure why she'd stopped, but Kate almost seemed in another place entirely. Now that her story had begun, she was already becoming lost within it.

"Tris wasn't there. He's Bea's partner, or ex-partner I should say, because of what happened with Zack. I mean, she denies it's *because* of what happened with Zack, but it doesn't take much to join the dots." Kate stopped again, perhaps noting that she was using the present tense for people who were no longer alive.

"Anyway, there were the three of us sisters, Bea alone, and Amber and I with our families. All of us summoned by Dad. Outwardly we were all pretending we didn't know what it was about, but actually we had a pretty good idea."

"And what was that?" McGee asked. "What *was* it about?"

She hesitated, glancing at the camera, as if aware for the first time that everything she said was being recorded, to be analyzed later.

"It was Amber who worked it out. Or thought she did. About three weeks earlier she'd visited Dad and found he was living with a new girlfriend, a woman who was at least twenty years younger than him. Susan, that was her name. Apparently Dad had been coy about her—which really wasn't like him." Kate stopped, biting her lip, remembering.

"At first, I thought this was good news. Mom had died a few years before, and we'd been encouraging Dad to find somebody who could be a companion in his later years. But Amber saw it differently. She didn't trust this Susan woman. She said there was something off about her. And she figured that this 'romance' was really about the money. Dad's money. Our money, I suppose. Our inheritance." She stopped again.

"Amber thought that Susan was going to steal it."

FOUR

THEN

"Amber thinks Dad's going to announce his engagement to this Susan woman." I say this to Neil, and he glances back at me from the driver's seat, his brown eyes slightly magnified by his glasses. He doesn't reply.

"She's super pissed about it," I go on, forcing him to reply, because Neil is often very measured and cautious, that's just his nature. This time it works, sort of. He shrugs slightly.

"Amber's always pissed about something." The Americanism sounds odd with his English accent. It's weird. Neil couldn't be more British if he were related to the Queen, yet he makes an effort to fit in. More than me anyway. I don't care that I'll always be stuck somewhere mid-Atlantic. English mom, New-Englander dad.

"If it makes him happy, surely that's the important thing?" he continues.

I pull a face. "Amber thinks the important thing is that she gets her share of the inheritance."

He frowns at me, too nice to talk about things like this. "Well, I guess you could argue she has to consider such things. She has her family to think about, the twins. It's not just her."

The thought of this makes us both move our heads. I turn mine, and Neil glances in the rear-view mirror, both of us needing visual confirmation that our own family, strapped into the seat behind us, is still there and safe. He's asleep, eyes screwed tight shut. It's funny how it changes you, having a child. Before Jack came along, I thought fighting over an inheritance was pure greed, especially one you didn't really need. But now there's a whole new life to think about—a whole life*time*— then maybe it isn't greed? Maybe there's something more noble about it?

Neil smiles back at me, sharing again the magical thought that *we've created* the person sleeping behind us. We conjured him from the sheer force of our love.

An hour later we pull into the driveway of Dad's house. I call it Dad's house; we used to call it the lake house, back when we were kids and spent every summer here. But after Mom died and Dad retired, he moved in full-time, so it's Dad's place now.

Whatever, it's a lovely old house. I think you'd call it colonial style, with high ceilings and big windows, and surrounded by porches and balconies on every side to make the most of the views. The best part is the location though. Out the back a long lawn drops gently until it meets a little stretch of beach at the edge of the lake, which is five miles long and about a half-mile wide. There's a jetty that juts out into the water, and a boathouse. When we were kids it was stocked with canoes, row boats and Dad's pride and joy: a wooden sailing dinghy that he would sometimes take up to the yacht club in the nearby town, and take part in their regattas. I liked it more when we would all pile in and go out to the island for picnics, or camp-outs with a fire, and toast marshmallows under the stars.

I don't want to give the wrong idea though. The setting is beautiful, but it's not a mansion. There's only four bedrooms, and it's smaller than the neighboring houses on either side. But I'm not complaining either; it was a wonderful place to grow up.

I look up at the house now, not moving from my seat in the car. We've been so busy with Jack that we haven't visited for a while, and it feels good to get here and see the familiar shapes and colors of the trees. The house itself though is looking a bit run down: there's paint peeling from some of the window frames, and the ivy needs cutting back. Amber's been nagging me about that.

I guess—from the cars parked around us—that we're the last to arrive. Brock's big BMW is there, and Bea must have picked up the rental Ford from the airport. Dad's Jaguar is there of course, parked in the garage with the double doors open because the wood's swollen and they don't shut easily anymore. There's also a little Japanese car I don't recognize, with a sticker on the back that says *Meat is Murder*. I guess it must belong to Susan.

"Well, here we are," Neil says, though like me he doesn't get out the car yet. He isn't really built for big social occasions, and I know that coming here with the whole family is a bit of an ordeal for him. But the reason he doesn't move has more to do with our son, still asleep behind us. Except that now he isn't. Jack wakes up and gives a beautiful yawn. I look across at Neil, expecting him to smile, but he frowns instead. I guess because there's no reason to put this off anymore.

Suddenly there's no chance of delaying anyway. The front door opens and everyone comes spilling out onto the gravel of the drive. I try for a moment to ask my family to stay quiet, to remind them that Jack's just woken up, but it's too late, and anyway he seems fine, his eyes super-wide as he stares into the faces of all these people cooing over him, as we're almost pulled from the car and into hugs—my family are more American than English when it comes to physical contact. With all the greetings it's hard to think, but I notice Dad seems older than last time I saw him. I catch the thought that he seems to be accelerating into old age now. Or maybe it's not that; maybe I'm now just so used to looking into the impossible smoothness of Jack's young face. Either way I find myself looking at Dad longer than I should, and I have to invent an excuse for doing so.

"You had your hair cut," I tell him.

"I did indeed." I'm reassured because his voice sounds the same, warm and kind. "A nice lady in the town did it for me." He means Stonebridge, the town on the lakeside, about three miles away.

"It looks really good."

"Thank you, Kate. You also look very good, if just a *little* tired." His eyes shine as he speaks, acknowledging how hard things are right now with Jack. I feel myself flood with warmth. I smile and give my father a hug. He feels thinner and more fragile than I'm expecting, and the same thought as before passes through me, but clearer this time. This man, who has always been here for me, cannot be here forever. And how can I possibly survive that?

"How was the trip?" Amber leans in for a kiss, and gives me her I-told-you-so look as she pulls back, inclining her head towards the Japanese car of our father's girlfriend. We've done almost the exact same journey since we live in the same town— Oakton, in southern Maine. About three hours south of here.

"Good. Yours?"

"Bit of traffic leaving town, but no bother."

She points with her eyes towards the front door where a woman is framed, watching us: Susan. She's in her early sixties —we think—which sounded old when Amber told me about her, but now, seeing her in person and in such close proximity to Dad, I can clearly see the years between them.

"This is Susan." Dad calls her to come out. "She's a... friend." There's just the slightest delay before he says the word.

I say hello, but we don't kiss. I don't know why, but get the sense that not doing so is a mutual decision. But I watch her, as Dad introduces her to Neil. Her hair is blonde, but shot through with gray. It's too long as well, the style better suited to a younger woman. Amber called her a stone-cold gold-digger last week, and there's something about her that does seem almost tailor-made for the description. A coldness. Anyway, I try to bury that thought. The way Mom passed was incredibly hard, and she's not coming back, so I don't begrudge Dad his happiness.

"Dad's put the three of you in the east wing," Amber says, watching me watching Susan. That's a joke by the way. The house doesn't have wings. What she means is the room at the back, but it's my favorite room since it has the best views out over the lake. "Are you OK sharing?"

"Sure." I smile. "Jack usually ends up in our room at home. We'll be fine."

I kiss Brock on both cheeks, getting a double dose of his cologne when one would have been more than enough. And then the twins sweep by. I get a mumbled hello from Eva, who barely makes eye contact, and then Aaron flashes his thousand-watt smile over me, before turning to Neil and complimenting him on the car.

"Is this new? It's a *beast!*" he says, nodding his large head enthusiastically. "What's it got, two liter? Two-five?"

I turn away, happy to know the question isn't for me, although Neil probably won't know either. It's not, by the way. A beast, I mean. Neil's Toyota is just an ordinary-sized family car, and it's got a hybrid engine because Neil wanted something environmentally sustainable. But that's Aaron. You could call him larger than life—most people do—but I've always seen it a bit differently. To me it's like he has to build up the things around him, to make them bigger and louder and more vibrant, just so that they match his own personality. I have nothing against Aaron, it's just that I've always found it easier to be around Eva, although she's always been almost as quiet as he is loud.

Finally, I greet Bea. Like Dad she seems to have lost weight, and there's a meekness to her expression. She was always the type to hang back a little—her and Eva are similar that way—but it's noticeable even so how she's standing with her back to the wall, almost in the flowerbed, letting everyone else say their hellos first. I have to step forward to her.

"Hello Bea, how are you?"

She answers with a shrug, and though she does make eye contact it's only for a moment, and I can see the pain is still there. I feel a rush of guilt. I haven't been there for her. I've been so consumed with my own life, with Jack, that I've ignored her... but then the self-castigation interrupts itself, confused. *She* was the one who moved away after what happened to Zack. And I did try to call, I *do* try, but so often she doesn't answer... I shake my head, *stop*. And just the thought of poor Zack makes me glance around to see where my own son is. *It's OK, Neil's holding Jack.* Showing him off with the quiet pride he has that I love so much, because I know it shows what a good father he's going to be, already is. Still, there's also a moment of—I don't know, fear? Because none of us know what the future holds. We all think we're safe, that we're building our lives, brick by solid brick. But it can all come crashing down at any moment. After all, it happened to Bea.

"Come inside everyone, it's cold out here," Dad calls out.

FIVE

I told you how we came here in the summers, but we came in the wintertime too, for Christmas and Thanksgiving. There'd be snow on the ground, and sometimes the lake would even freeze over. Dad would chop wood and build up great fires in the hearth downstairs, and we'd just have to hope the heat made it up to the bedrooms. Since then he's had electric heaters put in each room, but they've never worked that well. So I'm glad now to see a fire roaring in the big sitting room. I go to open the double doors that lead through to the dining room, maybe to see if there's a fire in there too, but more likely simply out of habit, because we never used to keep them shut. But Amber stops me.

"Nuh uh. Apparently we're not allowed in there until tonight."

I frown at her. "Why not?"

"Dad's doing us a special dinner. Or rather, he has *caterers* doing a special dinner." Again she gives me her knowing look, reminding me why we're here.

I turn away from the doors, wishing she'd stop hinting that all is not well.

"It's almost as if he has something important to tell us."

Amber's voice is laced with sarcasm, and she puts a hand on my arm, steering me back to the fire. Of the three of us, she's the most emotional. Or at least the one who expresses their emotions the most. I tell myself not to get swept up in it. Our father is no fool, and he cares about his family. If this really is about him marrying Susan, then he'll have thought of a pre-nup, or whatever that legal thing is that people do when they want to protect themselves in this kind of situation. At least I *hope* he will have done. The man he *used* to be would have done so. But there's something about how frail he looks this evening that makes me less confident than I'd like to be.

In between feeding Jack and settling him down—and in honor of Dad's special meal—we dress for dinner. Nothing formal, but I put on a knee-length dress in forest green, and even risk a pair of earrings when Jack actually falls asleep. If he was awake he'd just try to grab them, fascinated by the sparkle. Neil puts on a brown-and-white checked shirt, which makes his eyes look almost golden behind his glasses. Neil's not flashy, like Brock, or loud, like Aaron, but there's something about him. When we were dating I called him Superman, because he looked so handsome when he took his glasses off. I think he could look handsome with his glasses on if he wanted to, but when he goes to the opticians I think he just picks the closest pair on the rack, without even caring how they make him look.

We go back downstairs, me clutching the baby monitor, and I feel suddenly nervous. Maybe that's partly because it isn't just family here: the catering company has come with actual waiting staff to serve us all, which feels borderline preposterous. Actually, it's well over-the-line for this family, though maybe Brock had it when he was a kid, I'm not actually sure. I sense that Bea feels this too, and catch her raised eyebrows as I accept a glass of champagne from a boy not much older than Aaron. Then I notice my nephew is drinking too, sipping on a glass of red wine. I didn't know Amber was allowing that, but then both the twins are growing up so fast: Aaron already looks like a man. I catch myself wondering if he's already having sex, and then I wonder why on earth I would wonder that since it's clearly none of my business. I try to distract myself, listening to Brock regaling us with how he won a marketing contract that week. It seems to revolve around him and his sales team beating the prospective clients in a drinking competition. At the end of it he roars with laughter, then holds out his glass to the young waiter to top up.

"OK, we are finally ready for you!" Dad announces a little while later, and he pulls open the double doors to the dining room. It looks amazing. It's lit by candles and the flickering glow from a perfect log fire, and the crystal glassware shimmers with infinite reflections. We all coo appreciatively as we file in and take our seats, which are marked with our names printed on little folded slips of cardboard set out on the dinner plates. The three sisters have been put down one side looking out over the lake, where a full moon is reflecting in the still surface of the water. Neil, Brock and Aaron are opposite us, while Dad takes the head of the table. That leaves Eva and Susan to share the other end. All of which means that I'm sitting next to Susan, around the corner. Other than telling me she's a "friend," Dad hasn't said anything to explain her presence, and she wasn't with us while we were waiting to eat. Now I wonder if she feels uncomfortable being here, but the truth is I've been too busy catching up with my sisters, and with Jack, to think about her much. I turn to face her now we're sitting next to each another; there's no choice but to speak, though I can only think of one topic of conversation.

"The table looks wonderful," I say, as if we've known each other years. "And dinner smells divine."

"Yes," she replies. Her voice is clipped and cold. "Your father has gone to a lot of trouble." She turns to the front and pulls herself straight in her chair, as if cutting off further conversation.

I don't move for a moment. *I know he has,* I think, and I feel Amber's eyes on us. She waits a few beats, just until Brock has topped up everyone's glasses, before taking charge.

"So, Dad. We're all very happy to see you, obviously, and this is all very nice, but I'm sure I speak for all of us when I say we're *dying* to know what the occasion actually is?" Pointedly she leans forward to look at Susan as she says this. Dad doesn't reply, so Amber turns her gaze on Brock.

"I know my husband has been wondering, haven't you darling?" Knowing Amber, she probably gives him a kick under the table to back her up. Either way, he looks embarrassed, which is impressive, since Brock is almost impossible to embarrass. "And Kate is *full* of theories." Amber turns to me now, but fortunately Dad cuts in at this point.

"Would you believe, Amber dearest, that I simply wanted my beloved family to come over for dinner?" he asks, keeping his eyes on hers. Amber responds by swiveling her gaze back to Susan, who's watching this, before turning back to Dad.

"I think, as family, we have a right to—"

"I thought not!" Suddenly Dad is laughing. Not exactly *at* Amber, and in such a good-natured way that it lightens the atmosphere at once. But then he adopts a more serious tone.

"You're quite right, and I shouldn't have imagined that I'd get anything past you. Any of you." He smiles at all of us now. "But as an old man I do ask you one important indulgence. I *have* arranged tonight to be special, but I want it to be about *you*. All of you. And not about me—and whatever this weekend might ultimately wind up being about." He waves a hand as if dismissing that as unimportant.

"So, while I *will* tell you why I've asked you all here—uncover the big secret, if you insist on labeling it as that—I will tell you *tomorrow*. For tonight, you'll make me very happy if we can simply enjoy this wonderful food, and spend some time in each other's company."

There's a pause, and Brock cuts in. "Sure. Sure thing, Donny. I think that's a great idea, don't you Amber?" He glares at her, and I wonder how much she must have gone on about this to him, given how much she's pestered me. "Tomorrow Don'll fill us all in on... what's going on with..." Brock glances at Susan, but quickly looks away again. "But tonight it's all about the eating and the drinking and the good cheer!"

If Neil was a little more confident in social settings this is where he'd jump in with a "Hear hear!" or something similar, but he isn't, so I say it instead, raising my glass.

"Here's to Dad, whatever this is about, and to how nice it is to be here all together!" Everyone else lifts up their glasses, then I notice the look on Bea's face, and I realize how my words must have struck her. It's not just what happened with Zack, but Tristan's not here either. *Damn.* Sometimes being with family is so difficult.

SIX

Underneath our names is a menu card, which lists the first course as a "Fall Harvest Salad." After that is an explanation that this means a mix of arugula and spinach topped with roasted beets, candied pecans, slices of crisp apple and crumbled goat's cheese. And drizzled with a maple-balsamic vinaigrette. When the waiters bring it in it looks delicious.

"Amber, why don't we start with you?" Dad asks, once we've all been served.

"What do you mean?" She pauses, a forkful of apple and goat's cheese balanced in the air.

"Why don't you begin by telling us what's happening in your life? What you're up to."

"I don't understand." She stares at him. "You know what's going on in my life."

"Only up to a point. I'd like to know more."

She lowers the fork, clearly confused.

"I know *some* things, of course," Dad goes on. "About your life, and the lives that the rest of you are living. But I don't *really* know. I'd like to hear it from you—each of you. Because I'm sure there are parts that seem routine to you which I've managed to miss out on entirely. And even if there aren't, I'd like to hear it in your words."

Around the table we look at Amber, but she stays quiet.

"Here's what I thought would be nice," Dad tries again, his voice still good-natured and calm. "If each of you takes a few minutes just to say what's going on in your lives. What's important to you. Not just Amber, but all of you." He smiles around the table.

Amber's still frowning, and for a moment I realize I am too, and then I get it. I understand—sort of—what Dad's up to. I don't know if this is because Susan's really shy, or just a bit strange (clearly she *is* strange). But either way, this evening is Dad's way of getting her to know about each of us without having to actually speak to us directly. Or perhaps it's so that she *can* speak to us afterwards, when she knows a little more about us. It's like a weird way of breaking the ice. And it makes perfect sense. This is Dad all over. He thinks about things like this. Amber seems slower to understand though.

"I don't get it," she says slowly. "You know everything about me..." But Dad just opens his hands like he's some kindly deity.

"Humor me, Amber. Humor a silly old man like myself. Tell me what's going on in your life."

"OK..." Amber shoots a glance at Brock as if to say *I told you so*, and then begins. "Well, my name is Amber Langford, née Marshall, and I'm the oldest daughter of this crazy old man who lives in the house by the lake up at..." She looks around, and then pretends to jump, as if she's just realized where she is. "Oh, we're here *now*." She offers Dad a sarcastic smile, but she's getting into the flow of it now. "Of his three daughters, many say I'm by far the cleverest *and* the most beautiful..." At this Brock snorts with laughter and thumps the table, but Amber cuts him off.

"What? It's true. All the local boys thought so when we were growing up."

"As *I* remember it," Dad interrupts, glancing towards Bea and me now, "each of you had your admirers—"

"I was still the prettiest." Amber juts out her chin in a mock challenge, and Dad backs down.

"I do not doubt, Amber, that if prettiness were a virtue for which they handed out medals, you would still be in the race for gold—although young Eva here could soon be claiming your crown." He turns to her with a smile, which seems to surprise her—she's playing with the candle flame, running her finger through it one way and then the other. She stops at once, as if caught doing something she shouldn't. Dad turns back to Amber.

"But I'm more interested in what you're *doing* with yourself. What you're up to in your life. Whether you're *happy,* if you like." Dad looks hopefully at Amber, but when she still looks bewildered he goes on, turning to Brock. "Brock, feel free to join in, help her out."

There's another half-silence, and then Brock does so.

"OK..." He thinks for a moment. "So, you already know we set up Rocket! nearly... ten years ago now. And it's grown to be the biggest marketing agency in the state, with over a hundred and fifty clients. We're both very hands-on, running the business, but we have a staff of nearly forty now, so that takes the pressure off. And that's designers, account handlers, ad buyers—"

"Rocket!" Dad interrupts thoughtfully. "With the exclamation—"

"The line with the dot, yeah."

Dad seems to ponder for a moment. "You know, I always wondered what is the exclamation mark for exactly?"

Brock seems stuck by this, as if no one has ever asked this question before. But he sounds sure of his answer. "It's about rockets, right? They're filled with energy, literally. They're dynamic, fast moving. They get to where they're going. Fast."

He makes a fist and pumps it. "That's the line with the dot. It demonstrates that we're a dynamic, fast-moving company."

"Of course it does. Of course." For the first time that I notice, Dad casts a glance down the table at Susan, sending her a look I can't decipher. Then he looks back to Brock.

"Very good. Very good." Dad turns back to Amber, but then looks past her, down towards the twins.

"And my eldest grandchildren. Aaron, Eva, what of you? You're both at college now, of course?"

We all turn to look. For some reason Aaron has been subdued so far this evening—usually he's the loudest in the room. Even so, it's Aaron who speaks for them both.

"Just started our freshman year." He shrugs, like it's no big deal. "It's going OK."

"You've adjusted to the level of the schoolwork?"

"I think what you mean to ask," Brock cuts in, missing the point, "is how Dartmouth College has adjusted to Aaron." He grins as Aaron lifts off an imaginary cap, tipping it to his father.

"The work's not so hard. Getting up for the early lectures is tougher, but we're managing." Aaron grins now, white teeth and about a million watts, even in the candlelight.

"You're still swimming?" Dad asks.

"Swim scholarship. Yeah. I'm studying Business and International Relations. I could have gotten in anyway, just on my grades, but it's easier with the swim team." He pauses to give himself space for another smile. "Fastest one-hundred-yard breaststroke on the East Coast. *And* I've still got time to party." With this he leans forward to top himself up with red wine.

"Well, I hope you're not partying too hard." Dad smiles, then turns to Eva before Aaron has a chance to reply.

"And yourself, my dear? Remind me, you are studying...?"

Eva's voice is quiet. She's fiddling with the candle again, tipping it and letting the wax run down the side. She pushes it away, as if it has to be further away for her to resist it. "Just business administration."

Dad looks affronted. "Oh no."

She looks startled, and he goes on. "I wouldn't say *just* business administration. Actually, learning to run a business, not just lead one, is every bit as important. If not more so." He gives her a smile designed to encourage her to go on, but she doesn't do so, she just returns the smile and then looks down at her bread plate, which now has a drip of pale wax on its surface.

The waiters return to take away the dishes. I can smell the main now: Duck à l'orange. It's always been a favorite of Dad's. He waits until they've brought it in—ready-carved on two platters that are placed in the center of the table. Two large ducks, each covered with slices of orange. Then they bring in the vegetables too. This time there's a separate dish for Susan—vegan, I suppose.

"Wow Dad," I say. "This really does look amazing."

"It does, doesn't it?" His eyes are shining at the sight of it. "It really does."

We're all busy for a while serving up, but then Dad starts again.

"And what will you be studying, Aaron?"

Aaron stops what he's doing, taking another piece of meat. For once he doesn't look so sure of himself.

"Huh?" he asks.

"He already told you, Dad." Amber comes in, and this time it's Dad who frowns. He looks troubled for a moment. He sniffs, like he's getting a cold, but when he tries to recover, it only makes things worse.

"And are you doing any sports? You were a swimmer for a while, yes?"

For a second no one knows what to say, but at times like this Aaron's self-confidence can be a boon. The smile creeps back onto his face.

"I dabble, you know? I splash about a bit, here and there. Win a few medals." He's grinning widely now, and he glances at Brock to see if he's gone too far. Dad seems to sense he's being mocked, but it's like he's not quite sure how.

"I'm still playing hockey," Eva cuts in, changing the mood. She's clever, is Eva, she's good at reading moods, and she feels the same need to rescue things that I do. She's the younger of the two of them. Though I always wondered why that's even considered a thing, with only fifteen minutes between them.

"Oh. And where do you play? What position?" Dad asks.

"I'm a sweeper."

Dad's eyebrows go up; he's recovering his poise.

"And what does a sweeper do, besides, one would assume, sweeping?"

Eva's narrow face breaks into a rare smile. "I'm positioned behind the defenders, I'm like the last line of defense when someone attacks."

"Ah, now I see it." Dad takes a moment to chew on a piece of meat, reaching into his mouth afterwards to clear a scrap from between his teeth. Finally he gets it, and examines it in his fingers, frowning. He wipes it on a napkin.

"Bea. Why don't we turn to you next? How is everything?"

That's a pretty open question, given everything that's happened in her life in recent years, and I'm not surprised when she keeps her eyes on her plate and just carries on eating. After a few seconds I know she has no intention of answering, so I step in again.

"I'll go next if you like." I think I expect Dad to give me a grateful smile, but instead he looks annoyed. I recognize my mistake at once. Even when you have siblings—and you know that your parent loves them just as much as they love you—you still imagine they're really on your side just that little bit more. Right now, Dad really wanted to hear from Bea, and I messed that up.

"OK, Kate." He softens, as if instantly forgiving me. "You go ahead."

I take a deep breath. "Well, Jack is two and a half now, and as you all know he's not been the *easiest* child..." I understate it, for comedic effect. "But we think things are turning a corner now." I gesture to the baby monitor as I say this, which I put on the sideboard when we walked in here. Jack's stayed asleep the whole meal. I almost think he'll wake up now, just to prove me wrong, but he doesn't.

"We still can't get him to take a bath without screaming the house down, but he is sleeping through the night now. Most nights."

"And how about his speaking? Is that coming along yet?"

"Um..." In a way I don't want to talk about this in front of everyone. "He's just a bit late, but the doctors aren't concerned."

"You were a late speaker." Dad smiles at me. "You didn't say a word until you turned three, then told Amber that the mailman was coming; we all stared at you in amazement."

I've heard this before, and it does help. I mean, obviously I can speak now, so Jack being late isn't anything bad.

"He has a few words now," I say suddenly. "Maybe ten, twenty words? Mama, Papa, 'ack—that sort of thing." I smile at the thought.

"Ack?" Dad questions.

"As in Jack."

"Ack," Dad repeats, shaking his head a little, like he enjoys this. "Well, it won't be long now until he's babbling away just like you were." He looks at us all. "You were all very early talkers, if I remember correctly."

Again, there's a slightly awkward silence at how he's just contradicted what he said a moment before. Or maybe he means everyone but me? Again he seems troubled by our response, and he presses on quickly.

"Neil, how is your work going?" He turns to my husband. The two of them are both academics—of sorts. Dad was a lecturer, and wrote a really successful textbook on philosophy: it paid for this house. And Neil's more of a scientist, though he does give lectures as well. But Dad's always been interested in Neil's work.

"I read your recent paper, or tried to. It was fascinating."

"Oh really, which one?" Suddenly Neil leans forward, his shyness forgotten. Asking Neil about his work is a sure-fire way to get him out of his shell.

For a moment I'm worried that Dad's going to falter again— after all, Neil's work is incredibly technical, but he proves me wrong.

"You were using... now, let me see. Computational models to map out evolutionary trees, to discover how different species are related to one another. Is that a fair summary?"

Neil hesitates. "Ah, *that* paper." He chuckles at something, I've no idea what. "Yes..." I hope he's not going to go on to say it's an oversimplification, although I know that's what he's thinking.

"You were training computer algorithms to speed up the DNA sequencing of different species?"

"That's right. Thousands of them in fact..." For a second it seems like Neil is going to launch into a full-flowing explanation, speaking freely like he does when it's just the two of us. But then he seems to remember he's in front of my whole family, and he finds the most concise explanation instead.

"We begin with samples from tissues of different species. Then we use alignment software to find the optimal way of matching the DNA to the correct species. From that data we build what we call phylogenetic trees—graphical representations of evolutionary relationships."

"Fascinating. Really," Dad says. "And what happens next, where is it all leading to?"

Suddenly Neil goes from looking content to confused. "I'm sorry?"

"Where is it leading to? What's the end goal of the research?" This is where Neil and Dad differ. In Dad's world everything's geared to finding a practical application. Acquire knowledge, write a book, sell it to buy a nice house. Neil's world is much more theoretical.

"Well, it's not specifically focused to answer a particular question, if that's what you mean." Neil glances around the room; he's a strange mix at times like this, shy but also very proud of what he does. "Our work will help answer broader questions about biodiversity, the origin of diseases, perhaps the future trajectory of life itself." He reddens slightly, my shy scientist-super-husband.

"Good old Neil," Brock pipes up. "Out there curing cancer for the good of humanity." He and Aaron laugh. Dad too, but only a little.

"Actually, I have been offered a new position," Neil says when the room quietens, and I look at him in surprise. I thought he'd already rejected that job, and even if he hadn't, I wouldn't have expected him to bring it up here.

"Oh really?" Dad asks. "And what's that?"

He chooses this moment to take off his glasses and clean them on a napkin. I think of Superman again.

"It's a biotech company. Just a startup, but it's backed by one of the big pharma multinationals. They're looking at creating GMOs—genetically modified organisms—to help with, amongst other things, curing cancer."

This time there's an impressed silence.

"That sounds wonderful Neil," Amber says, her eyes widening in surprise.

"Yes. Well, it's not... *all* wonderful." Neil slips the glasses back on, and suddenly he's Clark Kent again, apologetic, looking for and finding the negatives.

"There are several issues. The gene therapies would be extremely expensive, and would have to be applied for a very long time, so they'll only be available to the wealthiest, which obviously has troubling moral implications. Plus, we don't know what the longer-term health risks are. It's difficult, I haven't..."—He looks at me—"*We* haven't yet decided which way to go."

There's another silence, this time more confused.

"But I bet the money's good, huh?" Brock asks. "If it's big pharma we're talking about?"

Neil almost winces in response, so I answer this one for him.

"They are offering quite a lot. But as Neil says, they're *asking* a lot too, so it's not an easy decision. And we're coping OK, and there's always the option of me going back to teaching. Part time."

"Life has a habit of throwing up difficult questions," Dad says, somewhat enigmatically, but he doesn't appear to be about to offer any help with the solution. Instead, he turns to me, as if Neil has said enough.

"And how about you Kate? Do you miss your teaching? You always said you wanted to go back, after your maternity leave?"

"I miss some things about it," I reply. I was teaching history in a high school before I got pregnant with Jack. Mostly it was OK, but sometimes the kids were little shits, and I don't miss that.

"Did they hold your job for you?" Amber asks. "You said before they were going to hold a place for you, if you want to go back?"

"Yeah. They have a place. But Jack's so little still. I think he needs me with him." I smile at her, expecting her to understand. After all, she didn't work for years after the twins were born. But instead her expression looks disapproving, as if Jack isn't *that* little anymore.

We're all done with the duck now. We made a good effort at

finishing it, but clearly there's going to be leftovers. Dad tells us the catering company are going to keep what we don't eat in the fridge, so there'll be duck sandwiches for lunch. Then the waiting staff whisk away the plates and come back with beautifully presented mini tarts. It's "spiced pear with vanilla-bean ice cream, laced with cinnamon and nutmeg," according to the menu cards. One of the waiters individually spoons a quenelle of thick cream onto each plate. I don't know how much this meal has cost Dad. I don't think it will have been cheap.

"Bea, darling. I know this is hard for you, but I would like to hear from you as well," Dad says. He's taken one bite of his dessert and then rested his spoon back on the plate. His voice is gentle, and the rest of us are kind of busy dealing with the tarts; the pastry is perfectly crumbly, but it's hard to get it onto the spoons. I glance up though to see Bea nodding.

"OK."

"How are you doing?" Dad's voice stays soft, understanding. "How are you coping with things?"

For a moment Bea closes her eyes. "It's still hard," she says finally.

"Yes. I know that," Dad says. "It will be. But is it getting easier? It's been... what? Nearly seven years?"

"Six years and ten months." She looks up, her voice suddenly and almost defiantly clear.

"But it's hard. Of course," Dad goes on. "I understand—up to a point of course. I never lost one of you." He seems to contemplate that thought for a moment, and then continues. "But it's still difficult for me now that your mother has passed away. And that was—I don't want to say expected—but she lived a long and full life. Zack was never allowed that, which is why what happened to him was such a tragedy."

We're all silenced. We don't talk about Zack that openly in this family. It's not exactly a rule, it's just how we've, I don't know, *evolved* to cope with it. Something makes me glance at

Susan again now. It must be weird for her as well, hearing Dad talking about Mom like that.

"But just as I had the years I had with your mother, you had the time you had with Zack, and no one can take that away. That's yours. Forever." He seems serious now. "Tell me, you're settled in your new house? I heard from Kate that you've sold some paintings?"

Bea hesitates at this, and it's not exactly what I said. I told Dad that a couple of art galleries had agreed to put some of her work up. Bea used to live not far from Amber and me in Oakton —Neil used to call it the Marshall Triangle—but after Zack she decided to move to the coast. I can sort of understand it—it's very beautiful, but it's not easy to get there, and it's kind of empty. Lonely. Amber is very dismissive of Bea's decision; she says she's given up on life.

"They haven't *bought* them," Bea clarifies. "They've agreed to put them on display."

"Well, I'm sure it won't be long before they do sell," Dad says. "They're very good."

I guess that's true enough. Or at least, Bea's work is *getting* really good. But that's not really how art works, is it? Even most of the famous painters never made any money until after they'd died. And her work isn't the sort of bland, nice stuff that you could put up in a normal room. It's all angry skies, storms off in the distance, moody, empty beaches.

"And how about Tristan?" Dad goes on. It appears no topic's off limits for him tonight. "Is that over for good, or is there any chance of a reconciliation?"

Bea opens her mouth to reply, but doesn't seem to know what to say.

"He's touring somewhere at the moment? Isn't that correct?" Dad goes on, as if this explains why he's not here, and it's not because their child died and they couldn't bear to be together because of how much it reminded them of this fact.

"I think so, yes," she manages.

"Tris is a musician," Dad explains, for Susan's benefit. "He can play just about anything, and he's played in the background for some pretty big names, isn't that right?" He glances at the twins for reassurance. "From REM to... The Food Fighters, is that the name?"

It's Eva who corrects him, stressing the lack of the last letter with an embarrassed look.

"Foo Fighters, that's it," Dad corrects himself. Susan raises her eyebrows, to show she's impressed.

"I think that, after Zack, he prefers to focus on his music," Bea explains.

"Well, you two were a good match, in your own way," Dad says tenderly now. "I hope you can find a way to work it out. Or failing that, I hope you find someone else to share your time with. It's very important to have someone." At this he seems unable to prevent himself glancing down the table again, towards Susan. We all look too. But she's not paying attention, just slicing into her pear tart. Dad kind of chuckles to himself, as if there's something funny about this.

Once dessert is over, Dad seems to be finished too. His eyes look really heavy now and eventually he stands, saying that at least the dishes don't have to be done. I don't know, I kind of get the idea he had some big speech planned, but in the event he doesn't deliver it. He just tells us he's going to retire to bed now, and then he goes to each of us, Amber, Bea and me, and gives us a kiss on the tops of our heads, like he used to do when we were children.

"Sleep well, my darlings," he says, and again it's like he's talking just to the three of us sisters.

And with that he quietly shuffles out the room.

SEVEN

"What the fuck was that all about?" It's obvious that Amber's been biting her lip the whole evening, and now she doesn't hold back.

It's just us sisters now. Neil's upstairs checking on Jack, and the twins have gone out to meet some friends—that surprised me, given how late it is, but Amber says they're basically nocturnal these days. Then Brock joins us. He's found himself a hefty glass of brandy and brought the bottle too, for top-ups. The fire has died down, but there's still heat there and I crouch down to rekindle it, building up a bed of smaller sticks and watching until they suddenly catch, then tossing on a couple of larger logs. I get a strange feeling as I watch them burn, like I'm being disloyal, or something similar. I can't trace where it comes from, until I remember that Dad mentioned how all this wood comes from the old willow tree that used to stand by the lakeside. It's still there in my memory of the house—we used to play hide-and-seek under its drooping branches as children—but when it stopped producing leaves, Dad had it cut down so it didn't fall on the boathouse. That was a couple of years ago. I don't know why disloyalty is the emotion this thought triggers.

Dad's careful with his firewood—the logs have been well dried and they catch easily, burning fast and without spitting.

"Kate, what do you think?"

I stand up, aware that I've completely missed what my sisters were saying. I stretch out my back from where I've been crouched down.

"About what?"

"About *Dad*. Do you think he's going to screw us over?"

This isn't a conversation I want to have. Not now, with everything else going on in my life.

"I think we should be happy for Dad," I say. "If this is what he wants, who are we to argue?" I shrug.

"Oh, *fuck off*," Amber replies. "You're happy, are you? That Dad gives everything to a woman who can barely even speak to us?" There's a cabinet on the wall where we keep glasses, and Amber strides over to take one out, then pours herself a drink from Brock's bottle.

"No." I hold out my hand, defiantly shaming her for not offering to make me a drink. In response she hands her brandy over and immediately makes another for herself. Someone—the caterers I suppose—has left a silver basket of ice cubes, and I tong two into my drink. I roll them around in the glass before sipping. The spirit changes me, as if the heat of it washes my away uncertainty. Tips me off the fence onto one side. Or the other.

"Of course I'm not happy," I say. As I speak, I think of Jack, all grown up, and basically destitute because of what Dad might be doing now. It's ridiculous, but it's the image my brain provides.

"Well then, what are we going to do about it?" Amber goes on. She joins me at the table and helps herself to ice, getting her own back with the same look because I didn't offer the bucket to her.

"I don't see what we can do," I reply. "If he wants to marry her, he's going to marry her. Though he hasn't actually *said* he wants to," I point out. "He hasn't actually said anything much."

"It could be Alzheimer's," Brock pipes up. He's taken the best chair, the one that gets the most heat from the fire. "The way he was talking tonight, I kinda thought he was trying to fix us all in his memory, you know what I mean? If that's the case, and he marries or changes his will now, then maybe we can get it overturned once he dies?"

"Don't talk about him dying," Amber scolds. "That's not what we're talking about here."

Brock shrugs, looking at her. "Then what exactly *are* we talking about?"

"We're talking about him making a foolish decision, because his head's been turned by a predatory younger woman. That's what," Amber says. "We're talking about a vulnerable old man who needs our protection."

There's a silence as we all consider this.

"If we don't give him our blessing, do you think it'll stop him?" I ask. I'm genuinely not sure. But no one answers me. Instead, Bea asks her own question.

"How much money does he have anyway?"

I'm shocked by how bluntly she asks it. And it's definitely not a topic we've ever discussed openly before. At least, not one that *I've* ever discussed openly. But by the way Amber answers, it's obvious that she's at least considered it.

"I don't know what he has in his accounts, but I'm sure they're very healthy," she begins, with one eye on Brock. "And he has his shares portfolio, which he's indicated to me as the—" She stops, but somehow I know she was going to say "eldest child." "They're pretty healthy too. But the largest asset is of course this house. We wouldn't want to sell it, naturally, but I did have a quick look and a lakeside property this size would be worth upwards of a million. And obviously that figure is a lot lower than it could be because of all the work that's needed."

I'm hit by two surprises in quick succession. First, how high this figure is, because it's not something I've ever looked at, or even thought about. And then what she says about the work. I don't see it needs that much. I open my mouth to ask what she means by this, but Bea is faster.

"What does 'healthy' mean?" she asks. "How much are we talking about?"

There's a pause, possibly reflecting the crudeness of Bea's question, but eventually Amber answers.

"It's a little more complicated than 'how much,'" she cautions. "And we don't know exactly how much he's got in his accounts, nor the value of the shares, but—"

"But roughly," Bea interrupts. "I'd like to know, and I know *you* know. I know you've worked it out." She stops, and almost begrudgingly she softens a bit. "I'm sorry. I know money doesn't mean that much to you. But I'm on my own. And I'm barely earning enough to get by. It would help me to have some idea of the figures we're talking about." She holds up her hands, as if to say: *go ahead, judge me.* Then she glances at me.

I turn to Amber in time to see a range of expressions pass over her face in the firelight. It's like she's grateful to Bea for acknowledging her own weak position in life, and that for Amber, this is much more about the principle than the actual money. Or maybe I'm reading too much into it.

"Well," Amber begins again, "we can make *some* assumptions. From what Dad's told me, I would estimate he has around a hundred in his accounts. In cash."

"A hundred what?" Bea asks.

Amber twists her face in annoyance. "A hundred thousand." There's a slight shake of her head at the need to answer such a question. "And then there's about a hundred and fifty more in shares. Obviously that varies as the market fluctuates, plus Dad likes to dabble. And then the house, let's assume a million for that. In total, that's one and a quarter million."

"What about inheritance tax?" Bea asks. "How does that affect things?" I sip my drink and stay quiet.

Brock joins in now. "Federal doesn't kick in until over ten mill. So, there's just the state tax, which is ten percent, but only over the first mill." He nods to himself. "So, assuming he leaves everything to the three of you, the state takes $25,000 and the three of you share the rest."

In my head I'm doing the math, but Bea's voice interrupts me, impatient.

"Well, how much is that?" She never was good with figures.

"Just over four hundred k. To each of you," Brock says. He clicks his tongue against his cheek. "But that's only if the old man doesn't do anything dumb, like getting married... If he does —then it all changes."

"How?" I hear my own voice joining in, then feel the heat in my cheeks when everyone turns to me. It's Brock that goes on to explain. He takes a deep breath.

"Firstly, you've got spousal rights, which kick in. That means she'd have a claim to fifty percent of the whole estate, even if he does nothing with the will. So that's your best-case scenario, if you like—you lose half of your share each. Four hundred thousand down to two hundred." He pauses, long enough for me to consider that.

And I do. *Two hundred thousand dollars*. I haven't ever thought about what I might inherit. I mean... that's not strictly true; in a sense it's always been there, the knowledge that at some point, the three of us will get *some* money. But I've never specifically calculated how *much* money. So it's a bit of a shock to hear it set out like this. Two hundred thousand dollars. Even if he does marry Susan. There's a lot we could do with that, Neil and I. Jack as well.

"Two hundred thousand is a lot of money," I offer, but Amber tuts impatiently, looks away and indicates to Brock to go on.

"I said that's the best case." He looks as though he's enjoying this. "That's assuming he doesn't change his will. But more than likely—if this woman is getting him to marry her—she's going to work on the will next. Then it's entirely possible he leaves *everything* to her."

"No way. He wouldn't do that—" I begin, but he talks over me.

"You haven't thought this through, Katy. It doesn't have to happen right away. She's at least fifteen years younger than he is. Now, I don't know if they're still..." He makes a vague gesture with his hands, which I don't understand at first, but Amber helps.

"Oh please, that's disgusting."

"*Sleeping together*. I was going to say sleeping together, not fuck—" He stops, resets himself. "But you don't know the power a woman can hold over a man by—"

"Brock!"

"I'm just saying it how it is! There's a lot she can make him do, you know, by withholding certain privileges."

I'm not convinced and I shake my head, but Brock goes on.

"OK, put it this way. What happens if she ends up nursing him, if he gets sick? That'll give her plenty of time to work on him, plus—and here's a kicker"—He holds up his glass—"If that happens, she can make a claim that's she entitled to the bulk of the estate, *even if he doesn't actually leave it to her.*"

We're all quiet, I think a bit shocked.

"I know, it sounds crazy, but there's precedent for it."

"You've checked this?" Bea asks.

"Yeah." Brock nods his head. She turns around and swears under her breath.

"Does that sound right to you?" I ask her. Bea used to be a lawyer, before she gave up to paint.

"I don't know." She shakes her head. "My expertise was in music rights. There's very little overlap."

"I told you," Brock goes on. "I looked it up. There's precedent for it. That means it's happened before, plenty of times. And you know what the lawyers are like? Fucking vultures. The messier it gets, the more *they'll* take." He glances at Bea. "Present company excepted."

Bea looks hotly at him but says nothing, and he drains his drink before going on.

"I tell you, if we're here because Donny is eyeing up marriage, your absolute best case is two hundred each. But realistically, I'd say you'll be lucky to get even half of that. And of course you can forget about this place." He glances around the room as he says this. This familiar room, which I've known for almost my entire life.

"We'll lose the house?" I hear my voice again.

"Are you kidding me? You lose it every which way. Did you meet her? You think she's gonna share this with you?"

I think of how cold she was the whole evening. How she didn't ask any of us a single question. It was like she just didn't care.

"Do you see now?" Amber turns to me again. "If he marries her, we *lose* the house. No more family gatherings. No more Thanksgivings, Christmases. No more summer breaks. It's unthinkable."

It is unthinkable. As in, it's literally too much to think about. So instead I turn to Bea. And I notice there's a strange look on her face. And I finally understand something I've not paid attention to for a very long time. I suddenly know that losing this house isn't quite the disaster for her as it would be for Amber. And maybe for me. The reason, when I think about it, couldn't be more obvious—what happened to Zack happened *right here*. Every time she comes here, she's forced to confront it, over and over again. The same happens to me, so I know something about it. When I go down to the lake, I still get flashes of that day—seeing his little body laid out on the lawn, his tight blue swim shorts, the expression on his face almost like he's still there, even though he's not. And that sense of just utter unreality as the paramedics zip him into that thick, black-plastic body bag before lifting him into the ambulance. Zack, dead, never coming back. For Bea those images must play in her mind every time she comes near this place.

"Kate, you must understand this better," Amber says to me, making me jump.

"What?"

"Now that you've got Jack, you must see how important it is to keep the house in the family? For his sake, and for the twins."

I try to focus on her question, if only to get Zack's deathly expression out of my mind. *Have I thought about it?* About Jack growing up, coming to visit here just like we did? Seeing him learn to swim in the lake, exploring the island in Dad's old sailing boat? Yes, I have, but who wouldn't? I've pictured how he might look, how he might *be*. And I've wondered who he might play with. The twins will be too old by then, but the neighbors have just had a grandchild, and maybe he'll be a playmate? Either way, Amber's right; whatever future I envisage, it does always revolve around this house. The thought of losing it hurts, almost physically.

"So, what can we do?" I ask.

Brock and Amber share knowing glances again, but it's him that answers. "Look, there might be something..." He pauses, rolling the ice cubes around his glass and looking to Amber, but she nods for him to go on.

"If he *is* suffering from Alzheimer's—or something similar, any kind of dementia will do—then there's an argument that he couldn't have made any decisions of sound mind. But in order to establish that, you're going to need to get him assessed. And that has to happen before any wedding: the earlier the better." Brock stops, and it takes me a second to notice why. It's because Neil's come into the room. Almost soundlessly. Brock looks to Amber again, as if checking if he should go on.

"Hey Neil, how's Jack?" Amber asks, sending an answer to her husband.

Neil nods. "He's asleep now." He looks to me. "He was awake, and kind of grumbling, so I read to him for a while, but he fell asleep before I finished."

I flash a grateful smile back, mixed with a dash of guilt. I'd almost forgotten they were up there.

"Fix you a drink?" Brock asks Neil, but he doesn't move from his chair to do so. Neil glances around, taking in that I'm drinking too, though my glass is nearly empty now. Maybe he takes that as a sign.

"No, I'm gonna turn in." He gives a rare, easy smile. "You never know with Jack, it could be a long night." He touches my arm. Just for a second, I feel my sisters' eyes on my good-looking husband. Both my sisters.

"You coming?"

"Sure." I lift my glass. "I'll just finish this."

It's not the answer Neil expects, and he hesitates for a moment before giving an awkward nod and walking away. The rest of us are silent for a moment.

"You were saying?" Bea asks Brock, when Neil is out of earshot. Brock leans forward.

"Yeah." He taps his thumb on his knee while he reorders his thoughts. "The thing about Alzheimer's, and similar... conditions. They're diagnosed by the way people *behave*. So, if there's evidence that—say for example—a family *think* an older relative is not of sound mind, that they're saying and doing crazy things, then a court is much more likely to conclude they couldn't have made a sound decision to do something like get married." He shrugs. "If there happened to be evidence that we were worried about how the old man was behaving—I'm talking emails, WhatsApp messages we were sending each other, discussing the weird things he was doing—just as an out-there example. Well, they could play an important role, further on down the line."

He fixes Bea with a knowing look, and Amber does the same to me. Then she joins in.

"And if we can get him to go and see a doctor," she says, "there's one we've found who might be more inclined to provide a diagnosis that... helps us."

Suddenly this is too much for me. I set down what's left of my drink without finishing it off.

"I'm tired. I'm gonna head upstairs too," I say.

And I leave before anyone can stop me.

EIGHT

"You're saying they were planning on fixing the will?" McGee sat back in his chair and stroked his chin.

Kate stayed silent, her head bowed.

"Kate? They were trying to set up some kind of scam, to get your father diagnosed as incapable of changing his will?"

"I don't know." Slowly, she lifted her head. "I don't know if they really would have done it, or if they were just floating the idea. I'm just telling you what they said that night." She bit her lower lip. "Before it all happened." Her eyes moved, taking in the interview room as if she were suddenly surprised to find herself there.

"I'm trying to show you that I'm telling the truth. About this, and about everything." Kate turned her eyes back and fixed them on McGee. For a few seconds he held them, green-brown, trying to read what was behind them. They might have stayed like that for longer if Robbins hadn't interrupted.

"Before what happened?"

Kate broke off eye contact. She glanced at Robbins, then looked back down at the table.

"Before all hell broke loose."

Both agents waited, but she didn't go on. And McGee was forced to say "Continue. Please."

The night isn't too bad. Jack wakes a couple of times—nightmares again—but not the really bad ones, and it doesn't take him long to fall back asleep. Even so, he's up and properly awake by seven, and so I take him downstairs to the kitchen. Breakfast for him, coffee for me. But I'm surprised to see that Susan is already up and about, setting the dining table for breakfast. I think about telling her there's no need, but that feels almost as awkward as her doing it in the first place. And yet... at the same time it feels like something in her has shifted. She's still odd, but it's not so much a coldness this morning. It's more like she's anxious, expectant. There's an energy shedding off her. A nervous energy.

I feed Jack at the kitchen table, while Susan is in and out ferrying an impressive spread to the dining room. It's obvious that her and Dad have thought almost as much about this breakfast as they did with last night's meal. She takes in fresh pastries, warmed in the oven, orange juice, a French press full of coffee. I take a top-up from that before it disappears through to the dining room. And slowly the rest of the house rises, and they stumble downstairs, and then it's like Dad's running a weird sort of hotel as Susan ushers them into the dining room. Eventually Jack finishes his breakfast and I join the others, who are now sitting at the table in the same seats as last night. All except that Dad isn't there. He hasn't come downstairs yet.

And then it happens.

I said we're all in the same seats as last night, but that's not quite right—Susan hasn't joined us at all; she's been more like a waitress and now she comes in again, only this time she walks around to each of us sisters and hands us an envelope. Our names are written on the outside, in Dad's handwriting. Before I open it, Susan clears her throat. Her voice is reedy, nervous.

"This is for each of you, from your father. He asks that you open it now." For some reason I glance up at her as she says this, and the expression on her face frightens me; her eyes are flared and wild. She looks like a junkie.

"What is this?" Amber demands, waving the envelope she's just been handed.

"Why don't you open it and find out?" Brock says, and I look past my letter at where Bea has already opened hers and is reading it quietly to herself. Suddenly her eyes widen, and she gasps.

I look at Neil and see lines of concern around his eyes. He nods, gently, and I slide a fingernail under the flap. I pull out a handwritten letter, again clearly written by Dad, his writing neat and compact. I begin reading, and the room around me fades away.

My Dearest Katherine,

Thank you for the lovely meal last night. It's quite clear to me that you have a wonderful family, and a superb boy in young Jack. I'm sure he will continue to delight you as he grows up into a fine young man. It's also very clear to me that you have made an excellent choice of husband in Neil. I'm proud of how you support him in his work, and I'm grateful how he supports you in the adventure of parenthood and perhaps your teaching career—or whatever else you turn your hand to. I wish you all every happiness going forward.

Alas, I must turn now to another matter. I have kept from you and your sisters an awkward truth. I have not felt myself for some time, and my doctors have now reached a settled opinion as to why. I do not wish to dwell here upon on the exact nature of my affliction; suffice it to say that I, and my doctors, have exhausted all possible options. Even with the best (and most expensive) medical treatment available, it will kill me, and it will do so gradually, painfully, and while robbing me of any remaining mobility. Simultaneously it will erode *who* I am, taking my memories—including those most precious to me, of my family. It will change my personality, preventing me from even attempting to be the tolerant, thoughtful man I wish for you to remember. It will make me angry, resentful, hurtful.

I do not wish that for you. Most certainly, I do not wish that for me. Therefore, I have—after leaving you all last night and writing these letters—taken a lethal dose of morphine, which will allow me to slip away from these earthly bonds in a painless and almost euphoric manner. Please believe me, this is what I wish to do. This is the way I choose to end my life, to avoid causing myself, and my family, any more pain than is necessary.

I am under no illusions that this will be extremely difficult to accept, and perhaps even to understand. For that reason, I have chosen to do this when you are all here, together, and I trust you will support each other with love and understanding. Furthermore, I have given instructions to Susan that she take care of the immediate practicalities, to make this difficult time as easy as possible.

My darling Kate, I wish there was another way, but simply, there is not. I could not have asked for better daughters than you and your sisters, and my love for you has been the over-whelming highlight of my life. But all good things must come to an end. Farewell my darling, and live brave—for life is short.

Your loving father,
Don

I read it through, and before I'm finished a droplet of water hits the paper, making the ink run, and I realize I'm crying. Then I look up and see the room's in chaos. Amber's on her feet, almost screaming, and Brock and Neil are both asking what the hell is going on. Eva looks terrified, and even Aaron seems scared. I hand the letter to Neil, and then just stare at him while he reads it too. I try to shut out the noise, but I can't: there are words ringing in my head.

"He's *killed* himself? Dad's killed himself?"

Then I realize it's not just in my head. It's what Amber is also screaming, and she's screaming it at Susan, who handed out the envelopes. So she must... she must *know* about it.

"Who the fuck are you? Did *you* do this?" Amber yells at her. Susan backs nearly out of the doorway with Amber moving after her, still waving her letter from Dad. I wonder—crazily—if this is some sort of joke. For a second I seize upon this idea, expecting that Dad is going to come in any moment, shouting "*Surprise!*" But of course he doesn't, he'd have to be a psychopath. Instead, Brock physically takes hold of Amber, wrapping his arms around her from behind and finally getting her to sit down. Neil's finished the letter now. His face is whiter than the paper.

"My name is Camilla Evans." Susan's voice suddenly cuts through the noise. "I've been using a pseudonym up to this point to prevent any possibility that you might research me, which might lead to you thwarting your father's plans. But I am now authorized to tell you my real reason for being here." We're all silent suddenly, listening open-mouthed as the shocks keep coming.

"I am a volunteer with an affirmative-action organization called The Final Choice Initiative. We work with selected individuals who have expressed a desire to control the means of their passing, and we assist them in doing so in a way that is both legal, but also in line with their wishes."

I stare at her. This woman, with her stone-cold eyes.

"So, you're not..." I close my eyes, trying to make sense of this. "You and Dad are not... together?"

"Absolutely not." She shakes her head and runs a hand through her hair, blonde shot through with gray.

"Your father chose to let you believe we were friends, in order that I could spend the necessary time here helping him prepare for his passing. And I would say we *became* friends during that time. But there would have been no question of anything more than that. It would be unethical."

There's another silence, until Amber nearly chokes breaking it.

"*Unethical?* Un-*fucking*-ethical... Are you actually shitting me? What are you talking about? What the hell did you *do?*"

"I assisted your father last night in assuring that his final wishes were carried out, but I did not help him in any way in the means of his dying. That would not be legal, and it's not what we do. However, I was with him, and I did hold his hand while he passed, so that he wouldn't be alone in his final moments."

At this Amber explodes. "You WHAT?" Her face is bright red and her chest is heaving. "You were *with* him? You could have stopped him? You could have called an ambulance?"

"That wasn't your father's wish—"

"*Fuck* his wishes," Amber spits back, struggling to break free of Brock's restraint. "You were *there*. You basically..." Her voice fades out, and this time she half turns and throws Brock's hands away. But she doesn't lunge for Susan—or Camilla, or whatever the woman's name really is. She just stares at her.

"Oh my God, you *murdered* him."

"No. That's completely incorrect. At The Final Choice

Initiative we work very carefully to ensure the Journeyer is fully able to make their own choices, free from any pressure. From ourselves, and as much as possible from any other source. What your father has done is to take his own life, but on his own terms, and for the reasons he has expressed to you in his letters."

Amber's mouth falls open again and she looks to the twins. Eva is crying. Aaron looks like he's been punched in the guts.

"I cannot believe you are doing this." Amber turns back to Susan/Camilla. "Telling me this *in front of my children*." She pauses, shakes her head and starts again. "You evil, evil, fucking *witch*." Suddenly her voice increases in pitch. She sits down heavily, and abruptly begins to cry.

A moment later she stops, almost as quickly as she started. She has another idea.

"Oh my God. How much is he paying you?" she demands. "Gosh. You're doing this for the money. Dad's inheritance! That's what this is about, isn't it?"

"Amber." Brock's voice cuts in at this point, urgent and sharp. He takes her hand, pulling her around to face him so she can't see Susan/Camilla anymore. But I keep watching the woman. She still looks nervous, and now I understand why. She knew all this was coming. In a fleeting moment I wonder how many of these she's done.

"Is this for real?" Neil asks her now, his voice oddly calm. I swing to look at him; it's the first real contribution he's made, but she seems to appreciate it.

"Yes, I'm afraid it is," Susan/Camilla replies, and then, after a silence, she goes on. "I am very sorry for your loss. I enjoyed last night very much, and you seem a lovely family." She hesitates, biting her lip, and it's like she's reading from a script in her head. "I am aware how much of a shock this must be, and part of my role here is to help you all to get through these most difficult hours. If you have any questions I am here to help."

"You're damn right I have questions—" Brock begins. He

seems to have forgotten his role in pacifying Amber, but Neil's voice cuts him off. He still sounds calm, authoritative somehow.

"The letter says Don has taken morphine. When did he do so? How did he take it, and how much did he take?"

Susan/Camilla nods at this. "Just after midnight last night, Don injected himself with 150 milliliters of morphine which, I should add, he researched and sourced himself, with no assistance from me or the organization. He then rested on his bed while I held his hand. Around ten minutes later, he slipped peacefully into unconsciousness. I checked for a pulse or signs of breathing, and found none. I believe he died at around twenty past midnight."

"And you did what? You didn't call the police, you didn't call the ambulance?" Brock seems angrier than Amber now. His voice is getting louder.

"That wasn't Don's wish. He asked that his body be left in his bed, until you were all informed about this over breakfast."

"Can I see the body now?" Neil asks now. I stare at him, but he gives me a look to say it's OK.

"Why?" Amber asks from beside me. I don't look at her.

"I need to confirm that what she's saying is true," Neil replies. Susan/Camilla nods.

"Yes. If you wish. But..." She glances at Eva. She's sobbing now, and no one's even comforting her. Amber seems to finally see this, and she pulls her arm free of Brock and runs to her, hugging her close.

"It probably shouldn't be all of you."

"No." Neil looks at me again. "I agree. I'll go and confirm." He starts to walk toward the door, and I can see how stiff his body is, like he can't believe what's happening, and it's making it hard for him to even walk. But he still goes.

We sit there, waiting in silence, breakfast totally forgotten, until Neil comes back a few minutes later. He nods to me, then stands at the head of the table.

"I'm very sorry to confirm that what... Camilla has said appears to be true," Neil begins. "Don is lying on his bed. He's left a further note confirming to the police what drugs he's taken and that it was his actions and his choice to do so. I also checked for signs of life, and there are none. I'm afraid Don is dead."

NINE

"Jesus H—" Agent Robbins began, but stopped himself. There was a moment of silence in the interview room, then McGee's voice broke it.

"That must have been a very difficult experience to go through. I'm sorry for your loss." As he spoke Kate squeezed her eyes shut as she forced back tears. When she opened them again McGee offered her a tissue. He took a deep breath, and carefully looked through the file he'd brought into the room. "The letters, the ones you described your father writing for you and your sisters. Did you read them all?"

"I... um, I'm sorry? Why do you ask?"

"It might be relevant."

Kate shook her head. "No." The tears were gone, and she looked irritated now. "No. This was all looked at at the time. The police spoke to all of us. They were interested in this Camilla woman, in whether she'd actually broken any laws but—"

"And what'd they decide? They press charges?" Robbins interrupted.

Kate shook her head, almost imperceptibly.

"No. The, uh... the organization that Camilla worked for—volunteered for—they were very careful to stay on the right side of the law, so there was nothing that the police could do. But it was all looked at. Back when it happened. It's not... it's not directly related to what's happened since."

McGee sat back in his chair, watching Kate as she answered. But then he leaned forward, finding the correct placeholder in his file of papers.

"The letters, did you read them all?" he asked.

Kate's face showed a moment's irritation again. "Um... yes. I think so. I saw them. Or at least they told me what they said."

"And what did they say?"

"Amber's one was similar to mine. He wished her well, he told her how proud he was of the business, and he explained why he felt he had no choice."

McGee nodded. "That was to Amber? How about to your other sister? To Bea?"

"The same." Kate paused. "He said again how sorry he was about Zack, and..." She shrugged, miserable. "He said how sorry he was that it had to be this way."

"Was that everything?"

"I think so."

McGee nodded again, and now he flipped open the pile of papers to reveal a photocopy of a handwritten letter.

"I have copies of the letters here," he said. "And your father wrote something in Bea's letter, something which just seems odd. Given the circumstances."

"What?" Kate asked.

McGee spoke slowly, carefully. "He said he hoped he'd be able to find Zack and look after him for her."

Kate said nothing, and after a while McGee continued.

"I guess what I'm curious about is what your father thought about these things. How he brought you up? Was he a religious man? What were you encouraged to think? About death?"

Kate took a while to answer, but when she did her reply was considered. "Dad was brought up as Catholic, Mom too, and I think that turned both of them against organized religion. It wasn't really discussed, but as far as I know, both of them were basically atheists." As she spoke, Kate's eyes lingered on the cross that Robbins wore around his neck. McGee saw her notice it.

"And that's how they brought you up? You weren't encouraged to be religious?"

"No. My father brought us up to put our faith mostly in science. But we were always free to believe whatever we wanted to believe."

"OK. That sounds fair."

"Yes." Kate smiled, just for a moment, then waited.

McGee's eyes dropped to the copy of the letter again. He turned it and pushed it toward her, a finger resting on the sentence he'd already highlighted.

"So this line about finding Zack: what's he saying here, do you think? If he doesn't believe it's true."

"I don't know," Kate replied. "At the time I supposed it was just meant to be comforting."

McGee nodded thoughtfully. "How about now? After everything else you say has happened?"

Kate thought a long time before answering.

"Perhaps when he came to contemplate his own passing—as he must have done in preparing for his own death—maybe he became more open to the possibility that it wasn't the end?"

"Huh." McGee nodded to himself, mostly satisfied. He thought about exploring the question further in light of the wider implications of the case. But he couldn't see where it might take them at this point. Better to let her just go on, in her own time.

"I could do with a coffee now," Kate said suddenly, interrupting his thoughts.

McGee's mind was brought back to the present and he nodded, quite pleased for the chance to get another cup for himself. He got up this time, glad to stretch his legs. After he placed the cup in front of her, she picked it up with two hands and hugged it in front of her as she blew on the surface. He watched her as he took his chair again.

"So what happened next?" he said. "After your husband—Neil—after he confirmed your father was dead?"

Kate nodded. "Neil wanted to call the police, but it turned out that Susan... Camilla had already done so, and called a doctor, to give an official—I don't know what you call it—certification of death?"

"And Camilla Evans, what happened with her? Was she ever arrested?"

"To be honest, I'm not exactly sure. She was taken away in handcuffs, but as I understood it, she wanted that to happen. When they do these things—this organization—they claim they want to help the person who's dying, but they also want publicity, to try and draw attention to their cause."

McGee sat back. He knew the answer to his questions, but there might be value in seeing if Kate answered them truthfully. Or there might not be. He rubbed a hand across the stubble on his chin as his other hand absently drummed on the file of papers. A large part of the file detailed the extensive police report into the death of Donald Marshall, including interviews with all members of the family present that day; the coroner's report, which had formally declared the death as suicide; and a note from the DA setting forth his decision not to file charges against Camilla Evans or anyone at The Final Choice Initiative, judging that this would only play into their hands. The file also contained newspaper articles which showed what a divisive issue this would have been had it resulted in a trial. McGee considered all this and compared it with what he'd heard, looking for inconsistencies. He found none.

"What about Jack?" Robbins asked suddenly.

"What about him?"

"You said earlier you had him in the kitchen, where you were giving him breakfast, but then you moved into the dining room, where Camilla had set up breakfast for the family, and where she gave you the letters from your father. But you didn't mention if you took Jack with you, or whether you left him in the kitchen." McGee wondered where his partner was taking this. Apparently Kate did too, as she frowned in response.

"I don't remember—" She stopped, her forehead creased in thought. "We took him, of course we took him. We wouldn't have left him alone."

"So where was he?" Robbins opened his hands into a shrug. "Was he sitting in a booster seat, perhaps? Was someone holding him?"

Kate opened her mouth, then closed it again. "I don't... remember exactly. I think Neil had him. Yes, Neil was holding him."

Robbins glanced down at his notes, shaking his head slightly now.

"But after you'd read the letter," he pressed, "you said the room was in chaos, and you handed your letter to Neil, and he read it too. How could he do that if he was holding Jack?"

McGee's eyes narrowed slightly as he watched the exchange. His face was blank, revealing nothing.

Kate's frown deepened, and McGee thought she wasn't going to answer at all, or perhaps simply say she couldn't remember—which would be reasonable; after all, this was several years ago.

"Bea took him," she said finally. "With all the noise, he was just starting to cry, but Bea was always really good with Jack. He always seemed to settle well with her. So she took him. She was holding him while it was all happening."

Robbins considered this for some time, keeping his eyes on Kate but saying nothing.

"You sure?" he said eventually.

Kate looked unsettled, which may have been the point of Robbins' questioning, but she nodded. "Yes."

Robbins shrugged, as if unsatisfied with her answer, or to emphasize that it hadn't been an important question in the first place.

"Okay then." McGee took over again, since his partner seemed to be done for the moment. "All this... family drama... how'd it end up? With regards to the house? The inheritance? I guess this problem of your father wanting to remarry, that never came to be in the end?"

Kate appeared to look inwardly a moment, as if remembering. "Well, in a way, that's where things really began."

"OK." McGee gave a little shrug. "We're still listening."

TEN

"My condolences Kate, I'm so sorry." The man who speaks looks even older than Dad did a week ago, when he was still alive—I still can't believe that was only a week ago. A mind-bending week, that's both flown by and dragged in equal measure.

"It was a wonderful service," he goes on, touching my shoulder. I recognize him now—I should have recognized him at the funeral service, which we've just held. He's one of Dad's friends from the sailing club in Stonebridge. I remember he was kind to me when I was little.

"I'm so sorry," the man says again, and shakes his head. "And the circumstances...." I'm not quite sure what he means by that—the way Dad died? The illness he had?

"It's so like Don to take things into his own hands," he finds a way to clarify, and his eyes are friendly, though I don't feel like connecting.

"I hope you can understand his choice. When you get to our age..." He stops, and I sense him sensing me. That I'm in no state to receive whatever wisdom he thought he was going to impart to me.

"Well, let's just say some things look a little different when you get to this age." He stops and lets his hand rest on my shoulder for a few moments, as if he's imbuing me with some healing power. I lift an arm to gently release him, using the pretense of wiping a tear from my eye. Actually, it's not much of a pretense. I've been crying on and off the whole week. During the service I couldn't keep my eyes off Dad's coffin. *Dad's coffin.* Two words that shouldn't sit together, that have *no right* lying side-by-side like that. Fitting together as perfectly as two puzzle pieces.

"Don would be very proud of you," the old man says now. With a final smile he moves on.

The next morning we're still at the lake house, but packing up to leave. I'm struggling to take down the travel cot that poor Jack's spent a whole week in, but the damn catch on the folding frame won't release. Meanwhile I've left the door open, and I'm worried he's going to escape and make his way to the stairs. They're not safe for a child his age. Then I sense Amber coming into the room. I can't see her, but I know perfectly well who it is from the way the air changes.

"We need to talk about the house," she hisses, presumably so that Bea can't hear her. She's in the room next door, but getting ready to leave too.

I glance up. "Could you keep an eye on Jack for me?" I ask her, and she nods, and comes and sits down on the bed beside him. She doesn't touch him though, just watches as he wanders over to the sink. He reaches up to turn on the taps.

"The house, Kate." She turns to face me. "It's important."

I know she's right, but it's daunting. The whole thing is overwhelming. And it still feels so sudden.

"First of all, there's Dad's stuff. That's going to need to be cleared out. Most of it will have to be junked, but maybe some of it can be given away. But the more pressing issue is the building works. We need to decide what exactly we're going to do, and how it's going to be funded."

"Building works?"

Amber sighs theatrically. "Kate, have you *seen* the place?"

I don't know how to answer this. *Of course I have.*

"Did you take a shower this morning?"

I feel my face crumpling into a frown.

"I'm guessing not—not because I can smell you," Amber adds quickly, but not out of any particular kindness, "but because you know perfectly well that there wouldn't have been enough hot water, not with this many people staying here."

"I took one last night, before I went to bed."

Amber is silent a moment, her eyes on Jack.

"That's not the point though, is it? Brock had to leave for work early today, and he went in without a shower because the whole plumbing here needs an overhaul. It's needed an overhaul for years, but Dad didn't want to face it."

I stare at her. I love my sister, but she can be a lot sometimes.

"I just... do we have to do this *now*?" I ask, and immediately she turns back to face me.

"*No.* Of course not. That's not what I'm saying. All I mean is that we can't just leave this. We have to speak, the three of us. We can't just..." She leaves the sentence unfinished, but looks around the room, and almost shudders. "We have to grasp this."

"No Jack, *no.*" He gets the tap on suddenly, and water goes firing all over the bed. The fact that the bedrooms have sinks but not full ensuite bathrooms has been one of Amber's bugbears for years. But I'm more concerned that I asked her to watch Jack and she didn't. I stand and lead him back to the little pile of toys we brought for him.

"Grasp what?" I say, turning back to Amber.

She clicks her tongue, like she's forgotten her thread. But not for long.

"Look, in his will, Dad left everything as simple as he could, everything he owned, just split three ways. But in a way that's *not* that simple, is it? I mean, who exactly is going to make the decisions? Who has the casting vote?"

"He explained that in the will," I reply. Dad planned it so there was no delay in learning his wishes. All his assets were divided in three; the house put in all of our names, so that we'd need a majority decision if we wanted to sell it.

"I was thinking we could go and visit Bea," Amber goes on. "In a couple of weeks, once the shock has passed. We could drive down, just the two of us, maybe stay the night in a hotel there since she doesn't have much room in her cottage. We could at least reach an agreement on how we're going to move forward."

I nod, then the obvious occurs to me. "The three of us." With my eyes I gesture toward Jack.

"Oh. Of course." Amber's lips curl up quickly into a smile. At that moment the catch on the travel cot finally releases and it collapses in on itself, going from large to seemingly impossibly small, like some kind of magic trick.

"OK," I say. I suppose we do have to decide what we're going to do.

"Great." Amber smiles gratefully. "It'll give me a chance to get some quotes together. For the building works." She's up on her feet before I can answer.

But just because we both have lives to lead, it ends up being nearly a month later that Amber and I are driving out toward the coast in her enormous four-wheel-drive BMW. Jack is strapped into the back seat, and next to him—thankfully out of reach—is a folder that Amber's brought with her. I don't know exactly what's in it; she just called them *plans*.

The car smells of leather, and something else which tells you it's new, and expensive. It's the first time I've seen her driving it, but neither of us comments on that. In fact, the stereo automatically syncs with Amber's phone and starts playing one of Adele's early albums—which I know she loves. After a period of driving without either of us speaking, she turns the music up so that speaking isn't an option. I don't mind; I'm lost in my own thoughts anyway. It's not easy to adjust to being without either of your parents, but on top of that, Jack's taken a step back in his sleeping. I don't know if it has anything to do with what happened with Dad, but the nightmares have come back worse than ever. At the moment it's almost every night that we have to go to him, sometimes several times. Neil's played more than his part; he even sleeps on the floor in Jack's room sometimes, but obviously he has to get up in the morning for work, so it makes sense that normally it's me. And it's so hard seeing Jack like that, seeing how much he's suffering and not being able to help him.

But then my mood suddenly changes. In the distance I get my first glimpse of the ocean. The afternoon sun is glinting off the surface, and it looks magical, otherworldly, the way it shimmers and curves to the horizon. I rest my eyes on it and feel it calm my soul as we descend the final long, shallow hill on the freeway. And then it's gone again, hidden behind the flatness of the land, and the beginnings of this strange little town that Bea's made her home. We catch a little traffic as we go past a McDonald's and a small shopping mall. They've made it feel nautical by placing a red-painted fishing boat at the entrance to the parking lot. Then the route takes us past the harbor—more boats, floating this time, but the same shade of red, a sharp smell of the ocean, old fish. I move my head close to the window to see down into the water, catching a glimpse of oily blackness, shim-

mering with color. Beyond a heavy rock wall, a tree-lined head-
land rises to a steep ridge.

We find a parking space right outside Bea's little cottage.
Ironically Jack's now fast asleep in his car seat, and I sit with
him, unsure what to do, just staring at the place for a while.
Amber doesn't move either, except for peeling off the gloves she
uses for driving and folding them neatly before placing them in
the glove compartment. The thought comes to me that I've
never seen anyone put gloves in a glove compartment before. I'd
never even registered that it's literally what it's for.

"What *is* Bea doing here?" Amber asks suddenly.

Before Zack was born, Bea was a lawyer. She specialized
in representing musicians in cases where one side or another
alleged plagiarism. That's how she met Tristan. He wasn't
accused of anything—nor accusing, for that matter—but with
his musical ability he made a good witness explaining to juries
how songs are written and what it means to copy one. Which
isn't as simple as it might sound. There's a lot of money in
music, and for a while it seemed that Bea might wind up
being the most successful of the three of us. But there was no
way that Amber would have ever allowed that, and she fought
like a cat to stay in contention. I remember those years; it
seemed to me like she demanded of Brock that he make a
success of their business—she gave him no choice. But then
Zack came along, and any sense of Bea and Amber being in
competition together just melted away. Bea loved motherhood.
Almost at once she declared that she wanted to be a stay-at-
home mom, and told us that her career had been horribly
toxic anyway. And Tris's income seemed enough to keep them
going.

But then of course Zack died, and everything went wrong.
Some of us wondered if Bea might go back to the law afterwards, especially when she announced that her and Tristan
were separating, but instead she told us she was going to move

out here, to this tiny town on the coast, and become a struggling artist. You can imagine what Amber thought of that.

In the end I unstrap Jack's seat and carry the whole thing in without him even waking. He's getting heavy now.

To be fair to Bea, her place is really cute. The outside is clad in wood, painted light blue, and the door and window frames are white. She's made the yard nice too, with little flowers dotted around a tiny lawn even though it's late in the season. She couldn't afford a place right on the water, or maybe she didn't want that after Zack—I don't know enough about her finances to really say. But she's only a couple of streets from the harbor, right in the heart of the town.

Bea calls down that the door's open and we should go inside, so we do so. I set Jack's car seat down in the living room, and then she comes down the stairs, which lead straight off the kitchen. I can see from her paint-smeared overalls that she's been working. Or perhaps, if I'm being less charitable, this is what she wants us to think.

"Hello." She kisses me on both cheeks, doesn't really make eye contact, and then pulls the overalls off, revealing a plain blouse underneath. She nods a hello to Amber, and then mouths the word "Jack" and holds out her hands in invitation. I point to him, and her expression changes as she sees he's still asleep. He's quite big for his car seat now, and his head has fallen on one side. For a long time she just watches him; it seems she doesn't want to stop.

"How are you bearing up?" Amber asks. Bea is still gazing hungrily at Jack. But reluctantly she turns to Amber.

"Fine."

"You left with Tristan, after the funeral?" Amber checks, and I know she knows this already.

"Yes."

"And?"

"And nothing. We got here, he had some tea. Then he left.

What did you expect? That we had wild, reconciliatory sex just after Dad's wake?"

"It's not entirely impossible."

"Except that I don't live in one of your *Fifty Shades of Grey* novels."

"I don't think that happens in those books."

"I wouldn't know, I haven't read them."

Amber falls silent and huffs a little.

We're still standing in the kitchen. Amber looks around disapprovingly.

"How about some tea?" I ask, before Amber can find something to criticize.

"Sure." Bea turns to a cupboard and yanks it open. As she does so I look around the pretty room. My eyes fall on the refrigerator. There's a calendar pinned to it with magnets. Today's November third, and there's nothing filled in for the rest of the month.

I'm distracted then because Jack begins to stir. I've noticed before how sensitive he is to tension between adults. It's strange; most kids aren't aware of it, but Jack picks it up somehow. And right now, there's plenty to pick up on. Bea and Amber are like two wary lionesses circling each other. Both of them well aware that an argument is coming, perhaps has already started. I wonder about my decision to accompany Amber here. Should I have just let Amber come on her own and found out later what the two of them had decided? Maybe, but it's too late now. Either way, Jack stirs, but then settles himself back down to sleep.

Amber sits herself down at the tiny kitchen table, and conspicuously drops her folder on it.

After Dad's death we all kept a key to the house, but Amber took Dad's set, which was the only one that had all the keys: not just to the front door, but to the side gate and the little boathouse. I kind of wondered about that at the time, but there wasn't really any opportunity to say much. In a way it was helpful—someone was taking control. But now I see there was a reason for it.

The tea made, we all take a seat around the table. It's small enough that our knees are touching underneath. Amber still has the folder, and now she opens it. Sometimes she and Brock personally present the pitches for Rocket! It impresses the bigger clients that the company bosses are giving them their personal attention. This has the same energy.

"So,"—Amber begins by clearing her throat—"I've spoken with three different contractors and talked through what we need done with the place. And I've got three quotes here. What I'd like us to do is make a decision on which one we choose."

She pulls out three separate documents, each several pages long and neatly stapled together, and lays them down in front of her. Then I see she has three copies of each, so they're not quite as big as I first feared. She hands out the first of them and begins to talk us through it. It lists repairs to the roof; a rebuild of the boathouse to include a patio area with picnic tables; pulling down and rebuilding the glass sunroom that sits out the back; and then redecoration of most of the downstairs. Total cost is $180,000.

"Why are you showing me this?" Bea asks, before I can decide what I feel about that.

"Well—" Amber begins, but Bea cuts her off.

"You know I can't come anywhere close to affording this."

"I'm not asking you to *come anywhere close*. But there is the money that Dad left you—"

"That's gone. I'm paying off the mortgage." Bea looks away, then goes on. "You know I don't even *want* this. I don't want anything to do with that place."

Amber frowns, like she's running through several possible ways to reply to this. Ways she's already thought about.

"I know you feel that *now*. I understand that. But I also think you might feel different, in time. In a few years, when things are better." Amber can't help herself from again looking around the little kitchen. She has a huge kitchen with a glass wall that opens out into her yard. She gives a bright smile. "And if you do feel differently then, you'll likely appreciate having the house—"

"I hate that house."

We're all silenced.

"You don't hate that house," Amber corrects her.

"How would you know what I hate and what I don't hate?"

With a start Jack's suddenly awake, tugging at the restraints on his car seat. I get up to release him; I offer him a coloring book and some crayons, but he shakes his head and looks around: it's clear he wants to explore. I keep a close eye on him as he moves around, curious. He hardly ever falls down now, and he's recently discovered jumping.

"Why *wouldn't* I hate that house?" I tune back in to my sisters, who are still on the same topic. "I lost my son there. *I lost my son*, and I lost my life."

Amber sucks in a deep breath and slides me a look, as if to say, *here we go again*.

"Bea, I understand—as much as it's possible to understand— but you used to love that house. You used to adore sailing on the lake with Dad. And you loved taking Zack there. My concern is simply that if we proceed in selling the house, it'll be gone and we'll all lose something precious to us. And I think we've all lost enough already?"

Bea doesn't reply, but I can see she's watching Jack now. The rooms are small and it seems he's already done with the living room. Now he wanders into the kitchen, takes a look at Amber and then comes over to Bea, where he makes a noise.

He's still not speaking much, but there's something in it that's a question. And somehow Bea seems to understand it. She reaches down and picks him up, sitting him on her lap. Immediately his face widens into a huge grin, and for a moment it looks like her face might match his. But in the end it's only a small smile.

"Tell me honestly Amber," she says after spending a few moments stroking Jack's soft cheek. Suddenly he's quite content not to explore, to stay right where he is. "Do you really want to do this for me, or is it about *your* family?"

"What does that mean?" Amber asks sharply.

"I think you know."

Amber doesn't reply, but she makes a shocked face.

"Somewhere for you to take the twins? For them to take *their* children. In the future, when that happens?"

Eventually Amber nods, but then shrugs as well. "Look I get it, you think I'm being a greedy bitch. Like always. And I don't entirely deny it; I *am* thinking of my family. But what exactly is so wrong with that? It's a horrible tragedy that Zack is gone, of course it is. But there are still other people in this family, and that house is important to them too. Would you deny it to them, just because of your own grief?"

I hold my breath; I'm thinking how I wish that Jack wasn't literally in the middle of this, but Bea stays very calm, teasing Jack by almost letting him hold on to her finger, then pulling it away.

"I remember Zack used to like this game," she says absently. "When he was this age." I smile at her, though it's not entirely genuine.

"Bea," Amber goes on, "having somewhere where we've been able to meet up as a family has shaped who we all are. If we just throw it away now..."—she shrugs again—"It's disrespectful to Mom and Dad. And we won't get it back. The money will be frittered away. *We'll* drift apart."

I'd never thought of this, and I turn to look at Amber. She notices, and flashes me an encouraging smile, as if we'd been talking this through and were already in agreement.

"Kate, you must agree? Surely? Now you have Jack, surely you can see how important this is?" I feel put on the spot, and I'm forced to nod, rather than really wanting to.

"Of course it's not *just* Jack," I hear myself saying—but I don't really know what I'm saying. I don't want to say anything, so I shut up. In response Amber reaches out and puts her hand on my arm, like she understands. Then she turns back to Bea, watching her letting Jack's little hands grip onto her fingers.

"Think about it, Bea, where else can we all meet up as a family? Certainly not here."

It might be a low blow, but Amber has a point. Bea's cottage has two bedrooms, one of which has been converted into her studio—and even that is tiny. We do have a spare room in our house but Neil uses it as an office. But then I think about Amber's house. She's never actually shown me around it, not really. But I know it's big.

Bea stays quiet though. She picks up one of the quotes. It has a design for the sunroom. It looks beautiful, but then don't these sketches always look amazing?

"What do you think of this, Jack?"

He grabs the paper, a frown on his little face. It's comical, it looks like he's really considering it. After a moment he gets bored and throws it away onto the floor. I reach down to pick it up again.

"Why does it have to be so expensive?" Bea asks.

"Because the house is very run down."

"So why not just fix it up? Why all the fancy new stuff?"

Amber gives a little exasperated sigh. "As I've been trying to explain, I've included a range of different options in each quote. They include simply carrying out the most basic work necessary —which incidentally we would need to do *even* if we were talking about selling the house—right up to adding on a few small elements, which it's sensible to look at while we have the contractors on site. The idea of coming here today is that we thrash out which of these options is going to work. For all of us."

Amber falls silent, and Bea's attention returns to Jack.

"*Ilk*," he says, looking up into Bea's face. I have to translate for him.

"That's Jack's word for milk. He's seen our tea and he wants his own."

I get up for my bag where I have all of Jack's stuff. As I do, he vocalizes more. "*Ilk, ilk, Mommy. Mommy.*" I know it sounds... backward almost, but it's just because he's a bit behind with his speaking.

I rummage in Jack's bag while Amber's voice floats through from the other room. "No Jack, that's not your mama, that's your Auntie Bea. Your mommy will be right back." She sounds brusque, business-like and it occurs to me she's never been very motherly with Jack. I mean, there's no reason why she ought to be—she isn't his mother. But I remember the change in her when the twins came along. It was like she switched, almost overnight, from the carefree party girl she had been, to the über-dedicated mother where everything suddenly revolved around them. I guess she's just moved on from that stage now.

I come back with Jack's cup, and though I intend to take him back and give it to him myself, he looks so settled on Bea's lap that I fill it up and give her the beaker. Her attention drifts from the paperwork Amber wants her to look at, and onto Jack. She strokes the short tufts of blond hair he has now as he gulps down the milk.

"I have some toys somewhere," she tells me suddenly. "Some of Zack's old ones."

I hesitate, just because Zack's toys will probably be for older children and Jack could choke on something, get hurt. I think she senses this, because she then says, "Most of them are from when he was older, but I'm sure there's something that Jack'd like."

I smile to say thanks and sit a while in silence, just watching Jack drink. Eventually he finishes the beaker and holds it out for me to take it off him. Then Bea hands him over, a little reluctantly, and goes upstairs. I hear her rummaging around up there, and Amber sighs, frustrated that neither of us are paying very much attention to her plans. But another thought occurs to me. It suddenly seems odd that Bea has a bunch of old toys in this house, when she moved here *after* Zack died?

She comes back down the staircase carrying a box, and I change my mind. Maybe it's not odd. Maybe it's just what people do when their son dies? They keep as much of them as they can, because every piece they get rid of is another piece of their child disappearing. It's certainly a big enough box to support this theory. Bea sets it down on the table—on top of Amber's plans—then starts rooting around, pulling out electronic gadgets, an Etch A Sketch and, as I feared, various toys with small parts. Then she pulls out a train, which I remember that Zack used to play with all the time. And I mean *all* the time, like it was his special thing. This was back in the days when Bea, Zack and Tristan lived just down the road from Neil and I.

"What do you think then, Bea?" Amber tries again to get her interested in the plans, which I understand, because we do, somehow, have to make a decision here; but I can tell my sister is lost to us, she's mumbling to herself, asking how the train got into this box instead of—I'm guessing here—a separate box where she keeps the more precious of Zack's old things. But then we're all taken by surprise.

"*Ain,*" Jack says, reaching up with one hand. "*Ain, ine.*"

"What's that honey?" I say to him, taken by an unusual urgency in his voice.

"*Ain!*" he repeats. He's insistent now. "*Ain ine.*" He can't really make the sounds at the start of his words yet—it's a sort of speech impediment, but the doctors tell me he'll grow out of it soon. Anyway, I know exactly what he's saying: *"Train mine."*

"No, it's not yours honey, that's Zack's train." I flash an apologetic look to Bea, meaning to signal that she can put it away if it's too precious to her to have Jack dribbling over it, and bashing it into the table leg.

"Ain. Ine," Jack repeats again. He's actually getting indignant now, his face flushing with color. He watches as Bea takes the train and puts it high up in a cupboard where he can't see it. Then he starts to cry.

"For goodness' sake," Amber says to herself, then she raises her voice. "Can't he just play with something else?"

And just as I feel a shaft of irritation at my eldest sister, Jack stops and begins to explore the other toys in the box. He's so young still that when something is removed from him, it's like it's no longer there. And in front of him is a whole box of colored, tactile toys. So he's happy.

"The plans? Bea? What do you think?" Amber tries yet again to capture our sister's attention. "At the very least we have to decide *something*. Are we going to sell, are we not going to sell?"

This does get Bea's attention, and she stops what she's doing and looks at Amber.

"Regarding that question," Amber goes on, "I think we should have a formal vote on it, as Dad envisaged. A simple two-thirds majority. If *both* of you want to sell the house..."—she opens her hands—"Well, I'll go along with that."

It's a grand concession, except she knows she won't lose. Bea knows it too.

"Kate doesn't want to sell."

They both look at me. I stammer for an answer.

"I haven't really thought about it enough," I reply. We haven't discussed this, Amber and I. She's just put me on the spot. But I know I don't want to sell. It's our future. It's where Jack's going to grow up. Bea looks away, shaking her head in disgust.

"Look, I understand that you don't have the money right now," Amber goes on, chasing her victory, "so what I'm proposing is that Brock and I fund the bulk of the work. For you,"—she turns to me as well—"For *both* of you. We've been very lucky that the business has gone through a good patch. And it means you both get to enjoy the house, with its improvements, and you won't be broke."

"How much?" Bea's voice is sharp. "What does 'the bulk' mean?"

There's a silence. We're actually negotiating now.

"Well, let's say Brock and I fund two thirds of the cost of the refurbishment, and you and Kate can split the final third between you?"

I'm shocked by the generosity of the offer, even more so when I work through the numbers in my mind. I'd expected to have to pay out almost everything that Dad left me, but this way I'll have some left over. Bea's surprised too.

"But the house still belongs to all of us, split three ways?"

"Of course." Amber screws up her face, as if that was always a given. "Absolutely. That won't change. That won't ever change."

Bea's quiet for a while, thinking. I am too.

"*Ain*, Mommy." Jack suddenly injects himself back into the conversation, tugging at my leg and pointing to the cupboard where Bea put Zack's train a few minutes ago. He's been through the box, and apparently nothing else in there will do.

"*Ain.*"

The three of us watch Jack, unsure how to respond. But then Bea gets up. She takes the train out from where it was hidden and examines it for a few moments. Then she looks to Amber.

"You're right, I did love that house. And I hate that I hate it now. And I don't think there's a thing you can do to change that, but I guess it's only fair that I let you try. So OK, you win." It's funny then, because Jack's still waiting for the train and he pulls on her pant leg to remind her. She looks down to him. "I guess both of you win."

Then with a smile she crouches on her heels and holds out the train to Jack, who is waiting anxiously to take it, both hands held out in front of him.

And it should be a nice moment, the argument settled, and even Jack happy for a while. But there's something about seeing the two of them there, looking so comfortable together, that feels really, really weird. I can't explain why exactly, and I know that if I tried, no-one would believe me. Not yet. Because the feeling I'm picking up from Jack, the signal that's now flooding into my brain, as clear as if it were lit up in headlights. It just doesn't make any sense.

It makes no sense at all.

ELEVEN

"I'm going to break in here," McGee said. He'd picked up a pencil and twirled it around his fingers, thinking. "I want to understand about Jack at this point."

Kate glanced at him, wary at the question.

"What about him?"

"You said Jack had trouble with the beginnings of his words. What age was this- the story you've just told? And can you—I don't know—give an estimate of his vocabulary at this stage?"

"He would have been two and a half. Maybe a little older."

"And his vocabulary?"

Kate shook her head. "I don't know. Like I said, he started speaking late. Maybe he had fifty words?"

McGee tried to think back to his own daughters at that age. It seemed a lifetime ago and he couldn't quite get there.

"And in any of those words, did you get any sense of what he would go on to say?"

Kate paused at this point. "There were some moments, some odd moments, but I don't remember him specifically *saying* anything at that point. That came later."

McGee let a silence stretch out.

"Odd moments?"

McGee kept his attention casually on Kate, pretending that the question had no particular significance, but in reality he was watching her carefully, looking for eye movements, where her pupils went. He estimated her blink rate, watched for signs of a dry mouth—licking her lips or swallowing, which might be caused by the release of the stress hormone cortisol. So far there had been nothing to suggest she was lying, but now they were touching upon the part that simply couldn't be true. Did that mean her demeanor would change? Would there now be tell-tale signs?

Sure enough her eyes moved, going up and to the left. McGee felt his own eyes narrow. Some experts claimed this was evidence of the brain accessing a visual memory—and therefore the truth—rather than the invented memory that the eyes going up and to the right would indicate. It didn't necessarily mean a whole lot—the best way to lie convincingly is to really believe what you're saying. But even so. It told him something.

"There were odd words."

McGee kept watching. "Go on."

Kate licked her lips. "Mostly he said the normal kind of words. *Mommy, milk, car.* But then there were some words that seemed to be more... complex."

"Such as?"

Another hesitation. She seemed reluctant to go on. "He used to say 'bigamy.'"

Robbins' head jerked up suddenly, as if he hadn't been paying much attention.

"*Bigamy?*"

"That's right."

"As in, being married to two people at once? That was one of your son's first words?" His expression clearly showed he didn't believe her.

"Yes—*no.*" Kate screwed up her face. "He didn't mean it as

'bigamy.' It's just how it sounded... And there were other words that he said, words that didn't mean anything at all, or that we didn't think meant anything."

"Like what?" McGee asked. Kate hesitated again. But she'd come this far.

"*Ay-ack-own.*"

McGee frowned at her.

"That's what it sounded like. And he said it a lot. And with what happened... well." She shrugged. "It began to seem relevant."

Robbins cut in again before McGee could respond.

"Is it though? Relevant?" This was more to McGee than Kate, but the target seemed to shift as he went on. "We're here to determine the cause of a fire which killed four people. I don't see how that can be related to her son's first words."

"Let's let her finish," said McGee. "This phrase, *ay-ack-own*? When would he say it?"

Another pause.

"When we gave him a bath. *Tried* to give him a bath." Kate's eyes were shot with anxiety. "Any time we tried to put him in the water, or near the water, he'd scream it. Really loudly, like he'd get super panicky and yell it."

This time McGee was able to conjure up a memory of his own daughters in the bath, playing happily together with their plastic ducks. It was hard to square it with what Kate was saying.

McGee took a deep breath.

"Kate, maybe this is a good moment for you to tell us about Zack, about what happened there?"

The suggestion seemed to sit heavy on her. Her eyes widened, but she bit her lip.

"OK," she said.

TWELVE

"Zack was Bea and Tristan's son. They weren't married, but they lived together; I guess they would've gotten married eventually, but it didn't happen that way."

Kate paused, gathering her thoughts.

"They were just like any normal family really. Even though Tris was, you know, the way he lived, the difficulties that brought."

"What does that mean exactly?" McGee asked.

"I guess I mean how Tris had to travel so much. For work. He'd play on tours, and sometimes that meant being away for weeks at a time. And that was hard on Bea."

"You mentioned that before. Are you saying he was actually famous?" Robbins cut in.

"I... no. He works as a session musician. Like a substitute. He can be switched in and out of the bands he plays with. But he's popular with them because he's very good."

"You ever meet them? The big names he works with?"

"No."

Robbins looked a little disappointed.

"What was Zack like?" McGee asked now.

Kate hesitated, as if pondering the question. "He was nice. He was a quiet boy. Kind of— thoughtful, if you know what I mean?"

McGee opened his hands in a non-committal gesture. "Not really. You're the one who knew him."

Kate straightened a little in her chair. "He was mild-mannered. He took an interest in the people around him. I liked that about him. Most children are much more self-centered."

McGee considered this. "You got anyone in mind when you say that?"

"No. Well... OK, maybe. I guess it's just that I remember him so much in the context of Amber's kids. They spent so much time together."

"The twins? Aaron and... Eva, right?"

"Yes."

"They were, what? Three years older?"

Kate nodded.

"OK. So what were *they* like? How was the relationship?"

She looked troubled for a moment. In the end she shrugged. "Eva was quiet then, too. She was always in Aaron's shadow."

"Did you like her?"

"Yes. Of course," she answered quickly. "She's my niece..." She stopped, her mouth forming into a "w" as if she were going to correct herself, but instead she shook her head lightly, as if that could erase the truth. She went on.

"I mean, they're very different, aren't they? Children, at different ages. So it's difficult to say whether you 'like' them exactly, when they're changing so much." She swallowed and fell silent.

McGee wasn't sure if he agreed with her or not. "And him? Aaron?"

Kate shrugged again, the smile already gone. "He was a big,

boisterous boy. Always. It's like he came out that way, and it meant he captured all the attention, and then he just... dominated every situation. But he needed more."

McGee drummed his fingers on the tabletop. "OK. Let's go back to Zack. How old was he when he died?"

There was a pause. As if Kate didn't like it described that bluntly.

"He was eight."

McGee noted her hesitation but pushed on. "And the twins would have been... what? Eleven?"

"They'd just had their birthday."

"So just eleven." He seemed satisfied with this. "Why don't *you* take it from here? Just tell us what you remember. Everything that happened that day."

Kate took a deep breath, gathering her thoughts. "It was summertime. It was a long time before I had to worry about these things, but for Amber and Bea, they had the problem of what to do while school was out. So they just kinda decamped to the lake house. For a month or more. But then, Neil and I were there too. Just for the week. To see..." Kate's voice faded out. She swallowed.

"It wasn't maybe as idyllic as that might sound, because that was the summer that Mom was going downhill. And we were all struggling with it. Dad of course, but also the rest of us. That's why Neil and I were there. To try to help."

"What'd she have exactly?" McGee started rifling through the file, but then gave up and looked at Kate.

"She had a disease called ALS. Amyotrophic Lateral Sclerosis." She bit her lip. "It affects nerve cells in the brain and the spinal cord."

"What does it do?"

"It's horrible. It means you can't control your movements. At first it's just your arms and legs, so you can't walk, but then you start to struggle with eating. Later on it even affects breathing. Everything has to be done for you."

"And she was in the hospital at the time?"

"Yes. Her disease was already advanced. She died about six weeks later."

"OK." McGee pursed his lips in thought. The truth was that he and Robbins had lost track in the early stages of their investigation of just who had died at the lake house, and when, but they had made a timeline to clarify it. First it was Zack, then the mother, then Donald. And now... He cleared the thought and listened as Kate continued.

"Brock wasn't there. He'd gone off on a golfing weekend; I don't know where exactly, but I think it was somewhere in Florida. I know that he flew, because there was a whole drama about him not being able to get a flight back. The rest of us were all staying at the house— Dad, Neil, Tris, myself, and of course the children. But it was a super difficult time for Dad, so some of us went with him to the hospital most days. We knew that Mom wouldn't have long, so we felt we ought to be with her as much as possible so she wasn't alone.

"It was Dad, Tris, Bea and myself who went to the hospital that morning. Amber stayed at home looking after the kids. And Neil stayed as well."

"Why didn't he go with you to the hospital?" McGee asked.

"He was working. He was writing an academic paper and there was a deadline he had to meet." Kate shrugged. "As a teacher I was on my summer vacation, but he still had to work. He wanted to be supportive and be with me, and Mom and Dad, so he was working when he could. It wasn't easy for him."

"OK. So... he's what? Working up in your room?" McGee asked. "The one that overlooks the lake, wasn't it?"

"No, Dad let him use his study. It looks out the front."

"Sure." He nodded. "OK. And Amber was down by the lakeside where the children were playing?"

"Yes."

"There wasn't any expectation for Neil to look after the children as well?"

"No." Kate looked momentarily lost in a thought, and it made her smile. "Like I said, he was working. And Neil's not... back then at least, he wasn't exactly the sort of person you'd ask to look after children, not when he had his head down in his books."

"What's that mean exactly?" McGee questioned.

"Think mad scientist. Totally lost in whatever crazy theory he was investigating."

"OK." McGee moved on. "The children. The twins and Zack. Where were they? Playing on the lakeside, or *in* the lake?"

Kate paused. "Do we really have to do this? It was all looked into at the time. You've got the file in front of you."

"I know. And I know this is hard, but I'd like to hear it from you."

She sighed and paused, as if resetting before carrying on.

"They were in the lake. But it's..." She seemed about to say "safe," but perhaps realized how that would sound with what went on to happen. "There's a part of the lake where the water is shallow, and that's where the children would play. We used to do it all the time when we were young. It's only further out where it gets deep."

"OK. Go on."

"So, as Amber told us afterwards, the children were all playing in the shallow part. They knew to stay there; she'd warned them. But they didn't stay there, not in the shallow part. At least Zack didn't. He kept going out, to where the water was deep."

McGee thought for a moment, running his mind over what she'd already said.

"Was it out of character for Zack to misbehave like that? You said earlier he was a good kid?"

"He was... I mean he wasn't, like, the *perfect* child. Sometimes he was over-excited, sometimes he was moody. He was just... he was an eight-year-old boy, you know?"

"So you don't think it's impossible that he was pushing things a bit? Testing Amber's authority? Going out further than he was allowed?"

"It's not impossible, no. Of course not." Kate sounded irritated, and McGee backed off.

"OK, thank you. Please continue."

Kate drew in a breath, composing herself. "So that's what Amber said kept happening. She would call Zack back in, and he'd come back, but the moment she turned around again, he'd keep going out into the deeper water. So she had to call him in *again*."

"I assume the children were wearing bathing suits of some sort? How about Amber? Was she in the water or on the lakeside?"

Kate was still for a moment. "She was wearing a dress. I remember because it was still wet when we got home, from where she'd waded out into the water. It just kept happening, and Amber told Zack that if he didn't stay in the shallow part he wouldn't be allowed in the water at all—the twins confirmed she warned him about this—but they said it made him angry, and that's why he went out again."

"And that's when it happened?"

Kate nodded. She sat in silence for some time. When she finally spoke, her voice was almost empty of emotion.

"She told me how he swam out the last time, like a long way out. And then he got into trouble. It happened really quickly. He started crying for help—and she knew it was for real, but as she was wading in to get to him, he disappeared under the water."

"What did she do?" McGee asked.

"She screamed. Really loudly. To alert Neil, and it worked, because he came running down from the house. He realized right away what was happening, and ran into the water too."

"And?"

Kate glanced again at the papers in front of McGee, as if wishing again that this was a story that didn't need to be told, but she didn't protest again.

"Neil saw Zack floating in the water. Face down. Amber had—I don't know, maybe she panicked—but she'd waded into the wrong part of the lake, so he was the first to reach Zack. Neil managed to get him to the shallow water, and then the two of them pulled him onto the shore."

"Did they try to resuscitate him? Mouth-to-mouth?"

"Neil did. For a long time. By coincidence he'd done a course on it just two weeks before, connected to his work at the university. The paramedics said he did exactly the right thing. But they also said it's very rare that it actually works. It's not like in the movies. I guess you guys know that?"

There was a long silence. McGee took another look in the file.

"And the twins were interviewed? They said that they witnessed the whole thing? They were able to verify Amber's report?"

"Yes."

"And Neil too? I mean, he was inside the house at the start of the incident, not looking out over the lake, so he couldn't have seen the lead-up. But he confirmed Amber's version of events as well? The parts he did see?"

"Yes."

McGee pulled the pile of papers over the edge of the table and onto his lap so that Kate wasn't able to see what they contained. He flicked through a few pages until he came to the photographs of Zack Marshall's body at the scene. His face was white, the lips a sickly-blue color. His eyes were open but the life that had existed behind them had very obviously gone. Even in the photograph they were empty and dead.

"Thank you, Kate. I know that won't have been easy for you." McGee closed the file.

THIRTEEN

"Kate..." McGee hesitated, trying to scan the details of the unfolding story in his mind. "I just need to clarify: how long after Zack's death was Jack born?" The atmosphere in the room had changed with the retelling of Zack's story. Even for hardened investigators there was something painful in hearing of the accidental death of a child.

"Just under three years. Zack died in the summer of 2016, and Jack was born in spring 2019."

"So obviously they would never have met." He waved a hand, as if dismissing his own comment as being too obvious, even though it still needed to be said. "But did you talk about him much? Would Jack have heard Zack's name being mentioned? Could that be how..." McGee stopped this time, unsure how to go on. The short conversations they'd had with Kate in the hospital, and the interviews with the surviving members of the family, had left them with a puzzle, and he still wasn't quite sure how to address it, how to bring it up.

Kate answered the question anyway. "It's not like we never mentioned Zack, but he was gone, and talking about him wouldn't bring him back." She frowned now, as if trying to be precise. "I mean, children die, they get ill, accidents happen. What happened to Zack was horrible—especially for Bea—but the crazy stuff came later."

"OK." McGee considered. "Well, maybe we can move onto that now? Could you perhaps say when..."—he considered how to phrase this—"When you first started to suspect there was something strange in what Jack was saying? Can you tell us about that?"

Kate remained silent, and McGee waited, giving her time to organize her thoughts.

"There wasn't really one moment," she began eventually. "That's not how it... It kind of built up, over time?" She flashed him a questioning look. "And it wasn't just the things he was *saying*. It was the way he wouldn't sleep, his mannerisms... But when he learned to speak, then yes, that's when we began to understand *what* he was trying to tell us."

"How old was he then?" McGee pressed.

She shrugged slightly. "He was a bit older than three. When he finally started speaking."

"OK. Why don't you tell us what happened then?"

It's three-fifteen in the morning. I can clearly see the contours of our bedroom illuminated in the pale green light from the monitor on my bedside table. Its little screen shows me what's happening in my son's room, as he writhes and twists in his cot. We have the sound turned down—we always do now, because the noise is almost constant. And anyway, he's usually so loud that we can hear him through the wall.

Right now he's only mewing, except every now and then when the sound rises to a scream that rasps against my heart. It's impossible to sleep; even when he's still and quiet, I end up anticipating when it might come again.

There's nothing new in this; he's had what the doctors call

"night terrors" almost from the day he was born. In the beginning we took him to all sorts of specialists, but nothing worked. We're told it's not uncommon, and that he'll grow out of it eventually, but that doesn't make it any easier now. The terrors seem to come in waves. For a few weeks it might not happen at all, and then he'll get them seven nights in a row, two or three times a night. That's when it's really hard. When neither Neil nor I can get any sleep either.

"Want me to go?" Neil rolls half-over in bed, but he doesn't open his eyes. He's hoping I'll say I'll do it and he needn't fully wake up. But I don't blame him; I've done the same to him. Anyway, we've been told not to wake Jack when he has his terrors, because the fear he's experiencing can actually last longer if we do. But usually we still go to sit with him, to make sure he's safe and doesn't hurt himself as he thrashes around. I like to talk to him too, tell him he's OK, even if he can't actually hear me.

"No, you've got work in the morning. I'll do it," I reply. I'm wide awake anyway. Though I feel anything but fresh: this is the second time tonight and I swear Jack's woken up like this every night for the last two weeks. It's like he's going for a new record.

"You sure? I don't mind." His hand moves onto my belly, searching for my hand, but I know he's already drifting away back into sleep. And I don't want Jack to be alone, so I force myself to sit up, rubbing the sleep from my eyes.

Fuck. I'm tired.

I turn the monitor away from Neil so the light doesn't disturb him—though he's already dropped off again—and I reach for my robe from the hook on the door. I feel destroyed, numb, acting on a sort of autopilot where a significant chunk of my brain is just not functioning, perhaps most of it. Yet I'm able to go to him.

I follow the noise into Jack's room and turn on the side light, glad to replace the sickly green of the monitor with the comforting yellow glow that explodes over his cot. He's in there, mewing right now, but I can see another episode is beginning. Suddenly his feet kick against the limits of his pajamas. His little hands punch up toward the ceiling, clenching and unclenching. He curls up, lifting both legs and his head into the air and twisting his body around, as if he's been physically hit. Then he relaxes, and he's quiet for a moment. I'm so tired I could just lie down here on the floor and fall asleep. But that would be disloyal, to be here with him, but somehow not here at the same time.

"Hey, little man. Hey, Jack." I speak quietly so I don't wake him.

"Jack. It's OK, it's Mommy. *Hush.*" I take the opportunity of his sudden stillness to place the back of my hand on his cheek, wondering even now at the softness of his skin, and he huffs and puffs in the cot as he works his way through another spell of it. Sometimes I think it's like an airplane, fighting its way through turbulence. It's the way you can't see it coming, the way it bucks and jerks his little body, just like air pockets buffeting a plane. I just have to sit with him now, and be here through the bumps and lumps until he gets through. I just have to stay calm and not get scared. Nothing bad is going to happen, nothing bad is even *happening*. It's just a natural thing that works out this way sometimes.

Then suddenly his eyes snap open—and this *is* new. I feel my own eyes widen, a sharp stab of alarm. Until I realize that of course this *does* happen—he's just woken up. He sees me then, and there's this visible draining of tension from his body, and I pick him up. His hair is wet with sweat, and his back too, soaked through the fabric of his pajamas. I cradle him to my breast, rock him from side to side, just wanting to be with him before I change him.

"Oh Jack, what is it? What's bothering you?"

"*Ig. Ig. Ig.*" He looks at me. His eyes look scared-wide, the pupils deep brown, almost black in the dim light of the bedroom.

"Ig," I reply, smiling. I have no idea what it means, but his vocabulary—after a very slow start—is now expanding rapidly.

"*Ig, afor. Ig,*" he says again, and my tired brain understands that he wants me to understand him. Needs me to.

"*Ig.*" His eyes are round, scared.

"*Ig,* Mommy. *Afor. Ig. Ig!*"

What's he saying? My brain starts to put letters in front of the sound, to form whatever word it is he's trying to say. But I can't make it work. *Gig? Jig?*

Suddenly it clicks. The only word it could be.

"*Big?* Before big?"

He nods quickly, relieved that I've finally got it. He holds tightly onto me, his eyes closed again. He's calmer now; I could maybe get him back to sleep, and maybe he'll go through until the morning. Maybe I'll even be able to sleep in myself. Get through to eight; that would give me... I'm too exhausted to work out how many hours that would mean. But rather than do the math, my thoughts go in another direction. The strangeness of what Jack has said connects somewhere.

"What was big before? In your dream? What is it that was big?"

He shakes his head now, "*Ee. I ig. Ack.*"

I feel the tension returning, like he's got this off his chest and now I'm bringing it back to him. Automatically I try to soothe it away.

"OK, honey, I get it. You were big. Jack was big. It's OK." He relaxes again, not fully this time, but even so, sleep soon takes him, pulling him away from me and into his private world.

I wake to Neil leaning over me, touching my arms.

"Morning, sleepy head." He pulls me gently from sleep. "I have to go to work."

"What time is it?"

"After ten," he says. He's dressed for work. He's putting a brave face on things, but his color is almost gray from how tired he is. I blink, squeezing the already-forgotten remnants of dream from my mind.

"*Ten?*"

He smiles. "I thought you could do with a lie-in. Jack's had breakfast and he's playing downstairs."

An emotion rolls through my mind, difficult to identify. Gratitude? Guilt? Perhaps just love.

"I'll get up." I smile at my husband and watch as he goes to the bathroom to brush his teeth. It's amazing what a few hours of real sleep can do for you. I actually don't feel too bad, and I go to push the covers back. Then I remember what Jack said in the night.

"Neil," I begin, without really thinking. "Has Jack ever said anything strange to you?" At once the stupidity of the question hits me. In the mirror Neil smiles.

"No, never, he's always made perfect sense," he replies. "Unusual in a three-year-old, as I understand it." As he speaks he starts brushing, which adds to the comedy in his reply.

"Seriously." I roll out of bed. I'm still in my bathrobe from the night's interruption. "Something he said last night was... I dunno. Weird."

"What kind of weird?" Neil's attempt at humor fades, and I get a strange sense, like he knows what I'm going to say.

"I think he said he was *big*."

Neil's still facing away from me, but I see his shoulders stiffen.

"Well, he is," he replies, without turning around. "He is getting bigger."

"No. He said he used to be big. He said he *was* big."

Neil bends over to spit. "Maybe that's what his nightmare was about?"

"What, that he used to be bigger?"

"Maybe. He could have been dreaming he was a dinosaur, or an elephant. Something like that?" Neil grabs the bottle of mouthwash, twists off the cap and takes a slug. I hear him rinsing the liquid around his teeth. He turns away again to spit out the mouthwash, and then he's done. He looks at me kindly.

"I've really got to go. You sure you're OK to get up and keep an eye on him?" It's a genuine offer; there have been days when I've just had to sleep, and he's gone to all sorts of trouble to rearrange his work to cover me. But today he's giving a lecture, and they're always harder to get out of.

"No, I'm fine." I stand up, showing him this is mostly true. But as I go to move, I think I might collapse onto the floor. Perhaps I do need more sleep after all.

He watches me a moment, then moves to stand in front of me. He grips my shoulders lightly, and then suddenly he kisses me on the mouth. It leaves a taste of mint on my lips.

"You're doing great," he says. "Call me if you need help?" He doesn't let me go until I nod my head.

"OK."

Neil kisses me again, squeezes my shoulders and tells me he loves me. Then he leaves the room. A few moments later I hear his voice again, calling up from downstairs.

"Jack's in front of the TV now, approved viewing only. Have a good day."

And the front door shuts. I get dressed, wishing that Neil had woken me just a little earlier so I could have had a shower while he was watching Jack. And then the question I didn't quite form comes back to me:

Has Jack ever told Neil that he was bigger?

FOURTEEN

It's about three months later, maybe more, maybe less. That's the thing about being a full-time mom, you kind of lose track of time. But then again, there are rhythms to the week that keep you kind-of sane. Like today: it's Tuesday, ten thirty, so it's time for Jack's gymnastics class. It's where they fill the local gymnasium with balance beams, and hoops, and fabric tunnels, and we moms run around holding their hands as they climb and jump and crawl. It's great fun, and I love it almost as much as Jack does, only today we're late because I couldn't find my car keys and now the traffic is a pain.

I get to the gymnasium five minutes after it begins, but hurry Jack through the entrance and down the steps to the main hall. Already I can hear the squeak of sneakers on the polished floor, and the squeals and laughter of the children. It's not a problem being late, but it does add to the sense of failing, coming in and seeing all those other mothers who weren't late, who look so much more put together than I do.

"Katherine Marshall." I turn at the sound of a stern female voice, thinking for a second I've transgressed some rule.

"There's no running in here," my friend Jan goes on, dead-

panning behind me. When I turn, her face is completely serious, as are the expressions of the two children who accompany
her. Daniel is about the same age as Jack; Holly is two years
older. As Jan gets closer a smile breaks out and she embraces me
in a full hug.

"You're joining the late gang?" She breaks away from me
and holds up a hand for Jack to high five. When he does so she
grabs him and pulls him in for a hug, as if it were a trick.

"Hey Jack, you enthusiastic to get in there?"

Jack squirms loose and nods.

"Go on then. Go with Dan and Holl; they'll show you the
way."

The three children run ahead together and we fall into step
behind them.

"How you doing, honey? You look great as always." Jan puts
just enough emphasis on the "great" so that I know she's gently
teasing me, but in an understanding way. I feel I ought to give
her a gentle push in return, say something sarcastic, but I'm not
relaxed enough for that.

"He still waking up every night?"

"Mmm," I reply. "Maybe a bit less. I think we're getting
better." I pause a moment, realizing I always give the same
answer. We're always getting better, but never quite get there.

"Yours?" I go on.

"No, they're both perfect." She makes a face, and I feel a
burst of camaraderie. Holly has her own issues: the doctors
think she's on the spectrum, though she's too young for a formal
diagnosis. We head over to where the bags are kept, and then
we're lost to each other, as we each have to head to our respec-
tive offspring and attend to their every need.

Half an hour later and I hit a problem. Sometimes they divide
up the hall to allow different sports to take place at the same time,
and there's this giant net curtain they pull across. Today there's a

trampoline session going on, along with the gymnastics class. Jack was fine when he didn't notice it—too busy with the tunnels and hoops—but when he gets bored of those and sees the older children bouncing on the trampolines, he wants to join in. He keeps pushing at the curtain, trying to find a way through.

"You can't do that Jack," Jan tells him. "You're too young."

At once he turns to her, shaking his head. Again he tries to find a way through the curtain. But Jan has a way with kids. She drops her head onto one shoulder. She speaks to him almost as if he's an adult.

"Oh yes you are. Holly wanted to do trampolining too, but they told me you have to be six years old. And you're only three."

I catch up with them, and Jack holds my hand.

"*Amp'ine!*" He looks at me imploringly. "*Ig me 'id 'amp'ine.*"

His words unsettle me, not because of what he's saying, which I understand perfectly well now: *Bigger me did trampolining.* What concerns me is that he's saying them in front of Jan. Normally he's careful about who he says things like this in front of—no, that's a crazy thought—of course he isn't. It's just coincidence that he doesn't say these things in front of people, along with the fact we don't see that many other people. But either way, I can't remember anyone else hearing him say this kind of thing. Jack looks at Jan now, suspicious, as if he's realized this as well. Fortunately, however, it doesn't look like Jan understands "fluent Jack" yet. He turns away from her and says it again. More defiantly.

"*Ig me 'id 'amp'line.*"

They blow the whistle to say the session's over, and we head to the café, where Jan unpacks a vast collection of small Tupperware boxes—chopped fruit and low-sugar cookies—and I line up for two cappuccinos. By the time I place them carefully on the table, the children have nearly finished eating and are already itching to get back to the play area.

"Go. And no murdering the other kids," Jan tells them, and she kicks off her shoes as she picks up the coffee.

"Damn I need this." She takes a sip.

"Were you by any chance exaggerating earlier when you said how well yours are sleeping?" I ask.

"God no. They really are angels. It's Gary; he had a work party and came home late last night. Woke me up wanting a blowjob." Gary is Jan's husband. I've only met him a few times, but I know his sexual habits in some detail. It took me a while to get used to how open Jan is, but I barely blink now.

"Did you give him one?"

She gives me a look, as if I ought to know the answer to this. "Yeah, but I got me done too. You gotta take it where you can once you have your second child." She drains nearly half the cup, and roots around in her bag for more Tupperware. This time she pulls out some full-sugar cookies.

"Come on, gorge yourself, before they see what we're up to."

I take a cookie, but don't bite into it. There's something I want to ask while I have her here alone. In truth I've wanted to speak to Jan about this for a while, but have never found the right moment. But with what Jack said down in the hall about the trampolines, it gives me a way in.

"Do yours ever..." I begin, and adjust, to make the tone of my voice more casual. "Do they ever say weird stuff, Danny and Holly, about being bigger?"

She looks at me sharply, her intelligent eyes piercing deep into mine.

"Like what Jack said earlier, you mean?"

I get a hit of alarm. She did understand, after all.

"Yeah. Like that." After the shock comes relief; it's only Jan, and for a beat I predict that she's going to say "yes, of course," and everything will be normal again. But she doesn't.

"I mean, kids do say strange things... but I agree—that was totally weird."

She reaches forward and takes another cookie, breaking it into halves and then quarters. She pops one quarter in her mouth and continues.

"I mean, he comes from you and Neil, and you're both weird as shit, so it's what I'd expect, but even so. Where does he get it from, I wonder?" She pops the second quarter into her mouth and chews slowly, waiting.

"I don't know." I'm really unsettled now, further unnerved by how interested she seems to be. "He just says stuff like that sometimes."

"Like what exactly?"

I pause, thinking. "He says he was bigger, before. And recently he's started talking about his 'other mom.' I don't know, I just thought that maybe that was something that kids said from time to time."

"If it is, I've never heard it." She looks to him now; Jack's climbing in the jungle-gym area, and he looks like any other kid in the world.

"Maybe he's reincarnated?"

I look across at her sharply, not sure whether to laugh or be annoyed. "What?"

"You know, that he lived before? Reincarnated."

I still don't know how to react.

"Why would you say that?"

"Because he's saying he used to be big and he had another mom? If he lived before, that would all make sense, right?" She eats the final quarters of her cookie, and immediately reaches for another.

"You don't believe in that stuff, do you?" As soon as I ask the question I wonder. Jan believes in all sorts of crazy things. Once a year her and Gary go away for a weekend without the kids and take MDMA—that's the drug that was known as ecstasy when I was young. I was never brave enough to take it, but apparently it makes you feel really strong sensations of love. She says they have the best sex ever, and the effects last for weeks.

"I don't know." She shrugs. Her body language is casual, but she's still watching me closely. "There's all sorts of things in this world that we don't know about."

Suddenly I sense that I'm about to get one of her conspiracy lectures. She spends way too much time on Facebook, which is where she picks up all this stuff. But I'm really not in the mood for it now. I signal this by turning away and eating my own cookie. Then I glance at my watch, even though I've got nothing on for the rest of the day.

"I should really get back," I tell her.

FIFTEEN

It's seven o'clock. Neil's downstairs cooking dinner while I'm putting Jack down. I've been waiting for a bedtime like this, when he's calm and I'm not too stressed out, and he's not doing that thing where his eyes are shutting with tiredness. I pick out a book, one I know he likes, and I sit next to him on our bed. But I don't open the book. Instead I just sit there looking at the cover, while he fusses a bit with his feet and waits for me to begin.

"Ready Mommy," he says, like he's unsure why I haven't started already.

"Jack honey, you keep saying that you used to be bigger. What do you mean by that exactly?"

He nods, but looks confused at the same time. I wonder what the hell I'm doing, putting ideas like this into his head. But then he nods again.

"Bigger."

"You were bigger?"

"Bigger, like Mommy."

"How were you bigger? Because you used to be a really tiny baby. Do you remember that?"

He shakes his head now. "Bigger, 'efore I die."

I feel a prickle of unease but force my voice to stay light.

"You died?"

"I die Mommy, then I 'ome back. I pick you."

My knuckles are white from holding the closed book too tight, but I tell myself to relax. This is just Jack, my Jack, and although the things he's saying don't make sense, he must have picked them up from somewhere. From some TV he's been watching that I should have paid better attention to. But it's still crazy to hear him say it.

"How do you mean you died, honey?" I ask.

"I died"—he really makes an effort now—"Before." He taps the book now, getting impatient.

"Who were you... before?"

"Bigger," he says, working hard on the first sound of the words. "Bigger me. Book now. 'ease?"

And so—with my head just about exploding with questions about what the hell is going on—I read him a story about a mouse packing his suitcase to go on an adventure.

"Bigger me?" McGee asked, leaning forward now, the connection he'd just made suddenly compelling him to interrupt. "*Bigamy*, right? You told us he had some unusual words when he was just learning how to speak; this was one of them?"

Kate half shrugged. "Yes." She glanced at Robbins' face, and it made McGee glance around at him too. Robbins shook his head ever so slightly, signaling he wasn't buying it.

"Look, I'm not saying you have to believe what Jack was saying," Kate insisted. "But you should believe he *was* saying it."

McGee turned back to her.

"And was there anything? On TV, or in books, that might have put this idea into his head?"

Kate shook her head. "Not as far as I know. He watched

normal kids' shows, and for a while I paid more attention to them, to see if there was anything there... But of course there wasn't." She shrugged, looking frustrated. "They don't tend to be about living past lives."

For a moment McGee thought back to his own years as a parent, but it was so long ago he couldn't isolate a single show his daughters had watched.

"How about books? You have any books on reincarnation in the house? For adults, I mean. I guess what I'm asking is, was this something that you were into? Yourself or your husband?"

"I mean, it's possible," Kate replied, "But I never found anything. And of course Jack couldn't read at that point."

"How about the TV?" Robbins interjected. "Netflix? Paramount? They always have shows on this kind of bullshit. Maybe we can go back, see what you watched?" The way he said it, it sounded more like a threat than an offer to help.

Kate didn't answer, and McGee found himself staring for a long time at his partner, lost in thought.

"OK," he said after a while, coming back to the present. "What was he like when he said this kind of thing? Was he excited? Was it like a game he was playing?"

"No, he was usually very calm. That's what made it weird. It was like he wasn't really himself, like he wasn't quite there."

"He go see-through?" Robbins cut in.

"Excuse me?" Kate turned to him, and McGee did too, feeling his partner had gone too far. Robbins held up a hand in apology.

"You don't have to answer that. I just find this kind of thing a little hard to swallow." Robbins didn't take his eyes off Kate as he spoke. "Especially when four people have burned to death. And we're trying to work out who's responsible."

There was a silence, Kate unwilling to go on and McGee unsure whether to encourage her or back his partner.

"So maybe I'm just checking if you want to drop all this..."—

Robbins paused, but then found the word he wanted—"*Super-natural* stuff, and just tell us who set the fire? It'd save us a lot of time."

Kate did answer this, her voice much quieter. "I told you, I didn't see."

But as she spoke she suddenly wasn't able to hold eye contact, and her face flushed. McGee's training kicked in at once, the result of decades of waiting for these moments. They told him so much more than anything she actually said.

But at the same time, something else happened too. From somewhere—he didn't know where—the idea formed that not only had she seen, but she was actually reliving the moment in her own mind, *right now*. It was strange. Almost like—if he could only bring himself to concentrate in the correct way—he'd be able to view the thoughts in her head as clearly as if he were in there with her.

"Or maybe you're just saying that," Robbins continued, "because it was *you* that set the fire? And all of this, the whole crazy story, is some weird attempt to cover it up?"

Kate didn't reply.

"You're just trying to gaslight us. Going for the sympathy vote?" Robbins shrugged, as if the precise reason for her story wasn't important.

The two of them stared at each other, and McGee's mind was his own again. He took a moment to try and examine what had just happened, but other than it having been a long week and the fact that he was getting too old for this shit, he had no idea.

"No," Kate said, sitting back in her chair.

There was silence in the room, and McGee realized they were both waiting for him to push things onward. He decided to start afresh. Let her tell a part of the story that wasn't so hard to believe.

"You mentioned there'd been complications with the house.

Something about the finances that your father had left you which put a lot of pressure on you and the family? But you never really explained it. Could you tell us about that now?"

Kate replied, her eyes still on Robbins. "Sure... but it wasn't really about the house, not exactly."

"OK," McGee said. "So what was it about?"

"It was about Aaron."

McGee frowned.

"What about him?"

Kate took a moment to look McGee in the eye before answering.

"It was when Aaron got arrested."

Amber calls me three times while I'm in the shower, and as I notice while toweling my hair dry that I've missed her, a text comes in from her.

> Where are you? The police have got Aaron.

I text back the single word '*What?*', and then try to call her back; when there's no reply I message again, telling her I'll wait for her to call me. But when fifteen minutes later my phone still hasn't rung, I try her cell again. This time she picks up at once, but she's in such a state that I can barely understand what she's saying. It's something to do with a girl—a stupid girl—Amber calls her.

"They're holding him for further questioning," she tells me; she sounds broken. "I can't get hold of Brock, and Bea isn't answering her phone. Can you get here?"

"Of course," I reply before I even think about it. I have Jack.

As soon as I hang up, I pause to consider. Jan's on vacation this week so she can't help, and Neil has a class this morning. I consider waiting until he's out so that he can come home and look after Jack, but then I hear the pain in my sister's voice all over again. And the twins' college is only a two-hour drive. If I leave now, I'll be there by the time Neil's finished. So I tell Jack we're going on an adventure, a little road trip. And I pack him in the back seat with some toys and pull the straps tight.

I try Amber's number several times while I'm driving, but it doesn't connect, so I end up following the directions she's texted me without being able to speak to her again. They take us to a hotel. I recognize the name; I think Amber and the twins stayed here before when they were deciding which college they wanted to attend, but I'm a little surprised at how expensive it looks. I carry Jack on one arm as I head to the reception desk, unsure exactly what I need to ask the girl there, but then I see Eva standing up from the seats in the lobby, coming over to intercept me. Her face is white.

"They're upstairs," she says, by way of a greeting.

"What's going on?" I ask her, but she turns away.

I notice the hotel has a bank of elevators—I do still have Jack on my hip—but Eva leads the way up a wide, carpeted stairway that dominates the lobby. I want to ask again what's happening, but her slender back is still turned away from me. We climb to the second floor, and then she leads me along a hallway before slotting a keycard into a bedroom door.

"Kate," Amber says the moment she sees me. "You came!" I catch just a hint of surprise in her voice.

The room is large; I guess you'd call it a suite—it has a sitting area with a sofa and two armchairs, one of which Amber is pushing herself up from. I'm surprised as Brock emerges at the same time, appearing from what must be the bathroom. He must have arrived after Amber called me.

"And Jack's here too?" Amber pulls my attention back.

"I had to bring him. Neil's at work."

"Of course." She nods, as if both pleased and displeased. But a watery smile seems to dismiss the confusion and she squeezes Jack's cheeks. "Thank you for coming." She kisses me on my cheeks and gestures for me to sit. I consider telling Jack to go and play, perhaps with Eva, who has thrown herself onto one of the double beds and is now looking at her cellphone, a dark look on her face. But he's clingy, so I just sit down and put him on my lap.

"What's this all about? What's happened?"

I direct the question openly, and I'm not sure if Amber or Brock are going to reply. I don't think they're sure either, but in the end it's my sister.

"They're holding him overnight," she says finally. "In a prison cell."

"It's a holding cell," Brock corrects her. "They're going to make a decision whether to charge him in the morning." He's pacing, walking to the wall, turning around and then walking back, as if he's not even aware he's doing it. I look back at Amber.

"But what's he been accused of?"

Before replying, Amber carefully smooths the line of one eyebrow, as if steadying herself.

"It's bullshit. Total bullshit, but they take these things so seriously these days." She looks to me as if expecting me to agree. But I can't. I still don't know what it's about.

"They always believe the girl."

Still I wait, but my sister looks away.

"Of what? What's he d—" I stop before completing the word "done" and correct myself. I think before she notices.

"What's he been accused of?"

My sister takes a deep breath.

"Last night Aaron went on a date with a girl from his class. They went to a restaurant in town. They ate pizzas." She gives me a look, like this demonstrates how normal it was.

"Everything was normal, except that Aaron says it didn't go particularly well—he'd already decided he wasn't going to see her again, it wasn't going to go anywhere—and when they finished he drove her back to her dorms. She's a student here just like he is." She pauses again as if she's picturing it now, but something catches my mind. I say it before I can think.

"Aaron has a car?"

Amber's eyes flick up, then she waves a hand dismissively. "A little one. We bought one for each of the twins. They need them to get around."

"Matching BMWs," Brock tells me, without stopping his pacing.

"That's hardly important." My sister sniffs, as if the crying has blocked her nose, and she reaches for a tissue from a box on the table.

"The point is he drives her home, and when they get there, she's expecting more—she wants him to kiss her, she probably wants him to come in with her—but he just thanks her for the evening and waits for her to get out of the car." Amber shrugs. "I don't know, maybe she's upset by that?"

I wait a beat, but she doesn't go on.

"That's it?"

"In a way yes, but..." Her forehead creases into a frown. "Eventually she gets the message, the silly girl, and she gets out the car. Then Aaron waits for her to get to the door—he makes sure she gets in safe, because that's how we brought him up? You know, to be respectful?" She looks up at Brock, and for a second he stops pacing and nods his head.

"And she goes inside, and he drives away."

I wait for more, but it doesn't come.

"I'm sorry, I don't—"

Amber shakes her head impatiently. "It's the next morning that it happens. This morning, first thing, these two detectives turn up at Aaron's door. They tell him that this girl has made a complaint about him. Aaron gets angry, as anyone would, and they end up arresting him."

Suddenly Jack's weight on my lap feels heavy. I wonder how much of this he's able to understand, and what I can do to make sure he doesn't hear any more. As my sister has been speaking, and actually the whole time I was driving here, a single word has been appearing in my mind, and now it's there, as if flashing in neon. The word is *rape*.

"Are we talking... are we talking about a *sexual* complaint?" I say the word quietly, trying to signal to Amber that Jack's here and we shouldn't say anything too explicit. But she frowns at me instead.

"A sexual... No!" She makes a face. "Oh my God, Kate. No. It's nothing like that." Amber gives me an incredulous look, as if she can't believe I'd even think such a thing. "No, the girl has a couple of little bruises on her face, that's all. And she says that she and Aaron had a disagreement and he hit her, then pushed her out of the car."

Her words don't make any sense.

"I'm sorry? *What?*"

"Exactly! It's completely crazy. The police say this girl has an injury on her face, and that it was Aaron who hit her. And now they want to charge him with assault."

I'm stunned. I don't know what to say.

"But why? I mean, why would Aaron—"

"He *wouldn't*. He didn't. Of course he wouldn't. And he's totally baffled as to why the girl is even saying it. I mean, like I say, the date didn't go that well, so perhaps she's upset about that?" She shrugs again. "But to make up something like this, she must be crazy."

I try to force my brain to properly connect with what she's saying. It really doesn't make sense.

"But Aaron didn't...? I mean, you've talked with him? And he says nothing happened?"

"Of course. I mean... talked is perhaps overstating it. We've spent the whole morning in the police station, and they let us see him for less than ten minutes." Amber turns away in disgust.

"We're bringing in our attorney," Brock interrupts. "He's on vacation in the Caribbean, but obviously he's cutting it short."

"Obviously," Amber repeats.

I don't reply to this, but I wonder for a moment what they actually mean. Do Amber and Brock have an attorney they keep on some sort of retainer? Or does she mean he's someone Brock's family have worked with? That would make more sense; they're that sort of family, but I didn't know Amber was now like that too.

"Brock's family have known him for years." Amber reads my mind, or part of it. "He's really good."

The weight of Jack on my thighs is beginning to hurt, so I lift him off and sit him beside me. He's clearly sensing the tension in the room and doesn't want to leave my side.

"I still don't understand. Aaron says he didn't do anything to this girl, so how come she's made a complaint?" I search for exactly what it is that doesn't make sense. "I mean, does she have actual injuries?"

It's Brock who answers me. "A few bruises. Nothing too serious."

I don't understand what he's implying here—that Aaron can't have hit her too hard?

"But Aaron didn't actually do it—I mean, he didn't do it at all?"

"*No*," Amber replies. She shakes her head, as if dislodging the thought that he could have.

"And there's nothing the girl could have misinterpreted? Misconstrued? An accident?" I go on.

"No. Nothing at all. He said goodnight, she got out the car and walked to her door. That was it."

"And she wasn't injured at that point?"

"No."

"So... Are you saying that someone else did it?"

This time Amber just throws her hands up in a dramatic shrug.

"I don't know. We don't know."

"Did you want to get some food?" Brock asks suddenly. "I can have something sent up?" The question surprises me since eating is the last thing on my mind, but then he goes on, "Or something for Jack maybe?"

I turn to my son and ask him. And Jack, who would usually have eaten his lunch by now, nods his head. So Brock gets on the phone and discovers there's a kids' menu, and eventually orders a burger. Then Amber cuts in and says she'll have one too, because they haven't eaten today at all. I've no idea how long I'm going to be here, so I get a burger too, and we sit for a while, waiting for the food to arrive.

"So what happens next?" I ask, and it's Brock who seems to have taken over the explaining.

"Jon—Jon Voight, that's our attorney—he's landing at eight tonight." He checks his watch and I'm surprised to see it's nearly five. "First thing tomorrow he'll try and get Aaron out, and then we'll have to start fighting this thing."

"And what does that mean, exactly? How do you fight something like this?"

Brock doesn't answer for a moment; he half shrugs, his eyes widen. I know why: this isn't like anything we've ever faced before.

"Jon'll know," Brock says finally. "God only knows what we'll have to do, but Jon'll know."

"The thing I can't bear," Amber says, "is how this will stay with Aaron his whole life. He's done nothing wrong except the decent thing and taking this nutcase on a date, and this is how she repays him? It's disgusting."

The room falls into silence. I have more questions, but I don't know where to start exactly. On top of that I'm also beginning to wonder why I'm here. On the phone Amber said she needed me, but aside from moral support, I'm not sure why. Except I'm beginning to suspect I was called when Amber was in the blind-panic stage, and she's already moved well beyond that. Maybe Brock senses this as well.

"Are you staying the night?" he asks now. "I can phone down again; I'm sure they have more rooms."

I look at my sister, but her face offers no clue as to what she's expecting. So I think about Jack and Neil instead. Neil's offered to drive up himself as soon as he's done with work.

"Eva knows her, by the way," Amber says suddenly.

"What?"

"The girl, the stupid..."—it looks for a second like Amber is going to swear, but she doesn't—"silly girl who's made these allegations. These *false* allegations." She breathes heavily, and it takes me a moment to unpack what she's said.

"Eva knows her?"

"Not to speak to," Eva says now, from the bed. "I've seen her around, is all."

"And what's she like?" Amber goes on.

"I dunno. Like I said," Eva protests. "She's a bit... full of herself. Like, she's really pretty and that. But we're in different classes. I've just seen her around."

Amber turns away, as if unhappy that her daughter hasn't done a better reconnaissance job.

There's a knock on the door, and a man's there with a cart. He pushes it in, and Brock thanks him and slips him ten dollars. Then he hands around the food. It's good to have something to distract Jack with, and it gives me time to think. When Brock asks again if I'm staying I have an answer this time.

"Amber, do you need me to stay? There's Neil at home and obviously I have Jack..."

For a second she looks confused, as if she can't understand why I would put this decision on her, on top of everything else she's going through. But then she hides the look under a caring smile.

"No. I mean, if you *want* to, of course we'll pay for the room, if you prefer to head back in the morning." She smiles at me. "But we'll be fine. Jon'll be here soon and he'll know what to do. Thank you, Kate. Thank you for coming to help, it means a lot."

SIXTEEN

"So what happened next?" McGee asked when Kate seemed to have finished. She ran her finger over an eyebrow before replying.

"Well, it all got worse before it got better. I wasn't involved, not personally. I drove up there that one time, but Amber told me about the rest of it in text messages and calls. And I had to piece it together, everything they did with the lawyer."

"OK." McGee made a steeple with his fingers and waited.

Kate took a deep breath, like she found the whole story distasteful. "First, we found out that Amber and Brock had underestimated the extent of the girl's injuries. They told me it was just a few bruises, but it turned out she had a broken jaw. Bad enough that the poor girl was unlikely to ever fully recover."

"And he still denied it?"

"His story never changed. He said she was fine when she got out of the car. The police arrested him the next morning, and that was the first he heard she was hurt."

"OK... But a broken jaw? That would be... aggravated assault, right?"

Kate nodded. "Yeah, that's what they said. And obviously Amber completely freaked out about it. All she could see was Aaron's perfect future going up in smoke."

McGee thought for a moment, trying to work out what pieces of this puzzle he needed to fit together. "You said what happened to Aaron was connected to your father's house, that it put pressure on the family. Can you explain that?"

Kate nodded but stayed quiet for a while, apparently lining up the story in her own mind.

"At first the case against Aaron seemed very strong. Voight —the attorney they used—believed they wanted to make an example of him. They put up this star prosecutor and they were going to link it to the whole crackdown on male violence thing. And it seems the girl's family were pushing for this too. Amber hated them, she called them 'crazy scheming hippies'; she thought the whole thing was a set-up just to hurt Aaron. But the point was, for a while it looked like it was going to cost thousands to defend him. Hundreds of thousands. It wasn't just Voight; he said they needed a whole team."

"Did they have that kind of money? Your sister and her husband?"

Kate shook her head.

"No. That was the problem. About a week after I drove up there, Amber called me. And she told me how all the plans for the house were over. We were going to have to sell it all. To pay for Aaron's defense."

"Did she ask, or did she tell you?"

Kate scoffed. "It was more of a tell. But I could understand it. In the circumstances."

McGee considered. "You sure about that?"

She frowned at him.

"What do you mean?"

"I mean, he wasn't *your* kid. You've already made it clear you didn't like him that much. And you've only got his word for it that he didn't hit this girl. Now you find out the house your father left you is going to be sold to pay to defend him. That can't have felt great?"

"Of course it didn't!" Kate snapped. "But I still wanted to support my sister. It was still the right thing to do. And to be honest, I didn't care that much. I was... preoccupied with the stuff Jack was saying by then."

McGee resisted a glance at his partner. "We'll get back to that in a minute. What happened next? Did they charge him? Did the case go to trial?"

Kate shook her head.

"No. Voight—the attorney my sister used—he turned out to be very good, very cunning. He came up with this alternative version of what must have happened if it wasn't Aaron that hit her."

"And what was that?"

"Well, if it wasn't Aaron, and if the girl wasn't blaming anyone else—which she wasn't—then it had to have been her. She had to have caused her own injuries, and be blaming it on him."

"Setting him up?"

"Exactly."

"She'd need to be pretty crazy to break her own jaw."

"That was Voight's point. Most people assumed that the worse the girl's injuries were, the more likely it was that Aaron did it, but he argued the opposite. You have to be crazy to make a false accusation for no reason, and what better evidence of being crazy than breaking your own jaw? And then he started looking for any evidence in her background of a history of mental health issues."

"What they find?"

"Somehow Voight got access to her social media history." Kate sighed. "Darcy, the girl's name was Darcy. It turned out that a few years previously, she had a friend who took her own life. And Darcy became sort of obsessed with it, posting all these tributes. Dwelling on it, longer than was... normal. Voight used it against her."

"How?"

"Apparently the poor girl went to counselling for months, and she was taking anti-depressants when the assault happened. The *alleged* assault. Voight put pressure on the prosecutor's office, on the family, they threatened that all this would come out, that they'd paint this poor girl as the real perpetrator, and Aaron as the victim."

McGee tried to see how this story connected, or intersected, with what they already knew. But it was just another piece of a jigsaw that he didn't know where to place.

"What happened then?" he asked.

"About a month later she dropped all the charges. That was it."

"So no trial..." McGee tried to connect the dots. "I guess that's how your family came to keep the lake house? Suddenly Amber didn't need to spend a ton on the lawyers?"

"I'm sure Jon Voight did well enough from the whole affair. But yeah... Actually, it was more than that. Amber and Brock had squeezed all this extra money from the business when it looked like they'd need every dime. And when they didn't have to spend it on defending Aaron, they decided to pour it into the lake house instead. But this time there was no consultation. It wasn't the three of us sisters deciding together what we were going to do. This time Amber just told us she was going to upgrade the plans. But she made it sound very generous. Her and Brock were going to pay, and we'd both get to benefit. We still had a third of the house each; it was just going to be a much better house." Kate smiled, but there was no humor in it.

"That bothered you?"

She shrugged. "I suppose, a little bit. But I was more

focused on my own family. What Jack was saying, what it *meant*."

There was no doubt in McGee's mind they'd return to that part of the story. But he decided he wasn't quite ready to move on from Aaron's role in events.

"What did you believe?" he asked.

"About what?"

"Aaron. You've got these two kids in the car. She says he punched her and broke her jaw. He says he didn't touch her, and she must have done it to herself. Which one do you believe?"

"I..." Kate shook her head. "That's hard to answer. I wasn't there."

"I'm not saying you were. But you've known Aaron his whole life. Do you believe this was the sort of thing he was capable of?"

She avoided his gaze for a few moments, then gave up. "I don't know. I didn't know. Neil and I talked about it obviously, and we weren't sure. We didn't even want to consider that he might have done it, but why would the girl lie? That's what we couldn't work out. We weren't sure."

"So what you're saying, if I'm not wrong," McGee pressed gently, "is that it wouldn't have been entirely out of character for Aaron to have done this? That he might have broken this girl's jaw in an unprovoked attack?"

It took Kate a few seconds to answer, and when she did so it was with a non-committal shrug.

SEVENTEEN

"OK, let's get back to Jack," McGee said then. "How were things going at this point? Was he still saying the same things?"

"More and more."

"How about your husband? With his scientific background? What was his view?"

In response a half-smile flashed over Kate's lips, conflicted. "I guess you could say things got complicated. You have to understand about Neil; he's not just a scientist, he's an *evolutionary biologist*. His whole career is based on how we evolved by blind luck from chemicals in a primordial soup. We come from nothing; when we die we return to nothing, that sort of thing. And he's quite certain that the evidence on this is clear. So what Jack was saying—that he'd lived before—it was like a direct challenge to Neil that was... *awkward*."

"How did you resolve it?"

"I'm not sure we did. For a long time I think we both tried to avoid it, but that was unsustainable because Jack kept saying things to me, more and more often. So eventually I knew I'd have to speak to Neil about it again.".

"Tell us about that." McGee settled back in his chair. "Tell us how it went."

"Here, take this." Neil holds out a glass of white wine, droplets of water condensing on the outside. "You've earned it."

"Thanks." I smile, my hand brushing his as I take the glass, but it isn't true: tonight's bedtime wasn't a difficult one. The only time Jack mentioned living before was when I read him his book, and he told me his other mommy read him books too, but that she didn't do it any better than me, or worse. Just different.

Neil's wearing an apron printed with bright red apples; there's a pan bubbling on the stove top.

"What's for dinner?"

"*Italiano,*" he replies, making a poor stab at an Italian accent. "Spaghetti carbonara." He lifts out a forkful of pasta as he speaks. "Ready in three minutes. How'd he go down?"

I don't answer for a moment. And then suddenly I know I'm going to say something. I can't keep this to myself any longer. We're not a couple if we can't discuss something like this. We're strong enough to face this together.

"He was fine," I say, and continue before my nerve goes. "He said something though, something weird again."

Neil stops, clearly intrigued, and maybe a little concerned too. "What'd he say?"

I take a deep breath. I can't keep my eyes on his face. "Neil, he just told me that he died before, and that he came back and chose us. I think we need to talk about this."

There's a sudden, heavy silence, with just the noise of the pasta bubbling on the stove. Before Neil replies.

"Wow! OK." He shakes his head. "Wow."

"I'm not saying I believe him, but ever since we first talked about getting bigger, he's saying weird stuff more and more often. I haven't wanted to bother you with it but... we can't just pretend it's not happening."

It takes Neil a long time to answer me, but when he does I feel a rush of relief. And love.

"No, you're right." He bites his lip. "We need to address it."

We're both silent for a moment; this isn't exactly something either of us expected when we dreamed of being parents. Yet here we are.

"What do you make of it?" I ask. And I don't know what I expect from my scientist husband. I don't know if my expectations are unreasonable, but I don't get the response I want. There isn't a moment when he even *considers* believing him.

"It's interesting," Neil begins. "He must have heard the idea from somewhere, and now he's repeating it."

"Where would he have heard an idea like that?"

"I really don't know." Neil takes a sip of his wine, and now he seems to be acting as though this isn't a big deal, as if this maybe isn't even the biggest issue he's dealt with *today*. "It could be something he's seen on TV or overheard somewhere. If you think about it, at his age, when he's just beginning to learn about life, it makes some sense that he should be thinking about the opposite, about death."

I try to think about this, but nothing makes sense.

"I don't understand."

"No, nor do I, not exactly. But think about it. We tell him all the time that he came from your belly, and he sees people all around him, of different ages... And then not so long ago there was all that business about your father dying, so he has been exposed to these ideas. I suppose this is just... just the way it comes back out again."

I don't know why, but his explanation disappoints me. It's so... banal. "So you don't believe him?"

Neil actually laughs at that. "Do I believe that he lived before? No. Of course not."

"But it does happen," I begin to insist, though I immediately regret the phrase. I've done some research and discovered that it's not completely unheard of for children to report memories of past lives. Or at least, that it's more common than you might think. But it's the wrong thing to say to Neil, to imply that *reincarnation* itself is real, when what I meant is that some children really do make these claims, for whatever reason.

But from the look on his face, he's not concerned about either point, and that makes me try to push things.

"There was a case in Oklahoma, a boy who claimed to be reincarnated from a man who died in a mining accident. And he knew all this stuff about mining, even the layout of the tunnels. And there are loads more cases in India."

He laughs again. Except it's not a real laugh, but a kind of self-satisfied chuckle that he uses when we're talking about people who aren't as clever as we are. As *he* is, I should say, since he's the one with the doctorate.

"I agree it's an interesting phenomenon, and some of these stories can appear convincing, superficially. But not once you understand the underlying mechanisms that are driving it—"

"Like what? What mechanisms?" The conversation is a little heated now, my voice taut, almost challenging. Neil's alert to it. But before he answers he turns off the pasta and drains the pan in the sink. Then he pours in a little olive oil and mixes it with the fork. By the time he speaks his voice is calm, compassionate.

"Kate, this is a subject that's been very carefully investigated. There are all sorts of well-understood psychological factors that can explain this phenomenon. For example, studies have shown that young children are remarkably receptive to the creation and implanting of false memories."

"What the hell is a false memory?"

Neil looks around the room a moment before replying. His eyes alight on his phone. He holds it up to show me.

"We think of our memories like the videos or photographs we record on our smartphones, but memories aren't accurate recordings of reality, just our interpretation of it, and they can change over time." He frowns, not content with his explanation. "Memories can be influenced by suggestion, by leading questions, or even societal expectations. Sometimes these distortions are minor, but they can also be quite significant and can convince you that something happened in a certain way when it actually didn't—or even that it happened at all when it never actually did."

I open my hands to show I'm not really following.

"Elizabeth Loftus." Neil snaps his fingers so they rest in a pointing motion, which I know I'm supposed to find dynamic and convincing. But I've no idea who he's talking about. "The cognitive psychologist? She's done a lot of work on this." He looks at me as if he's still expecting me to have heard of her. But I shake my head.

"She did a ton of studies demonstrating how easy it is to implant false memories. All it takes is a tiny little push—a suggestive question or a leading statement, and the mind can fill in the gaps. It creates these vivid, entirely believable 'memories.' It's really incredible."

I'm calmer now; the rush of blood has faded away, and I'm listening. Honestly with Neil it's usually better that way, he knows so much.

"But what would Jack have heard for him to be saying he's been reincarnated?" I can't help but picture Jan as I say this, and all the things she could totally have told him while my back was turned.

"I'm not sure we're at that stage yet." Neil's face crumples in mock surprise at my choice of words. "He is saying some strange things, granted, but he's not claiming *that*."

He pauses, suddenly thoughtful again. "Even that boy in Oklahoma you just mentioned—the one who claimed to be a miner? He was likely picking up tiny cues and prompts from his environment, words and conversations he'd overheard which he then stitched together to form a narrative. Human beings have an amazing capacity to seek out patterns, sometimes where they don't even exist. It's called 'pareidolia.' The boy's parents would have been just as susceptible. Without even knowing it, they're probably interpreting unrelated statements and actions because their brains are hardwired to find a pattern."

I break off for a moment and take a large sip of wine. Neil's left the pasta steaming gently in the strainer. I don't feel hungry anymore.

"That boy in Oklahoma knew the name of the man he used to be."

"The man *he claimed* he used to be."

I shake off the correction, irritated. "He knew all sorts of things about him, about his family."

"Which is entirely explainable by confirmation bias. Once the idea of a past life is suggested, once the parents are looking for it, every 'correct' statement is taken as confirmation, while the much more frequent 'incorrect' statements are ignored or forgotten."

"How does that explain the boy telling them things he couldn't possibly have known?"

"It doesn't—because he *didn't*. The things he 'knew' were simply coincidences or lucky guesses."

"But the boy described his death in detail—he had nightmares about it, just like Jack does."

We're both quiet for a moment.

"Jack doesn't have dreams of dying in a mining accident," Neil says quietly, and I screw my eyes shut.

"I didn't mean that."

He reaches out a hand and rests it on my shoulder, squeezing gently. "I know, I'm sorry. The point is, as strange as cases like this seem, in almost every instance the so-called mystery is perfectly explainable."

He's still holding my shoulder and I drop my head, looking down at the floor. Suddenly I'm feeling the cumulative effect of God knows how many nights in a row without sleeping properly.

"There are still things that can't be explained by coincidence," I protest. "The really specific things? The Oklahoma boy remembered that he had a sister, that the miner had a sister. He remembered her name, and that she had a dog called George." I watch Neil now; this is the part I just can't wrap my head around. For a moment it looks like he can't either, but then he shrugs.

"People lie, Kate. For all sorts of reasons. And for no reason. For all we know the boy in Oklahoma never said those things. Or if he did, his parents could have coached him to into it."

"But why? What would they get out of it?"

"Fame? Notoriety? After all, *we've* heard of them, and if they hadn't made those claims, we certainly wouldn't have."

He looks at the pasta and moves to the stove to stir the sauce.

"Come on, you look hungry. Let's eat."

EIGHTEEN

It's mid-afternoon, raining, and Jack's just waking up from his nap. Neil's still at work and won't be back till six, so it's just the two of us here. I was going to take Jack for a walk, but not with this weather. So instead I'm going to try and get him to say a little bit more about who he thinks he was. If that's what he really thinks.

He cries a little as he wakes, but soon he's rubbing his eyes and wanting to explore. He can walk really well now; actually he can run, and that seems to be his preferred method of movement. So it takes a while to get him to slow down enough to take an interest in his blocks, but finally I do, and we build a tower taller than he is, and then he knocks it down and we start again. I let him do it a few more times before I ask him.

"Did you build towers when you were bigger?"

He stops at once and looks at me suspiciously. I feel a shaft of—what? Guilt, I suppose. Like I shouldn't be asking him questions like this, like I'm going to mess him up if I do. And if he *does* tell me something, then all I've done is implanted the idea in his head in the first place. But on the other hand, how am I supposed to find out anything if I can't ask him?

"*Bigger me*," he replies, then turns back to the blocks, starting to pile them up again.

"Bigger you," I repeat. "Did you like making towers?"

"Sometimes," he says, offhandedly, but I know he's remembering now. There are times when it's clear he has no memory of this stuff at all, and when I ask him, he literally doesn't have a clue what I'm talking about. But other times I can see he knows.

"Sometimes? Did you do them with your mommy?"

"Mommy."

"But not me? Another mommy?"

He shrugs, non-committal.

"Not blue blocks." The set we have is wooden, and mostly they're painted in different shades of blue. It was a present from Neil's mother.

"What color then?"

"All 'ulor." For a moment he slips back into his old habit of not forming the beginnings of his words.

"All colors?"

He nods, and for a moment he meets my eye. I take his hand, keeping his attention on me.

"Do you remember who you were? When you were bigger?"

For a second he keeps his eyes on me, then nods very slightly, looking away.

"Who Jack? Who were you?"

"'Ack," he says, his attention on the blocks again. "Tower, Mommy, make 'ower."

Jack. He was Jack. Of course he was! He just thinks that he was Jack, but somehow bigger. It's just his childhood imagination. Just like Neil said. I'm somehow both relieved and disappointed.

My phone trings into life. A call.

I check the display before picking up, and feel a shaft of warmth.

"Hi Jan, how's your day?"

"Awful. We've been to the park, *in the stinking rain,* because Danny insisted, and then he didn't like it because the swings were wet—I obviously told him they would be—so we came back, and now I'm going to murder both my children. Unless you meet up for a coffee with me. I promise I won't swear in front of Jack."

I laugh. The truth is I was hoping she might call. "Do you want to come here?"

"No, your coffee is disgusting. Let's meet in the Flagstaff."

The Flagstaff Café is popular with moms, but it's late afternoon and it's thinning out a bit. Jan's already there—I suspect she might have even called me from there, judging by the amount of Tupperware pots and empty coffee cups on the table. Her two are lost in the plastic play area, and Jack's eager to get involved too.

"Take your shoes off," I call to him. Then I watch as he comes running back to me so I can do it for him. And then he's gone, running in his socks into the play area.

"What are you *feeding* him?" Jan asks, sarcastic. "He's getting bigger every day."

A waitress comes, a girl, who casts a wary glance at the table top. You're not supposed to bring your own food here and Jan's apparently emptied her pantry, but the waitress makes the wise choice to say nothing.

"What can I get you?" she asks me instead. I order a cappuccino, and when it comes I take a moment to enjoy it.

"So, how's your research going?" Jan eyes me as she asks the question.

We've talked, a bit, since she made the initial suggestion that Jack's comments could have something to do with the strange subject of reincarnation, and I get the impression she's done her own reading on the topic.

"Is he still talking about it?"

"A little..." I ponder a moment, taking another sip from my coffee. If it wasn't Jan, I definitely wouldn't want to talk about this, but there's something about how open she is with everything in her own life that makes me relax my guard. "I asked him today if he remembered who he was in his old life."

"Oooo..." Jan leans forward. "Go on, spill the beans! No, let me guess, he was that guy from Nirvana who shot himself—that would be so cool, and he looks like a rock star." She bites her lip, a habit she has when she's talking too much and wants to shut herself up. "Go on, what'd he say?"

I shake my head. "Nothing. He said he was just Jack."

Jan looks disappointed.

"That's boring. Can't you implant something? The Nirvana guy?" Now I *know* she's been reading about this, like me, because there's no way she would know about implanting memories.

"Hang on." Jan raises a finger in the air, interrupting my thoughts.

"What?"

"So did he say he was 'Jack' or did he say *'ack*?"

I think back. "I'm not sure. Ack, probably. But Ack *means* Jack. It's just what he calls himself."

"Does he though?" She waits a beat, and I get what she's saying just before she comes out with it. I hadn't met Jan, back when everything happened with my sister. But I've told her all about it.

"Ack could just as easily mean *Zack*."

Suddenly this conversation, which was kind of fun and light, makes me feel physically sick. I try and mask it with the coffee, but it's like someone's poured bleach into it. I put the cup down and it clatters onto the saucer, spilling a few splashes onto the table.

"That's ridiculous." Anyone else would see from my face that they shouldn't continue. But this is Jan.

"Is it though? Isn't that what the books say? That when a kid is reincarnated, it's quite often into the same family?"

"What books?"

Jan waves away the question. "Just something I got on Amazon. This Dr Palmer guy found loads of cases where a kid is reborn after a sudden or unexpected death in a family. Just like what happened with Zack."

I want to criticize her logic. But that bit at least is true. Amongst the several thousand cases collected by researchers, a fair number do involve children who claim to have memories of either older siblings or close family members who have died, usually quite recently.

"What's the gap between Zack's death and Jack being born? About three years?" Jan's eyes are alive now, filled with wonder. "*Ack—Jack—Zack.* Think about it?" She lays a hand on my arm. I think she finally gets that this is creeping me out now. "Hey, it's OK, you don't have to go so white."

We're both quiet a moment, but Jan doesn't let it rest. "Why don't you ask him again?" She bites her lip, but watches me. I can hear Jack now, playing with the other children in the jungle gym.

"You can't exactly *not* ask him." Jan gives me a knowing look, and she's right. "You're gonna do it, so you might as well do it with me here. For moral support."

I'm not about to call Jack over and interrogate him here in the café, but Jan quickly grabs my arm anyway, as if to stop me. "No, I've got a better idea. In this book I read, the scientist guy shows the children photos, and that way they can test if the child really knows who they were before, or if they're just saying so. We can do that now."

"How?"

Before I know it Jan has me browsing through my old Facebook photos, looking for an image of Zack. I don't recall specifically if Jack has ever seen any photos of Zack. We've said to him a couple of times that he used to have a cousin who died, but I don't know if he really understood. Or even really listened. Actually, I can't even remember if we *did* fully tell him, or whether we just planned to, at some point.

"Have you got one?" Jan asks, looking up from her own phone. "I'm gonna get a picture of another kid, a random one, and we'll see which one Jack says he was."

I scroll back in time through my texts. It takes quite a long time, but eventually I get back to when Zack was alive. In those days Bea kept me well updated with pictures of him, but quite a few were taken at the lake house, and I don't want to use them because Jack's been there and the background might give him a clue. In the end I select one from Zack's seventh birthday, where he's holding up a present just before opening it. It was actually the present I sent him, a water tower for a train set he was really into. Bea asked me to get it for him, and I guess she sent me the picture to say thanks. In the image Zack is staring right at the camera and looking happy. The background is Bea's old house, which she sold before Jack was born. Meanwhile Jan jokes about how her Google searches for "seven-year-old boy images" are going to get her arrested. I don't feel like joking now.

"Chocolate-chip cookies," Jan says.

"Excuse me?"

"Chocolate-chip cookies, that's what we need now," She yanks yet another plastic pot from her bag. Then she gets up and goes to the playground, sticks her head up the tunnel slide and calls the children over. Lured by the chocolate they come running, and she hands out the snacks. Her two stuff them in and demand more, but Jack sucks the chocolate from his. And that freaks me out slightly because I've just—literally moments ago—rejected a photograph of Zack sitting on the lake-house lawn, sucking the chocolate from a candy bar.

"No, that's enough you two, go and play, and you can have an apple later." Jan orders her children away. They're torn for a moment between pleading for more and the dubious attraction of the Flagstaff's play area, but the latter wins. Jack stays with us, licking his fingers. Jan weighs her iPhone in her hands, looking at me.

"Jack," I begin, my mouth dry. "You remember what we talked about at home. With the blocks?"

It's like he has no idea what I'm saying, but he stays put, chocolate around his lips.

"When I asked if you remembered who you were before, you said 'Ack.'"

He nods now. He remembers again. I feel the tension building.

"I've got some pictures here. Photographs of two boys. One of them might be the person you used to be. Would you like to take a look?" I glance at Jan, seeking reassurance I'm doing this right. She nods.

And Jack's interested now, I can see that. He moves closer, reaching for my phone. But I pull it away. This has to be done as scientifically as possible, I need him to see the two images at the same time. I hold the phone out of Jack's reach and tell Jan.

She nods. Getting it. Course she does. She's read the same book. We both hold our phones in front of Jack, our hands covering the screens, and when we're both ready I nod, and both of us take our hands away. Making it like a game. And Jack is suddenly faced with two images. Zack on my phone, and ten-year-old Daniel Radcliffe on Jan's. Harry Potter.

"*Jan!*"

Why the hell didn't I check who Jan was Googling? Jack hasn't seen *Harry Potter*, he's far too young, but it's certainly possible he's been exposed to it. Though thankfully he isn't dressed in the full wizard outfit. But I still think it's much more likely he'll pick that photo. I'm annoyed.

But that's not what happens. Instead, Jack barely glances at Jan's phone before his eyes settle on mine. He seems fascinated, then he stabs at it with his stocky little finger, which moves the image. So I pull it away from him, and at once his arms go up, clutching to get it back. He makes a noise too, an indignant, almost panicked gurgle. I hand him the device and this time he just stares at it. Suddenly I know, for sure, that this is the first time Jack has seen an image of Zack. His little eyes are wide open, and now the hairs on the back of my neck are literally standing up. I didn't know that was an actual real thing.

"'Ack!" Jack looks up at me, a blend of delight and confusion on his face. "'Ack. Bigger me. 'Ack!"

NINETEEN

It takes me a day or so to tell Neil, but I have to. I mean, you can't just pretend something like this isn't happening. And I sense that he knows anyway; it's there in the way he won't quite look at me when we talk, and how we avoid any subject that even comes close to the things Jack's saying. Even so, I wait for the weekend, when he won't have to dash off to work. Or be able to.

"Hey you, do you want eggs for breakfast?" It's a peace offering of sorts—though we haven't actually argued, we've just been off with each other. I notice suddenly that Neil's got his cycling gear on. He's not really into riding, so he doesn't wrap himself head to toe in Lycra; it's actually easy enough to miss.

"I was going to go for a quick ride." *A quick ride.* Code for *I don't want to speak about this.*

"Please. We need to talk."

He looks guilty for a moment, then nods. And then he's helpful, setting the table and being super attentive with Jack, who's also insisting on helping, carrying the plates from the kitchen and chattering the whole time. We sit him in his booster seat and give him an egg. When we're finished I put the TV on for Jack, and the coffee for Neil.

"Jack told me who he thinks he was, when he was bigger," I tell Neil, keeping my voice level and matter of fact. Rather comically, Neil has just picked up a copy of the *Journal of Evolutionary Biology*, which was delivered this week. The irony of the juxtaposition isn't lost on me.

For a few moments he continues to hold the journal in front of his face, before slowly lowering it.

"Oh really? Who?"

I wonder about making him guess. I wonder if he already knows. I'm certain, at this moment, that Neil will have asked Jack too—he's just too curious a person not to have done so—and he's smarter than me too. He'll have figured out the answer.

"Zack," I tell him. There's a silence between us.

"Yeah, I guess that figures."

I'm irritated by how casual his reply is.

"Don't you think it's interesting?"

"Yes. Very. I told you, I think it's fascinating."

"Do you think it's *possible*?"

He laughs at this. "No. Of course I don't." For a second his eyes return to his journal, as if he'd prefer to lose himself in it rather than have this conversation with me. But then the corners of his mouth turn up just slightly, and that tells me he's fundamentally a good person, a kind person, who loves me, and whom I love.

"Come here," he tells me, and after a moment I get what he means. He wraps his arms around me and pulls me tight. I didn't know that what I needed was physical contact, but now I have it I drink it in. I absorb his strength. I breathe him in.

"It's OK, Kate. I know it's... weird as hell, but it's OK. This doesn't mean we've done anything wrong as parents. It doesn't mean *you've* done anything wrong, and it doesn't mean there's anything wrong with Jack. This kind of thing just happens sometimes." He strokes my hair, smoothing it into my back. I feel his fingers on the strap of my bra, and it reminds me it's been a long time since we made love. His fingers linger a moment, as if he's thinking the same. Then he gently pushes me away from his body, but still holds me with his hands on my shoulders.

"Are you OK?"

For me the moment has passed. It's good—necessary, sometimes—to just connect physically. But I want to talk to him about this. I want him to accept it.

"Why don't you believe it?"

He doesn't answer at once, but he indicates that he will. He takes his coffee and sips it, before blowing out his breath in a noisy sigh.

"The concept of reincarnation requires for there to be some part of you, or me—or anybody—that exists separately to our bodies. However, that idea isn't supported by any evidence. Indeed, *all* the evidence out there suggests this *isn't* the case." He picks up the journal again as if he's about to show me something in it, but then drops it back on the table top.

"There are countless experiments that demonstrate how everything we know about consciousness, memory and personality can be traced back to biochemical processes in the brain. And *only* in the brain. On the contrary, every attempt to demonstrate the existence of a soul—or anything like it—has manifestly failed." He opens his hands into a shrug.

"There's no real evidence, Kate. You or I might not like that fact. It might not even 'feel' right. But I've been trained to follow the evidence, and to rely on it."

"I showed him a photograph of Zack," I say, my voice quiet. "Along with another photograph of a second boy," I don't tell him it was Daniel Radcliffe. "Can you guess which one he said he was?"

Neil hesitates. "I don't know. I would say it might be more likely that he picked Zack, but even so, it's a fifty-fifty guess."

His words take the drama from my reveal, but I say it anyway.

"He picked Zack."

Neil shrugs again. It's like I've proved him right.

"But it was the *way* he chose Zack," I go on, suddenly animated. This is my husband I'm talking to, my life partner, and I don't think there's ever been a more important moment in our lives. "You should have seen him; he looked so pleased to see the photograph, and yet so bewildered too. It was like he was being *validated*."

Please Neil, please see how fucking important this is to me.

"Kate..." Neil takes another deep breath. He's thinking hard. "I don't pretend to know exactly how this works, but Jack was born into a family that had recently suffered a terrible tragedy. Zack's death affected us all, but you three sisters most profoundly." He pauses, giving himself the time to choose his words carefully. "With Bea moving away, you could argue that you've lost a sister as well as a nephew. And she of course has lost almost everything." He glances at Jack as he says this, and I do too. Our son is sitting watching cartoons, oblivious, and the thought of losing him is simply unbearable.

"These circumstances, a child born into a family that has suffered the tragic death of a child, not to mention the way your father passed..." He pauses, as if unhappy with his choice of language. "They're *exactly* the circumstances most likely to result in the later child believing—or saying—that they once *were* that earlier child."

I don't reply. I guess I'm trying to listen to him. To not be stupid, not be one of those gullible people that get drawn into nonsense theories. But I get a flash of memory about Dad too. Is he sitting up above looking down on this conversation where Neil is saying he doesn't exist? It's too much.

"It sounds like a coincidence too crazy to be true, doesn't it?" Neil continues. "A family not only loses a child, but then goes on to have another child who claims to have memories of an earlier life? What are the chances of two unusual events like that? But the reality is the chances of the second event are far higher for a family that has suffered the first event. The earlier tragedy is *what produces* the second event."

I have to break off, and I go to Jack and sit next to him. He glances at me, then looks back at the TV, and I can't help myself. I pull him close to me and squeeze him tight, too tight. For a second he resists, but then he melts into me. *My son. My beautiful son.*

"Did you use to be Zack?" I ask him quietly. I don't expect him to reply, he seems lost in the TV show. But he responds anyway.

"Yes." He gives me a half smile. Just being a good boy, answering my question.

The weight of it—the situation we're in—hits me again. I squeeze him a moment more, breathing in the smell of his hair, then go back to where Neil's sitting at the table, watching us.

"What do we do then?" I ask him. I'm—not convinced exactly—but nearly. Almost sure that even though what Neil is telling me doesn't *feel* right, it must somehow *be* right, because he's smarter than me, and he knows more than me—knows more than almost anyone I know. "What do we do when he says things like that?"

Neil thinks again. I don't know what he's doing in those moments: checking what he's about to say against some database of evidence stored in his mind? If so the fact-checked answer is surer than I expect.

"We have to tell him the truth."

My face must tell him I don't understand, or maybe that I don't like what he's said.

"We don't have to use words like 'reincarnation' or 'soul,'

but we should tell him that he isn't Zack, and he never was." He pauses, softening his words. "The worst thing we can do is encourage him."

"What if he keeps saying it?" As I speak I know I'm hoping he will, and I don't know where that comes from. Why is that something I would want? Maybe I'm a crazy conspiracy theorist?

"We have to be gentle with him," Neil replies. He seems unaware of how his words are dredging through my mind, stirring up chaos in their wake.

"But we put him right. I don't think it's going to be a massive issue for him. From what I've read, children that make claims like this only do so for a few years, and then the supposed 'memories' fade away. It's quite possible we all start life with similar thoughts, and we all forget about them."

Something about this last statement screams at me, and it takes a moment for me to realize what it is. If we all start life with memories of past lives, then shouldn't we take it more seriously? Like, a hell of a lot more seriously? But I'm prevented from saying this, because my slow-witted brain has finally arrived at the answer to my previous question. I now know why I don't want Jack to stop saying he used to be Zack—it's because it's a part of who Jack is. And I love every single part of my son.

But that doesn't make what he's saying real.

TWENTY

"Who did you really believe at this point?" asked McGee. "Your husband, or your son?"

"I don't know; I wanted to agree with Neil that it was crazy, but I was kind of split."

"How so?"

Kate shook her head. "I spent so much more time with Jack than I did with Neil. But Neil was clever, he had all the answers. But it changed a bit when I made the connection with..."

McGee frowned. "With what?"

"I told you we didn't give him actual baths because of how much he'd scream, and by then it seemed normal. But it wasn't. It really wasn't. And I guess that's when I finally connected things up."

"Come on little man, time to go to bed." Neil scoops Jack up into his arms and carries him upstairs. It'll take him an hour to bathe Jack and get him to sleep, and momentarily I'm lost. Most nights this is my routine and I'm used to it, and when Neil takes over I sometimes don't know what to do with this extra, empty, almost unwelcome hour. A thought hits me: I haven't spoken with Bea in a long time, and I consider phoning her, but something stops me. Instead I go upstairs to read, lying on my bed while half listening to the sounds of Neil bathing Jack.

I should tell you: when we talk about bathing Jack, we don't mean what most parents do. We don't put him *in* the water, we don't even fill the bath—we just undress him and clean him with baby wipes. But Neil has this idea that we can gradually get him used to water, first by cleaning him in the bathroom, where he can see the bath, and later by leaving the shower running, so he gets used to the sound of water while we clean him. That's where we are now.

I listen to Neil's voice, calm and soothing as he gets Jack undressed, and then the sound of the shower. There's no question of Neil trying to put him under it: Jack would scream blue murder, and even though they both know that's not going to happen, I hear the familiar response from Jack: alert, but not panicking or screaming, just warning Neil.

"*Ayak, ayown.*"

I've heard this phrase so many times I almost don't register it, but for some reason this time—finally—the meaning suddenly appears, as if written in the air in front of my eyes.

Ayak—*I Zack*
Ayown—*I drown*
I'm Zack. I drowned.

I gasp, choking for air, as if it's me suddenly trapped underwater. Jack might have seen Zack's photograph, but there's *no way on earth* we ever told him that Zack drowned.

It suddenly feels like the temperature in my bedroom has plummeted. I try to think, desperately trying to remember if anyone could have told Jack how Zack died. Why would they?

He's *not even four years old*. From the bathroom I hear Neil giving up, shutting off the shower, and his soothing voice again.

"It's OK, Jack. Calm down, little man. Let's turn that off, shall we?"

How could he know? How could Jack know that Zack drowned? But as soon as I ask myself the question, doubts flood in. Might Bea have said something? She still likes to talk about Zack, and I know she's told Jack about him, how he used to have a cousin, and how he would have liked him. Could she have said something about how Zack died?

But then I think back to the earliest moments with Jack, and my knuckles whiten again as I grip onto my book. They told us in the hospital not to bathe him until the umbilical cord fell off, so our first try was... what, maybe three weeks after we brought him home? And that was the beginning of it. That was the first time we knew he hated water. He cried, he fought, he made tiny fists with his hands. Even if Bea *had* told him that Zack drowned, and for some reason that stuck in his head, that must have happened later. Yet Jack's had his fear of water right from when he was born. Not a fear, a terror.

I feel an urgent, angry impulse to burst into the bathroom and confront Neil with this. But I don't. Because right away the doubts come again, a new wave. I know what he'll say. It's just a coincidence. It's just chance that he has a fear of water; it's just a coincidence that poor Zack drowned. And if Bea really did tell him, then it's no surprise that Jack's fear got worse. There's a natural explanation. Every time, there's always a rational answer. There's always a reason to conclude that our son isn't telling us the truth.

I think about calling Bea again, this time playing in my mind how I might ask her. *Hey sis, just checking in—did you ever tell Jack that Zack drowned? Why? Oh, just because he's saying he's the reincarnated spirit of your dead boy, you know, the one whose death you're probably never, ever, going to get over*. I drop the book and bury my head in my hands. This is... this is too much.

"*Ayack, ayown!*" Jack reminds Neil for about the thousandth time, as my husband rubs him down with a wet wipe.

"That's enough now," Neil replies. "We don't say silly things like that."

A new thought crystallizes in my mind, and even though I'm exhausted, this one sticks. Bea *knows* things. Stuff about Zack that I don't know, things that I couldn't possibly have passed onto Jack in any of the ways that Neil's told me about. So if I *could* ask her, then maybe I could find something that provides me with certainty, a way of deciding whether I ought to believe my scientist husband or my infant son. But I can't ask her. I can't tell her what Jack's saying. It would tear her apart.

I pull in a deep breath, still listening to the sounds of my non-believing husband and my reincarnated nephew finishing off in the bathroom and about to come here for his book, as if we were just an ordinary family having an ordinary bedtime. And then I think something else. *Someone* else. Someone I *can* talk to, who would know things about Zack that Jack couldn't possibly.

Tristan.

TWENTY-ONE

I'm lucky, Tris is on a break from his latest tour. In a few days he flies out to Asia for six weeks.

"Where exactly are you playing?" I ask as he settles into his seat opposite me in a booth in Starbucks. I would have preferred to do this in his apartment, but he didn't invite me there.

He sighs, like he's weary just at the thought of it. "We're doing a couple of gigs in Japan—Tokyo and Osaka, Then Singapore, Bangkok, Kuala Lumpur, Jakarta..." I think he's stopped, but he's just thinking. "Then Manila, on to India—Mumbai and Delhi." He stops again. "There's a few more but I forget."

"Wow," I reply.

"Yeah." He raises his eyebrows. "Glad I'm only doing the Asia leg. Getting too old for the whole thing."

"What's she like?" I ask, pointedly not naming the artist he's supporting. Tris has often told us how important discretion is in his job, even with family. Previously I've taken this to mean he doesn't want us asking, and I've taken a sort of pride in not doing so. But suddenly it's an easier topic than the one I came here to discuss.

"She's cool," he replies, and I assume this is all I'm going to get, but he seems to mistake my subsequent silence for wanting more information. "I'm just one of a whole crowd on the tour, so I don't really know her that well. But she's cool." He gives an awkward shrug of his shoulders.

"Hey, what's this about?" he goes on, his voice artificially bright now. "You said you wanted to ask about Zack?"

At these words my eyes swing—like I'm some Pavlovian dog—to Jack. He's asleep in his stroller, which isn't an accident by the way. I arranged this meeting for after a double-play session in the gymnasium, where he ran around chasing balls and balancing on beams for an hour, and then instead of going to the café he did it again. Now he's flat-out exhausted, and I'll be able to concentrate more easily on what Tris tells me.

"Yeah. I did." I force a smile back. With all my preparation I'd somehow fooled myself this would be easy. Now I'm here I can see I was wrong.

"OK." His smile at the thought of his son fades into a look of sadness as he remembers that poor Zack is dead. It's a look I know so well from my sister's face. Although on Bea it's deeper, more pronounced, and it never really leaves her. Or maybe Tris is just better at hiding it.

"I just wanted to—I don't know—this is going to sound a bit... silly," I begin, starting my pre-prepared excuse. "But with Jack growing up so fast, it's made me realize how much of Zack's early life I didn't get to see..." Now that I'm saying this out loud it sounds stupid, so I go on quickly, hoping it will get better. "I just wanted to know a little more about him." The obvious lameness of my words is somehow highlighted by the bright bustle of the coffee shop, surrounded by normal conversation. Tris eyes me, still not sure what to make of this. I try again.

"He was here for such a short time... and he was Jack's *cousin* and I wanted to..." I pause, reassessing what I intend to say, coming up with a subtle shift. "I wanted to *actually* remember him."

Tris considers this a while, thoughtfully turning a spoon around in his cup while I curse myself for asking him here. What was I thinking? What do I actually hope to achieve, besides making him feel like shit?

"You talk to Bea regularly?" he asks, after a while. I focus back on the here and now. I shake my head.

"Yes, but not as much as I ought to," I confess, trying to make this whole thing sound less weird than it is. "She's not the easiest to talk to."

And suddenly we're on common ground. "Tell me about it." He smiles, just a little. Then he shrugs. "Well, shoot, what do you wanna know?"

I lean forward, then force myself back in the chair. *Casual, keep it casual.* I've prepared a list of questions, things that I think Jack might remember if he really *was* Zack, even though that's ridiculous.

"Did he have any favorite toys when he was younger? Anything specific you can remember?" I begin.

He gives me a funny look, but I try to bluff it away with a smile. There's nothing weird here, just a totally normal conversation a guy might have with his sister-in-law about his son, who died seven years before. He answers. Slowly.

"He had this train. You remember that, right?" He looks questioningly at me and I see it in my mind at once. Not just Zack with his train, but Jack, nearly a year ago now, in Bea's little cottage, holding out his hands for it.

"Yeah. I think so." I frown, as if he's just reminded me, but then focus again. "But I was wondering if there was anything else? Before that, maybe?

Tris looks at me again like I'm behaving oddly, but he answers the question. "I guess when he was a bit younger, there was a bear he liked. Maybe it was Paddington Bear? I don't know exactly, it had a blue..."—he thinks again—"A little blue waistcoat."

"Do you have any photos of it?" I ask. When I texted Tris asking to meet up, I said it would be helpful if he could bring along some photos of Zack.

"I... I doubt it, no," he replies now. "I told you, Bea's got more photos of Zack than me as I was away so much. And my phone got stolen that time in Berlin, you remember?"

"Oh yeah." Dimly, and quite strangely, I do remember this, the very mildest of mini-dramas that Bea made out to be a tragedy before she learned what that word actually meant.

"You must have *some* photos?" I say, because the thought unsettles me a little.

"Yeah, I have a few, just..." He tails off, then gives a false laugh, because it isn't funny. "Just not as many as I'd like." The laughter fades back to the sad smile, which looks so painful I hurry to move on.

"How about food? Did Zack have any food he absolutely couldn't stand, or any that he really loved?" I force my smile again, drop it at Tris's confused reaction, but carry on regardless. "Kids are so picky sometimes, I was just wondering."

He sighs and glances away. For a few moments I wonder if he's going to answer at all.

"He loved cheese," Tris says suddenly. "The real stuff, English cheddar, that Bea bought somewhere. Not the plastic type we get here." He looks back, flashing a smile. And I feel a shaft of... what? Something. Jack *loves* cheddar cheese, I put it on everything.

"He liked ketchup..." Tris goes on, but then he shrugs his shoulders. "Listen, Kate, I don't know what you want me to say here. I don't really get what this is about?"

I wave away his concerns, not willing to dwell on the fact that Jack also loves ketchup.

"How about sports or hobbies? I'm curious what he was into, what he liked doing?"

But Tris has had enough.

"Kate, what is this? Why are you asking all these questions?"

He stares at me, and I know he's not going to answer any more unless I come clean with him. I feel an upwelling of stress. Torn in two directions. What am I doing? Do I actually believe that my son might be the reincarnation of *his* son? For a moment the thought unhinges me slightly from reality. I feel the need to grip the edge of the table, anchoring me into this reality. I do so subtly so that Tris can't see what I'm doing, and it helps. I feel like I'm suspended over some vast, dark space that exists somehow underneath our everyday reality. It's nothing but a crazy thought, but it scares me, and I feel the fear etching itself into my face. It's not my intention, but it makes Tris back down.

"Look—it's cool. I don't mind, I was just..." He shrugs and looks away. It's like he can't bear to look into my face. "I get that it can be hard, when you're the one alone with a child, like *isolating*." He hesitates, and I don't understand for a moment. "I was away so much, but I know how hard it was for Bea. And she had your dad to help out. Your mom too, at least until she got sick. While you..." His voice fades out. "I'm saying that I understand," he goes on. "That it can be really hard, in your position."

I say nothing; for a moment I'm not sure I can. The sensation of the void is still there, but it's changed shape somehow, moved to another dimension.

"Thanks Tris," I say, feeling quite unreal again. "That's kind."

Tris puffs out his chest, still pondering how to answer a question I've almost forgotten asking.

"So, um, what else... He wasn't really one for sports. I tried to play ball with him a few times and it never really went anywhere."

I bite my lip, pulled right back to my mission. Again I'm instantly comparing, because Jack isn't one for sports either. A couple of times Neil's tried to teach him to catch, and I'm not sure which of them is worse at it. For a second I add this to the food questions and it feels like I'm winning, like this is a game I'm playing and I'm three up. But I remind myself I just want to know; I have nothing to prove.

"Spaghetti!" Tris suddenly says, breaking into the biggest smile I've seen on him in a long while. "Zack loved spaghetti. Made a real mess when he ate it, but he couldn't get enough."

"Did he like it with sauce, or just on its own?"

"Oh please. Cheddar cheese." Tris smiles. "All the way. Cheese and ketchup."

My mind fills with an image of Jack, a bowl of wriggly spaghetti worms in front of him, and to the left of him a second bowl of grated cheese. To the right—always—the ketchup bottle. I feel a wave of dizziness. Like I did in the Flagstaff with Jan. I take a second, then move on again.

"Was there a place that you might describe as somewhere that Zack really loved going?" The change of topic is too abrupt, and I try to soften it. "I'm thinking of taking a trip with Jack and —I could use some ideas."

The weirdness of the question nearly throws Tris again, but he does his best to answer.

"He loved the lake house, of course. With his cousins." He waves a hand but exhales hard; it's obvious that just mentioning the place still affects him. But he pushes it away. "He liked the beach. A lot. I'm pretty sure that's why Bea's moved there now."

I almost move on to my next question, but then I make sense of what he's just told me.

"You went there with Zack? To where Bea lives now?"

"We had a few weeks there; the last time was, I don't know, six months before he..." He doesn't finish the sentence. "Didn't you know?"

"No. I didn't. Bea never said." My mind swirls at the implications of this, the possibilities. "Where did you stay?" I ask. "You said it meant a lot to him?"

In response, Tris digs in his jean pocket and pulls out his phone. "I do have a few photos of that; they came up on my Facebook feed a while back, you know, one of those memory things they do?" He flicks the screen as he talks, and for a few moments, while I hold my breath, his attention is taken by the phone. Then he suddenly looks up.

"Here we go."

He leans forward, holding the phone out for me to see. The screen shows a young Zack, aged maybe six years old, building a sandcastle with the tide just licking at the edge.

"We used to stay in this awesome house," Tris says; his voice sounds distant again, as if he's in a different place mentally, but I am too. I can see there are other photos in the same set and I swipe to see them. I see a photo of my smiling sister crouching down to hug Zack on an impressive balcony with the ocean in the background. There's nothing between the house and beach, no road or other buildings—just steps that lead directly onto the sand.

"It belongs to a friend." Tris's voice interrupts me. There's something about the way he says "friend" that I take to mean someone famous. And at once I understand why Bea wouldn't have mentioned it. Tris would have needed to keep it quiet.

"It's a beautiful house, and Zack loved it there." Gently he takes the phone back and I think he's not going to show me any more, but then he slides the screen a few times and hands it back. Now I see the whole house, sitting right on the beach. Bea and Zack are sharing a hanging chair suspended from the upper balcony. It's like they've paused fighting for control of the chair to smile for the photos.

"Wow, what a place."

"Yeah it's..." Tris's voice fades out, as if he was about to tell me which of his superstar friends owns it, but he's too wise to make that mistake. But I don't care about that. I only want to know if it's something that Zack would have found memorable.

"You went there a lot?"

He looks a bit shifty.

"A few weeks. Over the years. Three, maybe four times?"

"Can you send me these photos?"

He gives me a look, uncomfortable with the idea. But he hasn't said who the house belongs to. And anyway, he trusts me. We're family. Kind of.

"I guess..."

TWENTY-TWO

It takes Tristan a while, and several texted reminders, to send me the pictures of the beach house. And by the time he does so I've already worked out where it is and who owns it. It wasn't hard. I know it's in the town where Bea now lives, and it's a big house right on the beach. Plus I have a pretty good idea of all the bands that Tris has supported over the years. I'm not going to say who exactly—and it isn't actually anyone from the band itself—but let's just whisper the name *Coldplay*.

Anyway, I Google, and pretty soon I come up with several photos of my own. I feel this is important, because I now have images of the house without Bea or Zack in them, and that would obviously have given Jack a major clue as to which image to choose. I then go to Google again and find several other beach houses—some of those stilt houses in California, a couple of places in the Hamptons, one big, the other a veritable mansion. I print them all out and put them in a file, along with some other photos that Tris has sent me and items that I think will be helpful. And I place it in Jack's room. I don't want to try this on him when he's not ready, but I want to catch him when he's in the right mood, when he seems to be remembering.

A couple of days pass before I feel the time is right. Neil plays squash on a Wednesday evening, so I do Jack's bath, and I don't put the shower on like Neil does because I know it still upsets Jack. And maybe that puts him in a better mood, and after I've wiped him down and put him in his pajamas he's chattering away and asking for his favorite book, so that's when I ask him.

"Jack, honey, did you have a favorite book, back when you were Zack?"

He looks up at me, sharply and suddenly, sensing the change in how we're interacting. His body stiffens a bit where it's touching mine on the bed. Eventually he gives a tiny shrug.

"You don't know? You don't remember?"

He shakes his head, like he's sorry for something.

"That's OK, honey. I was just wondering. Casually I reach for the file, which I've placed under his pillow. I don't open it, I don't make out that it's a big deal, but even so, I can feel him eyeing it.

"How about toys? Did you have any toys you liked?"

He nods now, on safer ground. "*Ain,*" he replies, then he tries a bit harder; he's working on the beginnings of his words. "*Tur-rain.*"

"Train? Big train?"

Happy now, he nods. "I remember Big Train too. Was there anything else? A teddy perhaps, that you liked when Zack was younger?" My voice is casual and soft, and I add, "When *you* were younger?"

He looks thoughtful now.

"A bear?" I add, and eventually he nods.

"*Air. Oo bear.*"

"Blue bear?" I feel my heart rate ratchet up a notch, and open the folder. The top three photographs are images of different teddy bears. Two of them are dressed in nothing but their own fur, though one of them is actually blue. The last one

is Paddington Bear, wearing the blue duffel coat that he's
famous for.

I lay the three photos on the bed in front of Jack. His eyes go
straight to Paddington. I almost don't have to ask.

"Do any of these bears look like Blue Bear?" I ask him. "The
one you remember from when you were Zack?"

He nods again, and his little finger stabs down on the image
of Paddington. He presses it so hard the paper bends, and he
looks up at me, his eyes round with surprise.

"*Ooo bear,*" he says again.

It's not, even *I* admit to myself, entirely convincing. After
all, Paddington Bear *is* famous, and it's highly likely that Jack
has seen him before; in fact it's almost impossible that he *hasn't*
seen him. So I wait a few moments, and then calmly I pick up
the three photographs and lay out three books instead. The first
two we've had for some time: *Where the Wild Things Are* by
Maurice Sendak, and *The Very Hungry Caterpillar* by Eric
Carle. These copies actually *were* Zack's, because Bea gave
them to us along with a load of others when Jack was a baby.
The third book I bought off Amazon. It's called *Goodnight
Moon* by Margaret Wise Brown, and it's about a young rabbit
that says good night to everything around it, from the moon to
the socks. According to Tristan, it was Zack's favorite. I told him
it wasn't in the box of books we got from Bea, and he said she'd
probably held onto it since it meant such a lot to her. Either
way, we haven't come across it, Jack and I.

"Moon," Jack says at once. "Moon!" He's excited suddenly.

"Do you remember that book, honey?" It's a ridiculous
question; it's plainly obvious that he does. It couldn't be clearer.

"Read Moon, Mommy. Please?"

"Do you remember it?" I insist on asking again. A part of me
is trying to see where the trick is. I can see the magic just fine,
but how does it work, how is this happening? But he just nods
enthusiastically before pushing the other books further down

the bed to get comfortable with *Goodnight Moon*. So I read it to him. He's never read it before, never seen it, I'm absolutely sure of it, yet I stop occasionally and let him finish the sentences. He's not even four. He's not reading; he's *remembering*.

Eventually we put the book away, and I'm trying to rationalize this. I *know* I haven't read this book to him. I'm completely certain that Neil hasn't either, since we didn't own it until Amazon delivered it here two days ago. But on the other hand he's been to pre-school twice a week for over a year, and isn't it possible that they read it to him there? I ask him the question, but I don't understand his response.

"Did you read that at one of our visits to the library, honey? Is that where you learned that book?"

He shakes his head, but then at the same time he says yes.

"Yes, 'ibrary."

What felt like total certainty dissolves again into confusion, and gently I take the book away. I reach for the folder again. I only have one more set of images, of the beach houses. I lay them out on the bed in front of Jack. This time I simply look at him as he looks over them, then glances up at me. I can see he wants to reach for one, but he doesn't know if he's allowed yet, so I tell him.

"Go on Jack, you can take it." He reaches for the picture, the right picture. The beach house where Bea and Tris took Zack, years before Jack was born.

"Have you ever seen that house, Jack? Have you ever been there?"

And Jack picks up the photograph and he stares at it, excited but confused. He nods, enthusiastically.

"'andcastle," he says. "'Ake 'andcastle."

Sandcastle. Make sandcastle.

"Have you been there, Jack? When you were Zack, is that where you went? On vacation?"

Again, Jack nods, but this time a different voice answers.

"That's a leading question, Kate." Neil is standing in the doorway, watching me. "John twisted his ankle, so we finished early." He gives me a meaningful look, and then— when I don't seem to follow what it means—he gives a tug on the handles of the sports bag he's holding, his squash racket protruding from the top. "Don't worry, it's just a sprain." Without pausing he changes gear.

"What you up to, little man? Can I get a goodnight kiss?"

He leans over me to kiss Jack on the cheek, then he pulls back, coolly telling me he's going to take a shower. A few moments later I hear the noise of the water running.

"*Ayack, ayown,*" Jack mutters, right on cue.

TWENTY-THREE

"Can I take a bathroom break?" Kate asked. They'd been at the interview for over three hours now, without stopping.

"Sure." McGee suspended the interview and put in a call for a female officer to escort her to the ladies' room. Then he went himself; the old bladder wasn't as strong as it used to be.

"She's lying. Has to be," Robbins said, as soon as he came back into the room. "Either that or she's crazy. In either case, she's our number-one suspect for starting that fire. And that makes her a killer."

McGee said nothing, just clicked his tongue against his cheek.

"Oh, come on, Jim. Tell me you're not buying this? We only have her word for it that he's picking the right photos. That's it. She's lying to herself."

McGee poured himself another coffee, thinking about this.

"I dunno."

"You can't be serious. You wanna explain to the DA that this woman's son is reincarnated? You really are keen on early retirement."

The lightest of smiles rose to McGee's lips at the thought of it.

"I'm not saying that. Just that I don't see she's lying. I mean maybe she's fooling herself. But are you really getting that she's actively lying?"

"Sure I am," Robbins replied. "I think she's giving us this firehose of bullshit to somehow mask what she did. That she set that fire."

McGee became more serious.

"I still don't get it. I don't get how one thing leads to the other. Let's say you're right on the first point—whatever actually happened with her son, he didn't literally come back from the dead. What I don't see is how it links to the second point. Why does that mean she set the fire? How do you get from one to the other?"

"If she's lying about her son"—Robbins leaned forward— "then how can we trust her? That's what I'm saying. How do we know she's not lying about the fire? And if she's crazy, then this is what crazy people do: crazy shit."

But McGee shook his head. "It still has to make sense. And the way I see it, none of it does. First of all I don't get the sense she *is* lying—even though what she's saying can't be true. Second, whether she is or isn't, I don't get the link to why she'd set that fire."

He was interrupted by a knock on the door and Kate was escorted back into the room. As she sat down Robbins got up, saying he had to step out for a moment before they restarted— maybe his bladder wasn't so young after all. But McGee barely heard him. His mind was still grinding around the central questions of the case. Did she start the fire? If not, had she seen whoever did? Nothing in her demeanor told him she was lying, but that didn't mean a whole lot. They'd discussed putting her on a lie detector, but he didn't like the idea. He believed that *she* believed what she was saying. And if she could fool herself into thinking her son had been reincarnated, she could certainly fool herself into thinking she didn't start the fire when she was actually guilty. And if she passed a lie test they'd have to disclose it to a defence attorney...

"I didn't start the fire," she said suddenly, her eyes fixed on his.

McGee froze. Robbins was still out of the room and the interview hadn't restarted; he hadn't actually *asked* her the question. Yet it felt for all the world like she'd just replied. Like she'd replied *to his thoughts*.

"What did you say?" he asked. Although he'd heard her just fine.

"I *didn't* start the fire." This time she stressed the word "didn't"—as if she were literally answering what he'd been thinking. Was that how she'd said it first time around? He wasn't sure.

"Why did you say that?" he asked. She didn't reply.

"Why did you tell me that, right then?" He met her gaze, until this time she was the one to look away, almost dismissing him. He continued to stare at her until his gaze faltered as he blinked the idea away. It was ridiculous.

"You want to tell me who did start it?" he asked then. From the way she sat there, her body turned away from him, he wasn't even sure she'd reply. And he certainly wasn't expecting her to tell him. But then something strange happened. For a few seconds she stayed silent, then she turned to face him again. She shook her head.

"I *didn't see* who started it," she said. And then she blinked. Three times in quick succession. Then her tongue appeared, touching the corner of her mouth for just a moment, before disappearing again. Finally she looked away, but to the right this time. A little up. Each action was tiny—easy to miss, but not for an investigator with decades of experience of studying the responses of witnesses and suspects. McGee's face gave absolutely nothing away, but deep inside his brain Kate's responses registered with a massive jolt.

She might have been telling the truth up to then. But that sure as hell looked like a lie.

TWENTY-FOUR

It's completely obvious that Neil's pissed off with me. I settle Jack into bed, then come back and gather up the photographs. But instead of hiding them away I head downstairs and lay them all out on the dining table. The books, the images. I wait for him to come down.

"Hey," Neil says, half an hour later.

"Jack's asleep," I tell him, though probably he'll have looked in.

He nods. "You must have tired him out."

I bite my lip, say nothing.

"What were you doing?" His eyes glance over the photographs on the table.

"I went to see Tristan last week. He told me some things I didn't know about Zack. Things he liked, places he went. And I wanted to see if Jack knew anything about them."

I think that Neil is going to roll his eyes, or sigh, or do something to show me how stupid I'm being. But he always surprises me. All he does is wet his lips with his tongue. But I can see he's thinking, hard.

"And?"

I feel like crying. I don't know why. I don't understand the emotion I'm feeling right now.

"There's a house on the beach where Bea and Tris went, with Zack. She never told me about it, because it was something to do with Tris's work. One of the bands he plays with. But they went there three times. First when Zack was five, and then twice more after that. I never even knew about it, so there's no way I could have told Jack."

"OK. And what happened? Did he pick the right house?"

"Yes. Right away! Neil, he recognized the house. I'm sure of it. And you heard him, he said *sandcastle*. Why would he say *sandcastle* if he didn't know the house?" I'm sounding excited now, and Neil comes to sit beside me. He points at the picture, the right picture.

"Is this the house?"

For a brief second I feel deflated, but I'm not even sure why. I nod.

"Wow." He raises his eyebrows. "Nice place." He studies it, running his hands through his thick brown hair. I watch him, waiting to see what he's going to say next. After a while he puts down the photo and picks up the next one, a beach house in California, up on stilts above the sand.

"How about this one? Who lives here?"

"I don't know. I found it on the internet." I wait as Neil takes the third picture and studies that carefully too. He turns all the images over, checking the paper they're printed on. Finally he returns to the first image. The house where Zack stayed.

"I chose this image, Kate, because it was the one you were looking at. Or trying not to look at, I can't say exactly, but I had a sense it was this house."

I don't reply. Maybe I *was* looking at it, or trying not to. But it's much easier for an adult. Neil would have known it anyway, from the style of the architecture.

"He *can't* know it, Kate. Jack can't know a house he's never been to, just because his cousin went there before he died."

Neil spelling it out like this confuses me. It's like there are two realities, and if I don't think too hard I can be in both of them at once. But Neil isn't like that. He has this ability to clarify things, into what's real and what isn't. Or maybe it's a need.

I push the house photos out of the way and stab my finger down on one of the teddies.

"Tris told me that Zack had a favorite toy when he was younger, before the train. It was this bear, Paddington Bear. He called him Blue Bear. *Zack* called it that," I clarify, "but *Jack* did too. Just now."

Again Neil studies the images carefully before responding. Again he settles on the correct image, picking it up and examining it closely—though it's obviously easier this time, because he knows who Paddington is.

"He's wearing a blue coat. Maybe he was talking about that?"

"But what if he wasn't?" I implore him. "Why can't you believe in this?"

Neil takes his time answering. He puts down the photograph and takes my hand instead, holding it in both of his.

"I can see how difficult this is for you Kate. But I just don't think it's going to help us if I lose my impartiality. I understand how convincing this feels, but that's how these things work. The phenomenon *is* how convincing it feels."

I don't say anything, and he continues. "I can't say exactly why he picked up that bear photograph," he tells me. "But there are all sorts of possible explanations. Maybe he's seen that bear on TV, maybe it was the closest one to him. Maybe he just liked it. But all of those are infinitely more likely than his having seen it before in a previous life, something there's no evidence *for*, and a huge amount of evidence *against*."

"But *this* is evidence, if you'll just accept it! You can't dismiss all the evidence we have, everything Jack says, and then say that because there's no evidence, that in itself is evidence he's not telling the truth."

I think back to the book. How Jack finished the sentences in the story as if he knew it really well, even though I've never read it to him. And then I remember how I asked Jack if he'd read the book at nursery, and he said he had.

"Everything you do now, asking Jack about this. What you're really doing is reinforcing these ideas in his mind. Maybe he came up with the idea first—he's smart enough to do that—but now between the two of you it's being built up into something it isn't. He thinks you want this to be true, and he loves you, so he's going to do everything he can to make it true. Even though it isn't true. Even though it can't be."

I stare at him. I don't know what to think. Again.

"OK, so what should we do?" I demand, a few moments later.

This seems to confuse Neil. "About what?"

"About Jack; do we just ignore him?"

He still seems unsure what I mean. "No, of course not. We continue as we are. We take the best care of him."

"I mean about what he's saying. Do we just ignore him when he says things like this?"

"No. We should tell him it's not true. And we should make sure we're not doing anything to encourage it. In a couple of weeks he'll probably forget about the whole thing."

"And what if he doesn't?" I ask, far from convinced.

"He will. I'm sure of it."

TWENTY-FIVE

It's Danny's fourth birthday. The party is being held in one of those plastic indoor play spaces, with the big jungle gyms and slides, and the smell of hot dogs and children's vomit. If it wasn't Jan's son I might have made up some excuse for not going, but she'd never forgive me. Actually it's near the end of the party, and most of the other moms and dads whom I don't know that well—are looking like they want to get the hell out of here. But first we've got to get the cake cut.

"Come on everybody!" Jan bellows, puffing out her cheeks at me as she goes out of the little side room we're in which they set aside for parties. A dozen overtired, sticky children make their way back in from the play space and sit down around the table, anxious for their next sugar hit. Jan seizes the moment and dims the lights.

"Here comes the cake."

I hold my phone out, recording as Jan comes in with four candles flickering over the icing of a shop-bought Minions cake. If you don't know, Minions are these yellow characters with one eye that star in various kids' movies. They're actually pretty funny; at least they are until you've watched the movie for the tenth time.

The children sing happy birthday like their lives depend on it, and I get one of those moments that parenthood gifts you. Where you feel simultaneously completely cynical about the ridiculous, consumerist nature of it, and—because of the angelic look on your own child's face, as if they're witnessing an actual miracle—like you want to burst into tears at the beauty of life too.

Danny blows out his candles, visibly spraying spit on the icing, and Jan holds up a knife, pretending for a second that she's a crazed killer.

"So, who wants a piece of murdered Minion?"

Most of the children scream that they do; a couple simply scream. But Jan doesn't mess around anymore. She stabs the Minion in the eye and divides it into slices, wrapping them in serviettes. I turn to Jack, laughing at my friend's energy. But there's a weird look on my son's face. It's earnest. I know it well by now.

"I had 'inions cake! For my 'earthday. I remember!"

I've made him a cake for each of his four birthdays. None of them had anything to do with Minions.

"No honey, you had Spider-Man this year?" Before that it was Peppa Pig, which Neil joked looked unfortunately rude. But Jack shakes his head, annoyed.

"No, 'inions. *Minions.*" He makes an effort with the "m".

"Hey, big boy." Jan hands him a slice of cake and he takes it from her, but doesn't say thank you, or immediately start stuffing it into his face like most of the other children around the table. Instead he stares at me, angry that I don't believe him. But I can't do this here, we can't do this now. So I turn away. I tell Jan I'm going to bring out the coats from the cloakroom, as more and more parents are turning up to collect their kids.

A half hour later and it's all over. I've stayed to help Jan with the clean-up, and she rewards me with a cardboard cup of coffee. We slump down in the main seating area of the play hall. Holly, Jack and Danny are sitting in the ball pool, lost in make-believe.

"You should ask your sister if Zack ever had a Minions cake," Jan says casually, sipping her coffee.

"I didn't realize you heard."

She shrugs. "Did he?"

"Did he what?"

"Have a Minions cake?"

"Not with me, no."

She sips again, then sighs contentedly. "So you gonna ask your sister?"

Reluctantly I pull out my phone, but then I pause. "How do I ask that without it sounding weird?"

Jan opens her mouth to reply, but then doesn't seem to know what to say. "Actually, I'm not sure."

I shake my head. "I'm not even sure the *Minions* movie would have been out when Zack was alive. Isn't it much more recent than that?"

For a moment I feel a surge of hope: that this is correct, that it proves Jack is wrong. If he remembers a Minions cake from before the Minions were a thing, then it shows Neil is right. I hold my breath as Jan slips her own phone out, Googles it, and quickly gets an answer.

"The Minions first appeared as bit-players in the film *Despicable Me*—I love that movie—in 2010. When did Zack die?"

I think for a moment. "2018. He was born in 2010." Jan reads on from her screen.

"The characters were a big success and featured more prominently in *Despicable Me 2* in 2013, and then in their own movie in 2015." She gives me a sharp look. "Just the right age for Zack's early birthdays then."

I don't answer. There isn't much to say.

"Hey, while I have my phone out," Jan continues, "what do you think of *this* guy?" She holds up another tab, this time showing the image of a man, and I frown at her, not understanding.

"He's a psychiatrist, and he specializes in cases like yours, where a kid remembers living before."

I look around, anxious at how loudly she's talking, but all the other parents are gone and it's too late for regular customers.

"What about him?"

"You know that Dr Palmer guy, whose book I told you about? Well, this guy used to work for him, and now he's taken over the research. He says he's actively looking for cases, especially in the US. He'll come and see you. I think you should contact him."

She hands me the phone, I look at it for a few moments, then hand it back and shake my head.

"I can't. Think what Neil would say."

Jan's silent for a moment and I follow her eyes; she's looking towards Jack and Holly and Danny, who are all sprawled out together in the ball pool, chatting.

"Fuck Neil," Jan says quietly. "I'll send you the webpage."

TWENTY-SIX

"There was no way I was going to do it. Contact some crazy pseudo-scientist about Jack? That was more than my marriage was worth." Kate shook her head.

McGee frowned, scrabbling in the papers he'd brought into the room.

"But you told us you did eventually speak with Dr Wells? What changed?"

Kate's mouth moved to a weary smile. "I guess Neil got shamed into it. Shocked and shamed."

McGee and Robbins waited for her to go on.

"I told you how British Neil was? How proper? Well, he really was. We were trying for a second child. Not that often if I'm totally honest, because of how damn tired we both were the whole time, but we wanted two..." She stopped again, as if losing the thread of her thoughts. Then she came back, present but saddened.

"Jack had this flashlight. A toy one, but obviously it worked just like a normal flashlight. And we both thought he was asleep. It was late, and both the bedroom doors were shut." She kept her eyes off the two men. "And I was... on top. We were—you know. *Trying.* And then suddenly this damn flashlight flicks on, from right beside the bed." She shakes her head at the memory of it.

"It was Jack?" McGee asked, carefully.

"Yeah. I didn't even realize he was there. The room was dark and suddenly I was bathed in light and I'm... naked—I just screamed."

There was an awkward silence in the interview room.

"And what happened then?" McGee asked.

I stop screaming when I realize it's just Jack, but Neil writhes out from underneath me—from inside me—as if I'm suddenly toxic. Somehow he manages to get the covers over us both.

"Jack! Hey little man." His voice is anxious and breathless. Totally false. He stretches over and turns on the bedside light, catching my eye as he does so. "Hey little guy! What're you doing here?"

Now that the lamp is on, Jack flicks off his flashlight and I can see his face for the first time. For a moment I hope that maybe he's actually still asleep after all, just sleep-walking, but he's not, he's wide awake. Curious, a little scared.

"I guess you want to know what we were doing?" Neil begins, and I can almost see him thinking. He's always been strangely coy about sex; I think it's the Englishness of him. He doesn't like to talk about it, but more than that, Jack's so young that we haven't needed to explain it to him. He knows he came from Mommy's tummy, and that Daddy gave her the seed, but that's it. He doesn't know the details.

"Is that making babies?" he asks, and his head falls onto one side, that familiar look of his.

Neil glances at me again, unsure. "Yeah. Um. Actually, yes, that's right. How do you know about that?"

"Mommy told me."

Neil hesitates, looking at me again. "She did?"

I don't say anything. I still haven't said anything since he turned on his flashlight.

"Not my now Mommy. Old Mommy."

At this Neil turns his head away like he can't look, and I suddenly lose my inhibitions. I open my arms and wrap Jack in a tight embrace.

"Go back to your room, honey. I'll be there in a moment to tuck you back into bed."

Obediently he flicks on his flashlight again for the long, dark walk down the hallway to his bedroom. I slide out of bed and find my robe.

Forty minutes later, and I leave Jack's room. I wonder if Neil's fallen asleep, but no, he's awake, glasses balanced on nose, an academic paper spread out before him. He drops the page he's reading and I catch the title: *Decoding the Brain: How Neural Networks Account for Human Experience*

"Is he asleep?" he asks.

I nod.

"Really asleep this time?"

"I think so; why, do you want to try again?" I give him a smile to show I'm joking, but also that I don't have to be if that's what he wants, but he shuffles the papers, as if work was all that was ever on his mind.

"Maybe we should put a lock on the door first?" I say, still trying to get him to laugh about what happened, because that would make me feel better.

But I can't. It's there, like an elephant in the room, ridiculous to ignore.

"Neil, I need to tell you: I haven't spoken to him about sex. I haven't told him about 'making babies.' Nothing like that."

He sighs, takes off his glasses and rubs his eyes. I think of Jan. Jan and her woo-woo pseudo-scientist.

"I think we need help with this," I say, before I can stop myself.

It takes him a long time to reply. "With what, exactly?"

"With Jack, with what he's saying." I realize that if ever there's a chance of getting Neil to agree, it's now. "There's this guy, a psychiatrist named Matthew Wells. He studies this kind of thing. I looked on his website and he's asking people to contact him if they have a child like Jack."

"What do you mean, 'a child like Jack'?" Neil's voice is cool.

"Someone who remembers a past life." I stop, correct myself. "A child who *claims* they remember a past life."

Neil stays quiet, but behind his glasses he blinks a couple of times. Nothing more.

"Look, I don't know if I believe Jack," I go on. I can't stand the silence. "Really I don't. But there's no doubt about *what* he claims, even you must accept that. And I believe that *he* believes it; I can't see any other explanation for it. He's not... playing. It's something else."

Neil finally moves, dropping his head. He's not a robot after all. "OK, I agree with that, it does seem different from when he's in make-believe mood."

"Exactly." I seize upon Neil's agreement, but then I'm not sure where to take it.

"I've read his website, Dr Wells's. He describes how he's met with lots of parents in our position. And how it *helps them.* They get to understand how other people have dealt with the situation, even if they don't believe that it's..." I don't finish my sentence, but as I'm speaking I scrabble for my phone on my bedside table, and find the website Jan sent me.

"Here." I hand it to Neil, and wait. After a while I realize I'm holding my breath.

Neil reads the page, and then looks at the rest of Dr Wells's website. It takes him a long time, but I'm used to my husband working like this. Careful, methodical.

Finally, he puts my phone down. "I don't think this is a good idea."

"Why not?"

"These people..." he begins, then sighs when he sees my face. We're both frustrated.

"What do you mean, *these people*?"

He picks his words carefully. "People who purport to be scientists, like this. They're often very good at disguising what they're actually doing, but when you examine them in detail, they're not really doing genuine science. They twist the facts, they cherry pick the data, they sensationalize... I've no doubt they're very good at it. But—"

"No." I reach for the phone. "He *is* a scientist; he works at this university out west. Look here—"

"A university doesn't control what someone on its staff works on," Neil explains patiently. "And they don't necessarily condone it either. And you have to ask yourself, why would he want to meet you? What's in it for him?"

I don't understand what Neil's saying, so he gently takes the phone from me. With a couple of clicks he navigates away from Dr Wells's website to a page on Amazon showing his books. "He may work for a university, but this is how he's getting rich. Selling the pretense of science to people who *want* to believe. If you invite him here, that's what he'll do. With Jack."

"No." I shake my head. "He guarantees anonymity if that's what the parents want. It says so." I want to show him, but being Neil I know he'll have already noted it.

"I would expect he wrote that part to make it easier for any parents in this position to make initial contact. He can still ask their permission to let him feature them in a book, once they've established a relationship and it's harder to say no. And I'm sure that's what he'll do."

Neil shakes his head.

"I'm really sorry Kate, but I don't think it's a good idea at all."

TWENTY-SEVEN

"So, what did you do?" McGee asked, when Kate fell silent. He smiled inwardly, already guessing the answer.

"I emailed Dr Wells," she replied, defiantly running a finger down the line of one of her eyebrows. "What else was I going to do? Jack wasn't stopping with his memories."

McGee allowed himself a chuckle. "And what did Neil say about it?"

Kate shrugged. "Neil was Neil. He didn't get angry. A bit disappointed maybe, but not even that for long. I think he was interested too. He had his own theories for what exactly was happening, but even for someone as settled in his views as him, it was hard to explain away everything Jack was saying as implanted false memories, or whatever Neil's theory was."

"OK. How'd it happen? With this researcher? Was he interested? Did he come?"

Kate nodded. "Oh yeah. He came. He came on the next flight."

. . .

"You mustn't coach Jack, just let him say whatever he wants to say," Jan says, her hands wrapped around a coffee mug as she waits on our sofa. Obviously I know this already, but I think she's just nervous, which is weird for Jan.

It's a Friday evening, and I'm not sure who's going to turn up first: Neil, or Dr Wells—who I emailed on Wednesday, explaining the situation we're in with Jack, and he replied the same day. He said how important it is for his research to visit the child as soon as possible, because most of the time he doesn't meet the kids until they've started to forget. After a bit of back and forth he booked a flight which got in today at four p.m. He and his associate—I don't know who that is yet—are going to be here for the whole weekend, maybe longer, and they want to conduct interviews not just with Jack, but also with myself and Neil, and with Jan, because she's heard Jack talking about his memories. Maybe they'll want to speak to other people too, I don't know.

It takes about an hour and a half to get here from the airport, so they should turn up around the same time that Neil gets back from work. So yeah, I'm kinda nervous too.

"*Obviously* I'm not going to coach him," I reply. "I just want to find out the truth."

"Yeah." Jan gives me a goofy smile. "Sorry, it's just..." She doesn't finish the sentence, but I know what she means. When this was just Jack saying strange stuff, it was odd, but it was possible to fool yourself that it wasn't *that* odd. But now, with a paranormal investigator—which is how Dr Wells is sometimes described—rushing to the scene as soon as he can, it feels like we've moved to another level. We're a literal scientific emergency. A *pseudo*-scientific emergency.

"You know what would be funny?" Jan goes on, with no trace of humor in her voice. "If Jack doesn't say anything when he gets here. If he pretends he doesn't remember any of it, the whole time they're here."

I glance at her. And for a few moments it strikes me that maybe she feels guilty about all this. That she thinks she played some part in encouraging me, and maybe somehow that *made* Jack say what he said. I don't know. I don't know what to think anymore. But maybe that's OK, because I'm out of time to think. The doorbell rings.

There's a shout of "doorbell" from Jan's daughter Holly. She's teaching Jack and Danny to camp under a blanket in Jack's bedroom. But I'm already up, trying to quell the queasiness in my stomach. Jan gets up too, playing her supporting role. We go together into the hallway. I open the front door.

"Katherine Marshall?" In real life he's taller that he looked in his picture. Lanky almost. Vivid blue eyes smile at me through tortoiseshell-framed glasses. "I'm Matthew Wells, call me Matt." He holds out a hand which I shake.

"This is my associate Charlotte Dean." He indicates the young woman beside him, and I shake hands a second time. "We're both very grateful to you for letting us visit." I catch a note of Charlotte's perfume. I notice that she's strikingly pretty.

"Come in," I say, though right now I don't want them here, but even more so I don't want them on my doorstep because of what my neighbors might think. I'm grateful now for Jan's offer to be here. Not just for moral support, but to help me kick them out if they turn out to be the weird hippies Neil thinks they are.

"How was the flight?" I say after I've fixed drinks. Wells takes a tea. The beautiful assistant has hot water, which I assume she's going to add something to herself, but then she doesn't.

"Oh fine, very easy," Dr Wells replies, glancing around the room. Charlotte sips at her water, and nobody quite seems to know what to say. I'm surprised by their hesitancy for a moment. Then I get it; they're wondering where the subject of their investigation is. Or maybe if he even exists at all.

"Jack's upstairs," I say.

"Oh, that's fine," Dr Wells replies. "We like to take our time when we first meet a family. It's an odd situation, but we try to make it as natural as possible." He glances around the room again, and I realize that he's not actually nervous, just studying the surroundings. Judging the room. I get it though; just like I'm wondering if he's crazy for the subject he specializes in, he's wondering if *I'm* mad for the claims I'm making.

"We tend to play it like we're distant relatives," Dr Wells goes on, smiling easily. "Here for a family visit. Or something like that."

"My husband will be home any moment," I reply, stupidly. I've already told him when Neil gets home, but it feels disloyal not to remind him.

"Yes, you said." He hesitates and seems to guess what I'm about to repeat next. "You mentioned he was a scientist? An evolutionary biologist?" His eyebrows go up, like this will be a novelty for him. "I'm looking forward to meeting him. It will be interesting to hear his views on the situation." Dr Wells smiles again and I feel a flutter of anxiety, like I might have misrepresented things in my emails.

"Actually he doesn't..." I bite my lip. "He doesn't believe in what Jack's saying."

I fear he's going to look irritated at this, or disappointed, or something, but again he flashes that easy smile.

"Please, don't worry. It's very common for parents in these situations to disagree on what's actually happening."

"What *do* you think is happening?" Jan asks, but he rebuffs her effortlessly, and I get the sense he's not going to tell us that, not until he's got what he needs, anyway.

"Hopefully we'll get a better idea of that while we're here." Again the smile, and again he sips his tea. And then I hear Neil's key in the door, which is a relief, of sorts. We all stand up again as he comes into the room.

I make the introductions and everyone shakes hands again, and then we bring the kids downstairs too, so that Jack can meet his "distant relatives." We don't tell him that exactly, just that Dr Wells and Charlotte are some people who'd like to talk with him. Wells is obviously comfortable with children, but he makes no special effort with Jack, showing an equally normal level of interest in all three children. And then, now that Neil's back with me, Jan gathers her stuff together to take her two home. I know that Dr Wells and Charlotte are leaving soon too. The plan is to do the first interviews tomorrow—this evening was just about meeting each other, after the rather rushed way we've come together.

"Thank you both again for agreeing to meet at such short notice," Dr Wells begins, when it's just us left. "And thank you as well, Jack. I must say it's very nice to meet you."

Jack doesn't say anything now that his friends have gone, but he eyes the tall man suspiciously. In response, Dr Wells crouches down and pulls something from his jacket pocket. "I hope your parents don't mind this," he begins, glancing up but giving a reassuring smile. "But I took the liberty of bringing you a little gift. It's only a small thing." He hands over a package wrapped in red and gold paper.

Jack looks at me now, questioning whether this is OK. I smile and nod permission, although his little arms are already reaching forward for the gift. He takes it and tears the paper gently away. Inside is a toy car. Nothing too expensive, but not super cheap either. Jack's eyes go wide with the thrill of it, and immediately he starts whooshing it up the side of the sofa. Dr Wells watches him a moment, then stands back up to his full height.

"I wanted to start by explaining how we usually operate. We'd like to conduct a series of interviews with each of you, separately if possible, so that we can reduce the risk of you influencing each other's responses. With Jack we may need to work up to that so that he's comfortable with the idea, but that's fine. We'll tape those interviews so we have a record of what was said, and how it was said. Is that OK with you both?"

"What will happen to those records?" Neil asks in a casual voice. "You gave Kate a guarantee that nothing we tell you is going to end up in any of your books. We've kept a copy of that." The warning is clear, but it's met by an easy smile.

"Yes, and that absolutely stands, Dr Reynolds. You can relax on that point."

Neil doesn't for a second. But then he nods. "Please, call me Neil."

Dr Wells smiles and then nods too. "Great. The most important aspect of this from our point of view"—he indicates Charlotte as he speaks—"is the research. It's better from our perspective to have you on the record, but anonymous data is better than no data."

At this Neil's eyes flick across to the assistant, Charlotte. I sense that he's thrown by her appearance here. Perhaps he wanted to be tougher on Wells, but he feels like he can't in front of such a beautiful young woman. He's like that sometimes.

"Hey Jack, is that a *drum* over there?" Charlotte catches my son's eye and points to a pile of toys on the side of the room. "I just love drums. Can you actually play it?"

Jack nods, and then he doesn't need much encouragement before he goes and picks it up and bangs it, at which point Charlotte claps her hands in pretend delight. So for five minutes or so we all sit here, not really saying anything and indulging Jack as he bangs his drum, and tells Charlotte over and over that she's pretty and has pretty hair.

Eventually I've had enough, and I tell him it's time for bed. He makes a fuss at first, but he's OK when he learns he's going to see Charlotte again tomorrow, and she's going to do an *actual interview* with him. I wonder if Dr Wells is going to ask to watch his bedtime routine, because I've already told him that this is when Jack tends to speak the most about his memories, but it seems that's it for the first meeting. They head off to their hotel, with a promise to be back at nine the next day.

TWENTY-EIGHT

True to their word they turn up right on time, with all their equipment. They set up the camera on a tripod in the lounge. Jack's so excited about it that we agree to start with him, with a plan to switch to interviewing me or Neil if Jack gets tired. It's all very informal, but there's a professionalism to it as well, and it's clear they're careful to avoid anything that might look like pushing us to give certain answers. I can see why Dr Wells needs an assistant, because there's lots of people-management going on, including a cool box containing food which I guess they bring so that we don't have to provide them with anything while they turn our house into their laboratory.

"So Jack," Dr Wells begins, when we get him sat on the sofa ready for his interview. "Is it OK if I ask you some questions?" Dr Wells is sitting on a chair from the dining room while Jack and I are both on the sofa. Jack nods, looking happy and confident.

"OK."

"OK then." *Enthusiastic.* "Let's start with this. Do you have some memories of having a different life? Before this one?"

Jack nods again.

"Will you tell me about it? I'd really like to hear."

He glances at me, and I half shrug and half nod. I don't want to look like I'm prompting him—I understand how important that is for the science. But I'm also his mom, and I want him to feel like he's doing well. Like the brave little boy he is, he looks right at the camera.

"Me 'igger. Before."

"That's really interesting. Can you tell me more about it?"

"Like what?"

"What was it like?"

"OK. 'igger. Do more things."

"What kind of things?"

Jack seems a bit perplexed by this question, and it takes him a while to answer. It's not something I've ever asked.

"Ride 'ike. Go school."

"You rode a bike?"

Jack nods.

"Can you remember it? Your bike, what it looked like? Could you describe it for me?"

Jack frowns lightly, and he shakes his head.

"OK." Dr Wells appears to think about this. "Do you remember how many wheels it had? Some bikes have two wheels, some have three. Some have those little training wheels on the back? Do you remember how many wheels your bike had?"

Jack bites his lip, thinks about it, and shakes his head.

"How about the color. Do you remember what color it was?"

Jack spends a few seconds apparently thinking, then shakes his head again.

"That's no problem." Dr Wells smiles encouragingly. "What about pedals?" he says, as if he's just curious. "Did it have any, or was it one of those you push along with your feet?"

"'edals," Jack replies at once. He doesn't need to think this time.

"OK." Dr Wells nods, like he's pleased. "Pedals. Do you remember riding it anywhere? Anywhere you can tell me?"

"In the 'oods."

"In the woods? That's *great*." Dr Wells seems pretty good at figuring out what it is Jack is saying. "What do you remember about that?"

Jack looks perplexed, like this is a weird question.

"Did the woods have a name? Was it just trees, or anything else?"

"Like what?"

"I don't know. Anything you can remember?"

"Don't 'member."

"OK, that's fine. That's no problem, Jack. Do you remember how you got to the woods? Was it on your bike, or did you just ride the bike when you were there?"

This time Jack doesn't answer. Instead, he starts playing with the toy car that Dr Wells gave him yesterday. And we go on like this for a half hour or so, with Jack saying a few bits here and there but not much, at least it doesn't seem much to me. And then we take a break. Charlotte takes Jack into the kitchen to give him something from their cool box, though he checks with me first to make sure I'm OK with that. I nod, but I feel a bit frustrated.

"I'm sorry he's not saying much, I think he feels a bit shy."

"Not at all. He's doing just great. The way this works, we want to record Jack giving as much detail as possible about what he remembers. Afterwards we'll try to verify if it matches with the person whose life he seems to remember."

"I'm not sure he's giving you much."

"He's told us he remembers a bike, and going to school. That's significant."

"It's hardly specific though," Neil objects, cautiously. It's the first thing he's really said all morning; mostly he's just watched. "After all, what child doesn't go to school or ride a bike? If he's imagining all this, then isn't it exactly what you'd expect him to come up with?" I know Neil's saying this primarily to gauge Dr Wells's response, and I feel myself wishing I could warn him how smart my husband is. But there's no need.

"Perhaps," Dr Wells replies. "But the idea is to fill in as many details as possible about what he remembers—or claims to remember—and then we'll see if anything can be specifically linked to one individual."

"Mostly he doesn't seem to remember anything," Neil observes, but Dr Wells won't be drawn. He smiles at Neil, but turns to me. "Kate, how about we ask you some questions while Charlotte and Neil stay with Jack in the kitchen?"

TWENTY-NINE

I'm there a long time, recounting everything I remember about what Jack has said, right from his earliest words. Dr Wells is also interested in other details, like Jack's nightmares, his fear of water, and whether he has any birthmarks. We break halfway through so that he can try again with Jack; this time it's just Dr Wells and Charlotte in with him, but he seems to enjoy it.

And then I'm back, sitting on the sofa, with Dr Wells folded into a dining room chair beside the camera and asking me about everything, questions that seem relevant and many that don't. He asks me whether Jack has a bike, and I explain that he does have one, a push-bike, without pedals. He asks me to get it and show it to him on camera. Finally, after what seems like a hundred more questions, we seem to be done, and I'm kind of amazed to see it's five o'clock in the afternoon. We've spent the whole day just talking.

They come back the next day, again at nine a.m., and we go on. Interviews with Jack, with Neil, with myself, and also with Jan who arrives without Holly and Daniel this time, because Jack hasn't ever told them anything about his memories. This time the day drags a little—I guess I'm tired. When five o'clock comes, Dr Wells asks if I have any objection to him witnessing and filming Jack's bedtime routine. We've come this far, so we say yes, but Neil insists on us having a break first, and the two of us take Jack out for a walk while Dr Wells and Charlotte sort out their equipment. Afterwards they promise to buy us a take-out. Dr Wells says it's the least they can offer after how much time we've given them.

When we're back, Dr Wells stands behind me as I wash Jack with the wet wipes. He's interested in what would happen if I tried to actually put Jack in the water, but he doesn't push me to show him. He films the bedtime story—by now I think that Jack might insist on it being filmed if Dr Wells didn't suggest it; he seems to have really taken on board how important the camera is. And when we're done (Jack asks for *Goodnight Moon*), Dr Wells encourages me to ask Jack if he has any new memories. He says that sometimes the act of interviewing children causes them to remember more details, or at least claim to. But though Jack is quite happy to repeat much of what he's already said, nothing new comes out. Eventually I tuck Jack in and Dr Wells and I go downstairs, where Charlotte has just walked in with the food.

In a way, although we've done nothing but talk all weekend, we've not really talked at all. And now I sense we're moving into a different phase. I feel it in Neil too, who's mostly kept to himself over the weekend and observed what's going on, but now he wants to have his say. I lay the table, and we sit down to eat.

"So," I begin, my voice artificially breezy as I pull the lids off the plastic containers. "What happens next?"

Dr Wells seems aware that something is different too. He nods, apparently to himself, before replying.

"We've carried out our preliminary interviews, but there's a lot more work to do. From everything you've told me, Jack appears to have what we call a 'solved' case—one where we're able to identify a specific individual whose memories he can apparently recall. Obviously I'm talking about his cousin Zack. So I'd like to speak with Zack's parents about him. The manner of Zack's death will be an important topic as well—"

I cut in, suddenly shocked I didn't see this coming. "That's not going to be possible."

Dr Wells looks up in surprise.

"Bea—my sister, Zack's mother—she doesn't know about any of this. She isn't aware of what Jack's saying."

I catch Dr Wells exchanging a look with his assistant, but then he speaks, cautiously. "We've documented Jack making several specific statements about his memories as Zack. It's critical for the case that we're able to verify—or otherwise—that they match with Zack's life."

I bite my lip. I've been so stupid. I briefly consider whether I could tell Bea. But she suffered so much, she's *still* suffering, and telling her that Zack's come back, in a way, is only going to tear those wounds wide open. And telling her after I've got someone like Dr Wells involved, that just seems impossible.

"No. I can't bring Bea into this." A solution presents itself; it feels like a lifeline. "And *I* can verify most of what he's said. I told you about the photographs—of the beach house where Zack stayed."

Again, Dr Wells and Charlotte share a glance.

"That's helpful of course, but we would still need to verify independently..." Dr Wells begins.

"No, I don't want to bother Bea with this." I'm firm.

"Mrs. Marshall, Kate..." Wells begins, but Neil cuts in.

"I think Kate's made her decision." His voice is cool. Authoritative.

Wells opens his mouth, looks at Neil, then turns back to me. Maybe he thinks I'll be easier to convince.

"Your sister—Zack's mother—she's best-placed by far to judge whether what Jack's saying matches her son's life. It will be almost impossible to continue this case if we're not given access to her—"

"Nevertheless, Kate has given you her decision." Neil interrupts Wells again and stares at him, as if daring him to ask again.

Wells looks down at the table for a few moments, then he looks up at me. I get a sense he's going to try for a third time, but then he glances back at Neil and nods.

"I understand," he says at last. "And the decision is yours."

I feel conflicted. A rush of relief, like I've dodged a bullet here, but also guilt that I've wasted Dr Wells's time. And a feeling that I've also let Jack down in not exhausting every avenue to find out the truth.

"I'm really sorry," I say. And right away Neil tells me that I have nothing to be sorry about, but I don't listen.

"Is there anything more you can do? Without Bea?"

Wells thinks a moment before replying. He glances at Neil again and holds up a hand, as if to restrain him.

"I would still like to speak to Jack about what, if anything, he believes he remembers about Zack's death. We've found that children with these memories often have vivid recollections of how they died. Even without your sister, it might be possible to match some details with official records."

He raises his hands, a gesture of disappointment. But for me it's something. Perhaps I can still get to the truth.

THIRTY

Neil goes to work before Wells and Charlotte arrive, so it's just the four of us in the house. Wells wanted to interview Jack on his own, but given the nature of the questions he's planning to ask, I said I'd prefer it if I stayed in the room. But I'm just here watching, keeping quiet. Dr Wells begins by going over some of the questions he asked yesterday, just to get Jack chatting easily. Then he changes the tone.

"Jack, you've said you remember that you drowned?" He keeps his voice light, but not too light; he's not pretending this isn't a difficult question. "Before, when you were bigger. Can you tell me about that?"

Jack doesn't reply, but I can see the gravity of the subject in his face. Disappointment too, like he imagined another day having fun with Charlotte. Instead, it's this.

"I know this isn't easy, but anything you can remember would be helpful. Do you know where you were?"

He shakes his head quickly, almost like a shiver.

"You don't know?"

"No," I interrupt from behind the camera. "He means he

doesn't want to talk about it." Dr Wells turns to me, a forced smile on his lips.

"Kate, thank you. But if I could ask you to just observe, that would be helpful." He nods, and I hold up my hands to apologize, but he's already turned away.

"Jack? Do you remember? It's OK if you do, but it's also OK if you don't. We'd just like to understand what you can remember, and how it feels to remember."

Jack has a cushion on his lap, and he's fiddling with the zipper, not opening it but flicking the little puller from one side to the other.

"Jack?"

"'Amma' and 'ampa house," Jack says suddenly. And this is something I've never heard him say before. *Grandma and Grandpa's house.* Dr Wells's voice softens a little, as if he senses this.

"What were you doing there? Do you remember?"

Jack shrugs at this.

"Do you remember who else was there?"

"Mommy. 'ampa. Not 'amma." He does that little shake of his head again.

"Why not Grandma, Jack, can you remember?"

Again the shake.

"Mom was in the hospital when Zack died," I say, almost as a whisper.

"*Ka-te!*" A singsong voice. This time Dr Wells doesn't take his eyes off Jack. "Please?"

"I'm sorry," I say at once, and resolve to sit quietly, whatever happens.

"Can you remember, Jack? Why your grandmother wasn't there?"

This time the little head shake is paired with a shrug.

"It's no problem if you can't remember. We're just trying to understand what you remember and what you don't. Both are absolutely fine. OK?"

He nods.

"Do you remember if anyone else was there?"

"'ron."

I hold my breath. I've never told Jack the details of Zack's death. I don't know how he'd know that Aaron was there.

"'ron un Eva. My c... cousins."

"Ron and Eva? Your cousins," Dr Wells checks, and Jack gives his little head shake again, only this time through frustration

"Not Ron. *A*-ron." He works hard on that first letter.

"Aaron?" Wells glances at me now, his eyebrows raised questioningly. I give a small nod and he turns back.

"OK. Anyone else that you remember? From your grandparents' house that day?"

Jack's eyes go up, he looks around the room, only he doesn't really; he's trying to remember. But again, he shakes his head.

"No one else?"

Shake.

"That's fine Jack, let's move on. Can you remember what time of year it was? Was there snow on the ground? Were there leaves on the trees? That sort of thing. Were you wearing short pants?"

Jack thinks a while.

"'wimming."

"You were swimming? Where were you swimming? Do you remember a pool?"

Shake.

"No pool? So where were you swimming, Jack? Do you remember the sea?"

I'm dying to help him, to tell him how Zack and the cousins, Aaron and Eva, were swimming in the lake every day that week, right up to when the tragedy happened. But I don't. I bite my tongue.

"Lake," Jack whispers, almost too softly to hear.

"Could you say that again?" Dr Wells asks.

"'wimming in lake," Jack repeats. "Every day, 'wimming in lake."

"That's really good Jack." Dr Wells smiles at him. "That's really helpful. And do you remember this yourself, or has someone told you about it? That Zack was swimming in the lake? That you were swimming there?"

I don't know what he's going to say to this, and I feel myself tense up. I lean forward, but all he does is the head shake again. Dr Wells goes back to the previous line of questioning.

"What do you remember, about what actually happened to you?"

Jack looks down again, resumes playing with the zipper. He mutters something under his breath.

"What was that, Jack? Did you say something?"

He half shrugs, half does his head-shake thing, but Dr Wells persists.

"It's OK, Jack. Whatever it is you have to say, it's OK. If you can remember it's fine, if you can't remember it's fine."

A thought strikes me; apart from his memories, Jack's just an ordinary little boy, with his own personality. And part of that personality is that he just hates being scolded. So he always tries really hard to do the right thing. So, with the way Zack died— swimming out too far, and not coming back when he was told— does that mean he's weighed down by this burden of guilt? After all, he knows how much it hurt everyone. As well as literally killing himself, when he was Zack. *Maybe that's why he came back to me? To try and put that right somehow? And at the same time,* I think, *could his desire to "do the right thing" make him more likely to make something up now, to please Dr Wells?* I'm held, trapped between two different versions of reality.

He mutters again. A little louder, but still too low for me to catch.

"What was that, Jack?" Dr Wells asks, patient.

"'*een*."

"Een? What does that mean, Jack? What's that word?" Wells's voice is still soft, questioning, but I get what he says, right away.

"'*een*. Ron was '*een*," Jack goes on, louder again.

"Ron was mean? Aaron was mean?"

Jack's still a moment, then he nods quickly, and his eyes drop back to the cushion. Wells turns to me again, a questioning look, but before I can answer he raises a hand to silence me. He turns back to Jack.

"You remember that your cousin Aaron was mean, Jack? Is that what you're saying?"

Nod.

Wells pauses, thinking.

"In what way was he mean? What do you remember about it?"

It's me that Jack looks up at now, an imploring look on his face. I think he wants to stop and I say so, the words tumbling quickly from my mouth.

Wells cuts me off. "Just a few more questions, then we'll take a break."

"Jack, your mom's told me how you get nightmares sometimes? Are they about what happened, when you died?"

Jack freezes, but finally nods again. He won't look at Dr Wells now, and he looks miserable and somehow smaller, like the sofa has grown, or he's shrunk.

"Are the nightmares about your death? When you were Zack?"

Nod.

"It's OK, Jack, it can't hurt you now. We just want to know about it. We just want to understand."

Nod.

"Jack, what did Aaron do that was mean? When you died? Can you remember that?"

I feel a burning need to stop this now. Aaron didn't *do* anything. *It was Zack, he swam out too far—*

"Head unnerwater." Jack's voice cuts into my thoughts. "'ron 'eld head unnerwater."

The tension in Dr Wells's voice is obvious. "Aaron held your head underwater? Do you remember that? Or is that a dream?"

"'emember. No breathe. O'er o'er."

"He did it over and over?"

Nod. Much more animated this time.

"O'er o'er. No breathe. It hurt here." He puts a hand on his chest. "No breathe."

A tear leaks from Jack's eye, and he pauses just long enough to wipe it away, as if he hasn't noticed that he's crying.

"No breathe. 'ron hold me unner water. Hurt. No breathe."

He sits, staring at Dr Wells, his hand still resting on his chest and rising and falling, as if even now he's grateful that he can pull in oxygen from the air, and not the cold muddy water of the lake.

"That's not how it happened," I tell Dr Wells, just a few minutes later. Jack's in the kitchen now with Charlotte, and Dr Wells is packing up the equipment. They have to leave now if they're going to catch their flight, but I can't let them go with things like this.

"I don't know where Jack got that from, but it wasn't Aaron's fault that Zack died. Zack was going out too far in the lake. My sister saw the whole thing; she was trying to call him in."

He keeps working, avoiding looking at me, but then he suddenly stops.

"You said you had two sisters? This was the other one, not Zack's mother?"

"That's right. It was my oldest sister, Amber. Bea was with me at the hospital when the accident happened. But Amber saw the whole thing. It wasn't Aaron's fault, it was Zack."

Dr Wells looks troubled, but he goes back to folding his tripod.

"Can't you ask him again, see if he gets it right this time?"

He stops again, shakes his head. "There is no right or wrong answer, Kate. All we can do is document what Jack remembers, and see how closely that matches the earlier life and death they claim to remember."

"But this doesn't match!" I try to think through swirls of confusion, and an idea presents itself. "Does that mean it's not true? That he wasn't really Zack?"

"I don't know. In my experience, children's recollections of their previous death tend to be the strongest and most accurate memories they have."

"But he's wrong. So what does that mean?"

He stops what he's doing and taps his finger thoughtfully on the tripod case.

"Look, without speaking to the rest of your family, without having the opportunity to fully investigate Jack's case, there's very little else we can do here. Are you able to reverse your decision, let us speak with Zack's parents, your sister?"

I shake my head, but then stop myself and try to think about it this time. What would that mean? But all I can do is hear Jack's words inside my head.

Aaron held head underwater.

The thing about Aaron is... I can believe he would have done that. Not deliberately *killing someone*—that's ridiculous— but playing like that? Holding someone underwater, just for a few seconds, to scare them? That's *exactly* the kind of thing he would have done when he was younger. That's what he'd do today.

No. I struggle to focus on my thoughts. *I literally remember him doing it.* Not on any particular occasion, but in the years before Zack died, I remember seeing him doing just that—dunking both Zack and Eva, and sometimes their friends who came around to play. I remember Amber having to yell at him about it, and even having to scold him myself—which I never liked doing because he usually didn't obey me, and would give me a funny look as if to say who the hell was I to tell him what to do?

I stop thinking, suddenly aware that Dr Wells is still speaking to me and I didn't catch a word of it.

"Kate? I said that this could radically change the dynamic of this case, from an evidential perspective. Jack has just given us a very different explanation for his death compared to the one you've provided for how Zack died. If Jack turns out to be correct, that would be compelling evidence that he's telling the truth."

"No," I say, the decision making itself from somewhere outside of me. "*No.* What do you want me to do? Go to Bea and tell her that her son was murdered? And tell Amber that her son's a killer? Oh, and by the way, the reason I know all this is because my son is actually the reincarnation of the victim? No way." I sense my voice running away with itself, like I've lost control of it. "This whole thing is fucking crazy."

For once it seems that Dr Wells doesn't know what to say.

"What should I do?" I ask him. Suddenly I hope he has an answer. "You must have come across this sort of thing, dozens of times? What do I do?"

He takes a long time to answer, and I can see from his face that he's going to disappoint me.

"This isn't a situation I've encountered before."

He falls silent, and I don't know what to say, so I fall silent too. I just watch him as he finishes packing up the camera equipment and then calls Charlotte from the kitchen. Several times he glances at his watch.

"I'm sorry we have to leave like this," he says at last. "But the flight leaves at—" I wave my hand to stop him. I don't want excuses. I don't know *what* I want. I don't even know why I wanted him to come. I thought it would help, but it's done the opposite. It's made everything much worse. I risk a glance at Jack. For some reason I expect him to look different somehow. But he doesn't. He's just Jack, my little boy, although he does look unsettled—like he senses that something isn't right.

"Are you ready Charlotte?" Dr Wells asks. He's checked his equipment several times already. She nods.

"Jack." Dr Wells turns to my boy. "Thank you so much for speaking to us. I hope that we'll get the chance to speak again." He looks at me, a final chance to change my mind. But I say nothing. There's nothing I can say. Sensing this, he holds out a hand to me.

"Kate. Thank you. If you change your mind..."

I walk them to the front door, and then Jack and I watch as they load their gear into the rental car and drive away.

THIRTY-ONE

The ensuing silence in the interview room was eventually broken by Agent Robbins.

"Jack claimed Zack's death wasn't an accident?"

Kate just nodded.

"Where'd he get it from? Had you ever discussed it with your husband? Or your sisters?"

"No." Kate's eyes flashed at him. "Of course not."

"But it *must* have been discussed? In the family? A major incident like that where someone died?"

"We talked about it. In the days after it happened, it was all we talked about. It was all anyone could think about. But it soon became... It was such a painful topic that we stopped talking. By the time Jack was born, it wasn't discussed at all."

"So where did he get the idea from?" Robbins ran a hand through his hair, frustrated. "I'm not gonna buy the idea that he actually remembered it."

Kate stared at him, her face impossible to read.

"And this Wells guy, if we contact him, he's gonna tell us the same story? That Jack actually said all this?"

"I don't know. I imagine so. Maybe he'll even show you the recording?"

Robbins was silenced.

"Could it have been..."—McGee cut in, his voice thoughtful —"the fact that you *didn't* speak about it that influenced Jack? If you didn't tell him anything about Zack's death, could that have encouraged him to make up a story about it?"

Kate swallowed, but didn't answer. Eventually she shrugged. "You tell me. I'm not sure I even know anymore."

I don't know whether I should tell Neil. When he comes home from work we sit on the sofa watching TV, not really speaking. I can still smell Charlotte's perfume lingering in the fabric. Present in the air around us. I let my brain fuss over problems I don't have, because they're preferable to the real ones. So I wonder whether Neil is also thinking about her, the way her golden hair fell on her shoulders, the curves of her breasts that even I noticed under her blouse. But I don't have to worry about those things with Neil. I'm lucky like that. But I do have to worry about what Jack said.

On the one hand, it feels disloyal not to tell him. We're supposed to be partners in life—and until very recently it's always seemed that we really are. Someone I can trust, and someone I can share anything with. So why can't I share this? The answer is obvious—because Neil didn't even want to bring Dr Wells in; he doesn't believe in the work he's doing. And despite everything that he's seen, he doesn't believe what Jack's saying. But I do. I think I do.

And if Jack's telling the truth, then have we got it all wrong about Zack's death?

"Neil," I say, before I think any more about it, "something happened today."

He picks up the remote control and turns down the volume.

He doesn't turn the TV off completely, but I can tell his attention is focused on what I have to say.

"Dr Wells asked Jack whether he had any memories of his death—Zack's death. And he did."

Neil opens his mouth to reply, but then closes it again. He nods for me to continue. I take a deep breath.

"He told us it didn't happen the way Amber's always told us. Aaron was bullying him, holding his head under the water, and he wouldn't stop. And he couldn't breathe, and that's how he died."

I watch him. I see the emotions shift and change on his face, like turbulence in river water, swirling. Finally he covers his face with his hands. He stays like that for ages. Hiding how he feels.

"Kate, this has gone too far," he says when he finally brings his hands down again. Forgotten on the screen, the TV show moves to a chase scene, a detective running wildly after a gang member. My eyes are drawn to it, because I don't want to look at my husband, I don't want to see him as he speaks.

"I'm sorry to say this, but I believe it was a mistake to contact Dr Wells. A serious mistake. You have to understand, the way he operates, it's designed to give the impression that he's studying a genuine phenomenon, but there's no evidence for it. On the contrary, there's an overwhelming body of evidence to show that he's simply collecting data to show how easily people can be mistaken about this thing."

"But how would Jack know anything about Zack's death?"

The question silences Neil again, but not for long.

"He doesn't. Not really. He knows that Zack drowned in the lake, because we've told him that he has to be careful there, and why. And he can imagine the rest. It's the way we tell him, to be so careful, how much it means to us. That's what's caused him to imagine these things."

"But why Aaron? Why would he come up with that?"

On the screen the scene changes to a shoot-out. I'm only seeing it out of the corner of my eye now. The detective at one end of a city alleyway, several gangsters at the other, sheltering behind a dumpster, taking it in turns to pop up and fire shots at each other. For a moment the cliché of it registers. I haven't seen this series before, but I've seen the scene, dozens of times. Neil lifts his hands in submission.

"Perhaps Jack overheard us discussing whether Aaron really did hit that girl? After all, we both know he's a bully; how hard would it be to imagine him behaving that way when he was younger?"

I try to make sense of this. "You're saying it's natural for Jack to imagine Aaron murdering Zack?"

"Not murdering. That's... Look, nobody's saying that Aaron murdered Zack, that's preposterous. No one's suggesting that Aaron did anything wrong. He didn't. We *know* what happened when Zack died, because Amber told us. And she was there. Jack wasn't."

I try to listen to him. The voice of common sense. The voice of sanity. Of course Jack wasn't there. Zack was, and they're not the same person. I know that, and I know there's been too much death in this family, with Zack and Mom and then Dad. So of course I've got death on my mind. But then I think about Amber.

"Can you imagine what Amber would have done though?" I say suddenly. "If what Jack said was actually true. Do you think she would have told us the truth if Aaron *had* killed Zack?" I look at Neil, my eyes widening. I know my answer to this.

"This is what I mean, Kate. Don't you see it? How this crazy idea just leads you further and further away from reality? And it's *dangerous*. Listen to me, the only evidence you have that Amber might have lied is a few words of Jack's. And he *wasn't there*. Categorically he wasn't there." Neil stares at me, imploring. "Please Kate, you have to believe me."

I say nothing, but my eyes are pulled again to the silent TV screen. It's easier to stare at it, watching the gunshots, the dramatic expressions on the faces of the actors. A place where unreality is served up to us every minute of every day. Is it any wonder it's so hard to tell the difference?

Sometime later—it's probably only ten minutes, but it feels like it might be hours—I speak again.

"So you don't think I should talk to her, to Amber?"

Neil snorts with hollow laughter. He's been back watching the show, but he mutes it again. "Absolutely not. Are you joking now?" He stares at me, but it's obvious I'm not. "I've told you. I think that what you should do is forget this whole thing. Children who make these claims, like Jack, they don't do it for long. Eventually they realize that no one believes them anymore, and they stop. Just like they stop believing in all the other childhood fantasies that we accept without wondering if they're actually real." He sighs, but when he realizes that the way he's speaking is hurting me, he puts an arm around me, pulling me closer to him. We haven't hugged much recently, we don't seem to fit as we used to, before this all began. A thought occurs to me.

"Why did you say it was a few words? What Jack said about Aaron?"

He gives up on the hug and looks at me, suddenly less assured.

"I didn't tell you *how* he said it," I clarify. "How Jack spoke about his death."

"You told me he thinks Aaron held him underwater."

"Yes but I didn't tell you it was just a few words—so why did you say that?" An answer forms in my mind, as clear as can be. "He's told you too. Hasn't he? You've asked him about his death."

"Kate, that's ridiculous, no. *No.* I haven't asked him, and he hasn't told me—and even if he had I'd know it wasn't true. I just assumed he said a few words because that's the way he's speaking at the moment. He's not exactly conversing in full sentences." He's red in the face now. "It's a few words from him, and ninety percent you filling in the gaps."

For a few moments he stares at the silent TV screen. I don't know who won the shoot-out, but now the crime-scene investigators have appeared, dressed in their funny blue suits. Only they're not really crime-scene investigators, because none of it's real.

"I'm tired," Neil says. "I'm going to take a shower." He goes to stand up, then hesitates, looking at me.

"You want this on?" He holds up the remote, inclining it towards the TV. I shake my head and he presses the button. The on-screen fantasy fades away, replaced by reality.

A cool, black nothing.

THIRTY-TWO

I have to know now. I have to get to the truth. The thought that Amber might have lied about Zack's death stays with me, this strange but suddenly possible other world, and I feel in limbo, not sure which world I actually inhabit. It's been a long time since I've seen my eldest sister. She was so preoccupied with Aaron's case, and once it was finally solved she threw all of her energy into the lake-house refurbishment, all of which meant she was too busy to come round or arrange a meet-up. We've texted and spoken on the phone, but face to face I've not seen her in over five months. I think I've encouraged this too, as a way of keeping her from hearing anything that Jack's been saying.

But now I find myself needing to get close to her, and I make a plan. She's been sending both Bea and I updates on how the building works are going—or not, since she focusses mostly on the problems—but I haven't paid them very much attention. But I decide I'll ask to see her. This is my idea: I'll talk to her about the house, but what I really want to know is what happened to Zack all those years ago. In my head it seems a viable idea, although it also feels like I'm losing the ability to make good decisions, or even to recognize what they look like.

I text her to suggest we go up to the lake house for a look, and she phones back five minutes later. At first, she's short with me. As if she doesn't have time to go all the way up to the lake, or that somehow she's gotten used to us not seeing each other in person, and actually likes it. But as she speaks, she changes her mind. Soon she sounds happy about the idea, almost as if she were the one to suggest it. The sister I know so well.

I don't take Jack. I drop him off at playschool, arranging for Jan to pick him up and stay with her until I get back. I don't tell Neil about it. I don't want him to know where I'm going.

I drive up alone. Amber offered to drive us both, but I wanted the time to think. Or I think I do. Actually all I do on the freeway up there is brood. Frustration that my husband isn't standing by me. Uncertainty—still—over whether I should trust Jack, when he's just a little boy and when so much of the world I know and understand will come crashing down if it turns out he's telling the truth.

The front of the lake house is masked by scaffolding and wrapped in plastic sheeting, so it's impossible to see how near the work is to completion. Although judging by the number of construction workers' trucks parked in the drive, and the pallets of bricks and stacks of plastic pipes, there's still a fair way to go. I spy Amber's BMW and park alongside it, but she's not in it. That means I have to go into the house alone, which I feel uncomfortable doing. I think it's because it doesn't feel like my house anymore. It feels like those days are long since gone. I check my reflection in the rearview mirror and try to pull myself together. I look like me, but not on a particularly good day.

I get out of the car and make my way to the front door. From inside I can hear banging, and male voices, and then a coarse laugh. There's overly cheerful pop music: a radio is on somewhere.

"Hello?" I call out, probably too quietly for anyone to hear. I'm almost grateful nobody seems to notice and I keep quiet as I step inside.

The house used to have a small porch, and then a fairly modest hallway which led off to the kitchen on one side, and then the living and dining rooms on the other. Part of Amber's project is to switch that around, so that the kitchen moves into the space that used to be both the dining and living rooms, to make a much larger modern kitchen. At the same time, an extension on the back will make the new living space much larger than it used to be as well. Amber sent us the plans, and while it all looked amazing, Neil and I did wonder whether it might be easier just to knock down the whole house and start again.

I step into the new kitchen, feeling the new sense of space. It looks almost finished, but the counters and units are all covered with blue protective film. There are two ovens, two dishwashers, and a huge island—even bigger than the one in Amber's kitchen. A long way away—almost an absurd distance, across beautiful stone tiles—the back wall is missing, replaced with a dozen sliding glass doors, which are also covered in protective film. Outside of *those* is a brand-new patio, where before there used to be flowerbeds. I get a sudden image of Mom pottering in them, and I bite my lip, wondering what she'd make of all this. And then the thought widens. It's not just the house: what would she think of Jack, and what might have happened to Zack? What would Dad think if he were still alive? But just thinking about it confuses me—as most thoughts about people who have died seem to these days. I'm almost grateful when I'm pulled back into the room by a female voice—obviously my sister's—and apparently angry. Before I can react she strides into the room trailed by an older man in overalls, a pencil behind his ear.

"No, this *isn't* the right floor." Amber gives me the briefest of welcoming looks as she strides past, then stands with her hands on her hips surveying the beautiful new floor.

"Mrs Langford, these are the tiles you first specified. You sent the name to me, we quoted for them—"

"Yes, but I *changed* them. Don't you remember? We spoke on the phone and you said they wouldn't allow an entirely flat floor with the doors open, so we changed them for the oak floorboards." She rolls her eyes at me before continuing. "If I can remember that, I'm fairly sure you can too."

"I definitely remember we discussed it, but you weren't sure, you were going to get back to me."

Amber shakes her head in disbelief.

"The point is, they're in now," the man goes on. "But if it's what you want, we can rip them up and put the oak down instead—"

"Of course that's what I want. It's what I told you I wanted in the first place."

"The second place. The first place was these tiles..." the man insists.

Amber gives an exasperated shrug before looking at the floor tiles, searching for something.

"Even if these *were* the tiles I ordered, the way they've been laid is just not up to standard." She moves suddenly to the wall, where the new floor butts up against it. There's a gap of maybe an eighth of an inch, neatly filled by grout, or cement or whatever they use. It looks fine to me.

"This shouldn't be here. You shouldn't be able to see this."

"Expansion gap," the man says, "You have to have it or the tiles'll crack in the summer, when it gets hot."

"A gap I could understand, but a *chasm*?" Amber replies.

"The skirting boards aren't in yet. You won't see it."

"No, Bill." Amber shakes her head. "I want the floor I asked for. Is that really too much to expect?"

Bill raises his hand, acknowledging me for the first time.

"Like I say Mrs Langford, whatever you want. But I can't not charge for it. You understand that?"

"Hmmm." My sister turns, finally addresses me. "Hello, Kate, good idea of yours to come here and check up on things. Bill, this is my sister, Kate."

I just smile, not quite knowing what else to do, how to feel – about the house, about what I now know about Amber. Or might know. Bill, who now looks like he's biting his tongue, nods at me. Even though he's won, he clearly feels he's lost.

"Well, if there's nothing else, I'll go and price up a new floor," he says, raising hairy eyebrows in my direction.

Amber sighs dramatically as he leaves. Then she shakes her head.

"What a nightmare."

"Hi Amber." I don't know what else to say. I was going to tell her how amazing the house looks, because, in spite of every-thing, it really does, but I'm not sure I want to. "What are the problems?" I say instead.

"What *aren't* the problems?" she replies. Then she starts ticking them off. "There's the floor in here. And then the glass surrounds in the other extension are the wrong color. And the roof clearly leaks—though they're denying that at the moment. They've turned the yard into a mud pit. And then the timbers for the new boathouse look far too new—they're supposed to match the older ones, or we're going to be in trouble with the Preservation Office, and we're already in lots of trouble with the Preservation Office." She shakes her head, but then smiles unex-pectedly. "Come on, let me give you a tour."

Amber leads me back out of the new kitchen and into where the old kitchen used to be. But that too is twice the size that I remember—no, maybe three times the size, once I get into

the room and appreciate the scale of the extension. And her
mood seems to have recovered entirely.

"So, this is the *other* new living space; it's coming along as
you can see. Double height here, and..."—she touches my
shoulder so that I spin around, and then points upwards—"Up
there is the mezzanine, which gives really lovely views of the
lake."

"Mezzanine?" I don't remember that.

"Yes, and there's going to be a wrought-iron spiral staircase,
just over by the wall, to access it." Her eyes widen in
excitement.

"I didn't see that in the plans."

She shakes her head. "It wasn't in there. We came up with it
afterwards. Had a hell of a job convincing the preservation
officer to accept it, which was ridiculous because we already
had the double height, and you can hardly see it from outside."
She sighs wearily. "Honestly you would not believe how small-
minded those people are. But we got it through." Her face lights
up in a smile again. For a moment she sounds scheming and
greedy, but then I remember how she's doing this for all of us,
fighting these battles—and the house is incredible. I decide to
give her some credit for that.

"Amber, this is amazing," I say, meaning it.

"You haven't seen it all yet." She looks touched. Suddenly
she takes my hands and pulls me back to the hallway, and then
up the old stairs—about the only part of the interior that I recognize—towards the bedrooms. It's clear from the noise that this is
where most of the work is going on. We come to the old master
bedroom, Dad's room.

"New windows, new floors, new walk-in wardrobe, new
ensuite." She steps past a man doing something with wiring,
and spins around in the center of the room. "We moved the
windows too so that you get a better view of the island. Brock
wanted to see it from in bed!" She laughs, and lingers a moment

before heading into the new bathroom. It's finished, and it's beautiful, with matching marble floor and wall tiles, and a huge walk-in shower set out with glass bricks.

"There were problems here too, with the lighting, but we put them right."

"Amber this is..." I'm about to say how stunning it looks, but her comment registers and I stop. "You've decided Dad's old room is going to be yours and Brock's?"

She stops, like she's sensing trouble. "No. Of course not." Then she breaks into a laugh. "Though it has to be someone's!" She touches me on the shoulder. "*All* the rooms are getting a major upgrade. It's just that Brock liked the look of this one." She shrugs. After a moment she leads me out of the master suite and down the hall into the three other original bedrooms, and one entirely new one, above the extension. The truth is they're all beautiful. She's done a great job, and I won't care which one I sleep in.

"It's really something, Amber. It's really lovely."

"It's *going to be* lovely," she corrects me. "When it's finally finished." I glance at her, and notice for the first time that she looks a little older. As if the project—nearly two years of it, since Dad died—has aged her.

"But my favorite part is the new boathouse."

There's a spring to her stride as she leads me back down the stairs, out through the back door and into the yard. Much of it has been churned into a thick brown mud, cut with tire treads. But a walkway has been constructed, half of it finished as a fine gravel path that curves elegantly down toward the lake where the old boathouse stood. But the old building—small, utilitarian —is gone, replaced by something unrecognizable, and quite stunning. The boathouse used to sit on the shore with the front open to the water, but now the whole building has been moved out onto the lake itself, where it appears to float on a platform of gorgeous hardwood decking. The workmanship is wonderful.

The wood is rich and smooth and the grain almost glows in the afternoon light. We step onto the deck—it feels solid, it must be on piles rather than floating, and Amber invites me to push on the double doors of the boathouse itself. I do so, and they swing open on smoothly oiled hinges.

"Oh my gosh. *Amber?*"

The front of the room is almost simple. The floor is laid with wooden planks, and a small kitchenette sits on one side, opposite a built-in seating area with large comfortable cushions. Beautiful, wooden windows give views out over the water. A little further back the floor drops away to where the lake laps at the side of a wooden dinghy. I recognize it at once: it's Dad's boat, moored inside the boathouse. It was battered and worn out the last time I saw it, but now it's gleaming.

"How does it get in there?" I ask, amazed.

"There're doors at the back. Electric, you just press a button." She looks at me, eager for my response.

"And that's really Dad's boat?"

"I had it completely restored. Obviously you have to drop the mast down to get it in, but it's easy to hoist it up again. And look." She spins me around, and above the entrance, in pride of place, there's a portrait of Mom and Dad standing together arm in arm, as if looking down on the room.

"I only wish Dad could have seen it." Amber looks wistful for a moment, then takes my hand again. This time we go through the boathouse and out a back door onto more decking, and I can see that a new wooden jetty—or perhaps the old one, restored and extended—now juts out into the lake.

"Come on!" Amber takes me along it until we're halfway out, water on either side of us, and then she turns around.

"What do you think?" she exclaims, swinging her arm to show me all that she's created. "It's a shame it's not dark; you see the lanterns—they're original brass—and they cast the most beautiful glow."

"It's perfect Amber, it really is."

"You think so?" She turns to me, and I can see how much she needs this, my overbearing and perhaps undervalued big sister.

"Yeah," I say. And I mean it. "It's great. Mom and Dad would have loved it."

THIRTY-THREE

We stay like that a while, her gazing back proudly at the boathouse she's somehow brought into existence, and the house behind—always large, and now almost overbearingly so.

"What was it you wanted, by the way?" she asks suddenly. "You said there was something you had to ask me?"

In a moment, like a vacuum when its seal is broken, everything starts to come rushing back. Every doubt and worry about Jack, and most of all, everything he said about Aaron, and how he drowned him when he was Zack.

"Um..." I glance to my left, at the little beach area where we used to base ourselves in the summer when we were swimming. And from there my eyes roam out over the shimmering water. I know it so well, I could point to the exact place where the bottom drops away and it gets dangerously deep. Even from this angle, with the light bouncing from the water's surface so you can't see beneath. From nowhere—or that's how it feels—an idea occurs to me.

"What?" Amber gives me a look.

"It's lovely, but..." I hesitate, climbing into a character that isn't quite me. "It's really special—and the portrait of Mom and

Dad is great—but..." I pause. I anticipate the effect of the final word on Amber's expression, wait until I see the frown.

"What?"

"It's just... I wondered if you put anything in for Zack?"

She looks perplexed. "For Zack?"

"Like some sort of a memorial?"

"Oh." A hand goes to her lips and she looks away.

"It wouldn't have to be much—" I start to press, but she cuts me off.

"No, that's a good idea." She's quiet for a moment. "I don't know why that didn't occur to me."

"It only just occurred to me," I tell her, which is true. And suddenly I feel bad, bringing it up like I have. But actually, it *is* a good idea. It would help Bea, regardless of... all this craziness with Jack.

"What do you think it should be?" Amber asks. Now I pretend to think about this for a while, but really I'm thinking about Jack, and what he told me about Aaron.

"Maybe it could be in the water?" I suggest. "At the point where..." I turn, my expression innocent. "Where exactly was it that Zack drowned?"

Amber looks away, out over the water, but doesn't answer. I feel my cheeks heat up at how obvious my question was.

What the hell am I trying to do?

"I'm not sure," she replies eventually. "But wouldn't it be better on the land? Perhaps in the yard somewhere?"

"How about the twins?" I keep going, now that I've started this. "Did they see where exactly it happened? Maybe they could tell us?"

She glances at me, clearly unsettled. "No, the twins were in the shallows. And I don't think they were looking and..."

Not looking? I want to interrupt her—you were shouting at Zack to come back in case he drowned, and then he *did* drown. And they *weren't looking*?

"Are you sure?" I ask, quietly.

"Am I sure of what?"

"That the twins didn't see it?"

Again she looks at me. "Kate, what is this? Some kind of inquisition?"

I don't reply, I don't know how to reply. But she seems to take my silence as a sign that she's the one who's overstepped a line.

"I can't say for sure," she tries to answer, "but they weren't close, when it happened." Her frown deepens; she's still clearly not understanding my sudden interest. Or maybe she's just thinking back to that horrible afternoon.

"They were in the shallows, and Zack was..." She pauses, and waves her arm vaguely out over the water. "Over here somewhere."

I want to ask her again, but I sense I've pushed her as far as I can. Again, I lapse into silence.

"I really think some kind of memorial on the beach might be better," she goes on. I'd almost forgotten the idea about the memorial. But now I see that's still the lens she's seeing this through. Though now it's almost like it was her idea. "Something small. Something tasteful." Now I can see her mind beginning to work. I know my sister too well.

"How's Aaron?" I ask suddenly, still watching her face.

She stops, and turns to me. "He's... doing well. Why do you ask?"

I think how to answer that. I wonder whether any other girls have accused him of hitting them. "Is he still swimming?" I ask instead.

Amber hesitates. "A little, we're not sure if he's going to pursue it," she begins. "He could get a place on the Olympic pathway, but it's such a big commitment, and he's looking more at going into business." I've heard this all before, so many times. I tune it out.

"He was such a good swimmer when he was younger, wasn't he?" I muse. Or I pretend to. "When Zack died, was Aaron already swimming competitively?"

My sister stiffens, pulling back slightly from the balustrade looking out over the lake.

"Junior competitions. Yes, he'd started by then."

"I remember how proud you were of him, even then."

"Why wouldn't I be, Kate? He's my son." I hear the edge in her voice clearly now. My sister knows me too, of course. "What is this? What are you talking about?"

We're both quiet a moment, and I wonder about actually telling her. The whole story. For a moment I can almost visualize it. I can almost see the shock on her face when I tell her the things that Jack says. How she might even believe him, because she was never into science—she thought that was what the nerdy kids did, and her business—Rocket!— is all about creativity, as if that trumps science in some way. But then I'll get to the part where Jack is saying how her son drowned Zack, and that she must have known, must have covered it up for all these years. And I know I can't tell her that, because that would be the end of us, we would no longer be sisters, it would tear us apart.

But she's still staring at me. So now I have to say something.

"I've been thinking about Zack a lot recently," is what I come up with. "And maybe I was just wondering why Aaron wasn't able to save him. You know? He was such a good swimmer."

Amber stares at me. When she answers her voice is cool, her words seem carefully chosen. "Aaron was just a boy. He was eleven years old. And like I told you, he was in the shallows, a long way away from Zack."

I listen, staying still and quiet. But the same thought just repeats itself in my mind.

"But he was such a good swimmer, even then..."

I see Amber's eyes dart from left to right as she calculates how to answer this. In the end she simply turns away and looks out over the water. And inside my mind I feel a huge clash, as if two huge forces have crashed together. On one side is everything that Jack has told me, impossible for me *not* to believe; on the other is my sister, and her version of events, backed up by everything I know to be true about the world. Neither can win, but neither can be defeated either, so instead there's just a furious, ever-present tension. A pressure that won't let up.

"Aaron and Eva were playing in the shallows," Amber repeats, unaware of the maelstrom in my head. "Zack was..." She waves her hand out over the deeper part of the lake again, but not to any specific area. "He was out there when it happened. I don't know what this is, and I don't know what else to tell you."

"I'm sorry." Suddenly I put my hand on hers, warm against the upright post of the carved handrail. I feel the bones of her knuckles through the skin, the faint pulse of blood through her veins. My sister. Telling me the truth about the tragedy that happened just as much to her as to our nephew. A boy who died, just a few dozen meters from where we're standing. A horrible accident that was nobody's fault. Which could not be helped.

And which had absolutely nothing to do with Jack.

THIRTY-FOUR

"Things got a lot more difficult after Wells's visit," Kate said. Her eyes were sad now, as though her story was drawing towards its natural conclusion. McGee waited, his hands pressed together in front of his chest. But she didn't go on.

"In what way?"

She sighed. "After Jack remembered how he'd died—how *Zack* died—it became one of his clearest memories. He became... sort of obsessed with it."

"How so?"

"It wasn't just that the memories came more often—though they did. By then it was almost always the way he died that he remembered. And he was so angry about it. He'd make little fists with his hands, tell me how he wanted to punish him."

"Punish... Aaron?"

After a moment Kate nodded. "Yeah. I know how it sounds. He wanted to confront him, he wanted *me* to confront him. To tell him what a bad thing he'd done." She looked up suddenly, her face weary. "Obviously it wasn't something I could do."

McGee stroked his cheek.

"Was he... seeing Aaron at all, at this time?"

"No, Aaron was away at college, but of course that couldn't last forever. But it almost didn't matter; I'd even stopped seeing Jan, I was so scared of what Jack might say in front of her, where it might lead."

"How about your sisters? Did they ever hear him talking like this?"

"No. Bea was away by the coast. I'd... send her pictures, pretend everything was normal. Amber was nearby, but... like I said, I was able to keep Jack away from her too."

There was a silence.

"I knew I couldn't do it forever—keep Jack away from everyone. But I thought that... maybe it could work until the memories faded?" She looked hopeful for a moment.

"This Dr Wells," McGee said thoughtfully, "did he help in any way?" He screwed his face into a frown. "I mean, after he'd elicited this... scenario about Zack's supposed death, did he... I dunno... offer any counselling, anything like that? I would have thought that was the least he could do?"

"Actually, he did. He sent me some names. But he didn't know anybody nearby to recommend, and I couldn't face going to a stranger and having to explain all of this. What was I going to say? I didn't know what to believe myself. And that was the worst of it. I didn't know whether my son was crazy, or my sister had lied to me—to all of us—about what happened when Zack died."

"What happened next?" McGee asked.

"I had one more idea. A way to finally prove it one way or the other."

THIRTY-FIVE

Jack and I are in the waiting room for the state medical examiner's office—a place I didn't even know existed. In his hands he's clutching a slip of paper with the number seven printed on it. The screen above us shows that the teller is currently dealing with number six, an elderly man with a walking stick. The desk is far enough away that I can't hear the purpose of his visit.

As Jack swings his legs on the plastic chair, I run through my own reasons for being here. It seemed less insane in the craziness of my private world, but now I'm here I'm not so sure. It has to do with Zack's death. Every time Jack tells me about it, it seems to affect him more strongly. He talks about how Aaron held him underwater, how it felt when he was fighting to get back to the surface. When he talks about it he moves, as if he's reliving it. He'll wriggle and shiver. Sometimes his arms will flail about if he's sitting down, or his legs will kick on the bed. And that's what made me think of this. I remember that in the days after Zack died, an autopsy was carried out. I think it's just a standard thing that happens in cases like these—I don't even know. I just remember that I never saw the report, or even heard what it said. Except that it confirmed what everyone already knew—that Zack had drowned. But then I wondered: if Zack really had been held underwater by Aaron, and if Zack really was fighting to get free—then wouldn't there be marks on Zack's body? Marks that would have been seen by the medical examiner?

So that's why we're here. The problem is, I was so fixed on the idea of seeing the autopsy report, anticipating what it might say, that I don't know they'll actually give it to me. Above my head the screen changes, and Jack nudges me in the side.

"Number seven!" He looks at me expectantly.

"Yes?" The woman sits behind a thick plastic screen, so I have to lean forward to be heard.

"I need to get a copy of the autopsy report for my nephew, Zack Marshall. He drowned in an accident about eight years ago."

"You'll need to fill out an application form. What's the reason for the retrieval?"

"Excuse me?" I swallow.

"The document retrieval. You need an authorized reason."

"Oh." I keep my eyes on her, and will Jack to stay quiet. "I just want to check something."

The woman's eyes— already narrow—become even more slit-like. "We don't just hand out autopsy reports."

I bite my lip, not sure what to say.

"No, I—"

"If you're a close relative you have a legal right to access an autopsy report, but if not, you'd need a valid reason."

I blink at the woman. "Oh. That's OK then. I'm his aunt."

She shakes her head again. "Definition of close relative is parent or legal guardian." She glances at the door, where a security guard is leaning, bored, against a wall.

"What counts as a valid reason then?"

The woman seems to consider calling him over, but decides to humor me, at least for now.

"Could be legal, to settle an insurance claim?" She sighs; suddenly I realize she's not angry like I thought, but bored. I've projected my own tension onto her, I've made her angry in my mind. "There's not exactly a list; you have to give your reason, and we decide if it's valid."

For a few seconds I consider telling her the truth. I'm sure if I let him, Jack would back me up, tell this woman how he was murdered by his cousin. But I'm just about clear-headed enough to know how that would sound. I can't go that way.

"Madam?" she presses.

"Um..."

"Do you *have* a valid reason?"

Another idea appears in my mind. I don't know where it comes from, nor do I have time to consider it before the words are tumbling out of my mouth. I lean closer, speaking in a hushed tone.

"It's about my son here. His diagnosis is... challenging," I begin, pulling Jack in front of me so she can see him better. I have no idea where I'm going with this, but once I begin the lie, the words just flow. "And I just don't know how he's going to cope with another stay in the hospital," I shiver and wait while the woman's eyes focus on my son, the very picture of health.

"However, my deeper concern pertains to a possible genetic connection between Zack's medical history and my son's condition. Unearthing this link could be of..." Finally I have to search for the words, but there are benefits to having a husband that never stops talking as if he's in a lecture theatre. "...*paramount* importance in refining his treatment plan." I fix the woman with a firm look and wait, holding my breath.

Her eyes go again to Jack. I don't know if I imagine it but he seems to be pulling a face now, as if trying to make himself look sick. Her face softens. She sees what I want her to see.

"Of course. I'm so sorry." She rolls her chair sideways to a bank of drawers and pulls one open. She spends a few minutes searching, and then scoots back with a three-page form. I catch her eye glancing at Jack again and giving him a kindly smile. When she looks back at me, her expression has changed completely; she's filled with compassion now, sympathy for me and my sick son.

"Fill this in; where it says reason for retrieval, just put 'medical query.' They're always accepted without requiring further evidence. But..." She bites her lip, as if she's sorry to bring this last part up.

"What?"

"There's a hundred-dollar fee,"

"That's fine." I breathe again, relieved, as I pull open my purse.

Even for a hundred dollars, I still have to wait two weeks, but then I get an email telling me to pick up the report. I don't open it there and then; instead, Jack and I end up in a coffee shop, where he falls asleep in his stroller. I sip my coffee for a while, delaying tearing open the brown A4 envelope which contains the details of my nephew's death. Eventually I gently prize it open and pull out a stapled document, about ten pages long. I read the cover sheet:

Autopsy Summary Report

Case Number: 2018-07-15
Deceased: Zack Marshall, 8 years old
Date of Examination: August 16, 2018
Pathologist: Dr. John Donald, MD, Board-Certified Forensic Pathologist

Autopsy Protocol: *The examination was performed upon the body of Zack Marshall, an 8-year-old male, at the State Medical Examiner's Office, following the standard protocols applicable to forensic autopsies. The external examination was initiated at 09:00 hours, followed by a comprehensive internal examination.*

Those last words give me pause, almost disgust me. I glance around, as if expecting to see the other customers staring: how could I be reading something so... invasive? But no one's looking. No one's paying me the slightest attention. I read on.

The cause of death is determined as asphyxiation due to fresh-water drowning. The lungs were markedly edematous, and water was found throughout the airways.

I stop again, this time to Google the word "edematous" which turns out to mean "swollen with an excessive accumulation of fluid." I keep going.

While external injuries were noted, these are suggestive of, and consistent with, aggressive resuscitative efforts post-extraction from the aquatic environment.

I feel a shiver at these words. *External injuries.* But I tell myself to stay calm. I think back to the day he died. By the time Dad, Bea and I got back from visiting Mom in the hospital, the ambulance was already at the lake house, and Zack had been pronounced dead. But Neil told all of us how he'd tried to resuscitate him, how hard he'd tried, so hard he was worried he might have even broken Zack's ribs because he was pumping his chest so violently. The paramedics praised him though; they said he did exactly the right thing, it just didn't work.

But could the report's assumption be wrong? Could the injuries it talks about, those *consistent with aggressive resuscita-*

tive efforts, actually have been sustained when Aaron was holding Zack underwater? When Zack was fighting to free himself? I turn quickly to the relevant section. I'm breathless, I have a strong hunch I'm on to something here.

It takes me a while, but I find the relevant passage:

Initial observation revealed the presence of superficial abrasions and contusions on the upper extremities and anterior torso. A notable finding was the presence of pronounced contusions and rib fractures on the anterior chest wall. These injuries are characteristic of forceful compressions, commonly seen in aggressive cardiopulmonary resuscitation efforts. The fractures are predominantly located in the mid-sternal region, with associated soft tissue bruising indicating significant applied pressure.

I have to check the meaning of several of the terms, but the sense of hope is short-lived. I read the words again, more slowly this time, and I realize I have the same problem here as I have everywhere. This might be evidence that Jack's telling the truth, or it might not be. There're always two explanations, and no one to choose definitively between them. I rub my face, suddenly feeling stupid. What was I expecting? Of course the report isn't going to conclude that Zack received injuries from fighting off an aggressor. If it had, then the police would have asked more questions at the time. I'm about to drop the report, certain that the whole thing has been a waste of time, when I notice the section immediately below where I've been reading:

Additionally, a significant laceration was noted on the plantar surface of the right foot, approximately 7 cm in length, with jagged edges characteristic of a cut inflicted by a sharp, uneven object such as a broken glass bottle. This injury appears to have occurred ante-mortem, as evidenced by the presence of minimal haemorrhaging around the wound margins, suggesting active

*blood circulation at the time of injury. The location and nature
of this wound are consistent with an accidental injury possibly
sustained in a panicked or agitated state, such as during a
struggle or frantic movement in water.*

Another memory bubbles into my mind, something I
haven't thought about for seven years. We arrived that day just
before Zack's body was taken away, placed into a black plastic
body bag and lifted into the ambulance. But I saw it. I saw how
shrunken his chest was, how his skin had taken on a horrible,
deathly-blue pallor. And I remember the cut on his foot. It
wasn't that bad, certainly nothing that would have contributed
to his death. But on another day—a happier day—we would
have bandaged it, and perhaps Dad might have complained
about the idiots who fished in their boats just off the house, and
the way they tossed their empty beer bottles into the water. He
used to keep a snorkel and flippers, and on still days, when the
visibility was good, he'd swim out and collect them. But you
could never get them all.

My heart is in my mouth as I scrabble through the pages,
past photographs of Zack's waterlogged lungs, until I find an
image of the cut to his foot. His right foot. A Y-shaped incision,
the flesh translucent around its edges. I give such a sharp intake
of breath when I see it that I sense people around me looking
over, wondering what it is that's upset me. But I can't tell them.
I can't tell anyone.

Jack has a Y-shaped birthmark on his right foot in exactly
the same place.

THIRTY-SIX

Kate fell silent, and after a while Robbins opened his hands questioningly.

"Jack had a birthmark on his foot? I don't get it. So what?"

Kate just stared, breathing heavily at the memory. It seemed that McGee had an idea of the significance of what she'd just said, but he didn't answer either.

"I don't get it. Lots of people have birthmarks, it doesn't mean anything."

Eventually Kate answered him.

"Some of the most compelling evidence for reincarnation —*claimed* evidence—is that many of the children who say they have these memories also have birthmarks or deformities on their bodies matching wounds or injuries on the bodies of those whose lives they remember. There are dozens of examples and some of them are very striking."

"The doctor guy mentioned it, Wells?" McGee asked.

"He provides many examples in his books. There was a case of a boy born with one side of his head horribly deformed. He remembered the life—and death—of a man who was killed when a shotgun was discharged at point-blank range, removing much of the same side of his face and skull. Another child had a mark on their chest which apparently matched where the person they remembered was injured in a knife fight."

"I have a picture on my phone," Kate said when neither of the agents responded. "Of Jack's birthmark. I thought it might be important. If you let me have my phone I can show you, and then you can get hold of the autopsy report from the state medical examiner."

"No need for that." McGee smiled briefly. "I already have a copy of Zack's autopsy." He ran his finger up the pile of paperwork on front of him, but made no effort to pull out the relevant pages.

"You want me to get it? The phone?" Robbins asked.

"I'll go," McGee said. "I could do with the break." He suspended the interview, and walked upstairs to where Kate had been processed and her belongings logged. After sitting for so long it felt good to stretch his legs.

When they resumed the interview five minutes later, Kate unlocked her phone, while McGee found the photograph of Zack's foot injury. It was a close-up, showing a Y-shaped cut, but lying on its side.

"Here," Kate said, placing the phone on the table and sliding it over toward him. McGee studied Zack's injury for a few more seconds before turning to the phone. The mark on Jack's foot wasn't clear, just a slight discoloration of the skin, but in location, shape and size there was no doubt it looked close.

"So this is what? Proof?" Robbins said, uncertainty etched into his voice.

"No." Kate shook her head dismissively. "You can't have proof. That's the problem. It could just be a coincidence." She shrugged. "It was more one thing. The weight of evidence just kept falling Jack's way."

"When was this?" McGee asked suddenly. "When did you request the autopsy report?"

Kate's eye's flicked to him, but then flicked away again.

"Recently. Three, four months ago."

"Did you tell anyone? Did you tell Neil?"

"I told Dr Wells. I thought he ought to know. He said it might be significant, but there was no point him coming back, not unless I'd changed my mind about him speaking to Bea."

"And had you changed your mind?"

"No."

"You didn't answer me: did you speak with Neil about the birthmark?"

"No. We weren't really speaking about what Jack was saying by then. We weren't really speaking that much at all."

"OK," McGee mused, "three or four months. So we're nearly up to date. You'd better continue."

THIRTY-SEVEN

There's a funny thing about life. You can be living what feels like a perfectly normal day, but actually be hurtling full-speed towards utter catastrophe. And you just don't know it. Even if the clues are there, all around you. You get exposed to the weirdest, craziest shit, and it ends up being your normal, so you just don't see it. And whoever you are, day-by-day, hour-by-hour, you take a step closer to the end. Whatever that might be for you.

It's Monday morning. Jack's swimming lesson. You might think such a thing would be impossible, and six months ago I'd have agreed with you, but now that Jack has explained to me why he hates the water so much, I've been able to explain to him how important it is to learn to swim, so that what happened to him before can't happen again. So now, twice a week, we go to the local community pool. At first we just watched from outside, holding our heads close to the thick glass windows and listening to the muffled whoops and shrieks from inside. And then we would go inside, but we'd sit high up in the steep bank of seats by the side and watch the other children, and the old people lumbering up and down in their lanes like graceless whales. Then finally we actually got changed into our swim-suits, and walked to the poolside, and sat there on the benches, watching, sniffing the chlorine.

I was self-conscious at first. I thought that people would be staring at us and wondering why we didn't go in the water, and I was fearful all the time that Jack might get into one of his states and just scream. But he didn't. He was cautious, of course, but very gradually he moved closer to the water, and finally he knelt down to touch it. He dipped his hand into the pool and moved it from side to side, marveling at how it felt. The look on his face was incredible, because you don't think of water as being anything special, but it really is. The next week I had him sitting in the water, his trunks finally getting wet, but his bottom firmly on the step so that there was no danger of his torso or chest going under.

And then we walked together through the water—the toddler pool is only thigh-deep for me, but that's chest-deep for Jack. There were a couple of nasty moments where other children would come too close and Jack would start to panic, but as long as I led him to the edge of the pool, and explained to the other children that Jack once had a bad experience in water, they stayed away. Eventually I got him to actually lie in the water, with his feet not touching the bottom. And that was strange, because as soon as he got used to that, he seemed to know how to swim, without actually being taught.

And once we conquered the pool, he became much better with his baths too. He was cautious still, but as long as we promised him that his head wouldn't go under, he wouldn't scream, and once he was actually in he'd begin to enjoy them, playing with his bath toys just like any other child.

I think this success made me let my guard down.

"Letter for you." Neil peers over his glasses as he rifles through the mail. If he's given a choice between receiving a bill through the mail, or as an email or an SMS like you can get these days, he'll always choose the former. Partly he likes to reduce screen time—he hates social media because he thinks the companies behind them are using science to hack our brains for their benefit. But partly, I think he just likes the mail. Even though neither of us get sent anything of interest these days.

"What is it?"

"The magic of letters, Kate, is that you have to open the envelope to find out."

I give him a sarcastic look and take it from him.

"Looks like a wedding invitation."

I open it, wondering who I know that might be getting married. And for a second, when I pull the card from the envelope, I still think that's what this is, because that's exactly what the card inside looks like too. But when I read the words my hope and calm evaporate.

"Oh."

"What is it?" Neil asks, a touch concerned.

"It's from Amber," I reply, already forming excuses in my head. "It's an invitation to a grand reopening of the lake house." I pause. "And it does look grand."

Neil looks up. Instantly I know we share the same concerns. I don't know exactly where Neil is on the issue of what Jack believes, and we're never going to agree. But we both know how awkward it will be if Jack tells my family about his memories. And the disaster he'll cause if he tells them his version of Zack's death.

"It's finished already?" he says in an attempt to continue with the sarcasm, and I actually do laugh in response over how long it's taken for Amber to get the upgrades done. But I guess I knew this day was coming—she's been emailing me about it— and I've just not wanted to face it.

"We can't get out of it," Neil says, as if we've somehow silently discussed this together. "You can't hide forever."

"Who says I'm hiding?" I snap back, suddenly angry.

"I'm not..."—he raises his hands in defeat—"I apologize. That's not what I meant. I just know how—"

"How what?"

"How... difficult this is, with Jack liable to say something inflammatory at any moment."

Inflammatory. I hate my husband's choice of word there.

"Maybe we should try to get out of it? Or not take him, could that work?"

"What? Like he's some sort of dog? We'll just put him in the kennel for the weekend, is that what you want?"

"No, of course not. Kate, that's not what I'm saying."

He glances at his watch; I know he has to go to work soon. "You're taking him swimming today?"

"Yes."

"Well, that shows how he can... improve, regarding this issue. So maybe it'll be OK. How exactly did you get him used to swimming? It was by gradually introducing him, wasn't it?" He knows it is, of course, because we've discussed it. "So maybe we can do the same with your family? Gradually introduce him to the idea of seeing them, but so that he knows not to say anything about what he claims to remember."

I feel a flare of anger again at his language choice—that Jack *claims to* remember. But it's old ground and the fight gets us nowhere.

"How exactly do we do that?" I ask instead.

"I don't know." He thinks for a moment. "We did it with the water thing, so maybe we'll start by showing him pictures and videos of them, and we'll..."

His voice fades out, perhaps because of the way I'm staring at him. He's driven me past a limit, an invisible line, and once I'm over it I have no choice but to respond.

"*We* did it, did we?"

He frowns, unsure where I'm going with this.

"*We* got him used to the water?" My mind fills with all the work I've done. All the near misses, when I felt that Jack was going to explode and I calmed him down, slowed things down. I feel so settled on the moral high ground here that I want to wallow in it, but he surprises me.

"Yes, *we* did. It was my idea to gradually introduce him to water by turning the shower on. I was the one who did his wipe-washes a little closer to the bathroom each time. You didn't do it at all, for a long while. Don't think I don't know that."

I feel my face heat up, and I have to look away.

"*I* took him to the pool, every week. You've taken him maybe once."

"I have to go to work, Kate. You know that. You can't possibly blame me because you have every day free to do things like this while I have to hold down a job."

I look away; I can't beat this point, but he knows it's not fair. He doesn't push it. I pick up the invitation again, turning it over in my hands. Along with the elegant, printed words there's a pen-and-ink sketch of the new-look lake house on the front.

"Who's going to be there?" Neil asks.

"I don't know," I reply. It's like the heat has been sucked out of the argument. "The invite says 'family and friends.'"

"So that means Aaron?"

I shrug.

"Because if it doesn't, and he stays at college, then maybe Jack won't say anything?" There's a hopeful note to his voice, and a little of it leaks into my mind too.

"It's right in the middle of fall semester, so maybe he can't get away?" says Neil. "Maybe he won't want to? I'm sure he still has his swimming commitments, and maybe he'll feel awkward, seeing everyone after what happened with the police?"

I think about this, but somehow I doubt it. "It's only a couple of hours from his college. And it's on the weekend."

From the other room I can hear Jack watching his cartoons

on the big TV. I don't know exactly what he's watching, but it's Netflix for kids, so I trust that it's safe.

"OK," Neil's voice becomes more decisive, "we'll just have to make sure he doesn't say anything stupid; we'll have to coach him."

It's probably the best idea. I'm about to nod, when an ironic thought hits me. "Isn't that your *actual* explanation?" I ask. "For kids like Jack who claim to remember past lives? Don't you say that their parents are just coaching them? But what you're actually doing is coaching Jack to *not* say these things?"

I give a half-laugh, honestly inviting him to join me in appreciating the irony, but his face is dark.

"This is serious, Kate, we can't have Jack accusing Aaron of killing Zack. That's the sort of thing that could tear your family apart. It could wreck your relationship with your sisters."

"I know it's serious." I feel ambushed, pushed somehow into saying something I don't actually mean. "*I know that.* I'm just saying, it's ironic that you want to do exactly what you accuse others of doing."

He doesn't reply to this.

"I have to get to work." He picks up his keys from the table. "If you have a better idea, text me. If not..." His look is dark again.

THIRTY-EIGHT

How exactly do you coach a five-year-old to not accuse their cousin of killing them in a past life? In some ways my life has become so weird that this doesn't even seem a strange question, and I decide to make a start before we go to the swimming pool.

To begin with I tell Jack that we're going to the lake house for a weekend with the family. Not today, but soon. His first reaction is to be scared. Not petrified, but worried. He hasn't been there since he was young, before the renovation. But I calm him down and tell him he doesn't have to go anywhere near the lake, not if he doesn't want to.

"I don't." He shakes his head. "Don't want to."

"That's fine honey, that's OK." We're in the living room. I think for a moment.

"The point is, we have to talk about what it's OK to say, when you see everyone from the family."

His face folds into a frown, concentrating on my words.

"What you mustn't do is tell them anything about what you remember, about being Zack."

I sense sudden anger at this.

"Why mustn't?"

"Because if you tell them it will hurt them, honey. And you don't want to hurt them, do you?"

Again the frown, but this time accompanied by a shake of the head. Thoughtful, maybe even decisive.

"No."

"OK..." I hesitate. Have I done it? Could it actually be this *easy* to coach a five-year-old into something so strange?"

"But you and Daddy say I have to tell truth. And my other mommy too, she said it important."

"It is, it *is* important Jack." I pause again; something else has occurred to me. I've been focusing on Amber's family, Aaron in particular—worrying what Jack might do when he sees *him*. And I have no doubt that this is driven by his anger at what Aaron did. But more and more these days he also mentions his other mommy, as if he now remembers her quite clearly. But I don't know if he's actually made the association between his "other mommy" and my sister Bea, his auntie. I realize I'm frowning too.

"So I have to tell the truth?"

"Yes. No. Not *that* truth." I stop, try again. "Sometimes you have to tell little white lies, just so you don't hurt people's feelings."

His frown deepens.

"Why hurt them?"

I pause. What he means is, *why* will it hurt them?

"Oh honey. It's hard to explain, but they won't believe you."

"Why no? You believe me? Charlotte believe me?" He still remembers Dr Wells's assistant. She clearly had an impact on him.

"I know. They're like—"

"Daddy believe me."

I stop, surprised.

"Daddy doesn't exactly..." I bite my lip. "He believes that *you* believe you have these memories. He definitely believes that. But he doesn't think they're... For Daddy, they're not actually real."

He shakes his head, clearly not accepting this.

"Daddy believe me," he says again, certain this time.

I try again. "Jack, this is a very difficult thing to explain, but the point is you mustn't tell anyone; it's like a very special secret that you can only talk about with me and Daddy? Do you understand?"

He looks wary.

"Do you see why you mustn't tell anyone, about your memories?"

This time he shrugs his shoulders.

"OK. Are you ready for swimming?"

I get another shrug.

A few days later and I try again, this time with Neil, when he's back from work. I cook Jack his favorite food—cheese pizza—and we eat it all together on the sofa, watching some cartoon series on Netflix that he's into. He stares at the screen, laughing at lines so bad I don't even recognize them as jokes. Neil sits stiffly beside me on the sofa, waiting for me to begin.

"Jack," I say, glancing at my husband, and wondering dimly why it's me that has to lead this. "Do you remember what I said the other day, before swimming?"

He looks at me reluctantly, just for a second, before his eyes switch back to the screen.

"Jack, can we have your attention?" Neil asks. He's a little more obedient with his father, he always has been. This time he looks pointedly away from the screen and nods his head. Neil picks up the remote and mutes the TV.

"Pause," Jack says, which goes over Neil's head.

"Pause the TV," I explain to Neil, "so he doesn't miss any of it." A little irritably Neil freezes the cartoon. He's taken over now, whether he wants to or not; Jack's eyes are on *his* face now, wary.

"Do you remember what Mommy told you the other day about going to the lake house?"

He bites the inside of his lip, but says nothing.

"About what you can say and what you can't say?"

After a pause, Jack nods.

"Can you tell me what you can't say?"

"Can't talk about Zack."

"That's right," Neil begins to say, but Jack hasn't quite finished.

"About how me was Zack."

There's a silence.

"OK nearly right," Neil corrects. "You *can* talk about Zack if you like, but you can't say you were him, or that you remember being him—or anything like that. Do you understand?"

Jack sort of half-nods, half-shrugs. His eyes flick back to the TV screen.

"There's one more thing." I hesitate. I'm not sure it's a good idea to tell Jack this now, but something drives me forward anyway. "Aaron's going to be there."

Immediately his face changes; first there's fear, completely obvious from the way his eyes widen and the color drains away. But then it looks more like anger. The color comes back, and his hands clench into fists.

"How do you feel about that, Jack?" Neil asks.

Jack's eyes look around the room. They settle on the TV remote.

"Unpause," is all he says.

THIRTY-NINE

The journey up is uneventful, but when we pull into the—newly resurfaced—driveway to the lake house I'm reminded of the weekend that Dad died. Except that everything's different now. It's amazing how fast things can change: change we don't see coming. Back then the house looked tired and old, like Dad himself. And now he's gone and in a way the house is too. I suppose that superficially it's prettier, but it's bulkier too, the large extension not just added to the back, but creeping around the side as well. Neil lets out a long, drawn-out breath.

"Well, here we are." Just like two years ago, he doesn't move to get out of the car.

"Do you remember this place, Jack?" I turn around to face my son, and he looks at me, unsure—he doesn't know what I'm asking. Maybe I don't either. "I mean, from when you came here as a baby? Not when—"

"It's OK Jack, you can talk about that," I hear Neil's voice beside me. "You can talk about your memories." I feel a flutter of concern about how confusing this must be for Jack. Whatever we think is going on, it's abundantly clear that Jack believes they're *all* his memories. But we're here now, and we have to make the best of it.

"Do you remember?" I ask again. "From when the Jack-you was here?"

I feel my husband's eyes on me, disapproving. But I keep looking at Jack, looking up at the house, regarding it with distaste. He doesn't answer.

We're here early—that was our plan: get here early so that Jack could settle in before Aaron or Bea arrived. But more importantly, so that we can get away early too. And just maybe so that we can skip most of the actual party, using the excuse that we need to put Jack to bed before it really gets going. But we are staying the night, there was no way to get out of that—it's a three-hour drive home and there's a brand-new bedroom reserved for us. But if all goes well, we'll be on the way home tomorrow before the rest of my family are even up. That's the plan.

I get out and unbuckle Jack from his seat, and then a little tentatively we head towards the front door. It's a new door: it looks expensive and my key doesn't work. So I have no choice but to ring the doorbell. The glass eye of a camera looks back at me as I wait.

"Katy! Neil! And little Jack!" Amber appears to explode outwards as the door opens.

"*Not-so-little* Jack, I should say," she goes on, gushing. "Wow, haven't you grown?" For a moment we all look at Jack, as if expecting a response, but he doesn't provide one, just moving closer to my legs instead

"Come in, come in, don't just stand there. Welcome." Amber steps back, allowing us into the hallway. Unlike my last visit some weeks before, it's all finished now and looks like a show home, or something from a magazine. A large chandelier now hangs next to the staircase, which is almost unrecognizable with its new banister and treads, the grain of the new wood glowing. A huge sideboard fills the other half of the room, topped with vases filled with flowers and cards.

Amber tells us that Brock is around somewhere and darts into the old kitchen looking for him, while Neil turns to me and mutters.

"Jesus, how much did this all cost?"

"I don't know." I shake my head. That question hasn't actually occurred to me, with everything else that's been going on. "But you know how well their business has been doing lately."

"Thank Christ we're not on the hook for it." He makes a sound, like this annoys him slightly.

There's no time for me to reply as Brock comes out, drink in one hand, cellphone in the other. He slips it into the pocket of his khakis and pumps Neil's hand.

"Guys! Welcome to our new home!" He gives the word "our" enough intonation to stress that he means all of ours, then crouches down to inspect Jack.

"Hey, buddy? Remember me? It's been a while, huh?" He ruffles his hair but stands up again before waiting for a response. "So, you want to get a drink first? Or do the tour?"

In the end we do both, with Amber and Brock together showing us around the finished changes as we sip on whiskey and soda while Jack drinks a 7UP through a straw. And the house looks incredible, it really does. Any resentfulness that Neil or I might have felt seems to evaporate as we're led around, and before long we're both cooing with appreciation.

The truth is, for the first time I think I *get it*. This was a lovely old house, with a sense of history—our history. But it wasn't without problems too. The doors that stuck, the damp on the walls. Before, I'd seen them as part of the character of the place, but really they were clues to the deeper underlying issues. And Amber, with her tenacity, and I suppose with her and Brock's money, have had to go deep into the structure of the building to put that all right. But it's the way they've put it all back together that's so amazing. The house still has that sense of history: the refurbishment has taken account of what the house was, but brought it up to date. It's turned the rustic charm into something spectacular.

"It's impressive, Amber, it really is," Neil says, when we're back downstairs in the huge open-plan living space. He sounds genuine, and she smiles.

"Thank you, Neil. That means a lot, coming from you."

The downstairs has been dressed for the imminent party. Tables are laid out in the living area, stacked with glasses. There are a dozen stainless-steel heated trays, ready to be loaded with food. Red and silver balloons hang everywhere. Brock reaches up and takes one down. He hands it to Jack.

"Why are they red?" Jack asks. "Why don't you have any other colors?"

"Because they're the colors of your granddaddy's favorite football team," Amber replies. "And this used to be his house." Then she turns to Neil and I. "If you think the house is good, you have to come down to the lake. The boathouse is super special."

I glance at Jack, and I think I catch a flash of anxiety on his face. The lake is where so many of his memories are centered. So I change the subject.

"Who's done all this? The party preparations?" I ask.

Amber waves her hand dismissively. "We took Dad's idea of getting caterers; it just makes things so much easier, don't you think?" She smiles at Neil.

"Come on, I want to show you the boathouse," she says. She's talking more to Neil than me, but something about it feels strange. And then I realize it isn't what she's actually said, but something else. It's her comment about Dad's idea of using outside caterers. How is that the one thing you'd remember from that weekend? The weekend when Dad killed himself?

Neil steps in, saving me from replying.

"Actually, we're all a little tired from the journey." He smiles at her. "Maybe we just need to get our bags in from the car and have a little rest."

Amber looks momentarily deflated, but she nods.

"OK, later then. Brock, you can give them a hand, can't you?"

Brock rolls his eyes, but rubs his hands together.

An hour later we come back downstairs, and the house feels busy already. People I don't know are buzzing around, still getting things ready for the party, which isn't due to start for a couple of hours.

"What can we do to help?" Neil asks, catching Amber's arm as she sweeps past.

"Oh nothing, it's all under control." She hesitates, but then eyes him reflectively. "Actually, you're taller than Brock, could you help put up a banner?" She takes his hand and begins leading him away. "Kate, why don't you fix yourself a drink?"

"Actually, I think I'm going to take Jack down to the boathouse," I say instead, hoping that no one will want to join me. I want it to be just the two of us when I introduce him to it. Make sure he feels safe there. After a moment's hesitation, Amber simply says: "Sure, good idea."

The yard has been landscaped now, and the scars are hidden beneath new flowerbeds and young plants. But it feels unnatural—too new for the setting, and it's like I can still sense the damage that's been done, the heavy machinery that ripped at the plants and the trees, wounds that will take time to heal. We make our way down the path to the lake. The doors are open on the new building, and it looks better than ever. The jetty juts out into the water invitingly, and it's hard to imagine a small boy not wanting to rush down and explore it. But Jack's mood is very different. He's staying very close to me, pressing up against my leg, both looking around and glancing up at my face for reassurance. To our left is the little beach, where Zack and the twins would have swum from on the day that Zack drowned.

Jack swallows audibly beside me as we reach the new building. We step together onto the wooden deck, and to the edge, beside the water. He squeezes my hand as we look out, urging me to squeeze back. He speaks quietly.

"That's where I died, Mommy." Suddenly Jack points to an area of the lake just off the beach, and then takes my hand again. His voice sounds earnest, confused, troubled.

"I know, honey," I tell him.

"We were playing there, and Aaron was being mean."

"I know. But we're not going to talk about it here? Not with other people listening. But I know."

He nods at me and squeezes my hand tighter.

"What do you think of the new boathouse? Pretty cool, huh?" I try to pull him around to look. "And the new jetty? The old one was much smaller and really rickety—"

"And that's where they laid me," Jack stays, looking now at the lawn just beyond the beach. "When I was dead."

This stops me. I look toward where he's pointing, and I can clearly see Zack's body lying on the grass—in a strange way it was like he'd been abandoned—after he'd been declared dead. Jack's pointing to that exact spot. A part of me wants to ask him how he knows this, but another part already knows the answer. I'm resigned to this now, to just accepting what Jack says, even if I know it doesn't make any sense. But then I realize something else. What he said just then is different to any of the claims he's made before. I turn to face him, then drop down to his level, one hand on the wooden railing to steady myself.

"Do you remember what happened *after* you drowned, Jack? Do you remember lying there?"

He doesn't respond in words, but very gently nods his head

up and down. I take in a deep breath and register the familiar smell of the lake, of the trees around the shore. Reality.

"Do you remember where you went, after you died?"

"Uh huh." He nods his head. "I was up in the air, watching."

"Up in the air?"

He nods. "I saw you too. That's when I chose you. To come back as your baby."

A new wave of unreality washes over me. But I just let it hit, not registering what it might mean.

"OK. Maybe we can talk about that another time? But you know you can't tell anyone about it here. You remember that, don't you Jack?"

He nods again, and I see his chest expand as he takes a deep breath.

"I know."

FORTY

When the party begins, a lot of the guests turn out to be linked to Amber and Brock's business. I suppose they're friends as well, and it's just the way the marketing world works, but I don't know them so I almost feel like a stranger as they trail in, and Brock hands them refreshments, and Amber embarks upon tour after tour. When they're done and they congregate in the living area, some of them even ask Neil and I how we know Amber and Brock. As if in their minds they're coming to *her* party, the reopening of *her* house, left to her when *her* father died.

It's more comfortable to slip outside where Amber has set up a game of croquet on the new lawn, and Neil busies himself teaching Jack to knock the balls through hoops with a mallet. Earlier I heard her telling people that we used to play it all the time as kids, though this isn't true. But then I see Bea arrive. She was flying in from the coast, and Tris picked her up from the airport. They're still not together of course, but it's the strange way they have of still doing a lot together. For a moment they stand alone in the busy room, looking like they're feeling as awkward as I did. I leave Jack and Neil playing, and go to speak to them.

"Hi Bea, Tris." I kiss him on both cheeks and give my sister a hug. Because of how Jack regards her, I feel a need to cling on to her, like she's a part of everything I'm going through.

"Hey Kate." She smiles back at me, but it's not warm. There's a distance between us, of course there is.

"Long time no see," she says, an edge to the words.

I try to pull myself together. To act normal. To be normal. I glance around, to see that Jack and Neil are still outside playing.

"What do you think of the place?" I ask.

"Not seen it yet." She shares a look with Tris, which I take to mean that I'm being too eager, that I'm getting this all wrong. But then she suddenly softens.

"But what I've seen is very Amber."

I want to smile and agree with her. A few years ago I would have done so, effortlessly. Back then we were so close that we often seemed to be thinking the same thing, and we would frequently finish each other's sentences. But I'm too stressed right now.

"I can give you a tour?" I say, realizing instantly that I actually sound like Amber now.

"I'd prefer a drink."

Tris is already making his way to the table where the drinks are laid out. He pours her a glass of rosé.

"There's champagne," I say, before I can stop myself. Bea doesn't like champagne, she never has.

We stand in silence until Tris returns and hands her the wine. Bea seems determined to give me another chance.

"She's fucking excelled herself, hasn't she?" She takes a deep draft of the wine. And this time I understand exactly what she means. For a second we're on the same wavelength, and it feels almost unbearably nice. Then I hear an interruption from behind me.

"Mommy?"

I turn, and there's Jack, keeping his eyes very carefully on me.

"Yes Jack?" My heart is in my mouth as I wait to hear what he's going to say.

"Daddy says you have to come and play crokey."

"OK." I sense Bea's eyes on my son. I want to get him away, but then I realize that she's expecting something—she hasn't seen him in over a year. "Say hello to Bea, honey. And Tris. They've just arrived."

Jack looks at my sister, the woman he believes is his old mommy. I can see the difficulty he has with not being able to tell her this: confusion and frustration pass across his face.

"Mommy," he says again, and he takes my hand and pulls me away.

Neil and I occupy Jack with croquet for a while in the yard, and then we eat, piling plates high from the buffet, just the three of us sitting there while Bea is caught speaking with old friends of Tris. After that one of Brock's clients comes up to us and entertains Jack by juggling with fruit and trying to teach him how to do it. Then Aaron arrives with some of his college friends, and it's like a small explosion rippling through the party. Or maybe a large one. They're immediately louder and brighter than anything else that's going on. I catch Jack staring at him. I wondered if he'd know who Aaron was, given that he must remember him as an eleven-year-old boy. But it's clear he does. It couldn't be more obvious. I shake my head slowly, warning him once again, and Jack returns a dark look.

But Aaron doesn't stay in the house for long. He and his friends decimate the buffet and then decamp to the boathouse, taking most of the booze—and the party's center of gravity—with them. I think Amber probably planned it this way, because of how carefully and beautifully she's decorated the boathouse with lights all along the wooden balustrade of the jetty, and lanterns hanging around the outside of the building itself. But rather than following the crowd down to the lakeside, we instead take the opportunity to make our excuses, saying that Jack is tired and we're going to take him to our room. Once we're there we don't go back out.

It's a shame to miss the party, but what choice do we have? It feels enough to have survived it.

FORTY-ONE

Jack wakes at seven, and though I try to keep him in the room for longer, he complains he's hungry, so we go downstairs. I find him a packet of waffles and some chocolate sauce while I try to figure out the flash new coffee machine in the flash new kitchen. I'm relieved that we're alone—there are no bodies passed out on the sofas, and someone's even made some effort to clean up: the left-over food has been put into the twin refrigerators, and most of the trash has been bagged and left by the back door. Still, I collect a dozen stray glasses and I'm emptying the dishwasher in order to load them when Amber glides into the kitchen. She makes a groaning sound, informing me of her hangover.

"Wow, my head." She stands at the sink and pours herself water, then sips it gently. She's dressed in an Asian-looking silk robe with flowers printed on it. Jack looks at her strangely.

"What did you think of the party?" She turns to face me. It's not a question but an invitation for a compliment.

"Great," I say, but I can see she's not quite satisfied with that.

"I had to take Jack to sleep a little early," I explain, and she glances at him, a little disappointed but mollified too.

"Of course." She smiles at Jack, then asks, a bit patronizingly, "Did you have a good time, Jack?"

He looks at me before answering, like he's still not sure what he can and can't say in this strange world. I flash a smile to tell him it's OK to reply.

"I learned to juggle."

"Oh yes,"—Amber's face lights up—"Guy Trone and his famous juggling. We're re-branding his gym-store chain." She sips the water again. "You know UltraGym? I think they have, like, two hundred and fifty branches nationwide." It's clear this comment is aimed at me, because then Amber moves closer to Jack.

"Maybe you can show me later on, when my headache dies down a bit." She rolls her eyes. "Have you got everything you need? There's pancakes in the refrigerator. And maple syrup."

I bite my lip; this is my moment to mention our plan to slip away early. When we discussed it on the journey up here; it didn't feel like this would be awkward, since we'd have got through the party. But now the time's come to tell Amber about it, I anticipate that she's not going to be pleased. Still. I don't have a choice.

"Um, we were thinking about getting on the road," I say weakly. Amber's face folds into indignation.

"Oh," she says, "I had planned we'd have a meal together. Tonight, just the family." She looks at me vacantly, like with her headache she can't compute what I've said. In my head I scramble for a reason why this can't happen, but since Neil and I didn't actually decide on an excuse, I don't have anything ready to use.

"You know, after such a big social *thing*," Amber goes on, making air quotes, "it would just be nice to do something a bit more intimate, don't you agree?"

I answer—of course it *would* be nice—before I realize it's a trap.

"Oh good." She brightens instantly. "I'm so pleased." Then she looks to the door, a little conspiratorially. "Actually, there's another reason why I need you to stay."

I wait, knowing I've already lost.

"Do you remember you had that idea for a memorial for poor Zack?"

At the mention of the name—his name—Jack's head snaps up from his plate. Amber notices it too, but it doesn't seem to register.

"I remember..." I say.

"I didn't think it was right to do this yesterday with so many people around, but I've arranged something for this afternoon, while we're all here." She gives me a sudden smile.

"What?"

"We're having a tree-planting. And I've had a rock with a plaque made—they're both turning up today." She looks at me, a little anxious now, like she knows that she's not the best of us at this stuff. "I wanted it to be a surprise."

I nod. I feel my throat constricting, like I'm being caught in a net, a trap I've set for myself. But there's nothing I can do to escape it.

"Sure. That sounds like... a really nice idea."

"So you'll stay?"

"Of course." I smile, as brightly as I can, and I keep my eyes on Jack. His forehead is creased in a small frown. For a long while Amber fusses around, making herself a coffee, and drinking it, and talking about the party. Apparently everyone gravitated to the new firepit that Amber has created out the back, and Aaron and his friends were there until at least six in the morning. I take some comfort from that; at least he'll probably not be up until midday.

When she's finished her coffee Amber goes for a shower, and Neil comes downstairs, still expecting that we're going to slip away, so I tell him the bad news. He takes it poorly, and he's still discussing whether we could still leave when Tristan wanders barefoot into the kitchen, and then Brock. Before we know it most of the house is up.

It's still early in the year—not yet summer—but the day is already hot, and Brock suggests a swim. He doesn't seem to make any connection between the planned memorial for Zack and undertaking the same activity that killed him, but maybe that's unfair. Either way there's a hungover push to get as many of the family into the water as possible, with Brock working on Neil until he relents. I'm asked several times if Jack and I would like to swim, but I remind them all that Jack isn't comfortable in the water yet.

So we all head down to the boathouse. The back of it—facing the jetty and the lake—opens up, and Amber slides the glass wall across so that the seating area is bathed in the fresh morning sunshine.

"Come on, diving competition," Brock calls out. He's already in his trunks, his ample stomach tanned and waxed clear of hairs. Neil has his trunks on too, but a shirt over his top, and he looks uncomfortable as he unfastens the buttons. Eva is swimming too, and I'm surprised by how little is left of the child I've always known her as. She now has the figure of a woman, lithe and taut-skinned. When Amber de-robes, her body looks bloated and flabby in comparison, and I'm glad for another reason that I don't have to join them. All of them—Brock, Neil, Eva, Amber and Tristan—line up on the jetty, and on the count of three, they jump and dive in together. Jack grips my hand tightly as they splash into the water, and when they surface, Bea, myself and Jack, are supposed to judge them.

"What do you think, Jack?" Bea laughs when they're in the water, and wet heads are surfacing left and right.

He looks up at me again, obviously still uncomfortable. I nod to tell him it's OK, to try and coax him into relaxing.

"Eva's looking good," Bea says, and I'm not sure whether she means generally or referring to her dive.

Jack nods, and Bea calls out, "First round to Eva!" Brock groans and splashes the water in mock frustration.

"Come on, we go again!" He heads to the ladder and hauls himself out. A few moments later and they're all lined up again, this time with water dripping from their hair and swimming costumes.

"Ready?" Bea calls out. "Go!"

Again they dive, and this time Brock tries to up the ante by performing a somersault. It's not particularly elegant, and causes a lot of splash, but when they surface Bea announces him as the winner, and although he demands a third round, the others refuse and instead begin swimming around. I'm glad the attention is off, and I relax a little into the new sofa. A question forms in my mind.

"Has, um..." I stop, momentarily unsure how to phrase this. "Has Amber mentioned what she's got planned for later?"

Bea glances at me, a little sharply. She nods quietly. "Zack's tree?"

"Yes. What do you think about it? I hope she didn't spring it on you...?" I begin, but she shakes her head.

"No. We discussed it a while back. Tris and I chose the tree. I think it's a nice idea." From the tightness of her voice, I regret bringing this up now. Clearly it's already difficult for her. Or she's anticipating that it will be.

"OK. Yeah, it's a nice idea." I smile encouragingly, meaning that the conversation is over, as far as I'm concerned. But she surprises me.

"Amber told me it was your idea, if that's what you're wondering," Bea says. I feel a burst of heat, as if she were accusing me of fishing for the compliment, but before I can reply she shakes her head.

"It's OK, Kate. I think I'd already guessed." She smiles kindly and touches my hand. "Thank you."

And then I have to look away, to where they're still splashing in the water, and I wonder what the hell is wrong with me. Why do I suddenly feel so alien in the presence of my own family? Why is it I can't relax here, at the house where I grew up, and which Amber has rebuilt for all of us? And then my eyes fall on Jack, keeping his eyes fixed firmly on me, but every now and then sneaking a glance at his other mom, Bea.

That's why.

FORTY-TWO

The swimmers climb out, and Amber fusses around, handing out brand new towels from a locker.

"Maybe you'd like a go in a speedboat?" I hear her say to Jack at one point. It's not just me that the comment registers with, because Bea replies.

"What speedboat?" she asks. "You haven't bought one of those as well?"

Amber gives her a slightly irritated look, but shakes her head.

"No, Aaron's borrowing a boat from a friend today. You remember Martin? Jim's son?"

I do. They have a house a few miles away, also on the lakeside.

"He said they're going to do wakeboarding," Amber explains. "I don't think you're old enough for that, but they also have inner tubes which are really fun."

When Jack doesn't reply she continues. "They're these inflatable rings that get pulled behind the boat. Super fun. I'm sure Aaron would love to give you a ride."

"I don't think so," I answer for him. "He's not good about the water, I told you—"

"Yes Kate, but you have to encourage him a little. You have to push him." She gives me an older-sister look. Amber knows best.

I try to signal to my sister that this isn't the time or the place, but she misreads me.

"He's very quiet, Kate. Don't you think?" As she speaks Jack presses tighter against my leg. "Bea? Have you noticed how quiet Jack is?"

But Bea doesn't side with her. "Perhaps that's just how he is? A bit more like Eva than Aaron?"

The comment stops Amber, and at that moment Eva happens to walk past us on the jetty, using the towel to dry her hair. I sense all three of us sisters eyeing her figure—the figure we all had once. Tris is sitting down next to us, and I notice he glances up too as she moves by.

"Well, see how you feel, Jack." Amber touches his shoulder, then looks back at Bea and I.

"We're doing the tree planting at twelve," she mouths.

The tree is smaller than I imagined. It arrives on the back of a truck, which also carries a mechanical mini-digger-type machine. Two men get out from the cab and lower it to the ground, and then, following Amber's instructions, carry the tree to the location she has chosen, just above where the sand of the beach gives way to the lawn. Then the digger returns to the truck and makes a second trip, this time carrying a large granite rock wrapped in cellophane. They scrape away at the earth to form a base and set the rock up, with the inscription facing the water. Neil and Brock help unwrap the rock while the workmen dig a hole for the tree, the metal bucket on the digger slicing easily through the earth, which is piled up on one side. Then they drive the digger back round to the driveway, but they don't load it back on the truck. Amber explains that after we've ceremonially planted the tree, they'll come back and do it properly. They do leave us a half-dozen shovels though.

At twelve we're all gathered around waiting for Amber to begin, but she looks anxious. It takes me a moment to understand why, but then I realize that Aaron still isn't here. She tries calling him on her cell but doesn't get an answer. But then it doesn't matter, because from the lake a distant buzz has become a nearby roar. We all turn to see a large red-and-white speedboat slicing through the water toward the jetty, clearly exceeding the speed limit which covers the part of the lake near to the shore. The engine note changes and it drops down off the bow wave.

"Oh, thank goodness," Amber says.

Aaron is driving, his friends seated comfortably in the stern seats. He steers the boat toward the jetty, mooring it with more throttle than he needs, sending a roar across the water towards us. Finally he kills the motor. The peaceful silence of the lakeside settles back. Aaron jumps athletically up onto the jetty, and he must see us, gathered around waiting for him, but he doesn't hurry; instead he speaks with his friends for a while, too far away for me to hear what they're saying. Eventually he leaves them there and saunters over casually. He's wearing a baseball cap turned round the wrong way, and as he walks he pulls out a pair of aviator sunglasses and puts them on.

"Did you hear that engine?" he says to Brock as he reaches us. "Four-fifty horsepower, it's a god-damn *beast*—" but Amber stops the conversation going any further.

"Aaron, honey, we're doing the thing?"

"Sure, Mom, that's why I'm here." He smiles at her, perfect white teeth, and finally he acknowledges the rest of us, standing there waiting for him. "Let's do it."

Amber has made herself master of ceremonies. She begins by reminding us why we're all here, and thanks Tris and Bea for helping to pick out the tree, a sugar maple, which apparently will give beautiful red colors in the fall. She also jokes that because maple syrup comes from sugar maples, Zack would have liked it. I look at Bea as she says this, and I'm surprised to see that she's crying, because she's doing so silently. One of her hands is tightly gripping Tristan's. His face is fixed and tight.

"Mommy?" Jack asks in a tiny voice.

"What?" I whisper back.

"I don't like maple syrup."

"That's OK, Jack," I raise my voice a little, in case anyone heard him. "She's talking about Zack, not you." Then I squeeze his hand to remind him of his promise.

"Actually, Amber,"—Tristan clears he throat awkwardly— "If I could just say, we picked the tree for the colors. Zack was more into chocolate syrup." He shrugs at her, and she acknowledges him with a tight smile.

"Sure. Of course."

Amber moves things on and leads us in a minute's silence, which Jack does really well at, and then we all take a shovel, except Brock, who lifts the tree into the hole, and then together we fill in the earth. Jack doesn't get a shovel of his own, but I let him use mine, and Neil helps him, telling him to be careful of the roots.

After that the idea was that Bea and Tristan were going to say a few words. Tris does so, talking about what a great son Zack was, and how his loss is the tragedy of his life, but I guess it proves too much for Bea because, when Amber calls her forward for her reading, she shakes her head and then she runs back to the house, followed quickly by Tris.

I look at the little card that Amber gave me for the service; the next item after Bea's tribute is a reading by Aaron. He comes forward confidently and looks in amusement at Tris, still hurrying up the lawn after Bea.

"Well..." Aaron says. He flicks the card against his thigh thoughtfully, then looks hopefully at his father. "Maybe we could just ditch this whole thing and go wakeboarding?"

FORTY-THREE

"How are you doing Jack?" I ask, when we're alone again. I made an excuse to take him upstairs, away from the others.

In reply he puffs out his chest in a big sigh. When he's finished, he nods.

"Is it weird? Seeing the memorial?"

Jack combines a shrug with another nod.

"Did you like the tree?"

He thinks about this, before shrugging a second time. "It's just a tree."

"Well. I think you're doing really well," I tell him. "Just a few more hours now and we'll go home, and you won't have to worry about it, at least for a while."

He pauses at this, but eventually nods again.

"Can we really not tell my old mommy? Just a little bit?"

"No honey. That's not a good idea."

His head drops as he sits solemnly on the bed.

"Do you remember Tris?" I ask suddenly. I've never really thought of this before. "As your daddy?"

Jack bites the inside of his cheek, but then gives a little shake of his head. "Maybe. But only a little bit. Not like Mom."

"He wasn't there much. He had to travel a lot for his work. Maybe that's why?"

"Maybe."

I smile at how serious he is. "Was she a good mom, Bea?"

"Yeah," he answers very seriously. "Really good."

"Better than me?"

His head goes onto one side, really giving this some thought. "Different," he says in the end. "But I was different then."

I smile again, this time at the wisdom of my boy. And then something makes me stand up and walk to the window. Far out on the lake now, thankfully a long way off, I can see Aaron and his friends wakeboarding. Much closer, the jetty and the decking around the boathouse is now bathed in full, warm sun. Eva and Amber are both sunbathing there, laid out in nearly matching white bikinis, though one is fashionably skimpy and the other much larger, but still straining to hold onto my increasingly ample oldest sister. Just off the jetty I see that Tristan and Bea have brought out Dad's old sailing boat, although there's barely enough wind to get it moving. I'm pleased that Amber had it refurbished—Dad would have liked it. I'm not sure what he'd have thought of the rest of the house, but he'd have liked that.

We keep watching a while, but soon Bea and Tris give up, paddling the dinghy to get it closer to the jetty, where Tris drops the mainsail and pulls the rope that quickly furls the jib. They leave it like that; I guess because they're planning to go back out if the wind increases a bit.

I used to sail here when I was little. And I always assumed that my children would too, just like Amber's and... I stop myself; suddenly I realize where my thoughts are going. Seeing Bea and Tris together in Dad's boat like that, it's brought back a memory of mine. I've watched the two of them sailing with Zack, before he died. I turn to my son now.

"Did you like sailing? When you were Zack?"

"Yeah," he says. Not crazy eager, but it's a clear yes.

"Would you like to go sailing now?"

He drops off the bed and pads barefoot to the window. Then he stares out at the world laid out below.

"Do you remember that boat? The one tied up on the jetty?"

He nods this time. Taking it in.

"Would you like to go for a ride in it now? With me?"

There's a long pause.

"What about the water? What if I fall in?"

"You won't fall in, honey. I promise you." But as I speak, I wonder if I'm able to truly promise that. Even on a calm day like this, if I'm sailing the boat I'll need one hand on the tiller and one on the mainsheet, controlling the sail. But I have an idea.

"Bea's in her sailing gear. Maybe she'd like to come as well? Would you like that, Jack?"

I don't quite understand the look that passes over his face. Maybe he doesn't either. But then how weird must it be to think about going sailing with your mother, and with your previous mother from your past life? I wait, trying to see which emotion wins the battle.

"Would you like that? You'll be wearing a life jacket, so even if you did fall in, you'd float. But Bea won't let you fall in. She'll hold onto you the whole time."

"Can I really go? With my other mommy?"

I try to analyze what I'm doing. It feels like it's more than just suggesting a go in Dad's old boat. Something much bigger than that. But I don't confront it. I kid myself this is a good idea.

"You have to promise you won't say anything to her. About Zack. But you can go. If you promise me."

"I already promised," Jack reminds me.

I bite my lip again. "Yes, you did. You did promise."

"I promise again." Jack puffs out his chest.

. . .

I intercept Bea and ask if I can have a word. Tris seems to sense he's not wanted and leaves us to it.

"What?" Bea asks, looking at Jack again. There's a way she has of looking at him, and out of nowhere a word comes to my mind to describe it. *Motherly*.

That should be a warning, but I go on nonetheless.

"I know you've just come in, but I asked Jack if he wanted a go in Dad's old boat. And he said yes."

Her head dips to one side, like she doesn't quite understand.

"I need an experienced sailor with us. To make sure he doesn't fall in."

Realization dawns, and with it a deepening smile.

"Me? You want me to come?" She bends down to Jack.

"If you wouldn't mind. Just for a bit. He's still a bit wary of the water."

"Mind? I'd love to take you, Captain Jack. And I'll look after you, I promise."

She spins around at once, ignoring me now. "We'll have to get you a life jacket. There's some in the boathouse. There's probably one somewhere that Zack wore that'll fit you." She leads him away, not looking at me, and I'm left standing there, wondering if this is a good idea or not.

It takes them a surprisingly long time to find the life jacket, and I wander down to the boathouse. Amber and Eva are still sunbathing and Eva is playing music on her phone, a horrible tinny sound coming from the little built-in speaker. But I suppose it's to mask the drone from the water, the buzzing, rasping sound of the big engine on the wakeboarding boat, even though it's right out in the middle of the lake. Bea and Tris's life jackets are drying on the handrail where they left them, though when I test one with my hand it's not actually wet. As I'm putting it on, Neil spots me from inside the boathouse, where he's sitting reading, probably one of his academic papers. He gets up, walks over and lightly touches my shoulder.

"What's up? You going boating?"

"Yeah," I say, wondering if I should have asked Neil to come. He's not a natural sailor, but he could have easily helped hold onto Jack.

Before he can say anything else, Bea and Jack come back, her still chatting away to him as he pulls at the foam collar of a bright orange life jacket. I see the expression on Neil's face. Surprise and concern, but I say nothing. The four of us walk up the jetty to where the little boat is tied up.

When we get there, I climb down into the boat to hoist the mainsail. I know this boat—I sailed her hundreds of times myself when I was younger, and my actions are automatic as I listen to Bea tell Jack what I'm doing, and where he should sit, and how he has to keep his head down when the boom comes over if we tack, or gybe. But we're not going to gybe—we're going to keep everything incredibly steady. Safe and easy.

I pull the sail up by the halyard, and the wind is so light it barely flaps, just lazily hangs there above our heads. Then I help Jack down into the boat, careful to keep my weight inboard. I sit him in front of the centerboard casing. Then Bea climbs in too, and gives her attention to Jack, making sure he's comfortable and telling him where he can hold on.

"Neil, can you untie us?" Bea calls out. And Neil hesitates a moment, but then does what she asks.

"That's it, put the bow around." Bea gives Jack a squeeze. "Ready, Captain? Captain Jack."

Up on the jetty Neil bends down to unwind the rope from the cleat, and then he pushes at the front of the boat to point the bow out into the lake. The sail fills now, and we edge away. Bea keeps on talking to Jack, telling him to pull out the little jib. The gentle wake foams out behind us, and I turn to catch my husband's unsettled face.

FORTY-FOUR

"Where do you want to head for?" I say, my eyes on the sail and not on my sister or Jack. We could head toward the town and even tie up and get an ice cream. Or we could sail west where the lake narrows and there are a series of little bays. They're fun to explore.

"I want to go to the island," Jack calls out, interrupting my thoughts. He points out in front of us, at the small humpbacked island that lies opposite Dad's house. "There's a castle on it." He sounds happy, excited.

"There is," Bea replies, and there's a tiny bit of confusion in her voice; I guess because you can't see it from the shore, and we haven't talked about the castle for ages. It's the only building out there, but it's hidden behind the spine of the island.

"It's not a real castle, but you can go in it!" Jack continues. "There's a place to put the boat underneath, around the other side." He bounces up and down on the seat, forgetting himself.

For a second I say nothing, just concentrating on steering toward the island and adjusting the mainsail. We glide into a small patch of good wind, and the boat responds primly, gaining speed, the wake now gurgling out behind us. Bea adjusts the jib, letting it out to reduce the power.

"How do you know about the castle, Jack? Did your mommy tell you?" Bea asks when she's finished. I can hear from her tone she's been considering this while she was working. Then she turns to me before Jack can answer. "Because they sold the castle, there's a couple who lives there now. I thought you knew?"

I start to answer, meaning to tell her that I did know. But decide it's better not to.

"Oh," I say, instead.

And then she goes on, explaining things properly to Jack. "A few years ago—back when Zack was alive—we used to sail to the island all the time. There wasn't anyone living in the castle then, and it wasn't even locked up. We used to go in there and pretend it was a *real* castle." She smiles at him, then shrugs. "But then it got bought and turned into a proper house. So we can't do that anymore."

I can only see Jack's face in profile, but I notice his expression, a mix of disappointment, confusion and just this need to absorb these changes in the world he thinks he once knew. Suddenly he looks around, as if noticing the water again, but sits up straighter, like he's telling himself to be brave about that.

"There's a place for camping," he says suddenly, "at the other end of the island. Is it still there?" I haven't told him any of this, and I know he's remembering it. But I can't respond, because I don't actually know the answer. Bea shoots me a strange look, before she answers.

"I'm not sure. I haven't been there for a long time." She turns to me again. "Tris and Brock used to take the children there, do you remember?"

I do. I remember standing with Bea in the little back bedroom, looking out with binoculars to check all the tents were up on the little pocket of flat land at the south of the island, this very boat pulled up on the tiny beach below.

"Maybe when you're older you could camp there?" Bea asks Jack. But she looks confused as his face darkens at this idea.

Up ahead, the patch of wind we've been cutting through disappears. It's like that on the lake. Some places you have a nice breeze, but elsewhere it drops to nothing. As we lose the wind, the pressure on the sails eases but we continue to glide forward entirely on the boat's momentum. Both Bea and I adjust our positions almost automatically to keep her balanced.

"Out of wind," I say. Up ahead of us the island is still a few hundred meters away, but you can just see the pretend battlements of the castle rising up over the ridge. There's a flagpole too, which is new. A flag moves lazily from side to side.

"They've got wind there," Bea notes, and she's got a point. If we can get through this calm patch we can tack up the back of the island. We can see if the old camp spot is still there, and maybe even put ashore on the little beach and investigate it. I'm sure Jack would like that.

"Look out." A note of alarm in Bea's voice snaps my attention back to the present. She points downwind of us, hidden a little behind the mainsail. I see the heavy red bow of the wakeboarding boat that Aaron and his friends are on. It's heading toward us, and although it's still a good distance away, it's moving fast and the bow is riding high, so that we can't see whoever's driving it.

"Can they see us?" Bea asks.

"They should see the sail."

But as I speak I push and pull on the tiller, trying to change direction, to make sure we're out of the way. But it does nothing; our boat is hardly moving now, and the wind line that we've come from is disappearing away behind us, leaving us totally becalmed. But it's OK; whoever's steering the powerboat can't fail to see our mast and sails. As long as they're looking. And it is

OK; a moment later the powerboat turns a fraction to avoid us. But still, it comes close.

"Horrible things," I hear Bea mutter as the powerboat roars past. It's only about sixty feet in front of us and towing an inflatable inner tube. Two young men are sitting in it, holding on tightly while Aaron tries to use the boat's wake to throw them out. I see his face, his wide, toothy smile as the boat zips past. As soon as he's clear of us, he throws the powerboat into a deep left turn, as if using us as a buoy to steer around. This causes the inner tube to accelerate out of the turn, skidding away over the flat, calm water. But then it catches on something and flips over, throwing the two young men into the water. Jack watches the whole thing, his eyes wide. As soon as the boys fall in he grips on hard, where Bea told him to.

"It's OK, Jack. They're just having fun," I tell him.

He nods, and I spot a concern. The wake from the powerboat has formed into a set of short choppy waves, and they're coming right toward us. There's no time to do anything except tell Jack to hold on. Then the waves hit, causing our boat to rock violently from side to side. The mast and the sails—empty of wind—flap noisily, and the heavy centerboard bangs in its casing as the waves pass underneath. Aaron has stopped the boat now, waiting while his friends swim back to the inner tube.

"Hey!" Bea shouts over to him. "Keep away!"

Aaron can't hear, or pretends he can't. He cups a hand over his ear.

"What's that?" he shouts out, grinning at us.

"Keep away please!" Bea shouts again. But this time Aaron ignores her. Just as the two boys are about to reach the inner tube he revs the engine, making the boat leap forward in the water, and whisking the inflatable away from them again. As he does so, he roars with laughter, and shouts to his friends to swim faster.

"What was that?" Aaron asks us, as he slows the powerboat again. He's close to us now, almost alongside.

"I said, will you keep away?" Bea says. "It's dangerous to come too close."

"Sure." Aaron shrugs, like it's no big deal. But he doesn't move away. Instead he points at the boys in the water, as if inferring that he'll just wait for them to climb back aboard the inflatable. As he waits, he observes us—that seems the best word for it—it makes me uncomfortable. How comfortable he is, I mean.

"Hey, Jack, you wanna go for a ride? Take a spin in the inner tube? It's super fun."

"He's four years old," Bea snaps back. "He's much too young to ride that thing."

"I can take it slow."

"No."

Aaron gives Bea a long look, like something in him is enjoying the confrontation, and then he drops an insouciant shoulder.

"Sure," he says. "Whatever. Just give us a wave if you change your mind." He glances up at our sails, still hanging uselessly in the still air. "Or if you need a tow." Then he shouts out behind him to where his friends are sitting in the inflatable, almost on top of each other.

"Hold on, boys."

Then he's really reckless. He sends the throttle all the way forwards, and the boat responds by creating and rising up a steep wedge of water. We're left in a cloud of stinking gray smoke, and a few seconds later the inflatable whips past, the boys screaming as they hold on. A moment later the sailing dinghy is rocked again, this time more violently. Aaron was so close this time water splashes over the sides.

"*Fuck,*" I hear Bea say as she holds on tight, one arm around

Jack. Then she mutters "What an asshole," before turning to me. "I'm sorry. I shouldn't say that in front of Jack but..."

I don't reply, but I keep my eyes on Jack and keep my voice as soothing as possible as I tell him it's OK. His face is white. He's really spooked.

"Did you see he doesn't have a spotter?" Bea continues. "When you're towing you're supposed to have a spotter—someone to watch where you're going and someone to watch the people being towed."

I don't answer. Instead, I watch as Aaron's boat arcs around the back of the island, out of sight.

"I want to go back now," Jack says in a tiny voice. All the fun, the wonder he was expressing is gone. He's really scared. I nod at once, sharing the sentiment.

"We'll turn around," I tell him. But Bea is still talking about Aaron.

"It's just a stage he's going through—that's what Amber said the other day—but how long is it gonna to last? The *asshole* stage." She shakes her head. I can't remember her ever openly criticizing Aaron like this before, and I'm not sure what's making her let rip now. If I had to guess I'd say it's something to do with Jack.

Up ahead—a few feet away—I see the beginnings of a puff of wind, darker ripples on the otherwise calm surface of the lake. Once it reaches us, I can use it to gain enough speed to tack, and then maybe stay within it as we head back for the shore. And yet, before we get there, I see Aaron's boat emerge from the south of the island. I'd thought—assumed really—that he'd gone behind the island to tow the stupid inflatable there, to keep out of our way. But now I see he's just done a circuit, and now the powerboat leans into another deep turn, lining up once again so that it's heading almost directly toward us.

"Oh, for fuck's sake!" Bea says. She actually sounds scared.

Uselessly I wave a hand, but I've no idea if Aaron can see me; I can't see him because the bow of the powerboat is so high.

"Go a bit faster Kate," Bea tells me. "Get out of his way."

But that's impossible. I can only move if there's wind, and right here, there isn't. From the front of the boat I hear Jack reacting to our concern: a moaning sound, sickening to hear.

"It's OK, Jack, he'll make a turn."

"He won't. He won't. I know he won't," Jack replies. He keeps saying it, and every time he does he sounds more panicky and scared. All the while the damn powerboat is heading right toward us.

"*Jesus Christ!*" Bea says. She takes hold of Jack and pulls him towards the back of the boat, since it looks like the powerboat is going to hit us side-on just in front of the mast. She manhandles Jack roughly, and he cries out afresh, this time in pain as his bare shin hits the block that cleats the mainsheet. I notice the fresh crimson of blood, but my attention is elsewhere, on the powerboat that's now just moments away. Suddenly I see Aaron's grinning face, and he makes the smallest of turns on the wheel so that the huge craft changes course by a few degrees, just enough not to hit us but to go flying by just feet from our bow. A few seconds later it's followed by the inflatable, the boys inside looking nearly as alarmed as we are at the near miss that Aaron's engineered.

The waves hit us next, but because we're facing into them the boat rides them better, though the hull bangs as they roll under us and the mast rocks in its step, as though the whole rig might come crashing down. And by then the powerboat is almost out of sight, off on another lap of the island.

Neither Bea nor I speak for a few moments, and then we hit the breeze. Now there's just enough for the boat to start making forward progress again, still out to the island.

"I want to go back," Jack says again, and I nod to him.

"We are honey. We just have to turn around." I tell him to

keep his head down, and then tack the boat so that we can point her back to shore. As the sail comes over and we swap to the other side, I know I'm going to do it. I don't know why, and I don't seem able to stop myself.

I turn to Bea.

"Jack thinks he was Zack."

I stare at her.

"What?" She looks at me, not sure she's heard right.

"Jack. He thinks he was Zack. Before. He has memories of being Zack."

"My Zack?"

"Yes."

There's a silence. Bea looks from me to Jack, who looks even more scared now. Unsure if he's allowed to say anything.

"What do you mean?"

"Exactly what I say. He has memories of being Zack. He talks about being Zack. He talks about it all the time. He almost never stops talking about it. He thinks he was him... before."

It takes her a while to reply, but she gets it now.

"What, like in a past life or something?"

"Yes. Exactly that."

"Kate, that's crazy. Why would you say that?"

And now I start to regret it. I think how hard I've worked to keep this from Bea, and why—because of how much it would hurt her if she knew. But now I'm just telling her. It's flooding out of me whether I like it or not.

"I don't want to keep it from you anymore." My voice cracks as I speak. "I've been keeping this a secret for over a year. I can't do it any longer. I need you to know."

Again Bea is silent, obviously unsure how to respond. Several times her mouth opens and she begins to form words, but then stops. Finally, she settles on a question.

"Jack, is this true? Do you have... memories of being someone else?"

He looks at her, clearly miserable now, and too scared to speak.

"It's OK Jack," I tell him. "You can tell her."

"You used to be my mommy," he says.

"Oh my God," Bea clasps her hand to her mouth, and moves physically away from him, as if he's electrocuted her, or she's going to throw up. She turns to me.

"How long has this been going on?"

"Ever since he could speak. He used to say '*Ayak Ayown*'— do you remember? When he was little and we tried to give him baths?"

Bea nods, her eyes wide. This was when we still used to see each other fairly regularly.

"We worked out that what he meant was: 'I'm Zack. I drowned.'"

"But that doesn't mean..." She stops, shaking her head. "Have you, I don't know, *seen* someone about this?"

Could I walk this back? Should I walk it back? I don't know.

"There's an expert in children who remember past lives. He works in a university out on the West Coast. He came to check him out."

"I don't mean..." She's breathing hard now, alternating between staring at me and sending wild glances toward Jack. "I meant a psychiatrist or something." The life jacket rises and falls with her breaths. "Well... what did he find? This... expert."

"He thinks it's possible Jack lived before. He can't say for sure, obviously. But he's seen lots of similar cases. He says it's possible that Jack's telling the truth. That he was Zack."

"Oh my God," Bea says for a third time. But this time she stays quiet afterwards.

"There's more," I say. My core feels as hard as steel. I don't care where this leads for now. I just have to say it.

"He says that when he drowned, it wasn't an accident." I

pause just for a moment, to let it sink in, then I deliver the killer blow. "It was Aaron."

Bea's face is completely white now, her knuckles too where they're gripping on the side of the dinghy. She looks first at Jack, and then back at me.

"What do you mean?" she asks, her voice hardening suddenly. "What do you mean it was Aaron?"

"Aaron held him under the water. It was like a game they were playing, only Zack didn't want to play. He was trying to get away, but Aaron kept holding him down. And he did it for too long."

We're moving along briskly now, well into the patch of wind that tends to run along the shore. I have to let the mainsail out a little to slow us on our approach to the jetty.

"But that's not what happened," Bea tells me. "That's not what Amber told us happened."

I bite my lip. "I know."

Bea's silent again. And we're getting closer.

"Can you furl the jib?" I have to ask, because I need to slow us down more. She does what I ask, and I steer a little downwind so that we can head up onto the jetty. Bea reaches forward to take the painter, ready to tie us up.

"What memories do you have?" she asks Jack now. He looks at me again before answering, but I suppose he's worked out it must be OK to tell her now.

"I remember the island. Going in the castle. And camping with Dad and Uncle Brock."

"Dad, do you mean..."

"I haven't told Jack anything about that island. He's never been there. He's never even been out on the lake until today."

Bea swallows. "When you say Dad, do you mean Tris?"

Jack nods.

"I don't remember him that well. I remember you much more."

It's like Bea doesn't hear this. "And on the day that Zack... the day that you died? You really remember that?"

Jack nods again.

"And it was Aaron. He held you under. You weren't swimming where you weren't allowed?"

There's a tiny shake of Jack's head.

"I knew," Bea whispers, under her breath. "I always knew."

FORTY-FIVE

Bea ties up the boat and helps Jack out onto the jetty while I drop the sail, bunching it loosely around the boom and shoving it down into the cockpit. Neither of us speak—it's like coming ashore means a watershed has been crossed. I see that Amber and Eva are still sunbathing, though our eldest sister seems to be waking up. She pulls away the book that's been covering her face and sits up a little inelegantly on the lounger.

Then she watches while the three of us walk down the jetty toward her.

"Hello." She smiles almost patronizingly at Jack. "Have you been in a boat?"

He doesn't reply, but Bea does.

"He nearly wasn't, thanks to your asshole son."

"What?" Amber's voice is sharp, shocked by Bea's words.

"Aaron, in that damned powerboat. He nearly rammed us. We could have been killed."

"*Bea*." Amber's voice is scolding, as if telling Bea this isn't a conversation we should be having in front of a child.

"Seriously, did you see it? He was seconds away from hitting us."

"Beatrice," Amber says—our mother used to use Bea's full name when she was in trouble, and Amber's doing it now. "I'm sure you're exaggerating. Aaron's a very good sailor, and he's very careful."

"The hell he is. He's a menace and someone ought to have the damn guts to say so."

She stops, her nostrils flaring like an angry bull. Now Eva wakes up too—there's something interesting for her to observe. She sits up too, her taught stomach creasing into two neat lines.

"Beatrice, I do not appreciate you talking about my son like that."

Bea's about to explode, I can see it in her face. "Oh, really? You don't *appreciate* it?" But she bites her tongue, I think literally. Then she calms herself down just enough to go on.

"Well, I don't appreciate him nearly *fucking* killing me. And neither does Kate. And most of all, neither does Jack. You know he's scared of the water. And Aaron knows that too."

There's a silence. Eva uses it to pop open the top of her sunscreen bottle. With a squelch she squirts some into her palm, then carefully applies it to her thighs.

"Beatrice, this isn't a conversation we should be having here."

"What do you mean? Not in your nice new house? Is that it?"

I don't know why she says this, maybe because she can't say what she's really thinking. Either way it makes Amber pause.

"It's *our* house." Amber looks suddenly confused. "What do you mean?"

Bea takes a couple of breaths.

"You know what I mean. You say it's our house, but then you turn up with all your friends, and it's like Kate and I are just random guests. Welcome here until we're not. It's obvious what you've tried to do here, and I don't appreciate that either."

There's a silence. I wonder what I've unleashed. I wonder

how far it's going to go. Bea looks at Jack as if she's about to tell Amber what I've told her. But something stops her.

"Are you coming to the house?" she says to me instead, clearly meaning we're going to continue our conversation there. And not knowing what else to do, I nod.

We take off the life jackets in silence, while Amber sits up on her sunbed watching us, her mouth still open in shock. Fortunately Neil isn't at the boathouse anymore, I'm not sure where he's gone to, or what he'd make of this. Then I follow Bea as she stalks up the yard. In the house she makes the mistake of heading into the room that used to be the kitchen, before stopping, backing out and stepping into the new room. Without asking me, she switches on the electric kettle and takes down two mugs for tea. Then she crouches down in front of Jack, who's followed us here silently.

"Can I get you anything? An orange juice?" She thinks a moment, and the shadow of a smile passes across her lips. "Zack used to like orange juice."

"Mmmm." Jack nods. "Yes please."

She watches him a moment, then leans forward and plants a kiss on his forehead. Then she stands and goes to the refrigerator.

I tell her everything—as much as I can anyway—about what Jack's been saying, and how Jan suggested we should contact Dr Wells, and then about his visit, and the tests he carried out. I tell her about Neil's attitude to it, and his continued disbelief that Jack is actually Zack. I don't try and hide anything, and all the while Jack is sitting there, sipping his orange juice and nibbling his way through a packet of chocolate cookies that Bea finds.

"So, you actually believe it?" she asks in the end, when I've finally brought her up to date.

I pause. I still don't know the answer to this.

"I believe 100 percent that Jack believes it. And I don't believe Neil's explanations. I haven't deliberately coached him, and I think that the idea I've inadvertently fed him information —so that he's been able to build this up into a fantasy all on his own—I don't see how that's possible. There are just too many things he knows, things *I* don't even know. Like the campsite on the island."

She listens, and thinks.

"Can *I* ask him a question? About Zack?"

I look to Jack. He goes very still, looking at me.

"Jack? Is that OK?"

He nods, and I do the same to Bea.

"OK." She stops to think.

"Who was your best friend? At school?"

Jack says nothing, but blinks several times. Then he gives a little shake of his head. "I don't remember."

"Did he have blond hair or brown hair?" She tries again, but this time Jack shrugs a little. "I don't remember."

She looks disappointed.

"Horses..." Jack says.

"What?" She frowns at him. "What about them, honey?"

"On the walls. Under our house. There were horses. I remember the horses."

I have no idea what Jack is talking about, but Bea's face has changed. "Do you mean the basement?"

Again he shrugs. "I remember the horses. It scared me a bit."

Bea turns to me, animated now. "In our old house we had a basement, do you remember?" She doesn't give me time to answer. "I don't think you ever saw it; it was super damp, so we blocked it off. But it had this peculiar wallpaper, with these pictures of horses on it." She turns back to Jack. "Is that what you mean Jack? Are you talking about the basement?"

But he just shrugs a third time. "I just remember the horses."

"Show her your birthmark Jack," I say to him, after a short silence.

Again Bea's face creases into a frown, and I go on.

"Do you remember, when Zack died, there was a cut on his foot? A really deep one, and they thought he might have stepped on a broken bottle, how that might have contributed in some way to what happened?"

She nods, and watches Jack as he pulls off his shoe and sock. He holds up the inside of his foot so she can see.

"Dr Wells explained how it's really common with children like Jack—children who claim to remember a past life—that they have marks in the same places that the previous people were injured."

Bea studies it, and then she drops her face into her hands.

"Oh my God. This is too much. Just too much."

Suddenly we're interrupted. I hear the unmistakable sound of Aaron's voice, confident and over-loud, speaking with Amber. They both come in through the rear doors, and though he must be able to see the state we're all in, he pays no attention and cuts straight into the conversation.

"Hey, guys. Mom told me you were unhappy about what happened out there on the water. So, I just want to apologize. I was just trying to give Jack a bit of a thrill. A bit of fun."

Bea opens her mouth to reply, but says nothing.

"And buddy," he points a finger at Jack, "if you do want a ride, you just say the word. I have to get the boat back later, but I can still take you out." He grins. "It's way faster than that old tub you were in earlier."

"Aaron..." Amber implores.

"What's up? Anyway, I'm hungry. What we doing for dinner?" He spots the packet of cookies by Jack, and picks one out. He doesn't offer one to anyone else, and he's now so large the cookie looks abnormally small. He quickly follows it with a second, still not quite getting a mouthful. Amber sighs.

"Actually, regarding food..." she says. "I had the idea that we could order takeout. Save anyone having to cook, does that sound OK?"

I'd totally forgotten her plan for a family meal. I'm not remotely hungry, and frankly I don't care what we eat, so I stay quiet. Bea doesn't reply either.

"Good, that's settled then. I'll send Eva around to take people's orders. About seven OK with everyone?"

Aaron wanders over to the fridge and pulls open the door, then stands there contemplating, so Bea and I get up to leave, her taking Jack's hand to lead him away too. I imagine we're going to keep talking, but when we're in the hallway she asks me quietly if I mind her telling Tristan about Jack. I really have no idea what to say, so I simply nod, and she does the same, gratefully. And then she climbs the new staircase to their room. I don't want to risk running into Amber or Aaron, so after a few moments I follow her, taking Jack up to our room. I find Neil there. I ask what he's doing and he tells me he's been packing, still hoping for an early getaway.

"We're having dinner at seven," I tell him. "Takeout."

He sighs. I think he's going to argue that we should leave earlier, but he just nods. "Fine. But maybe we can actually leave? After that?"

"OK," I say. I don't tell him that I've told Bea. Nor that she's telling Tris right now. And I certainly don't tell him I have a strong feeling about how this is going to go. How this whole family is about to explode.

FORTY-SIX

Not long after, Eva knocks on the door. She comes in, holding a menu from a nearby Chinese restaurant named Wok U Like.

"Mom told me I have to get your orders." She looks uncertainly at the three of us lying on the bed, as if she's wondering why we're up here. It's like we're hiding. Then she holds out the menu. Neil gets up and takes it from her.

"Have you been there before?" I ask, more to make conversation than anything. There's something awkward about the way she's standing there, her face blank.

"Yeah. A few times."

"Is it good?"

She shrugs. "It's OK."

Eva was never really one for conversation and I give up, not wanting to make her even more uncomfortable. Meanwhile Neil is examining the menu as if it's one of his scientific papers. He tells Eva his order and holds out the menu for me.

"Can you order something for me?" I ask him, before turning back to Eva. "And don't worry about Jack, I saw some chicken nuggets in the kitchen. I'll give him those and get him to bed."

Eva sighs, as if this is somehow a drag for her. Then, when Neil selects a dish for me, she writes that down and wordlessly leaves the room.

It feels wrong, staying in our room—like we're skulking or hiding in our own house, so I tell Jack we're going to go downstairs and see what's happening. We find the whole of Amber's family in the main living space. Amber herself is poring over her laptop, presumably putting the food order in, while Brock and Aaron are having a lively discussion—I quickly gather it has to do with whether they should buy their own powerboat, and they pay Jack and me no attention. All three of them are drinking. Amber has a large glass of white wine, while Brock and Aaron are drinking beers. Only Eva looks up from where she's curled up on the sofa reading a book. She scowls slightly, as if to warn us not to invade her space. So, after standing there a moment feeling awkward, I take Jack to the kitchen and give him his dinner. As the nuggets cook, I bitterly wish I could just eat with him, and then, like him, sleep until it's time to leave.

After he's eaten, we sit at the kitchen table for a while. I should have brought some more toys for Jack. For years there used to be a box of them here in a cupboard in the dining room. When Zack and the twins were Jack's age, they would pull it out and sit on the floor and put the train set together or play cars. The box was still there when Dad died, but it disappeared for the rebuild and if it's come back I don't know where it is.

"We could do a jigsaw, if you like?" I suggest to Jack, and he nods, while Amber—who's now on the phone—points to a new cabinet, mouthing that there are some in there.

I grab the easiest one I can find. When I turn back around, Bea is standing in the doorway. Looking at us all. She's drinking too—gin and tonic—and she clinks the ice around the glass before taking a long draw. Amber glances up, but apparently doesn't notice the black look on our sister's face.

For half an hour Jack and I fiddle with the jigsaw, but we get nowhere and then have to pack it away so the table can be set. I get Jack to say goodnight and take him upstairs. And Aaron leaves too. He has to take the boat back. Or refuel it, something like that. There's a moment when he and Amber clash; she's annoyed he's going now, just when the food's arriving. But he tells her to chill out. I'm pleased. I hope we can get through the meal before he comes back.

The food arrives. We lay out the plastic trays and gather around the table. There's a rush to open the trays and ladle the noodles and stir fries onto our plates.

"Well, this is nice," Amber says, when everyone has been served. There's a sweet, slightly sulfurous smell of soy sauce in the air, but I'm still not particularly hungry.

"Isn't it?" Amber presses.

"Is it?" Bea replies, and I glance at her. Maybe it's a warning look, but I just don't know anymore. I can see how her hand is shaking as she's serving herself fried rice.

"Well, *I* think so," Amber concludes. "We're all here together, as a family." She smiles sweetly.

"No we're not," Bea says, after a moment.

"Well OK, but Aaron won't be long." Amber rolls her eyes. But Bea glowers at her.

"Zack's not here."

"Well no, of course." The look on Amber's face changes, implying that this is a stupid comment, like she only meant to include people who were *actually alive*.

And then Bea says it. She just comes out with it, like I know she's going to, even though I can still scarcely believe this is actually happening.

"Did you know that Jack thinks he was Zack?" Bea says,

mirroring Amber's smile. I jump so hard my knees knock into the table, spilling some of my drink.

"What?" Amber's face screws up in a baffled scowl. "What are you talking about?"

"Hasn't Kate mentioned it? Apparently he's been saying it for years. Ever since he could speak." She looks at me, a look I don't understand, like she's equally angry with me for keeping this from her. Amber follows Bea's gaze, as if to see whether I'm going to deny it.

All the blood has drained from Neil's face. He freezes, fork halfway between his mouth and plate.

"What's Bea talking about?" Amber asks me.

"Jack thinks he's Zack?" Brock pulls his face into a half-sneer, like this is an attempt at a joke which he doesn't understand.

"He doesn't..." I search for a simple way to explain this. There isn't one.

"He has memories," Bea goes on. "And he says they're from when he lived before. When he was Zack."

There's a silence, and I wish I could crawl away. I risk an angry look at Bea, but she isn't having any of it.

"Why don't you tell us more about it, Kate?" she continues. "It really does sound fascinating."

I push my plate away—the thought of putting food in my mouth now makes my stomach churn—and I hold my head in my hands.

"Bea—" I begin, but she cuts me off; suddenly she's shouting, loud.

"What? You think I should keep this to myself? Or you think it maybe doesn't concern us? Doesn't concern *me*?" She puts her hands on her head, disbelieving.

"I didn't think you'd blurt it out like this."

She drops her hands again. "Well, it looks like you got that wrong." Now her chest rises and falls quickly with her breaths.

Suddenly I notice that no one is eating. Everyone is just staring at Bea. Bea and me.

"I'm sorry, I don't quite understand what's going on?" Amber speaks slowly, breaking the silence. "Are you saying that Jack likes to play make-believe that he's Zack? Is that what you mean?"

I don't answer, so Bea does it for me.

"No." Her lips are thin. "What she's saying, is that Jack might actually *be* Zack. She had him checked out by a specialist, a scientist or something, who confirmed it. And that's not all. He doesn't just remember Zack's life; he remembers his *death*."

"Well, that's preposterous," Amber says.

"Isn't it? Wouldn't that just be *so convenient* if that were so?"

"Well, it is so, Bea. It just is. I know you're a bit prone to these kind of... mystical ideas, but you have to understand they're not actually real."

"Of course they're real!" Bea cuts in—and I realize in a flash what's happened here. Bea's *believed* me. Not just believed that it *might* be possible that Jack is telling the truth. I mean she's totally accepted it. Maybe because it's finally given her some relief from the pain she's lived with since Zack died, or whether her way of life—the fact she's been turning herself into some sort of new-age hippie for the last five years—is what's behind it. But she's *believed* me. And she's believed what Jack said about Zack's death. She's swallowed the whole thing.

"Would you like to know what else Jack said?" Bea says now, her voice artificially sweet, laced with bitter sarcasm.

"What?" Amber asks, coolly.

"He says that, when he was Zack, he didn't die because he swam out too far. The way you told us." She smiles again; she's simmering, just moments away from a volcanic explosion. The tension in the room has almost made the air crystalline.

Amber opens her mouth to reply, but then closes it. I look

around, hoping that someone is going to stop this, but Tris looks helpless; he has one hand over his face like that's going to protect him. I look imploringly at Neil, and bless him he tries.

"Bea?" He holds up his fork, breathing hard. "If I may?"

It's not clear for a moment if she's going to let him speak: somehow she holds all the power in the room. But then she gestures with a hand, like a queen momentarily staying an execution.

Neil starts with a desperate glance in my direction.

"Bea, it *is* true that Jack has been saying these things. And for what I hope are obvious reasons, we *have* been keeping it from you. From all of you." He glances around the room. "But it's *not true* that Jack is the reincarnation of Zack. Categorically not true. From a scientific perspective that's completely impossible. And therefore we shouldn't listen to the things he says about—"

"Is it?" I hear my own voice, interrupting him. He glances at me, thrown out of his stride. "Is it actually *impossible*?"

"Well, yes. It is. Of course it is..."

But I'm not having that. I'm not *fucking* letting him get away with that. "Is it not just the case that it goes against the current scientific *consensus*?" I ask.

"Kate, this is not really the—"

"So it could be like when everyone insisted that the universe revolves around the earth, and when Galileo said otherwise they actually *cut off his head*?"

"They didn't..." Neil frowns deeply at me, his face imploring me to stop. "Galileo was put under house arrest because of his work on heliocentrism; he didn't have his head..." He stops, his eyes wide, a little wild. "And anyway, that was the *church* who did that, not—"

"But you get the point?" I'm angry now. Furious, angrier than I can ever remember being before in my life. Livid at Bea for betraying the trust I put in her, at Amber and her spoilt, ungrateful, nasty children, but more than anyone at Neil, for refusing to ever, *just once,* give our son the benefit of the doubt. "Everyone thought it was impossible, until it wasn't impossible anymore?"

He tries to reset. "It isn't *impossible,* that is correct. But the issue is that there's absolutely no evidence that it's true."

"Except that your own fucking son is telling you it's true. In plain English. Over and over again, since before he could even fucking speak!"

I thought the explosion would come from Bea; it's a shock to realize that I've said these words. Bea reaches out and puts a hand on my arm. I don't much want it, but I don't shake it off.

"Woah," Brock says. "This evening's taking a turn for the weird."

Amber ignores him. "What kind of things is he saying?"

Flatly, I tell her. Just a summary, about how we worked out what his early words were, how we linked his hatred of the water to the fact that Zack drowned. How he was able to identify the beach house where Zack had been on vacation, which I didn't even know about. Tris gives me a look at the point, I guess finally realizing why I went to see him that time.

When I'm finished, Amber turns to Neil, who's been listening in silence, his face pale and still.

"And you don't believe any of this?"

He shakes his head. "No."

"But it's true what Kate's saying? You've heard it all?"

He sighs a little before answering. "Some of it, yes. For the rest I only have Kate's word."

"But do you believe her?" Amber's eyebrows rise up.

Again, he takes a moment. "Yes," he says at last, but without conviction. "I believe Kate, and I have no doubt that Jack believes he's telling the truth as well." He sighs. "But there are many examples of people believing things that are simply not true."

Amber looks around a moment, as if stunned by everything that's happening. While I was speaking some of my family had been picking at their food, almost as if some things were getting back to normal.

"OK, so what is the explanation? How does he know all this stuff about Zack's life?" asked Amber.

"It's difficult to give a precise answer." Neil begins his now well-practiced explanation and I feel my anger bubbling back. But then suddenly there's an interruption from the least likely of sources. The normally silent Eva.

"What exactly did Jack say about Zack's death?"

As she asks, her cold eyes are locked right on mine.

FORTY-SEVEN

Eva waits in silence. For a second she glances at Bea, but then turns back to me. Just waiting. Everyone else is silent, as if Eva has now absorbed all the power in the room. She controls everything. Still I say nothing, but opposite me, Bea starts to speak.

"Jack says that Zack wasn't swimming too far out in the lake, but..."

She stops, takes a sip of her drink—another gin and tonic—and her hand is surprisingly steady.

"But you and Aaron were playing with him, closer in. He was dunking him under the water, holding him down." She stops, and there's total silence in the room. "And Aaron held him under too long. And that's why he drowned."

This time it's Brock who finds the words. "That's a hell of an accusation, Bea. I know you're still having a hard time with it all, but—"

"That's bullshit," Aaron himself interrupts suddenly. Shocked, I swing around to see him standing there, in the doorway. He must have returned from his boat errand, but I have no idea how long he's been there, no idea what he's heard.

"Total fucking bullshit. And I'm not gonna take it." He turns to Brock, obviously angry.

"I got the gas. It's outside the front door," he snarls, then slouches to the table and sits down. He reaches for the nearest takeout container and spoons rice onto his plate.

"You can heat that up if you like darling," Amber says.

"Don't you dare," Bea interrupts. "Don't you fucking dare pretend this is all normal. A happy fucking family."

Amber runs her hand through her hair. For a moment all three of them—Bea, Amber and Brock—are speaking together, three furious voices, until Eva suddenly cuts in, her quiet voice somehow silencing the rest of her family.

"It's true."

"What?" Amber says.

"It's true. What Bea said about Zack. And Mom *knows* it's true."

Amber swallows, but doesn't reply.

"What do you mean it's true?" Tris asks now. His eyes flick around the table, but come to rest on Eva.

"It's true. We *were* dunking Zack. And Aaron *was* holding him underwater. That is what happened."

"Eva, what the fuck are you talking about?" Aaron turns on her now. This time I catch something; beneath his casual words he tries to send her something, a look, a signal. There's panic too. But she just shakes her head, her face set into a cruel snarl.

"No Aaron. *Fuck you.* All my life I've kept this. All my life I've kept your dirty secrets—like that girl you hit. I know you did it, I fucking saw you. And I can't do it anymore. I won't do it. Jack *knows*. I don't know how he knows, but he knows."

"He was there," Bea says. "That's how he knows."

Now there's so much going on around the table it's hard to keep up with what everyone is thinking, but somehow my attention falls on Tris.

"Eva, this is really, really important," he's trying to say to her. "Are you saying that you remember Zack's death differently to how it was officially recorded?"

"Do you think I could ever forget? And Mom knows. I told her at the time, but she said we had to lie. She said we had to, otherwise we'd get into trouble. Aaron would get into trouble."

All of us turn to Amber. All the blood has drained from her face. Her matronly warmth has completely gone.

"Is this true?" Bea asks her. But Amber can't reply. She tries for a moment to shake her head, but it's not convincing. Then she drops her head into her hands.

"You're such a liar, Mom," Eva snarls at her. "You've always been a liar."

"You told me..." Bea begins, "...you told me how Zack wouldn't come back to shore... you had me believe he died because he was being disobedient."

"I thought it was for the best," Amber finally manages to say. "I didn't mean..." But then Aaron interrupts. He stands with such force that his chair is pushed backwards and tips over.

"I'm not sitting here and listening to this bullcrap." He's furious, I've never seen him like this. Then Brock shouts back at him, more assertive than I've ever seen as well.

"You sit the hell back down, Aaron." For a few moments they glare at each other, but then Aaron angrily resets his chair and sits back down.

"You saw the whole thing!" Bea turns back to Amber. "Why didn't you stop Aaron bullying him? Zack *died*. My son died." She's crying now, just full-on crying. "Why didn't you stop it?"

The significance of the question seems to focus all our attention on Amber's reply. When it comes it's quiet, her voice unnaturally reedy.

"I didn't... I didn't see. I wasn't looking, I was... working on something. I wasn't paying the attention that I should have been."

Bea's sobbing so hard now she's finding it hard to breathe.

Then she reaches forward, picking up one of the trays of noodles, still nearly full. She balances it on her right hand, and then suddenly turns and flings it at the wall. Some of it spills as she launches it, falling on the table and floor, and a huge greasy smear of chow mein splatters over the fresh paintwork. No one says a word.

"It was an accident," Amber says, her eyes following the dripping noodles, but it's like it's happened in another world. Not worthy of mention. "The twins were only children, I thought it was the best thing to do. What good would it have done for him to get into trouble?"

"An accident?" Bea repeats. "Aaron held Zack underwater until he drowned. That's an accident?"

"It was!" Aaron protests now, still somehow sounding like none of this should be a big deal, like he can't believe we're even angry. "It was a game we were playing. I didn't mean for him to drown."

Bea turns to him, struggling to maintain her dignity. "But you held him underwater, until he did?" she replies. "You held him under the water, while he panicked and kicked out, desperate, and you just *fucking* held him there?"

For the first time I see Aaron acknowledge it with a guilty shrug, like he's admitting to sneaking a cookie.

"Oh my God," Bea says.

For some reason I look at Neil. He's silent, his eyes wider than I've ever seen them. For a second I want to yell at him, to ask if he's prepared to believe Jack now, or if I've somehow still primed him to make all of this up. But I don't, and instead my eyes slowly shift focus to the doorway behind him. And I see that Jack is standing there, scared, staring at us all. It takes me a moment, but I realize the noise must have woken him.

"Why didn't you stop him, Amber?" Bea laments again. She hasn't seen Jack, and doesn't think anything has changed. "You could have stopped him. You *should* have stopped him! Aaron was always bullying Zack and you never did anything about it. Why the hell couldn't you have stopped him?"

"I was working," Amber replies, recovering a little of her poise. "I just stepped away for a moment to answer the phone. I was a working mother, and look what that work has brought you?" She sweeps her arm around, meaning to indicating the beautiful new room, but she stops dead still when she sees Jack as well.

"That's not true." Jack's tiny voice cuts through from the doorway.

"Jack, you shouldn't be here. You should be in bed." Neil gets up, moving toward him. He speaks with the voice he uses when Jack's been bad, and it takes me a moment to work out why it sounds so bizarrely out of place. Jack just ignores him though.

"Where was Amber, Jack?" Bea asks him, and she puts out a hand to stop Neil. He can't get past without pushing her away, and he's too English for that. Everyone turns now, to look at my son. "Where was Amber, when you drowned?"

His little face is pinched into a look of hard anger, a look that shouldn't be on a five-year-old, that *couldn't* be. And he delivers his next line with the sort of poise that should only come from a much older child. Yet the words are entirely of his age.

"She was upstairs. Making babies."

FORTY-EIGHT

"Making *babies*?" Brock asks. His face has stilled, and he stares at Amber. "Who the hell was she making babies with?"

Like in some sick tennis match we all turn back to Jack, to see if he's going to tell us this crucial fact. And I recognize the look on his face: he's remembered. He's just remembered something new.

"With Daddy."

"Daddy?" I say. Without thinking I turn to Tris, my eyes wide open. But he opens his hands defensively. "I was at the hospital, with you guys, I wasn't... *what the hell?*"

Daddy—my mind flares and fuses, white flashing blinding light—*what does Jack mean by Daddy?* Very slowly I turn to face my husband, Neil. The image I expect to see, of him preparing to explain this away, to tell me how this is impossible; even—crazily—of him laughing at how absurd this is. None of that is there. Instead his mouth is open, his eyes tired and defeated.

"Neil...?"

"Look, Kate, it wasn't like—"

"*You?* You were having sex with Amber? When Zack died?"

. . .

I don't know what happens next. There must be fifteen, twenty minutes, maybe even half-an-hour that are entirely unaccounted for in my mind. I can see that another carton of noodles has gone up the wall; maybe it was even me that threw it. Out of nowhere I actually vomit, the undigested food landing partly on my plate and partly on the table, where it drips onto the floor. There's not much, but I look at it in disbelief, the utter absurdity that we could all just be here while someone is throwing up at the dinner table. But it's the least insane thing that's happening. I turn to Neil. This must be a dream. This cannot be real.

"Neil, were you having sex with Amber, when Zack died?"

I really did lose some time; he must have already answered this, because now he's already trying to excuse it—not deny it —*excuse* it. At some point he must have stood up, because now he moves towards me, his hands leading the way as if to physically stop me talking, stop me thinking.

"Kate, I told you, it was only a couple of times. I was stressed at work, you remember that time, how—"

"*You were stressed at work so you fucked my sister?*"

He stops. He sits back down heavily.

"It was a couple of times. That's all."

I lose time again. When I'm back, to some extent present again in my mind, the room has changed. Bea is sitting with Jack on her lap, hugging him tight and rocking him back and forward. Amber, Aaron and Eva have disappeared. Neil too. Only Brock is still sitting as he was before, but he doesn't meet my eye.

"How did you know, Jack?" I ask my son. "About what Amber was doing?" On some level I'm used to how he remembers new facts, how you can ask him to explain them, and sometimes he can, sometimes he can't.

"I didn't mean to see, but Eva said I could borrow her swimming goggles. On the day I died. That's when I saw them, in their room. I'm sorry."

Bea smooths his hair, wet from her tears.

"That's OK, honey. It's not your fault. Not your fault at all."

FORTY-NINE

"Thank you," McGee said quietly. "It can't have been easy to tell us that." He paused, his thumb and little finger drumming lightly on the table top. "And I'm sorry I have to press a little deeper, but I need to in order to understand a possible motive for what happened next. You understand that, right?"

Kate stared at him, her face devoid of expression, but she nodded.

"The affair between Neil and Amber. Did you have any idea of this, prior to what Jack said?"

She shook her head.

"You never suspected?"

This time she stayed still, but it told the same story.

"And did either Neil or your sister give any further explanation for what happened between them? Either at the meal, or afterwards, before..."

She shook her head. "If they did, I don't remember."

"OK." McGee was pleased to get her speaking again. He chose his next question carefully.

"It's no small thing to have an affair, but to do it with your sister-in-law or brother-in-law... Do you have any thoughts about *why* they did it?"

"I've been wondering about it. Since the fire," she began. "I think they had different reasons." She paused, and McGee waited.

"Amber is nearly ten years older than me, I think that's part of it. When I was still just a kid, she was this beautiful young woman. She'd be chased around the lake by all these boys, good-looking, rich boys like Brock. And she loved it. She always said she was the prettiest of the three of us, and it was true. At least, until it wasn't anymore. By the time she'd had her own kids, and with the stress of the business, I guess that began to change. When I met Neil, I knew she was jealous. He had this..." She stopped, her face briefly breaking into a smile. "I used to think he had this Superman thing going on. He wore his glasses, but sometimes he took them off, and it was a shock how good-looking he was."

The smile faded.

"I don't know for sure, but Bea and I used to suspect that Brock sometimes cheated on Amber. If nothing else, he was that type. The day that Zack died he was away golfing in Florida with his buddies. I don't know exactly what that means but I wouldn't be surprised if women were involved somehow."

She stopped again, shook her head.

"What I mean to say is, I think she was jealous of me, because I still had my looks when she was losing hers. And she was bitter about Brock, and maybe she just... maybe she just wanted to see if she still had it? You know? If she could still make a man chase her, around the lake." Kate shrugged. "I don't know. I wish I did."

McGee considered her answer. Slowly he nodded back at her.

"And Neil? Why would he have done it?"

Kate took a deep breath and puffed out her cheeks. "That's

a little more difficult to understand." Her eyes flicked to Robbins, as if she would have preferred to explain this to McGee alone. He waited, the silence stretching out, giving her time to speak. "I think it comes down to how he viewed the world."

"I don't understand."

"Neil's belief in science was incredibly strong. It was like a religion, or even more so. You know—the universe begins with the big bang, and all these elements go flying outwards. And over time they get organized by these blind laws of physics, so there ends up being this lump of rock that we call a planet. And on that lump of rock, certain chemical elements just happen to bump together in such a way that they start to self-replicate. And that's life. And once you've got life, you get these tiny random changes each time it renews itself, and that drives evolution, so that eventually you get elephants, and mole rats, and us. But there's no *point* to it. There's no reason. It's just all blind chance." She stopped. Swallowed. "Neil believed that, more than anyone I've ever met."

McGee didn't understand where the explanation was going, but he trusted that she would get there. He waited, and was grateful that his partner did too.

"So if we're just here by blind luck, then what does it matter if he has an affair? If no one finds out, I mean. With that mindset there's no judgement from above. There's no judgement from anywhere. So you might as well do whatever you like. Have sex with your sister-in-law, have sex with your students—if they're offering it."

Her eyes flicked up to his, wounded.

"You might as well maximize your pleasure, because there's no moral reason not to."

"You think he slept with his students, as well as Amber?"

"I don't know." Kate shook her head. "Not for sure. I know

there were women who were interested. But if he did fuck them, he was careful."

McGee was surprised by her sudden use of the expletive. He sensed Robbins' surprise too.

"What I mean is," Kate went on, "I never suspected him. I trusted him, until I found out about Amber. But since then, I've reconsidered. I don't think it's impossible."

"Sleeping with your sister-in-law is hardly careful," McGee reasoned.

"No." Kate shook her head, more forcefully this time. "No, it's not. But for all Neil's conviction that his belief in science made him better than the rest of us, he was still human. He still made mistakes."

McGee couldn't keep a doubtful expression from forming on his face. Eventually he gave voice to it. "But why take the risk?"

"I guess I'm saying that if Amber came on to him, a woman in a bikini—still good-looking—making it clear that he could have it, with absolutely no consequences... I can see him going for that. Thinking with his dick for once, instead of his brain."

Again McGee let his hand drum on the table, thinking. "But this is... speculation, for want of a better word. You don't know this?"

She shook her head again. When she stopped she wiped her eyes, even though there were no tears there.

"I don't know. And I don't suppose I ever will know now."

To McGee it felt like she was drawing a line under the discussion, and he nodded now, more to himself than her.

"I guess you'd better finish the story," he said.

FIFTY

It's late now, the house is quiet; in a way it's weirdly peaceful. It's how I imagine it must feel after an earthquake, or some other terrible disaster: the initial violence has finished, but no one can bring themselves to face the utter destruction that's left. The world shattered into broken pieces. I don't even know who's here and who's not. I'm in our room, with Jack asleep beside me. I think Neil is in one of the spare rooms at the front of the house. We were going to drive home after the meal, but obviously that didn't happen and we're all just here, waiting to see what might come next.

I heard Brock getting a cab earlier. Maybe he's gone to a hotel somewhere, I don't know. He left alone, so I suppose Amber and the twins are still here, though I don't know for sure. Bea and Tris are here though, they're in the room next door. For a moment my lips nearly form into a smile at the thought; we've long wondered—Amber and I—if Bea and Tris still sleep together, and now the house is big enough for Tris to have his own room, but he's not using it. But then the full force of reality eviscerates the smile. It's like a punch in the stomach. Whatever Bea's doing is irrelevant. Because my older sister was sleeping with my husband. And their sordid carelessness caused the death of my middle sister's only child. And then, in the way that thoughts in the middle of the night can twist and turn themselves into things that aren't real, that don't fit together in the harsh light of day, my mind goes on. Bea's dead child then became my child. My Jack.

I feel hot. I push the covers back, careful to not disturb Jack, and after a while I get up and go to the bathroom and pour myself a drink of water. But instead of drinking it I just stand there, looking at myself in the mirror. My eyes follow the lines in my face that weren't there a few years before. The streaks of gray that are appearing in the roots of my once glossy dark hair. I don't know. I ponder the meaning of time, what it means to be alive. To grow old. To die. And then... to return? I think it's the first time that I connect what Jack has been saying to me. If he has memories of living before, and I accept them as real, then it follows—at least it seems to me—that we've all lived before. The only difference with children like Jack is that something goes wrong with the process of wiping the memories of it. And even then, by the time the child grows up, they tend to forget it all. At least that's what Dr Wells said.

This time a real smile does form on my lips. Will I tell Dr Wells about what's happened this weekend? I can almost imagine him and his assistant, setting up their cameras and interviewing all of us. Collecting evidence from Aaron about how he murdered his cousin. From Amber, about how she was so careless that she let it happen, and then covered it up. From Neil, about how he cheated on me, and lied about it. The smile's gone again, replaced this time by a ghostly vision that stares back at me in the mirror, a hot, empty heat in my head. Now I lift the glass and sip the water, but that's hot too. Unnaturally hot. I must have accidentally run the hot water, and I flick the faucet the other way, but that only makes it hotter. Confused, I turn it back to the cold marker, but it clearly isn't.

Maybe it's a problem with the plumbing? Amber has a list of small problems with the build—she called it her snagging list—and apparently the contractors are coming back in the next couple of weeks to fix them all... Suddenly my nostrils twitch: a smell, like wood smoke, but chemical too. And the noise, the roar inside my head seems to have moved, so that now it's outside my head. Outside the bathroom.

I turn, move back into the bedroom, but in the dark there's nothing to see. For a moment I hesitate, still not wanting to disturb Jack, but then I click on the main light, and like a nightmare, snake-like coils of smoke are easing their way though the cracks between the door and the door frame.

I blink. Disbelieving. Everything about this night—about my life—cannot be real; this is surely just the next stage in my descent into madness. For a moment I simply stand there, marveling at it. But I don't stay still long. Jack is here. Even though this isn't real, I have to act, to save him, or pretend to save him. To show whomever or whatever is watching that I'm trying to do the right thing.

I go to the door. At that moment a distant, ancient memory comes to me. I'm sitting on the floor, young fingers tracing the herringbone pattern of wooden floor tiles, while, at the front of the hall, three firefighters are sitting, looking out at us. They're all men, in smart uniforms. In those days they were just called firemen. And one of them is explaining that if we ever find ourselves in a house fire, we should check the temperature of the door before opening it. He shows us how by using the back of our hands, because the skin there is thinner, and it registers the heat quicker without burning us. How do I remember that, so clearly, decades later? There's no time to consider. Instead, I do it now.

Ouch. I pull my hand away. The door is hot, burning hot. And still the smoke trails silently in, underneath. I'm horrified, in a way; terrified but without fear... for the time being. But I know the only way out of the house is down the stairs; I know I have no choice but to open it, to face whatever is on the other side of that wooden door. More memories from the firemen return to me, and I rush back to the bathroom. This time I fill the sink and plunge the hand towel into it, meaning to soak it. While the faucet is running I go to wake Jack. I shake him gently at first, but then quickly, much harder.

"What?" he moans, still half asleep.

"Wake up Jack, you need to wake up."

"Don't want to." His eyes close again, drifting back off.

"Jack, we have to go. The house is on fire."

Still his eyes stay closed. But it doesn't matter. I'll carry him. I pause to pull on my shoes, and then go back to the bathroom. Leaving the faucets running I pick up the sodden towel, not caring that it soaks my nightdress and floods water onto the floor. Then I slip my arms underneath my son, who's asleep again, and I heft him onto my shoulder. He's heavy these days, but at this moment it's like he weighs nothing. I hold him against me with one hand, while with the other I bundle the sodden towel around my wrist. I take a moment to wonder at the unreality of my life. Then I pull open the door.

I scream. It's like I've opened the door to hell. The top half of the hallway is filled with thick smoke, illuminated from below in horrific violent-orange from the firestorm that is consuming—so fast it's actually visible—the front of the house. The stairway is obviously, terrifyingly, completely alight. Flames are streaking from the treads and reaching uninter-rupted into the smoke that obscures the ceiling; the banisters are already almost gone, charred black sticks disconnected and falling down into the yellow-black flames. Just as I'm about to step backwards into my room again, the door next to me opens, and I see Tris, wide-eyed and terrified. For a moment our eyes connect, and then he's moving, crashing into me and pushing me back into my bedroom. With his other hand he's pulling Bea, and when we're all inside the room she slams the door.

"Get the comforter, block the smoke," Tris says, but Bea's already doing it.

"What's going on?" I ask, stupidly.

"Fire," Tris replies. "We have to get out."

"We can't," I say. "The staircase is on fire. It's more than on fire, it's—"

But he shakes his head. "I tried, it's impassible. We have to get out the window. There's a trellis outside. Bea, be careful."

Bea's at the window, one of the original wooden windows, restored by Amber. She jerks at it; maybe it's already swollen with the heat, but it's hard for her to open it. She screams now, a yell of frustration and rage, and the wood gives, the window lifts up, leaving a space where we can escape. I rush over to join her, but the view outside is sickening. The trellis, which leads down towards the sunroom roof, looks incredibly flimsy, and below us, the dining-room window is glowing hot and flickering orange from the flames within.

"What about the others?" I say to Tris. He hesitates.

"Maybe they got out already?" Then he shakes his head. "If not, there's nothing we can do. They're all in the front of the house; we can't get there."

I pause, trying to think. There's no question he's right. You hear about people, heroes who fight their way through the flames to save their families, and I would. I really would, but this house is made mostly of wood. It's already a raging inferno. No one fights their way through that. But there must be some way out of this nightmare. "The fire department. Maybe they can save them?"

"I called them, they're on their way," Tris says, and for a beat my hopes surge. But his voice brings me back to reality, the awful, terrifying reality. "Kate we have to get out. We have to get Jack out. *Now*."

I know he's right. And I go back to Jack—I dropped him back on the bed when Tris pushed us back into the room, and he's awake now, sitting up, scared and still.

I pull him toward the window and look out. Some sort of maternal instinct takes over and I see a route.

"Tris, climb down to the roof of the sunroom, I'll hand Jack down to you."

He scans the trellis, then nods. And then he's climbing out of the window, with Bea pleading with him to be careful.

There are two windows in this room, and Bea and I go to the second one to watch. The trellis reaches right up to the window that Tris is climbing out of, and when he puts his weight on it, gingerly at first, it holds. Maybe it's more substantial that I feared. Casting a quick look at Bea, he climbs down, using it like a ladder. Seconds later he's on the roof of the sunroom below.

"Now pass Jack down!" he calls up.

I don't think too much. I just do.

"Are you ready for this?" I ask my son. His eyes are round with terror. Bea twists a bedsheet into a kind of rope which she tries to tie around his waist, but it's too thick. Even so, she's able to drape it out of the window, to help Jack climb out. And actually, it's almost easy for him. All those hours he's spent in jungle gyms, I know he can do this. And he does. He only needs to climb a few steps down the trellis before he reaches Tris's outstretched hands, and from there he can turn, slide down the cherry tree and onto the ground.

Bea goes next, and I watch until she too hits the ground and immediately wraps Jack up in a hug, waiting and watching until Tris and I make our escapes too. He's still on the sunroom roof. But I take a last look around before I climb out of the window. I look at the door, smoke now pouring thickly through the gaps. To my amazement the whole ceiling is gone, hidden by a swirling, black cloud of vicious smoke, lit up by the bedside light. For a final time I again consider being a hero and rescuing the others—if they're still there. But it's suicide. If I opened that door I'd be dead in seconds, overcome by smoke or literally consumed by those flames. Then I actually consider staying here, and letting the heat overcome me. Taking me out of this body to who knows where. But then I look out the window, at Jack on the ground below me, his face turned upwards, looking for me. And I know I'm not dying today.

I step over the windowsill, and my foot finds the solid edge of the wooden trellis. I start to climb, and through the smoke I see the flashing red lights and hear the sirens of the fire trucks, thundering down the road toward us.

FIFTY-ONE

Robbins leaned forwards in his chair, then sat back. Finally he turned to McGee. "Jim, you mind if I take a minute to sum things up here?"

McGee glanced across, considering the expression on his partner's face. It seemed the woman's story was done. She'd said all she had to say.

"Go ahead."

"Sure." Robbins leaned forward again and drummed his fingers on the table top.

"There were eight people in the house that night. The only people who escaped were Bea and Tris, yourself and Jack."

He paused, apparently considering this.

"Your husband Neil, your sister Amber and her two children—Aaron and Eva. They all died. Four people, dead. From the fire marshal's preliminary report, we think they were all in separate rooms, upstairs at the front of the house, right above where the fire started." He opened his hands. "But there was so little left of them, it's gonna take a while to be sure."

"We tried to tell them..." Kate covered her mouth with her

hands; she seemed suddenly on the verge of tears. "The fire crew who found us. We told them the others were still in the house, we begged them to do something. But it was impossible to get inside, even with the equipment they had. The whole house was an inferno."

"No argument there. The fire marshal confirms that by the time the crew arrived, the whole house was ablaze. So much of it was made of wood it went up like a bonfire." He stopped and nodded to himself. "We also know *how* the fire started."

As Robbins spoke, McGee made sure to watch Kate carefully. She dropped her hands and shook her head, as if trying to clear her tears. Robbins went on.

"The fire marshal says a large volume of propellant—gasoline—was poured around the hallway, and then set on fire. The remains of two metal ten-gallon gas tanks were found by the stairs. You said Aaron had left earlier that evening to refill the gas tanks for the speedboat?"

"That's right." Kate snuffled as she replied. "Brock told him to; they'd used so much fuel that day and he wasn't supposed to return the boat empty."

"And I am correct that they were metal tanks? Ten-gallon?"

"I think so. We'd had them for years."

"OK. And when Aaron came back, you said he didn't refill the boat right away, he left the cans by the front door. Why is that?"

"I don't know. Maybe because you can't drive down to the boathouse; you have to use a wheelbarrow, and Aaron probably meant to do it the next day, or after he'd eaten. Or maybe he was hoping he could get Brock to do it because he was lazy. I don't know."

She fell silent, and Robbins nodded again.

"Alright. The point is this. Aaron leaves the gas tanks outside the front door, and everyone's there when he does so, so you all know about them. You all know where they are. Then Aaron comes in, he sees the argument, and the whole place erupts. And then later on, in the middle of the night when everything is finally quiet, someone carries the tanks inside the hallway, empties them and sets the place on fire." He stroked his chin. "But you didn't see who?"

"No." Kate shook her head. "I was in my room."

Robbins gave her a look, as if to say, *we'll see about that.*

"Let's think this through," Robbins continued, speaking almost rhetorically now. "We've got eight people in the house, when the fire starts." He began counting off the names on his fingers. "That's yourself, Jack, Bea and Tris—and all of you escaped down the trellis at the back of the property. But Amber, Neil, and the twins, Aaron and Eva—they didn't make it." He paused a moment, thinking. "Brock wasn't there. He left earlier in the evening, like you said." He paused a beat. "But he didn't go to a local hotel, like you guessed. Instead, he paid $500 for the taxi driver to take him the three hours back to the family home. They were still driving—and over a hundred miles away —when the fire started. So I think we can rule out Brock. But as for the rest of you... Someone set that fire. Someone killed those four people. You all knew where the gas tanks were. With the possible exception of Jack, you all could have moved them in. So, what about motives?"

No one spoke, so he continued.

"Let's start with Amber. She's got this dark secret she's been keeping, which she believes is totally under control, and suddenly it's anything but. Her whole world explodes. I'm not going to say I know exactly why, but let's call it shame. People have been known to kill for less."

Kate stayed quiet, her eyes downcast.

"Same goes for Eva. The way you've described her, half her life she's had to keep this secret that she and her brother killed their cousin. That's a lot of guilt, a whole lot of stress. And she was the one who confirmed what Jack was saying, so in a way—maybe in her mind—she was the cause of all this?" A half-smile appeared on Robbins' lips. "She was the spark that lit the fuse, metaphorically speaking, so why not take the metaphor out of the equation and set the place alight for real?" He looked around, as if to see how this explanation was landing, but McGee kept his eyes on Kate, watching.

"And then there's Aaron..." Robbins continued. "From everything we've discovered about the boy, your description is on the money." He nodded to Kate. "He had a ton of self-confidence, which a lot of people have said sometimes spilled over into arrogance. He probably had a liking for violence, as shown by nearly getting charged for assaulting that girl. And if your story is true—which I have to say is a big 'if' in my mind—then he was also responsible for the death of his cousin at a very young age." Robbins pursed his lips, clearly thinking. "Plus, he definitely knew where the fuel was."

He seemed to let the thought settle for a while before continuing.

"Bea and Tristan. After the argument they say they went to the room they shared together—the next room along from yours." He nodded to Kate. "And they both say they stayed there—talking—until the smell of smoke alerted them the house was on fire. They first tried to escape down the stairway but were forced back, and then they came into your room, and finally escaped out the window. Like you just told us." He paused, thinking. "Each of them says the other was never out of their sight—they're effectively giving each other an alibi. But arguably they both have a motive too; they both learned that their son was killed by Aaron, and that his role in Zack's death was covered up by Amber and Neil."

He leaned forward, went back to drumming his fingers on the table.

"And then we have Neil." Robbins paused again, becoming

more animated. "Like Amber he's suddenly shamed, his affair uncovered in front of the whole family. So maybe he just couldn't take it?" Kate shook her head and raised her hands in a slight shrug.

"I don't know. I've told you everything I can."

"Have you, though?" Robbins replied. "And have you told us the truth?"

Kate shrugged again.

McGee watched them and wondered if his partner had missed anything. It took him a moment.

"Neil would have been professionally humiliated as well."

"Huh?" Robbins turned to him. "How'd you mean?"

"He was adamant throughout that Jack couldn't have been telling the truth. But in this final moment it appeared that he actually was. That would have been tough to handle. As a scientist. His whole worldview disappears."

"Uh huh. Hang on." Robbins held up a hand. "You're not accepting that it's *true*? That Jack really was Zack, all along? Because I'm going to struggle with that—"

"No." McGee shook his head. "I'm not saying that. Just that's how it would have appeared. Once Eva confirmed Jack's version of Zack's death—Aaron's involvement—it made it seem that he was telling the truth. That would be tough for a man like Neil to deal with."

Robbins was silent a few seconds; then he grunted, as if reluctantly accepting this. "Whatever. But there's still one person we haven't considered."

Kate waited a moment, then replied. "Who?"

"You."

For a few seconds Kate buried her face in her hands, pressing hard; when they dropped her expression showed sheer exhaustion.

"Why would *I* do that? What's my motive?"

"I don't know. I have to say that with your story about your son being reincarnated, I don't find you the most convincing witness. But..."—he shrugged—"How about revenge? For your husband sleeping with your sister? I think a lot of juries would call that a motive."

She shook her head. "Why would I put Jack at risk?"

"It's not that uncommon for parents to take the life of their children. Maybe you meant to kill yourself and him, then lost your nerve?"

Kate shook her head. "No."

"Or maybe you knew all along that you could escape down that trellis? You knew it'd be obvious you'd started the fire if you walked Jack out the front door, but escaping out the window... you made it look like you were trapped, but all the time you knew you could get out?"

"No," Kate said again.

"It wasn't you?"

"No."

"And you didn't see? You didn't hear anything? You have no idea who it was that poured gas around the hallway and set the place alight?"

"*No.* I've told you that, a hundred times."

Robbins wasn't finished.

"Mrs Marshall, I want to remind you that this is a formal interview under oath. If you say anything here that is subsequently shown to be a lie, that will constitute a federal offense. Even if you're just staying quiet to protect someone, that could land you in prison. Do you understand that?"

"Yes."

"And you didn't set the fire?"

"I've told you."

"And you have no idea who did? After all, you were there, you saw how they all acted, how they seemed after it all went off?"

She shook her head. "I don't know. It was like a bomb went off in my own head too."

"So, you don't have any idea?"

"No."

"And there's no one you're protecting here? You're quite sure about that?"

Kate was silent for a moment, just staring at Robbins.

"No."

He stared back, obviously frustrated. But finally, he shrugged.

"OK, then I figure we're done here." He turned to McGee. "Unless you have any other questions?"

It took a very long time for McGee to respond. His partner was correct, the interview had gone on long enough, and they needed to halt it to decide what to do next. But something inside was telling him there was more to this. He tried to think through everything he'd heard, and he searched Kate's face for any final clues. Her expression was impassive, she showed none of the obvious signs of lying, and she returned his gaze, so that for a few moments they were staring deep into each other's eyes. And that's when it happened again.

As their eyes locked together he became aware of a thought, or a feeling—no—that wasn't it. It was more like a *certainty*, something he knew to be true without knowing how he knew. He frowned, tried to shake up his mind and understand it better. And the focus sharpened. As he looked into her face, and she stared back at him, he was suddenly quite sure that she wasn't seeing him but was somehow visualizing what happened that night. How the flames had looked, the fear she'd felt when she opened that bedroom door and found there was no way to escape down the stairs.

He touched his temple, almost as if he was checking his head still felt the same from the outside. Inside, he felt alarmed by the clarity of the thought, and more—how unprofessional it was for him to be experiencing it. But he couldn't take his eyes off her. He knew if he did the picture would fade away. And slowly the vision seemed to shift. Gradually the flames died back, as if the way they had consumed the wooden house had been videotaped and he was now watching it in reverse. He heard his partner say something, but the words didn't register. Now he was concentrating only on what he saw in his head. A figure appeared, struggling through the front door of the house, a heavy jerry can of fuel in each hand. From his point of view—from Kate's point of view, that night, from the top of the stairs—he saw what she saw. How? He didn't know. All he knew was what he saw. The figure struggling through the door, then stopping, aware that they were being watched. And then looking up. The face illuminated in the moonlight flooding through the new windows.

"Jim? Jimbo?" Robbins' voice cut in, urgent, and concerned. "You alright?"

At that moment Kate suddenly looked away, and whatever had been happening, the vision, the hallucination—whatever it was McGee thought he was sharing with her—was torn away from him. And when she did look back a moment later, it failed to return. Moreover, from the expression on her face it was quite clear—or at least it seemed that way—that whatever had happened, whether or not she really had been seeing in her mind whoever carried the fuel cans into the house, she hadn't known that McGee could see it as well.

"Hey Jim, you sure you're OK?" Robbins asked again. "You need a drink of water or something?"

Finally, McGee shook his head, but he still took the bottle that Robbins was holding out to him, and he frowned at the concerned look on his partner's face.

"Yeah, I'm fine." His voice was croaky, and he swigged at the cool water, feeling it slipping down his throat. It reconnected him somewhat to the room, to the real world.

But as he blinked, he realized the vision in his mind hadn't quite disappeared completely. In the darkness behind his eyelids he could make out a face, looking up the stairs at him. A passive, guilty face. A face he recognized from the photographs in the file that sat in the desk in front of him.

FIFTY-TWO

"I say we go for her," Robbins began ten minutes later, once Kate had been led away. "It's not watertight, but we can get the DA to buy it. And a jury too, I don't know what they're gonna make of her crazy god-damn story, but there's a good chance it'll work against her."

McGee said nothing. All that was left of the image in his head was the memory that it had been there, and the confusion over exactly what it had been. And, of course, what the hell he should do about it. For a while he'd toyed with the idea of telling his partner, but he disregarded that almost at once. He tried, as well, to disregard it in his own mind. To find instead the place where his trust in forensic science was stored, his experience and training. But it lingered, the sense he had, like a bad smell. A strange smell. After a few moments he scratched at what was left of his hair.

"You really think we have enough to charge her?" he asked the younger man.

"Yeah," Robbins replied flatly. "I do. Everyone else is dead or has an alibi. Who else is it gonna be?"

McGee thought again, trying to run through the suspects one by one.

"Bea and Tristan could be lying, protecting each other?"

Robbins shook his head. "They could be. But both passed lie detector tests."

"OK." McGee squeezed his eyes shut for a moment, trying not to see what his mind continued to show him. The face at the bottom of the stairs, looking up at him. "The four that died, you're ruling them out just because they died? What about a murder suicide?"

"It could have been them. Just like it could have been some random who walked in off the street, set the fire and ran off into the night. You can never be one hundred percent sure."

"OK, so give it to me in percentage terms. How convinced are you that Kate did it?"

Robbins stared at him as if he didn't understand the question. "You can't put a number on it. It doesn't work like that."

"Yeah, but you just did," McGee persisted, unsure exactly what he was doing, but leaning in. If nothing else, it distracted him. "Come on, humor me. What would you give it? If you had to? Fifty percent? Sixty?"

Robbins kept staring, irritated now. "I'm... maybe eighty percent," he replied. "Close to that anyway."

"And you think that's enough?" McGee went on. "To charge her with felony murder? Where she'll be looking at decades in jail? No possibility of parole?"

Robbins stared at him, clearly angry now. "I don't know, Jim! Maybe, yes. Four people *died* that night. Four people, burned alive. What are we here for, if not to give them justice?"

McGee closed his eyes again. He felt suddenly exhausted, as if the cumulative effort of the dozens of cases he'd put forward over more than thirty-five years of service was suddenly weighing down on him. He considered them now, cases where he'd been certain, where his ambition had led him to push hard for a prosecution. It felt different now, at the very end of his career. Or maybe it was this case that felt different, the damn uncertainty that lay at its very core. Was Kate telling the truth about her son? He had no reason to doubt her. Was Jack telling the truth? Surely not. But then how had he known about Zack's death? And did the answer to that somehow reveal the identity of whoever had set the fire? The core of the case was unknown, perhaps unknowable. It didn't make any sense either way

He shook his head. Sat still for a long moment, deciding. "It's not enough."

"Come on!" Robbins banged the desk with his palm. "Jim—"

"It's not enough," McGee spoke over him. "Sure, I've had cases where I've been eighty percent sure, some of them with you. But then we've had witnesses, we've had physical evidence —DNA. Here we've got none of that. We hoped that talking to Kate like this she'd crack and give us a confession. But we knew it was a long shot. And it didn't pan out. We just have to accept it. It's not enough."

"So, what?" Robbins pressed his fingers against his eyes. "We're giving up? Letting her go? Is that what you're saying?"

McGee thought again for a moment, this time visualizing how Kate would be reunited with her son, who'd spent the last few days in the care of the Child Protective Services.

"What I'm saying is, we just don't know. Clearly you're right that Kate might have done it. She might have sneaked downstairs and set that fire, but so might Bea or Tristan—it's not that hard to beat a polygraph. Or it could have been Amber, or Eva, or Aaron. It could have been Neil. Christ, for all we know, it could have been Jack himself who dragged those gas tanks into the house and set it on fire." As he spoke the image he'd seen was almost lit up in neon inside his brain, the person he could literally see doing it—but he did his best to ignore it. He questioned himself for a moment, then carried on.

"Every single one of the people in that house had some kind of motive. At the same time, none of them gains that much from setting it on fire. So the way I see it, we're never going to know the truth. And I'm sorry if that means my last case is left as a god-damned mystery, I really am. But that's just how it goes sometimes. Not everything in life makes sense."

Robbins stared. "So that's it. You're just giving up?"

McGee sat still for almost a minute before he replied.

"It's a puzzle who set the fire. But you take any puzzle, and if you don't have all the pieces, you can't finish it. And one of the pieces—the biggest piece—of this puzzle is the mystery of whether Jack was telling the truth, or was... making the whole thing up. We don't have an answer to that question. And by my thinking, we're not gonna solve the puzzle until we solve the mystery."

He stopped.

"You want to call that giving up, be my guest. But I think it's the only honest way to end this."

With that McGee stood up, stretching out his back as he did so. Then he gathered together the documents in front of him, replaced them in the file, and walked to the door.

EPILOGUE

FIFTEEN MONTHS LATER

Former FBI Agent Jim McGee stopped the car a little way down the street and walked back to the blue-and-white painted cottage he had just slowed down to pass. Above, a few gulls wheeled in a near-cloudless sky. In the front yard of the little house a red bicycle was leaning up against a yellow plastic slide; there was something pleasing about the primary colors sitting together in the pure, bright sunlight. He lifted his sunglasses, squinting a little, and looked around. Not far away there were flashes of aquatic blue, the water in the sound seen through gaps in the buildings. The air was fresh and tinged with salt. He felt refreshed—not just from having given up the job, and a few months of resting and finally beginning the process of turning his backyard into a garden where he now grew onions and lettuce and peppers. He breathed deep, opened the gate, walked up to the front door and rang the bell.

"Kate?" For a moment he didn't recognize the woman who answered the door. Her hair was shorter, and she looked different—or perhaps she just wasn't gripped by the twin claws of shock and fear, as when he'd interviewed her almost a year and a half before.

"Agent McGee," she replied.

"Actually no," he corrected her. "I'm retired. You can call me former Agent McGee." He offered a smile. "Or maybe just Jim?" From inside the house came the sound of the TV, the high-pitched voices of cartoon characters, and then another voice, a woman's this time, calling out.

"Who is it?"

Kate turned around to reply, but seemed to think for a moment. "It's, uh... it's the FBI. Sort of." She gave McGee a half-apologetic smile, as Bea Marshall came into view.

"Oh right. You said he was coming," Bea said.

"You mind? I hope I'm not interrupting?"

Both women hesitated, but Kate quickly shook her head. "No. Not at all. What's it about?"

McGee thought for a moment before he answered. There was the excuse he'd already given her, and then the real reason he was here. The question that had plagued him almost every day since Kate had walked free from the police station. The question his mind had turned over and over, just as he'd been turning over the soil in his yard. The possibility that seemed to have germinated and sprung roots, and which now seemed to have permeated and changed every part of his being. He went with the first reason.

"I just wanted to follow up on a few loose ends."

At first Kate nodded, as if this stacked up, but then she hesitated.

"But how does that work, if you're..." Her eyes narrowed, more confused than concerned. He finished the question for her.

"Retired? It's not... official exactly. Just some questions I still have. I'm hoping you can clear them up."

Kate looked as if she were considering telling him to leave if she had no obligation to speak to him, but after a moment she stepped back from the door and held it open.

"I doubt there's anything I can add, but you've come a long way."

A few minutes later he was being poured tea from a pot bearing a faded picture of the Queen of England.

"That was Mom's," Kate told him, seeing him notice. "It was in the lake house when it burned down, but right at the back of a cabinet. It's amazing how some things were completely destroyed and others survived almost untouched."

McGee didn't answer, but his mind wandered back to the afternoon he'd spent being shown around the still-warm charred remains of the building. The feeling it had exuded. There was no memory of the smell though, that was gone.

"Is there any news about the case?" Bea asked. She stayed standing while Kate and McGee sat at the small kitchen table.

"It's an open verdict," he replied, knowing they already knew this. "The fire was ruled to be suspicious, but we don't have enough information to determine who set it. No one is actively investigating, but in the event that someone comes forward with additional information..." He shrugged, leaving the sentence unfinished.

"That's not going to happen," Bea replied.

McGee didn't respond to that. Instead, he held out his mug —handle first—towards the sound of the TV coming from the other room. "How's Jack doing?"

Kate nodded. "He's OK. We moved in here with Bea, after the fire. It's only temporary. We'll probably stay in the area though; Jack loves the beach. He even likes swimming now." She made a face. "Just not in lakes."

A smile formed on McGee's lips. He looked at the two women, two sisters, both in some way mothers to the same child. It was kind of fitting that the three of them had ended up together.

"Does he still remember?"

There was a pause, almost awkward.

"The research into children like Jack shows they begin to forget their past-life memories around the ages of five or six." It was Bea who answered him, and he was struck by how matter-of-factly she talked about it. "By seven or eight the memories are mostly forgotten altogether. That's around the same time that most adults begin to retain memories." She shrugged, as if there were a clear link here.

"And Jack is...?"

"He's seven." Bea's eyes moved to the other room, where presumably she could see him watching TV.

"Do you mind if I..." McGee hesitated. "Say hi?"

He sensed that Bea was about to give an excuse why he couldn't, when Kate answered.

"You can say hello. But I don't want you bringing up the fire. It's not fair to make him go through it all over again."

"Sure." McGee nodded. He got to his feet and followed Bea into the little living room, where Jack was sitting in the corner of a sofa, his eyes fixed on a colorful cartoon. He looked completely ordinary.

"Jack, could you pause that a moment?" Bea asked.

He did as he was told and then looked up at McGee, who crouched down, holding out one hand to steady himself on the coffee table.

"Hey, buddy, you remember me?"

There was no reason he should. McGee was just one of a dozen officers who had spoken with him during the investigation, while the detailed interviews with Jack had all been carried out by specialists in child psychology. The boy nodded though.

"You're the one who talked with Mommy after the fire."

"That's right."

Jack glanced at Bea, and then Kate, then shrugged.

McGee glanced at Kate as well. "Just a couple of questions."

"Two questions," Kate said. "No more."

McGee nodded to himself, thinking. Two questions. He thought about all the questions he'd like to ask. What it was like to have memories of having lived before, or to genuinely think you did? Had anybody coached him? Had anybody told him how Zack had died? All questions that had been asked already, but the answers were lost to the enigma inside this boy's head. An enigma that was itself fading rapidly away.

"I just wanted to ask if you were doing OK?" he said in the end.

Jack looked a little worried by the question, but he shrugged again and mumbled something, and when Bea asked him to, he repeated it, a little louder.

"I'm fine. Thanks."

McGee smiled at the politeness, and felt his eyes follow Jack's to the image frozen on the TV screen. A cartoon lion was shown in profile, looking up at a sky full of storm clouds; in it was the shape of another lion. For some reason the subtitles were on, and the words "Remember, I am your father..." caught mid-sentence. The title of the film was shown too, Disney's *The Lion King*.

"My granddaughter is coming to visit me next week," he said, jerking his thumb at the screen. "She's nearly four. I was wondering what to watch with her; you think she'd like this?"

Jack seemed to consider the question carefully. "Probably," he said eventually. "Or you could try *Frozen?*" He turned to look at McGee. "That's pretty good."

McGee considered it for a moment, then pushed himself to his feet.

"I'll check it out," he said. And for a second he felt an almost overwhelming desire to be there now, watching TV with his granddaughter, with her unruly curly golden hair and the funny mannerisms she had, some of which he recognized from older members of his family, and others which seemed wonderfully new. "Thanks a lot, Jack. I'll let you get back to your cartoons."

He watched as Bea sat down beside him, putting one arm around the boy's back as if protecting him from any further interrogation. He smiled again, went back into the kitchen and picked up his mug. The tea was half-gone now. Once it was drunk there would be no reason to stay.

"Who's going to supervise Agent Robbins with you gone?" Kate asked him.

He smiled at the joke. "He'll figure it out."

She gave him a look which might have meant that he hadn't exactly figured out *her* case.

"And Tristan?" McGee asked. "He still around?"

"Bea and Tris are still together." Kate glanced through the open doorway again, lowering her voice. "But they're also still *not* together. Just like old times."

McGee nodded. "And Brock?"

"Still running the business. He took it hard, but he's dating again, so there's hope."

"It's funny, how life goes on."

"Isn't it just?"

"For those who keep living," McGee concluded, but from somewhere a second half to the sentence hung in his mind. He wasn't surprised when Kate finally said the words out loud.

"And maybe for those who don't."

There was a long silence, that Kate finally broke.

"Why did you really come here?" she asked. "After all this time?"

There was no way he could put it off any longer. McGee knew he had to ask her.

"I guess it's because I had an idea who it might have been," he said. "Who started the fire."

Kate didn't say anything, but from her expression his

answer wasn't a surprise. Finally, she drew in an awkward breath.

"Who?"

McGee let his mind fill with the image that had infused so many of his thoughts since it had arrived there, perhaps courtesy of Kate's mind, and perhaps as a result of some other mechanism: his tiredness? His own imagination? Either way, once again he saw the flames consuming the staircase. He played the image backwards—effortlessly this time—until they shrunk back down to a dark nothingness. And he kept playing it back, now focusing on the open front door, and the figure that walked through it, a heavy gas can in each hand.

"Who set the fire?" Kate asked again.

This time McGee let his eyes roam up the body, the slim waist, the straight shoulder-length hair. The youthful face, fixed in a frown. He puffed out his cheeks.

"I think it was Eva," he said, quite calmly. And he watched Kate. This time she did look surprised. She glanced away, seemed to notice the still-open door and pushed it closed, giving them more privacy.

"How did you know?" she whispered.

He swallowed. He wanted to tell her. He wanted to say that he had somehow intuited it from *her* mind, that he was sure she had seen her that night.

But instead he said, "When we interviewed you, we only had the preliminary report from the fire marshal. We knew who had died, but not the full details."

She waited, silent.

"The final report came later. It gave the locations of the bodies. Of Amber, Neil, Aaron and Eva."

Kate's eyes narrowed, just a little. "Go on".

"Neil's remains were found by the bedroom door. Maybe he tried to escape that way, but he was overcome by the smoke. Amber and Aaron, they were found in different rooms, but by the windows. It was clear they'd both tried to get out too. But not Eva. Her remains were found on what was left of her bed. It seems she never got up." He shrugged. "Maybe that means she just never woke up. But I figure it could also mean she was relaxed about it. She'd set the fire herself: she knew she was going to die. She embraced it."

Kate avoided his eyes when she finally replied.

"That doesn't sound like enough to reopen the case."

McGee shook his head. "It's not." He kept his eyes on Kate's. He saw her considering what to say next.

How did you know? That's what she'd asked, a few moments earlier. Not "How do you know?" Not "Why do you think that?" McGee tried to breathe lightly, to keep his body language calm and not put too much pressure on Kate. Inside his mind he roamed the vision he'd shared with her.

"You saw her? From the top of the stairs?"

Her eyes flashed back to his, questioning. He thought for a moment she was going to deny it, but instead she simply seemed to accept it.

"She hated us," Kate said, carefully, quietly. "She hated *herself*. Can you blame her? She was eleven when Zack died. She had to grow up keeping her brother's secret. And then there was that girl at college who Aaron attacked. How many more would she have to cover up for? I think after what Jack said, she just wanted to start again."

He wanted to ask her again, to have her confirm it, but he sensed now that if he did so, if he pushed her, she would simply shake her head instead, and only repeat the claims she'd made earlier that she'd stayed in her room, seen nothing.

"I think she thought she was doing the right thing," Kate went on. "I know that sounds crazy, but you can't know. If you weren't there that night. If you didn't see how nothing was normal. It's not fair to judge her by the standards we live by, the rest of the time."

He nodded. Understanding what she meant, on some level at least.

"What happens now?" Kate asked a few seconds later. Even though almost no time had passed, it felt as if the moment had. "Does it have to become *official?*"

He paused, drew in a deep breath.

"That's up to you. Obviously there's no chance of a trial. But if you wanted to change your testimony and say you saw something that pointed towards Eva being the arsonist..."—the words felt crude to him—"Then maybe they'd reopen it." He paused again. "If that would help you, of course. To know the truth."

Kate glanced out through the still partially open doorway, where she could see her son sitting on the sofa, his other mother next to him, an arm around his shoulder. McGee looked too, watching as Bea whispered something to the child and he smiled in response. Kate smiled too. Then she shook her head.

"I don't think this world can quite handle the truth," she replied. "Do you?"

A LETTER FROM THE AUTHOR

Dear reader,

Huge thanks for reading *The Lake House Children*, I really hope you enjoyed it. What follows is a rather detailed note explaining how this book came to be. But before that, if you'd like to join other readers in hearing all about my new releases and bonus content, you can sign up here:

www.stormpublishing.co/gregg-dunnett

I also run a slightly more detailed newsletter, where you can hear about new releases and get a bit of insight into how I came to be a writer, and how publishing has allowed us to move to Spain. You can sign up to this on my website at www.greggdun nett.co.uk

If you could spare a few moments to leave a review that would be hugely appreciated. Even a short review can make all the difference in encouraging a reader to discover my books for the first time. Thank you so much!

Thanks again for being part of this amazing journey with me and I hope you'll stay in touch – I have so many more stories and ideas to entertain you with!

 facebook.com/greggwriter

HOW THIS BOOK CAME TO BE

This book is a work of fiction. We can say with absolute certainty that Jack was not the reincarnation of Zack, because neither actually existed. But large elements of the story are based upon the very real children who actually do claim—clearly and unambiguously—to have memories of living before. Before you go, I want to take a few pages to explain what it was about these children that fascinated me, why I thought the stories they tell might make a good underpinning for a suspense novel, and why I think we ought to pay them just a little more attention.

Until recently, reincarnation wasn't a subject I knew much about, nor had much interest in. But it came up in a casual discussion with my brother, and something about it made me curious. In his view, stories of reincarnation could be explained quite simply. They happened because most of us are unaware of, or misunderstand, various psychological effects that are well understood by scientists. For example, we might pay a lot more attention to where someone's claim of past-life memories appears to match a previous person, but much less to where they don't match. In my brother's view, this explanation, along with various others, account for almost all cases where reincarnation is claimed. And where there are cases that seem too incredible for such factors to explain, then we can simply conclude that the people who claim such memories are lying—either deliberately creating a hoax, or they've convinced themselves of something that just isn't true.

We could take my brother's view as broadly representative of the mainstream, scientific view, which is not surprising because he's an intelligent, well-informed individual, and he studied biology and psychology at university. But within his argument I noticed something that struck me as odd. My brother claimed that he was open to the idea of reincarnation being true in theory—if that's what the evidence supported. His view was simply that the evidence *wasn't* convincing. It took me a while to spot the issue, but I think I finally got it. The problem was he hadn't, and didn't need to, actually look at the cases in detail. The explanations he relied on—those psychological factors, or failing that, outright fraud—covered every case, and every *imaginable* case. He *knew* the children were wrong, without even needing to hear what they had to say. Surely that couldn't be right?

We wouldn't accept criminal trials where the judge doesn't consider the case for the defense before declaring the accused guilty. Yet to me this seemed a clear analogy for what was happening with cases where children claim to remember living before. OK, they're not being thrown in jail, but their claims are largely ignored by "serious" scientists (and certainly the claims they make play no part in our current theories of what it is to be human). I wanted to understand why.

I should point out here that it wasn't that I *believed* in reincarnation. I just thought that if we were relying on a system of judging that could only ever come to one conclusion—that it wasn't real—then that would be obviously problematic if it then happened to be true.

I had no plans to write a book about it at this point, but for some reason this logic (or what I thought was logic) stuck in my head. I decided to do some proper research to find out where I had got things wrong (which to my mind must be the solution).

Researching reincarnation proved to be challenging. There are many books on the subject, but almost all are written by those who believe in it. I chose a couple from the more "scientific" end of things, written by researchers who had studied children making these claims. On the other side there are a few books where reincarnation is considered along with other so-called pseudoscience topics—such as the existence of UFOs or ghosts—and then "debunked" by skeptics. But there's surprisingly little out there—certainly not an easy-to-find and fully comprehensive explanation of why science rejects it. In a way this matched my "logic" above. These cases really did (and still do) seem to be largely ignored by mainstream scientists. Ultimately, I did find some arguments from the scientific community, but not the organized, detailed and evidenced rebuttal that I'd assumed must exist.

So, I did my reading, and unsurprisingly began to discover that the situation is far more complex than in my first imaginings. To begin with, while I'd assumed that most people thought (a bit like me) that reincarnation *wasn't* real, a majority of people globally probably do believe in it. Large swaths of the Far East almost routinely accept it, and even in Western nations a big chunk of the population think it might be real. But in very general terms, my original sense of the subject, as seen through scientific eyes, wasn't too far off. Most scientists do view reincarnation as demonstrably false, and relatively easily explained by psychology, or failing that, by fraud.

However, the "insight" that sparked my interest had kind of

missed the point. The key reason that most scientists reject the possibility of reincarnation has little to do with the actual evidence for or against it. It's something else. They believe in "materialism" or "physicalism". This is the idea that everything in the universe can be reduced to what is (or isn't) physically there. It's what, apparently, underpins almost all modern science, and it nicely explains why imagining eating a cheese sandwich doesn't fill you up as much as actually eating one.

It all gets philosophical quite quickly, but essentially it boils down to this: most modern scientists believe that consciousness — our sense of being "us"—comes from the brain, and from nowhere else. And, because everything can be reduced to what is physically there, there is nowhere else that it *could* come from. Once we die, our brains stop working, and very quickly stop existing at all. No brain = no consciousness. That's why there's not much interest in investigating, or even bothering to debunk, individual claims of reincarnation. Scientists assume the claims aren't literally true because we are just our brains. Once our brains are gone, so are we. We can't move from one body to the next.

At this point I was a little disappointed. I may not have really believed in reincarnation, but I kind of *wanted* to. After all, the thought has occurred to me that one day I'll die, and I'm not exactly thrilled about the idea. So maybe the concept of coming back—maybe that's better than being dead for the eternity of time? (Incidentally this is one of those psychological factors that people point to: we *want* reincarnation to be real, so we're more inclined to think it is.) But let's be strong. Let's be scientific; it *isn't* real, it can't be—because science *knows* that our consciousness lies in the brain. Right?

I was also disappointed because by now I'd been wondering if there might be a book on this topic. Something that perhaps combined the mystery of reincarnation with the story beats of a good crime thriller. But physicalism put the brakes on that idea.

The scientists had closed the case. There *was* no real mystery in reincarnation.

Out of a sort of stubborn due-diligence I kept reading, just to see *why* scientists are so sure that consciousness comes from our brains, and not from anywhere else. And just like that, the book was back on.

It turns out there are a range of reasons why most scientists believe that consciousness comes from the brain. They point to a strong link between brain activity and conscious experiences. Put (very) simply—"prod" an area of someone's brain, and we can predict what that person will feel (presumably irritation at being prodded, if they do it enough). In some cases, we know which areas of the brain are linked with different aspects of consciousness—for example, the visual cortex is active during visual perception, while the pre-frontal cortex is involved in decision-making and self-awareness. What's more, brain damage can drastically change or impair consciousness. It's all evidence, I read, of the incredibly strong correlation between consciousness and the brain—which shows that the former must emerge from the latter.

But hang on. Sure, there is a correlation between the brain and consciousness, no one's doubting that. But the dangers of assuming correlation to be the same as causation are well known. If you were to attend a lot of house fires, you would soon notice that every time you saw a house on fire, you also saw firefighters. But should you conclude this means firefighters *cause* house fires you would have the situation completely backwards. Nine out of ten Olympic athletes drink milk as children, so our kids should drink milk to grow up just as strong. But then nine out of ten serial killers also drink milk... And not to push the dangers of this too forcefully, but one hundred percent of people who mistake correlation for causation wind up dead.

It's not that correlation *isn't* evidence for the idea that the brain produces consciousness, it's just that it isn't final proof. So, do we have final proof? If it exists, I couldn't find it. The boldest claims from the materialists seemed to be that they accept they don't have such evidence yet, but that it will come soon, perhaps in ten years or so. Until then, we just have to take their word for it.

But to me it felt that the more I dug into it, the less sure the whole thing looks. Most notably, you don't have to delve very deeply into consciousness studies before you come up with the famous "hard problem." I'm sure many readers will already know what that is, but just in case you're like me and didn't have a clue, I'll do my best to explain.

The hard problem of consciousness is the name given to the fact that, no matter how closely scientists study the brain, they are none the wiser as to how the wet, sloppy mass of gray matter gives rise to the experience we all have of what it is to be "us." Put simply, we don't know how the brain does it. The name's a bit ironic too. There are "easy" problems—such as how the brain integrates information, controls our behavior—which we also don't know the answer to, but are considered easier because there seems to be a path toward the answers. With the hard problem—how the brain creates the sense we all have of being "us"—we just don't know. Now it would be wrong to say we don't have theories. There are plenty, but they're all just that, speculative theories of what *might* be happening. None of them are well supported, and certainly none of them have been proven by evidence.

So how is it that we (or really they, the scientists who do this work on our behalf) have such confidence in the notion that consciousness *must* come from the brain, and that it cannot come from anywhere else? I think this can partially be explained by the elephant in the room—and arguably the gaping hole at the heart of this novel—religion. Whatever your views or beliefs about religion, from a historical perspective it's been locking horns with science for hundreds of years. During that time, most people would accept that science has got the better of things. Darwin's theory of evolution is more accepted today than the Bible's explanation of God creating the world in seven days. Religion told us the earth was at the center of the universe, but science said otherwise. But it hasn't been easy. The advance of science and retreat of religion has been bitterly contested, and the debates continue to this day, for example in the resurgence of creationist views. The point is not to comment on which side is right, but to understand why it might be that "mainstream science" has such an unshakable certainty that the brain creates our consciousness, even when it acknowledges that we don't know how. To do otherwise would give space to a religious-sounding notion that the mind can live on after the body has died. It sounds like a reference to us having a soul, and that's a battle science feels it won a long time ago.

But does this matter? Isn't it just obvious? Even if correlation is not the same as causation, everyone knows we do our thinking with our heads and not with our feet (otherwise, foot-amputees wouldn't be able to play chess, and they can). To put it another way, even if we don't have solid proof that the brain creates consciousness, we know it must do so, because what else could be happening? Well, there are other theories out there. For example, some people believe that the brain might be acting more like a TV set. It might be receiving consciousness from some external source, in the same way your TV receives the signal, and isn't creating the programs you watch, all on its own. This is not a mainstream view, yet in such a model we would still expect correlation between areas of the brain and consciousness, because different areas of the brain are working to receive our consciousness.

So why is the idea that the brain produces consciousness preferred over this model? It seems to come down to an argument that there's no evidence for consciousness existing outside the brain, and thus no reason to consider it. But that brings us back to the children who are claiming, very clearly, to have memories of when they were in another body.

Hopefully the problem is now clear. It seems that we are both discounting that phenomena such as reincarnation can be true *because* we know that consciousness comes from the brain, but at the same time using this knowledge (that reincarnation is false) as our reasoning for claiming that it must be the brain that creates consciousness (because there's no evidence to the contrary).

To put it another way, most scientists believe that reincarnation cannot be true, because it doesn't fit with the accepted theory that consciousness comes from the brain. And they believe this must be the case, *at least in part*, because there is no evidence that suggests otherwise. It's not quite a catch-22, but it's in the same ballpark.

But perhaps the words I'm putting into the hypothetical mouths of "most scientists" isn't really fair. Perhaps when asked the question "Is reincarnation real?" they would give a nuanced answer, something like:

> *We don't think reincarnation is likely, because the evidence we have so far strongly suggests that consciousness is in the brain, but there's a lot we don't yet understand, such as how the brain actually produces consciousness.*

If you've seen the movie *Dumb and Dumber* you might remember the scene in which Jim Carrey's character (The "Dumb" in the title) asks a beautiful woman about the chances of them ending up together. She politely turns him down by saying: "not good," but he presses for clarification. Does she mean *one in a hundred*, he asks. She turns him down again, this time saying: "more like one in a million." But at this point his face lights up and he says: "So you're telling me there's a chance?"

And maybe I'm being even dumber, but from the nuanced answer given by my hypothetical scientist, it sounds like *there is a chance*. It may be unlikely that reincarnation is real. It may be that science, in the years or decades to come, will close the door on that possibility, by solving the "hard problem" of consciousness, and showing exactly how and where in the brain it creates the sense of "us." But we don't appear to be there yet, and maybe not even close.

You don't have to take my word for it here—frankly, I wouldn't. But it turns out that while there are lots of scientists from impressive-sounding institutions who think the mind comes from the brain, there are others who are less sure. In fact, the more you read on the subject of consciousness, the more you realize there is no established consensus of ideas; in a way there is no "most scientists" at all. Instead, there's a muddle, with claims and counter claims, and a whole lot of uncertainty. Still don't believe me? Consider this. Here's a short list of questions that neuroscientists are still a long way from having settled answers to: Where do dreams come from? Why do we dream? Why do we sleep? Where do thoughts come from? Why do we have them? Can I choose what thoughts I have before I have them? How are memories stored? Why do none of us remember what it was like to be a baby? Do babies have consciousness? What does it mean to fall in love? These are experiences we all have, and yet, from a neuroscientific perspective we are, at best, in the earliest stages of understanding them.

And that's where I realized the opportunity for this book lay.

There are already plenty of books reporting on real-life

cases where children claim to have memories of past lives, and they're fascinating. But when you read them, you have to choose whether you're going to believe the person telling the story, or if you're going to conclude they're either fooling themselves or you. It's the problem presented right at the beginning of this note—we cannot exclude the possibility that they're lying to us. But in a work of fiction you *know* the whole thing is made up. Maybe such a book would give the space to explore the muddle that lies, still unresolved, at the heart of the question? Maybe it would help us consider what it might be like as a parent to have such a child? So I tried to write one.

By far the most famous researcher into reincarnation was Dr Ian Stevenson, the former head of the Department of Psychiatry at the University of Virginia. Almost no one doubts he was academically rigorous, and he kept that reputation even after he decided to dedicate his career to searching for children who claimed to have lived before (it all started when one such child was brought into his consulting room). He discovered thousands. In many cases he was able to link the life that the child seemed to remember to an actual person who had died. In others, the child appeared to have knowledge of the dead person that they wouldn't have obtained by any other means. Throughout his career Stevenson pulled together a database of over 2,500 cases of children who claimed to remember past lives. The work continues today, still under the department that Stevenson set up, and now over 5,000 such children have been studied.

For my story I tried to invent a character that was, as far as possible, an "average" of this database of actual cases. For example, in almost all of Stevenson's cases the child begins to make the claims as soon as they're able to speak. They almost always lose their memories by the age of seven or eight. In about 70 percent of cases, they remember that the previous person died suddenly and usually violently (which by the way is pretty perfect for a psychological thriller). In a significant subset of cases, they remember the life of a person in the same family, and in almost all cases it's someone who was both geographically near (as Stevenson put it once, no passport required) and near in time. In fact, the average time between the death of the previous person and the birth of the new person is around three years—by no coincidence the time between Jack and Zack in the novel.

I wanted to show a typical case, but I also wanted to tell a good story. So, I decided Jack should have information about the death of his previous personality—Zack—that didn't fit with the story accepted by his family. This *isn't* typical, but that's the advantage of fiction—I can make things up without being unscientific.

You may have already guessed, but Dr Palmer, whose book is briefly mentioned in this novel in a conversation between Kate and Jan, is loosely based upon Dr Ian Stevenson, and the character of Dr Matthew Wells—the researcher who comes to Kate's house to interview Jack—is loosely based on a psychiatrist named Dr Jim Tucker who is continuing Stevenson's work. It's by no means a full explanation of how they work, but I wanted to give a flavor of it. If you're interested to read more, Dr Stevenson published dozens of books detailing the children he studied, and Dr Tucker's own books continue the work. These are in fact the first books I read on the subject.

As I worked my way through my own book, I wasn't sure how to end it. I often write this way, coming up with a possible ending, but leaving it until I've got there before deciding if this is actually how I'm going to end things. In this case however, I really wasn't sure if I wanted readers to believe that Jack really was Zack.

For a long time, this bugged me, and I tried out my usual

tactics of going for long thinking walks, moaning to my family that writing is really hard, and generally being the annoying person I am to live with. But I finally realized this was actually the best way to end it. And maybe the only way to end a fictionalized story of a reincarnation case. We don't know exactly what happened with Jack, precisely because we don't know what happens in real life. I may have done a bit of research into the subject, but that doesn't mean I can tell you if reincarnation is real or not. I just don't know.

So it *might be* that Jack really is the reincarnation of Zack, but (for me at least) it seems incredibly hard to accept in a world where airliners stay in the sky, and the microwave in my kitchen works every time—because scientists are really smart people, and don't often get big things wrong. So we're forced to consider the ordinary explanations. Jack *isn't* Zack. But that's almost equally implausible. It *might* be that Kate is secretly coaching Jack, telling him to pretend that he was Zack, and feeding him information that he couldn't otherwise have known. But why would Kate do this? What would she get from it? I just don't know.

Perhaps Jack is making it up? Maybe he gets lucky, and guesses right every time he's asked a question about Zack's life? But again, why? And what are the chances?

Or maybe the truth is weirder still? Neil did know the truth about Zack, so maybe he's the one who coached Jack to say what he did? Or Eva? Amber? Or even Aaron himself?

As the author it feels weird—unprofessional even— to say I don't know what really happened in my own book. It's a pretty important part of the job. And if this is your first time reading one of my stories, I want to stress that I don't make a point of not telling you how it all fits together. But, in this instance, I don't know. How could I, when none of us know what is really happening in cases like these?

And I guess that's maybe a second reason why I wanted to

write this book. It came out of a sense of frustration that even though we don't know whether reincarnation is real, we treat it as if it's not. When cases do come up in the media they may be featured in the popular press, but they're ignored by science. There's almost zero research effort going into the area, and those who do show an interest certainly risk their reputations as serious scientists. I guess what I'm saying is I had a personal desire to know the truth, and if mainstream science isn't even looking, it felt like I was less likely to get to know how the story ends.

So where am I? After writing this book, and falling down this particular rabbit hole? Ultimately the whole thing has made me wonder if we as a species are all guilty of a bit of arrogance. With our access to technology, our easy and cheap air travel, with the news filled with advances in space exploration and Artificial Intelligence, it's perhaps too easy to believe that we have a pretty good handle on most of the world. To think that the big questions have been answered, and all that's left is a mopping up of the details. But perhaps this is just an illusion, born of familiarity? We're so used to our tech that we don't see how incredible it is in historical terms, how jaw-dropping it would have seemed to our ancestors. In the same way we have a familiarity with living itself—we do it every day, we think, we feel, and at the end of the day we lie down and switch ourselves off for eight hours, without really understanding why. So that most of the time we think nothing of how bizarre it is to be on a spinning ball of mostly melted rock, hurtling through space, and even more bizarre to be able to contemplate those facts. Perhaps we need a bit more humility, an acceptance that we don't have things mostly worked out. Life is still one big mystery. Perhaps it always will be.

Gregg Dunnett, 2024

ACKNOWLEDGEMENTS

I haven't typically put acknowledgements in my books, in part because the received wisdom of self-publishing (as I understood it) was not to include anything that might interrupt the reader in the search for their next book, but really because by the time I get to the end of a book I'm just knackered. But I always thought it was a shame because I liked reading them in other books, and I always felt a bit jealous if the author found a way to make them funny. So, having now set myself up to fail, here goes.

I'd like to thank my partner, Maria. I really have been a pain to live with while researching for and writing this book. I've excitedly shown her the latest neuroscience articles at three in the morning, insisted upon listening to weird podcasts on long car journeys, and spent hours explaining the thoughts of obscure philosophers. She's taken it with very good grace. As such she's contributed so much to this book and deserves a lot of credit if you liked it, and no blame if you didn't. Thank you, Maria, and I promise the next book will be less weird (and shorter).

I also want to say thank you to my editor, Kathryn. Several times she diplomatically steered it away from being too filled with the results of my deep dive into science and philosophy, and made it more like a psychological thriller. Several times I steered it right back off the rails again. But in the end, I decided to trust her, and hopefully between us we've got the balance just about right.

Finally, I have to say thank you to my brother, Jono. I know there's a lot here that you don't like, and will never agree with, and I hope you don't feel misrepresented. That was never the intention. And if it turns out I have got the whole thing wrong, I'm content that it's better to regret doing something than not doing it at all.